THE SECOND WORLD

Published by jk lawlz LLC, California

Cover design by Andrew Colaprete
Maps by Andrew Colaprete
Interior design by Books Fluent
Edited by Andy Meisenheimer at NY Book Editors

Hardcover ISBN: 979-8-9996390-1-1

Paperback ISBN: 979-8-9996390-0-4

eBook ISBN: 979-8-9996390-2-8

www.jakekorell.com

THE SECOND WORLD

A NOVEL BY

JAKE KORELL

For Mom, who never got to read this,
and Dad, who better—
this book wouldn't exist without them.

DOMES OF MARS

SATELLITE'S EYE VIEW

(NOT TO SCALE)

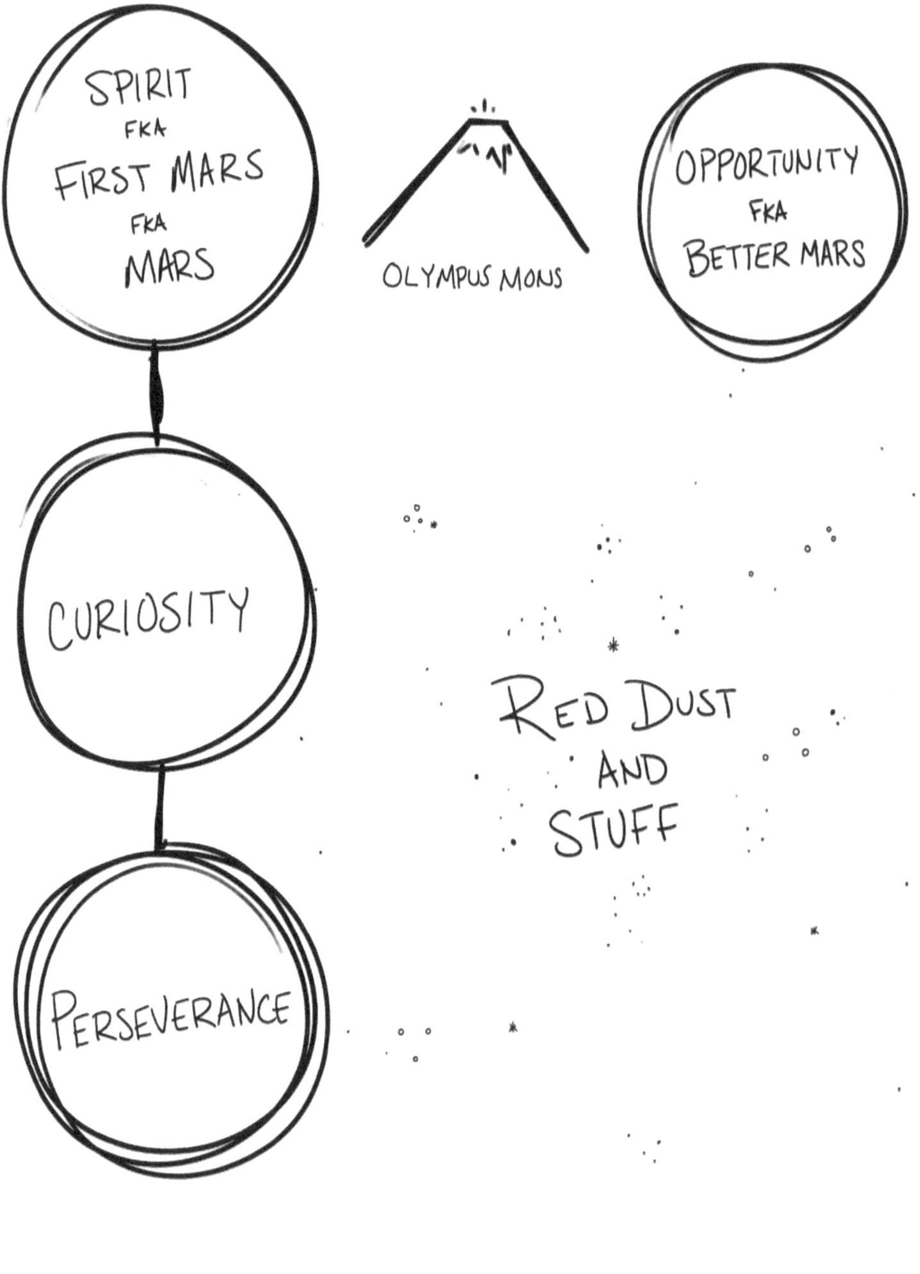

Original Biosphere Map

ALSO SATELLITE'S EYE VIEW

(ALSO NOT TO SCALE)

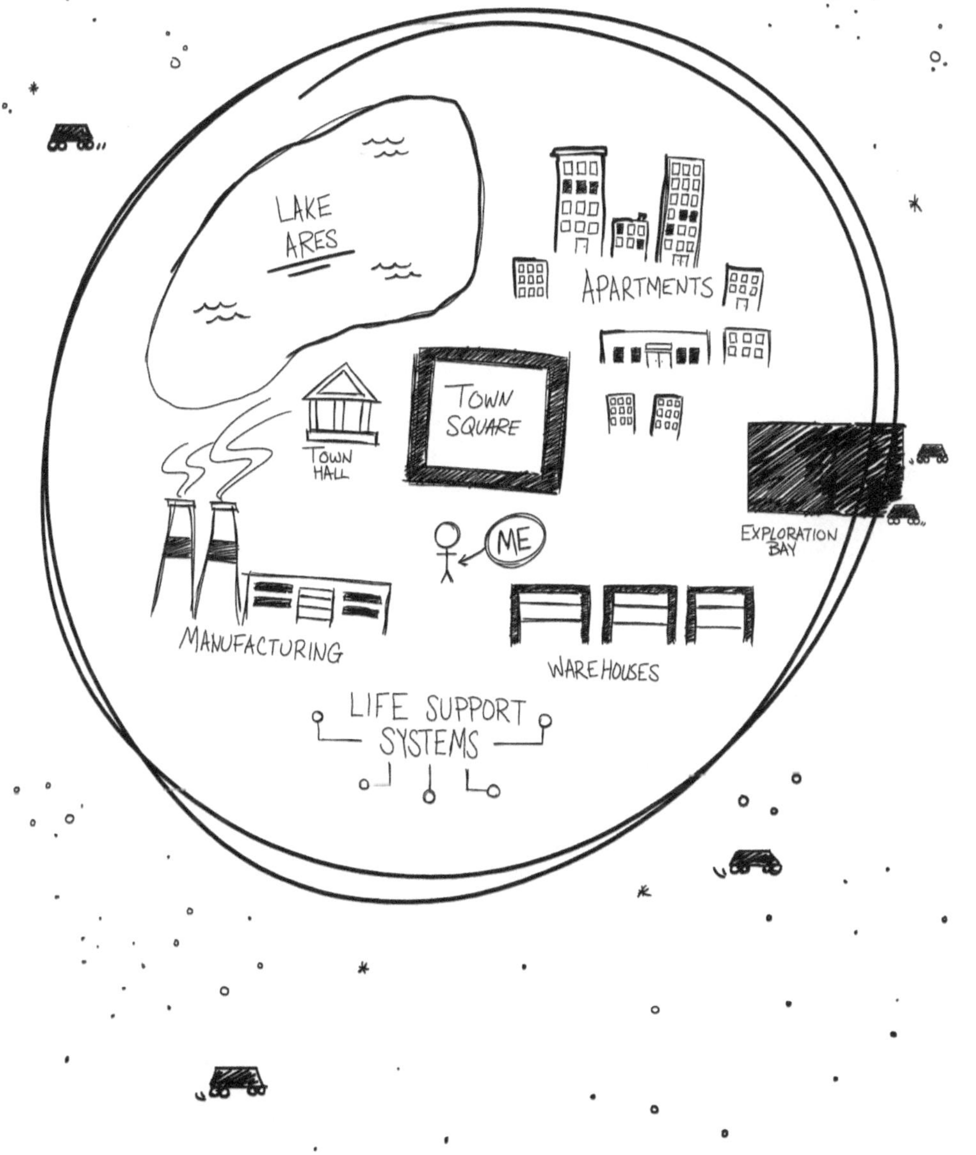

THE SECOND WORLD

PROLOGUE

THE FAMILY CURSE AND THE CURSE OF FAMILY

It's nearly impossible to disappoint someone before you even shoot out your mom's hoo-ha. But I did. Not on purpose—I was just born five minutes too late. Five minutes after the first. I was second.

Maybe that's why I'm here now, ascending to space on an elevator, watching the Martian biosphere shrink below me, the glass dome resembling a single water droplet in the middle of an endless red rusty desert.

To properly reflect on the chain of events that led me here would take time, but time is all I have. A Mars space elevator climbs the equivalent of nearly six million building floors, and let me tell you, the ride is uncomfortable. I'm just staring straight ahead, avoiding eye contact with the strangers crammed in beside me, pretending I wasn't responsible for the undeniable stench of poorly contained farts.

With no escape and no distractions, all I can do is think about how I got here.

Like so many others, my extreme adequacy isn't my fault—its genesis can be traced back to long before I shot out my mom's hoo-ha, before she shot out my grandma's hoo-ha, and before my grandma shot out my great-gradma's hoo-ha.

A long line of hoo-has before 2117—one hundred and forty-eight years' worth—it began on July 20, 1969.

As the story goes—one I've heard a million times—on that day, Buzz Aldrin became one of the first people to walk on the moon. Emphasis on "one of." Because he wasn't the first. Neil Armstrong was. Neil got the glory, Neil got the fanfare, Neil got the quote.

No one remembers a Buzz Aldrin quote. No one cares about the second guy.

Second. It ate and ate at him. For the rest of his life, his mission was to be first at everything. First to arrive. First to answer a question. First to orgasm. His children inherited the obsession—pining to be first in their class, first chair in the band, first place in the race. At dinner, plates were piled to the brim, no one daring to grab seconds. The word "second" wasn't uttered in the Aldrin household. They told time in hours, minutes, and sixtieths-of-a-minute.

It didn't work. It was as if a mystical, wrinkly traveler who only spoke in riddles with an unplaceable accent and a demented giggle had put a curse on the family name—a curse that was passed down through generations. One descendant was the Miss Universe runner-up. Another received the silver medal in equestrian dressage. A third, quite literally, played second fiddle in the Boston Philharmonic Orchestra.

Then came Penelope Aldrin, determined to break the hex, presented with the perfect opportunity to right generations of wrongs—becoming the First Human on Mars. She volunteered for the one-way flight to the Red Planet in 2050—a launch originally scheduled for 2035, but cancelled due to an "inopportune strong breeze" and postponed fifteen years.

For the entire nine-month journey, Penelope never shut up about her destiny to lift the curse that plagued the bloodline.

A day before landing, Penelope staked her claim at the exit hatch, glaring at anyone who floated by.

As the ship descended, everyone else strapped in for impact—except Penelope. She held her spot—that was, until severe turbulence tossed her from the floor and slammed her down, snapping her left, most favorite leg.

Didn't matter. Adrenaline surging, Penelope pulled herself up, pried open the hatch, and hobbled down the stairs. Step by step, she was about to break the family curse.

Then on the second-to-last step, her favorite leg gave out.

She collapsed backward, watching helplessly as another passenger weightlessly hopped over her and touched the Martian surface first.

And not just anybody. Naomi *Armstrong*, a descendant of the jazz trumpeter—not the astronaut—but it still stung the same. On November 1, 2050, humans landed on Mars, and the name Naomi Armstrong would be remembered until the end of time.

A kind young man named Eddie Buchanan bent down to help Penelope to her feet, supporting her as she became the Second Human on Mars. That moment sparked their passionate yet short-lived romance.

On July 16, 2051, Penelope gave birth to the First Baby Born on Mars. In that sixtieth-of-a-minute, Buzz Aldrin Buchanan broke the family curse at long last.

And that was always my father's grand finale to his origin story—a tale he could somehow fit into any conversation, flaunting his humanity-wide fame at every opportunity.

Of course, I never understood why he got all the credit. My grandmother did the conceiving, the gestating, the hoo-ha shooting.

Likewise, I got the credit—the blame—for being the Second-Born Second-Generation Martian, while my father expected me to be the firstborn, like he was in his generation. But they weren't my shortcomings—they were my father's shortcummings.

Still, when my father was growing up, my grandmother paraded Buzz around as the golden boy, the chosen one who redeemed the Aldrin name, pushing him to be the first, the best, number one in everything.

And he was.

Back then, Mars was different—or so I've been told by my father, who constantly reminded me he had to hike up a crater to school both ways. With so few people, firsts were abundant. Buzz was the First Person to Ride a Bike on Mars. He was the valedictorian of his class (of three). And, thanks to his undeserved fame and the accompanying brand deals, he was the Richest Person on Mars.

Firsts rolled in, one after the other—until they didn't. As Mars grew, firsts ran out. More people meant more competition. The family curse had simply skipped a generation—and returned to haunt me.

I never had a chance.

I was born five minutes after the Firstborn Second-Generation Martian, screaming, placenta bits getting wiped off me, looking at my father—my entire world—and seeing only indifference.

Of course, I don't remember it, and I'm wildly inferring, but I'd seen that look on his face for twenty-eight years. A look I've tried to please, rebel against, accept, please again, rebel against again, and, at some point, just learn to live with.

It was how the rest of Mars looked at me too—with passionate uninterest. As more important people did more memorable things, I was always the secondary character in the room. Stars lit up the night sky, the occasional meteor soaked in its fifteen minutes of fame, while I lived in the darkness between. Always orbiting.

But I still had value. I contributed. I inspired Martian independence—as an anonymous revolutionary. I discovered alien life and rescued the clones—as an uncredited advisor. And I saved Earth and Mars from oblivion—as a confidential wrestler. All stories the Martian government will never disclose. All stories destined to be erased by the passage of time.

And that's exactly why I'm in this space elevator, ascending to a ship that will carry me to another planet.

It matters, but it also doesn't. Not anymore.

Not after everything I've been through.

PART I

CHAPTER ONE

ORIENTATION

By the time I turned eight in 2097, I was already over my grudge against the Firstborn Second-Generation Martian. Instead, she became my best friend—two kids in our gang of five.

Our amateur organized crime syndicate specialized in phishing scams, hacking virtual wallets, and digital identity theft. We called ourselves the Catfish Trolls. The gang's main grift was raiding local networks and swiping crypto coins, Martian crimsons, and personal data. The loot was decent—and the ransom payments were even better. With stolen IDs and pooled funds, we bought whatever we wanted—trading cards, candy bars, and when we got older, mostly booze. They were the kind of friends you don't remember meeting—they had just always been there. More family than friends. More family than my own family.

At the time, my parents weren't around much, so I was left to my own devices. When I wasn't with the Catfish Trolls, I was wandering the streets, kicking pebbles and hocking loogies like a real badass. It was one of my phases of rebelling against my father—I remember it fondly.

One afternoon, I was experimenting with curse words.

"Fuck, fuckity, fuck." I glanced around, expecting an authority figure to reprimand me. Nothing. Nobody was paying attention to me. As always, I was invisible.

"Shit, shit, shit . . . Fuck . . . Pussy, dick, bitch."

I giggled, like a true rebel would.

Suddenly an arm wrapped around me, almost knocking me to the ground.

"Hey, Flip-Flop. I got a surprise for you."

Since Rizz was the oldest by two years, he was our gang's de facto leader. Even at ten, he had slight definition in his muscles and a naturally straight, pearly-white smile. He was like my cool older brother.

"Come on," he said as he skipped backward, leading me.

Cyber-pickpocketing was on hold that afternoon—new arrivals from Earth were flying in, and we were determined to sneak into their orientation. As a native-born Martian, I was never allowed in. And that simply wouldn't do. Once we met up with the rest of the Catfish Trolls outside the exploration bay, we all climbed to the roof and slipped in through a maintenance entrance.

Everyone in the gang was roughly my age. Pockets was the smallest, his oversized, hand-me-down baseball cap making him look even younger. Beneath the cap, his thick black hair stuck out in uneven tufts and his warm brown skin was perpetually sun-kissed.

Cheese was a dark-skinned girl on the rounder side, the funniest of all of us. Even when she wasn't making a quip, her delivery could still make anyone laugh—flat, deadpan, like she was in on some cosmic joke the rest of us hadn't figured out yet.

After we dropped down into the massive exploration bay hangar, we hid under conveyor belts, behind robotic arms, between cranes, peeking out as the gigantic depressurization chamber opened and a skyscraper-sized spaceship capsule was towed in from the Mars surface.

"That thing is huge," Pockets whispered.

"Reminds me of your mom," Cheese jabbed.

"Shut up!"

Cheese cackled.

"Quit it," Rizz murmured. "You're gonna get us kicked out before we get to the ride." Part of me wanted to get in trouble—I'd get reamed out by my father, but he would at least be giving me some sort of attention.

I was the palest of the group, my brownish-red hair matching the Martian surface. At that age, my face was covered in orange freckles—they've faded over the years, but my hazel eyes still get compliments. The name Flip was nickname enough for the Catfish Trolls, though occasionally someone would tack on "-Flop."

My best friend was Two-Shoes. She had dark brown hair in a loose ponytail, tan skin with golden undertones, and a button nose. Undeniably cute—the effortlessly beautiful kind.

Not that I'm attracted to eight-year-olds now, obviously. But kids think kids are hot, and I'm working off memories here.

At the time, nobody had much, but she could afford a pair of shoes—a matching pair—so we called her Two-Shoes. As the Firstborn Second-Generation Martian, she got paid a few crimsons from celebrity endorsements and ad cameos. Same way my father did, which meant my family had money too—but he didn't spend a single crimson on me he didn't have to.

We were best friends with two footwear-related nicknames, connected from the jump. A pair of pairs.

The spaceship intercom echoed through the hangar.

"And may I be the first to welcome you to Mars. The local time is 2:12 p.m. Please remain seated with your seatbelts fastened until the spacecraft comes to a complete stop. We hope you've enjoyed your flight, and as always, thank you for choosing Astral Destiny."

As a couple hundred passengers eagerly deboarded the spaceship, we blended into the crowd, dodging the wandering eyes of the crew.

We were ushered through double sliding doors into a grayish-white room with cost-effective carpet. High ceilings and tall windows along the outside-facing wall kept the space from feeling too claustrophobic. Below the windows, a cheap plastic red cloth was draped over a long table holding light hors d'oeuvres and themed cocktails—the Cosmos-politan and the Dark 'N' Starry, according to the small placards in front of them.

Six staff members in formal uniforms—black button-ups, maroon slacks, and matching bow ties—greeted the crowd as we squeezed into the congested space.

We wasted no time snatching drinks and snacks. But after overzealously grabbing both, I found myself stuck—a drink in one hand, a plate in the other, no third hand to get the food to my mouth. I stood there, salivating, wistfully eyeing my unreachable tasty treats while scanning for somewhere to set my drink. No luck.

Then the windows shuttered, the lights dimmed, and a hush fell over the crowd.

"Shh, shh—it's starting," Two-Shoes whispered to those of us still snickering.

A video projection flickered onto the back wall.

"Hi there, I'm Paul Kingsley. And welcome to Mars!"

An older, well-groomed man with a salesman's smile filled the screen. The grin belonged to the most recognized figure in the solar system—Paul Kingsley, owner and CEO of Astral Destiny.

"We're so glad you could make it. Earth . . . Mars . . . Look at us. Ha! Who woulda thought? I guess *I* did!"

He chuckled at his own joke.

"When I first built Astral Destiny, it was for one simple purpose: making humans an interplanetary species. With global warming, warring nations, and any number of unforeseen threats from the far reaches of our galaxy, it was important to me—to everyone, to all of humanity—that we have another home. A fail-safe."

The backup. The understudy. The second choice in case things went to shit with the first. Turns out, I had more in common with Mars than I ever knew.

Though he looked like a sprightly sixty-something, Paul Kingsley was in his early one-hundred-twenties. Whether or not you agreed with his politics or eccentric antics, you couldn't deny his accomplishments—but those antics certainly made you want to.

"Now, here on Mars, things are just a little different," he continued. "But I'm going to show you everything there is to know about the Red Planet, the biosphere, and our home under the dome."

Slow-motion clips crossfaded over each other—residents strolling together at sunset, chatting on benches, "collab-ing" on work projects.

"I know it's been a long journey to get here, but it'll be worth it," he said, puttering around the biosphere.

That's when I remembered—he had never actually visited Mars. By the time it was safe for him to go, his medical staff refused to let him make the trek.

The younger-looking man on screen had to be a deepfake. Even back then, it was crazy what CGI, AI, GANs, and all the other letters could do.

"Whether you're an immigrant, a tourist, or just in need of some well-deserved vacay, we're glad to have you on Mars. And so is our adorable Mars mascot! Say hi, Pluto!"

Trotting beside Paul Kingsley, Pluto the donkey let out a cheerful hee-haw.

"Yo! It's Pluto!" Pockets whispered, nudging me.

Not only was Pluto a household name and a hometown hero—she was our childhood idol. The only animal on Mars, Pluto owed her place on the planet to a technicality: her designation as a therapy animal. If not for that anxiety-ridden Earthling migrant, we'd never have known the tranquility of nuzzling the four-legged SSRI.

In my eyes, Pluto was the unofficial Second Jackass on Mars—the first being my father.

The orientation video cut to a laboratory where Paul Kingsley, wearing a white lab coat, stood behind a workstation. He lowered a pair of goggles from his forehead and lifted a model solar system into the frame—painted Styrofoam balls connected by flimsy wire.

"It may not look like it here, but on average, Mars and Earth are a whopping two hundred twenty-five million kilometers apart. If you pointed a flashlight from one planet to the other, it would take anywhere from four to twenty-four minutes for the beam to arrive."

He cupped his hand to his mouth and whispered conspiratorially. "But that would have to be one hell of a flashlight!"

Then Paul pressed Styrofoam Earth and Styrofoam Mars together. "Mars has 10.7% of Earth's mass, which means a one-hundred-kilogram person on Earth would weigh just thirty-eight kilograms on Mars—the best weight-loss program in town." He stuck out his gut and patted his stomach. "I could use one!"

"So could I!" Cheese joked beside us.

We all giggled, and Rizz threw his arm around her neck, pulling her into a playful headlock.

Even as a Martian native, I didn't know half the information in the video. It wasn't like anyone on the street could recite how much they'd weigh on Earth or how many times Mars fits inside the sun.

From beneath the lab workstation in the video, Paul pulled out a pair of bulky, dense boots. "That's why every colonist and visitor gets a pair of custom-made shoes that weighs sixty-two percent of their body weight—brought to you by Crocs. 'On a New Rock? Slip On Some Crocs!'"

He set the shoes down on the table. "We don't want anyone flying away on us, so grab yours now!"

At this point, in the orientation room, the uniformed welcoming committee handed out designated boots to each new arrival.

The Catfish Trolls and I tugged our pants down to try and hide the non-matching shoes we'd been wearing our whole lives.

"Without these Crocs," Paul Kingsley continued, "our muscles would shrink up—something called muscle atrophy—because we aren't using them as much as we would be on Earth. And if you don't use it, you lose it! The boots also prevent uncontrollable bouncing around and gymnastic tomfoolery. But Pluto couldn't get any that fit her hooves, so you'll see her hopping around the dome all the time."

The Crocs actually became a trendy sneakerhead collectible. The boots even sold out on Earth, where the company recreated them exactly the same—each pair weighing sixty-two percent of the wearer's body weight. Ankle injuries and widespread plantar fasciitis led to a colossal class action lawsuit, and the footwear company was fined $1.6 billion.

The orientation video cut to a basketball court. Suddenly in a jersey, Paul jumped with a basketball, soaring higher and farther than would be possible on Earth—especially given his age—and dunked it.

Hanging from the rim, he shouted, "I should've gone pro!"

After he dropped down, he picked up another basketball and spun it on his finger. "Check this out . . ."

The ball crossfaded into a spinning animated Earth in space. Paul Kingsley's voiceover kicked in as animations of Earth and Mars matched his explanations.

"All planets in our solar system rotate, and one day on Earth is one full rotation of the planet. But the rotation of Mars is a little slower. One Martian day—what we call a sol—is twenty-four hours, thirty-nine minutes, and thirty-five seconds. Nothing like a little extra time to hit that snooze button in the morning!"

Rizz tapped each of our shoulders and nodded toward a staff member eyeing us. We squeezed through the crowd to avoid her suspicious gaze.

The video cut to a playground, where Paul spun around on a carousel, speaking only when he passed closest to the camera and pausing as he circled away.

"A year is defined by one revolution . . . around our sun, or one full completion . . . of a planet's orbit. It takes Mars . . . almost twice as long as Earth to make it . . . all the way around, meaning if I'm . . . one-hundred-twenty years old on Earth . . . I'm only sixty on Mars . . . Can't you tell?"

Everyone could tell. Not that it explained why he looked sixty.

Paul stumbled off the carousel, dazed and wobbly. "Coordination between planets can get a little wonky, so Mars goes by Earth years and all twelve Earth months. Some months get an extra sol here and there to balance things out. To help keep track, even-year Earth dates are given a plus symbol. Like this . . ."

January+ 01+, 2094+ appeared in shiny text on the screen.

"Even though seasonal changes make no difference in the controlled climate of our biosphere!"

Still dizzy, his legs gave out, and he collapsed onto a patch of grass. Semi-translucent images of clocks and calendars crowded the screen, tackily emphasizing his disorientation.

"I know it can seem complicated at first, but you get used to it. And I'll tell you what, it makes way more sense than an ancient timekeeping tradition in the United States that caused the 2033 Daylight Savings Riots of the Seasonally Depressed."

I always rolled my eyes when my parents jokingly calculated their age in Martian years—probably to ease the existential dread of their inevitable, ever-approaching death. Everyone else sticks to Earth years.

I was eight in 2097. So if you've done the math, you know I'm twenty-eight. If you haven't done the math, I'm twenty-eight.

In the video, Paul Kingsley meandered through the same orientation room we were in, sipping on a Cosmos-politan. "Now that you have your bearings, what do you say we have a little bit of fun? Come on! Let me show you around. Just remember to buckle up and please keep your arms and legs inside the vehicle at all times."

Right on cue, the wall to our right gradually ascended—revealing a fully functional roller coaster. Short poles rose from the floor, firing thick lasers toward each other, forming a boarding queue.

It was the moment we'd been waiting for. The orientation coaster shut down between landings, so even though we were all over one and a half meters—technically tall enough, according to the sign—we'd never had the chance to ride.

We shoved our way to the front of the crowd and boarded the coaster. Two-Shoes took the seat next to me, and we grinned at each other, breathless with anticipation. My feet couldn't stop swinging back and forth above the coaster floor.

The over-the-shoulder restraints lowered and Rizz patted us all on our arms. The new arrivals murmured excitedly alongside us.

A small screen on the back of each coaster seat flashed on, and the orientation video continued. Paul Kingsley boarded the same roller coaster, pulling down his own restraint like he was riding with us.

"There isn't a better way to see the whole biosphere." He grinned and winked.

"Ready? Let's hit it!"

CHAPTER TWO

THE RIDE

The roller coaster shot forward into the darkness and we screamed. The track tilted at a forty-five-degree angle, the only light coming from the tunnel's end—where I assumed a plunge awaited. A chain mechanism clanked beneath us, ticking as it pulled the coaster higher.

I didn't have to pee, but the building suspense was convincing me otherwise.

"Oh man, I love roller coasters," Paul Kingsley said. "The anticipation is the best part."

At the peak, the coaster emerged from the tunnel and a blaze of sunlight burned my eyes.

"Can you believe that's the same sun you see on Earth? Space is crazy," Paul continued. "And that very sun powers everything in the biosphere. Astral Destiny runs entirely on clean, renewable solar energy."

We crawled over the crest of the first drop, then nosedived. My stomach plummeted, and Two-Shoes and I squealed, along with our fellow squinting passengers—until primal terror and the force of acceleration pressed the air from my lungs.

At the top of the second incline, my vision finally adjusted, revealing the entire Martian colony beneath us, encapsulated in glass. I had lived there my entire eight years of life, but I had never seen it all at once.

The sunlight shimmered off Lake Ares, which spanned a fourth of the dome's floor. Beside it, skyscraper-like apartment buildings—the homes of every Martian on the planet—rose in height, growing taller from the biosphere's outer edge to its center. Our warehouses and manufacturing plants filled nearly every remaining square meter.

Everything converged at the heart of the dome, where Town Hall sat on a green lawn beside our bustling town square.

"Wouldya look at that? Amazing," Paul marveled. "Just under a hundred thousand Martian colonists live under the dome, and our population continues to grow. We're all protected by a glass shield 800 meters tall and spanning 6850 meters—about eight FIFA-regulated football fields high and sixty fields across, for those more familiar with a different, nonsensical system of measurement.

"The dome is like one giant snow globe! And if you're looking for a little memento or a present for a loved one, you can purchase a model snow globe as you exit through our gift shop after the ride."

Two-Shoes and I locked eyes and smirked, knowing we'd be getting our sleight of hands on one of those snow globes.

Paul Kingsley nodded to our right. "Now, if you turn your attention to that big building right there—that's our exploration bay, the same place you entered from! Weighing in at thirty thousand kilograms, our Martian rovers go in and out of the attached depressurization chamber—or massive airlock—charting every centimeter of the planet and gathering samples on the surface. So cool. I love free samples."

He gestured toward a cluster of bulky facilities. "And check out those factories recycling the air we breathe." Paul took a deep breath in. "Smells great!"

After three banked turns, the coaster glided over the glistening surface of the lake.

"Right now, we're riding over Lake Ares, the massive man-made reservoir that provides the entire colony with drinking water and necessary irrigation systems—not to mention indoor plumbing! Speaking of Ares, he is the Greek god of war, though the Romans called him Mars—our planet's namesake. Our two moons were named after his two sons, Phobos and Deimos, the Greek gods of fear and panic."

No matter what your boyfriend says, the two moons don't affect menstrual cycles. Or at least, that's what a couple of my exes have screamed at me over the years.

Grinning at the camera, Paul continued, "Late at night, if you're at just the right angle and Pluto is still hopping around, you can see a donkey jumping over the moon—one of the moons, anyway."

It was a rare sight, but it did happen. Whenever we saw it, my mom would say, "Make a wish!"

Above the narrow roads, the coaster weaved between towering apartment buildings. Unsurprisingly, serving fried finger foods and alcohol between a spaceship landing and a roller coaster was a bad idea. Stomachs aboard the ride couldn't handle it—mine included.

Unable to hold it in, I shamefully contributed to the barrage of undigested projectiles showering down on the pedestrians below. But, as if expecting a sixty-percent chance of stomach-acid rain, the would-be victims calmly popped open umbrellas, shielding themselves from the splattering spew. That's when I finally understood why some of my neighbors owned umbrellas in a glass-covered town.

"This biosphere is super compact," Paul continued. "Every centimeter is used for something essential—life support, manufacturing, entertainment, living space, you name it. And don't get jealous of your neighbor's place—every cookie-cutter apartment is identical, leaving little room for feng shui."

In 2097, there were some larger two-bedroom apartments available for families, but most people only had one or two kids. Larger families from Earth usually couldn't afford the additional spaceship tickets, seat selection fees, and luggage costs. Not to mention, their mental health couldn't withstand nine straight months of traveling with kids.

We hurtled over the center of the biosphere, catching a glimpse of the main square.

"If you're in need of a little pick-me-up, grab a pumpkin spice latte from Marsbucks. And if you're feeling peckish, In-n-Outer Space Burger has you covered. Or if you're more in the mood for pizza, Dome-ino's delivers hot pies straight to your door!"

These sols, it costs six crimsons for a cup of coffee at Marsbucks—which I always thought was a lazy play on words. Plus, everyone confuses the name with the Martian monetary system. Locals rave about In-n-Outer Space Burger, but I've never thought it lives up to the hype. And with a not-so-clever pun on the glass dome, Dome-ino's Pizza became a hook up spot for teens giving each other head.

"Wondering where those places get all their ingredients?" Paul Kingsley asked me and the other riders, gesturing to our left. "Good question! Over there is where we keep our vertical farms—since there's limited space under the dome, traditional horizontal farms aren't feasible."

He pointed to our right. "Next to those buildings are the labs where we grow our beef, poultry, and every other kind of meat—from just an animal biopsy and a petri dish! And in the same area, we have the manufacturing district—Warehouse One through Warehouse Four, and Warehouse Six through Warehouse Ten." Something in his voice shifted—it cracked. His eyes dulled, his expression clouded. All while we barreled through a few loop-de-loops.

The roller coaster zipped back to its start. As we waited for the cars ahead of us to unload and reload, the video continued on the small screen in front of us. Paul lifted his shoulder restraint, stepped off the ride, and stretched his arms. "Oh man, that was fun! Let's do it again sometime."

He sauntered through the gift shop, grabbing a silly pair of glasses from a knickknack rack, tossing a few shirts over his arm, and shaking a mini dome snow globe, sending glitter swirling around the tiny dome. "Thanks for coming along and letting me take you on a journey around the dome."

The video zoomed into the sparkling snow globe, and in a seamless transition, crossfaded to an aerial shot of the real Mars biosphere.

Paul's voiceover continued. "And from all of us living in the biosphere—"

The video cut to clips of smiling Martian residents, waving enthusiastically at the camera.

"Welcome to Mars!"

"Welcome to Mars!"

"Welcome to Mars!"

It crossfaded back to Paul Kingsley petting Pluto. The camera zoomed out, revealing fifty colonists crowded behind them, all grinning and waving.

"Welcome to Mars!" they shouted in unison.

Pluto hee-hawed. The screen faded to black. Our coaster car glided into the boarding platform at the edge of the orientation room, and with a soft click, our over-the-shoulder restraints lifted.

"That was amazing," Two-Shoes exhaled as we stood and exited on the opposite side of the platform, following the signs to the gift shop.

"Better than I ever imagined," I added.

"Think we could go again?" Pockets asked.

"Once was enough for me," Cheese mumbled, visibly green and queasy.

A voice shouted from the platform.

"Hey! You kids can't be here!" a member of the welcoming committee screamed at us in a very unwelcoming manner.

We'd been had. We froze.

"Scatter!" Rizz shouted. We all bolted in different directions. I doubled back, swinging under the coaster restraints to the other side of the platform, blending into the boarding crowd. Hoping Two-Shoes was right behind me, I glanced over my shoulder—only to see her on the opposite side, pushing toward the exit.

I didn't have time to change course. Two staff members closed in, shoving through the mass of newcomers. Using my kid-sized size to my advantage, I ducked down, wove through dozens of legs, and squeezed out into the empty half of the orientation room.

Pockets, Cheese, and Rizz had done the same. True to form, Pockets shoved more handfuls of finger food into his pockets before we slipped through the double doors and back into the hangar. Behind us, the automatic doors opened again, and two enraged men charged at us.

We spread out—dodging rover charging stations, weaving past repair welders, and tiptoeing over the assembly belts. A staffer lunged—arms out, fingers grazing my sleeve. Barely avoiding his reach, I dropped to the floor, slid between his legs, and clocked an emergency exit door out of the corner of my eye.

I bolted for it.

The door swung open into a narrow alleyway outside the hangar. I was the first one out, but I wasn't sticking around. I dashed right—

—and nearly slammed into a glass wall.

I screeched to a halt, gasping, as a cloud of red dust swirled just meters from my face, in the barren rusty desert outside the dome.

Heart racing, I spun around and kept running. I collided with Pockets, Rizz, and Cheese as they threw themselves through the emergency exit. The four of us sprinted down the alley, rounded the corner, and made it to the front of the building.

Panting, we caught our breath on the street.

Then forty meters away, I saw her.

Two-Shoes—arms full of gift shop merchandise—being escorted back inside.

Still wheezing, I could only tap Rizz and point. Rizz tapped Pockets. Pockets tapped Cheese.

"She's done for," Cheese coughed.

"Toast," Pockets added.

"But we have to do something," I pleaded.

"It's a lost cause," Rizz said. "She'll be alright. She's connected. I bet she only gets a slap on the wrist."

I hesitated. "But . . ."

Rizz threw an arm around my shoulder, steering me away, but I dipped under and scurried toward Two-Shoes. I shoved the staff member off her, sending Pluto plush toys flying. I grabbed her and yanked her into a scamper.

Glancing back, I saw the rest of the welcoming committee step outside, watching us flee with an armful of gift shop merchandise. They exchanged looks, sighed, and gave up on the chase.

Two-Shoes grinned and showcased her loot. "I got this *Mars: Best Place on Earth* tote bag for Cheese and these *I* ♥ *Mars* tees for Pockets and Rizz."

"Oh . . . cool," I mumbled, trying to mask my disappointment—she hadn't stolen anything for *me*. "They'll love those."

I was plenty used to people forgetting me, but not Two-Shoes. She was my best friend. She was the one person who was always supposed to remember me. She was the one person who was always supposed to put me first.

Distracted—secretly pouting in my mind—we smacked directly into a hulking, dark-haired, stern-looking man standing at the intersection.

"Pepper?" he snapped.

"Hi, Dad," Two-Shoes muttered.

"What have you gotten yourself into this time?" grilled the tomato-faced madman.

"We didn't steal anything this time, I swear!"

He snatched the tote bags and tees from the back of her pants. "Really, Pepper?"

From then on, when we were with the Catfish Trolls, I called her Two-Shoes, but when we were alone, she was Pepper.

"Where do you live, son?" her dad asked, his voice sharp. "I'm sure your parents would like to know what you've been up to."

His tone was meant to be strict, even intimidating. But my father had never called me "son" before, so I immediately warmed to him.

"Building P, floor seventeen, room 1704," I answered obediently.

"You're right above us. You're Buzz Buchanan's boy?"

I nodded.

"Come on. Let's get you home."

I knew Pepper and I lived in the same building, but that's when we figured out we shared a floor-ceiling—or ceiling-floor, depending on your perspective. We walked about three-quarters of a kilometer to building P and knocked on my front door.

No answer.

Without a word, I pressed my thumb to the fingerprint scanner. The door unlocked, and I stepped inside.

"Hey." Pepper's dad placed a firm hand on my shoulder, turning me back around. "Tell your parents that I don't want you and Pepper hanging out anymore. And neither of you should be a part of that fish gang."

"It's the 'Catfish Trolls,'" Pepper corrected.

"I don't care what you call yourselves, Pepper, you're going to return everything you stole, and from now on, I'm not letting you out of my sight."

I stared at Pepper as the door closed between us, but her dad stopped it before it shut.

"Are you okay being alone?" he asked. "Will your parents be back soon?"

I nodded.

"Alright. Come on, Pepper. Let's go."

The door shut. A sixtieth-of-a-minute later, three light taps sounded.

I cracked the door open. Pepper stood there, finger to her lips. From her pocket, she pulled out a model snow globe, shook it, and handed it to me. The tiny biosphere twinkled with a blizzard of glitter.

She wanted to surprise me with the best gift shop plunder of them all. And after that, I never questioned our BFF4L status again.

"Pepper!" her dad's voice boomed from down the hallway.

She kissed me on the cheek and flashed a mischievous wink.

Then she disappeared.

CHAPTER THREE

MR. BIG MAN HOTSHOT KING OF THE CASTLE

Though I wasn't technically home alone, it wasn't much different—my mother was passed out in the living room with a nearly-finished bottle of white wine.

Her red hair—the same shade as mine—had clearly been done up earlier that sol but lay in a tangled mess on the arm of our couch. Her pale, freckled complexion was smooth, vibrant, unscathed by wrinkles.

As a kid, I thought of her as *old*-old. But looking back, she was the same age I am now, and I don't feel much different than I did then. She was a kid with a kid.

I picked up the wine bottle from the coffee table and sniffed it—immediately jerking my head back. The sharp smell shot straight up my nose and burned. It was rancid. I couldn't understand how adults drank the stuff—though it wouldn't take me long to figure it out.

The cramped living room connected to a narrow, open-wall kitchen. To the right, a compact eating nook sat untouched, its small table mostly gathering dust. The walls and floors were as bland as every other apartment—rusty red, the color of Martian soil and basalt used in construction.

Most people decorated. Hung up art. My parents never got around to it. Once things were unpacked just enough to make it livable, the last ten percent was impossible for them.

I grabbed a jar of Mar(s)malade and a box of Crater Crisps from the low kitchen cabinet—always stocked where I could reach them—and sat next to my mother on the couch. I queued up an episode of *NCIS: Mars*. Right when Special Agent O'Shea was about to reveal the killer, the front door burst open.

"Have I got news for you!" My father didn't even glance in our direction as he headed straight to the kitchen for a drink.

He wasn't chiseled, though he claimed he exercised frequently. Maybe there were bulging muscles under the layer of fat, but I never saw any evidence. Still, he had a handsome, welcoming face, and hazel eyes that matched mine. I always thought our dimples were our most charming feature. His light brown hair was styled up and to the right—making his thinning hair on that side less noticeable, or so he thought.

Looking back, he still looked pretty good for forty-six.

"Where's your mother?" he asked.

I lifted her arm above the back of the couch and let it drop.

"Iris? Iris!"

No response.

"Huh. Guess she started celebrating without me again. That's fine—I'll tell *you*." He grabbed something from the fridge, slapped it onto a pan, and tossed it in the oven. "Your father got a promotion tosol! Martian Executive Officer. I'm now the head honcho at the top of the corporate ladder. Numero uno."

He beamed, puffing out his chest. "It was destined to happen at some point, and that point . . . is right now. Ivanov passed away a few sols ago, so the opening was there for the taking. And I sure as hell wasn't going to let Madison Chen take it from me, I'll tell you that much."

Buzz took a deep swallow of his red malt—whiskey made on Mars.

The Buchanan family had a long, interplanetary history of alcoholism. My grandfather, Eddie, had dutifully hauled it with him across two hundred twenty-five million kilometers. Even by traveling across the expanse of space to an entirely different planet, people can't seem to escape the human condition.

That's not the theme of this chronicle, though I wish authors would state such things outright—we'd all be spared from pretentious educators wasting our time pointlessly dissecting some silly green light across a lake in an outdated piece of literature.

So, naturally, Buzz inherited our family's genetic weakness of knowing how to have a really good time.

The kitchen buzzer dinged. I heard him shuffle around, clinking plates and glasses. A moment later, he plopped down in the living room sofa chair, balancing a full plate of food and a refilled drink.

"You know, Flip, if you put in a little more effort and quit fooling around so much, you could achieve the same kind of success."

"I'm eight," I reminded him.

Buzz took a bite of his dinner-for-one. "By the time I was eight, I had already knocked out a dozen firsts. And that work ethic has a lot to do with why the First Baby Born on Mars is now the top-ranking official on the planet."

"I thought it was because someone died?" I prodded, like a real bad boy.

"Everything's just a joke to you, isn't it?" Buzz pursed his lips, tilting his head to look at me disapprovingly. "Listen, that's politics, pal. Those obsolete geriatrics in charge will always clutch onto their power, only giving it up when pried from their cold, dead hands. You'll learn that somesol."

He took another bite, washing it down with red malt, sitting back in his chair, swirling the glass in his hand. "Hey, since your mom can't celebrate with me, it looks like that responsibility falls on you. Want to try a sip of my drink?"

"I'm eight," I reminded him again.

"Just a sip. Come on. It's okay. You have my permission. Come on."

He held up his glass, smiling, then shook it slightly, clinking the ice cubes against the sides. I looked at the glass.

People warn you about peer pressure—parental pressure, on the other hand, you never see coming. It was rare to have such a golden opportunity to gain his approval. Most nights, I went to bed before he came home—he was always off doing more important Mars "business." I couldn't pass it up.

I walked over, grabbed the glass, and took a sip. The red malt burned more than the white wine, and I couldn't help but cough as saliva filled my mouth.

"Atta boy!" My father grinned and slapped my back. "That'll grow some hair on your chest."

He stood, taking his dishes to the kitchen. "Well, I think I'm going to turn in for the night." And there I was thinking my father and I were about to become drinking buddies. "What do you think, Iris?" he asked, knowing he wouldn't get a response. Which he didn't.

"Great. I'll see you in bed."

Halfway down the hallway, Buzz turned back. "You got dinner, right?"

I held up my box of Crater Crisps.

"Good boy. Way to take care of yourself. No one else will do it for you." Then he added, "Don't stay up too late."

After I found out who the *NCIS: Mars* killer of the week was, I put the crackers away, draped a blanket over my mother, and turned off all the lights.

My bedroom across the hallway from my parents was as claustrophobic as every other—though back when I was younger, it felt a little bigger. Most of the walls were bare, but I had managed to get my hands on a poster of my favorite rackethand player.

Rackethand had been played on Mars since the early sols of colonization. Very few Earth sports transferred well to a low-gravity environment—balls flew way too high and way too far. Still, in a brazen money-grabbing scheme, the NFL desperately tried to expand to Mars. Everyone knew American football would never catch on outside the USA, but the league kept pushing the greedy fantasy on uninterested fans for years.

Having grown up with rackethand, my father was the number one ranked player on the planet until he retired early—before he declined. If you ask me, his play was uninspired . . . but no one has ever asked me.

Years later, I came onto the scene, reaching the top ranks myself. I was on the fast track to going pro—raking in millions of crimsons in sponsorships—until I dislocated my shoulder diving for a ball, launching myself into the court wall.

My shoulder healed quickly, without any permanent damage—except, of course, for the deep psychological trauma and newfound fear of walls. I haven't been the same player since. Now, instead of being an interplanetary rackethand legend, I write mildly successful books—famously just as lucrative.

Underneath the poster of my favorite rackethand player, I placed the snow globe Pepper had generously stolen for me.

At almost the exact same moment, a loud thud came from below my feet.

Thud thud.

I smirked as I remembered—Pepper and I shared a floor-ceiling.

I stomped twice.

CHAPTER FOUR

Y2K1H

For the next two years, Pepper and I were only allowed to see each other at school, but we still talked all night, every night—through thuds and stomps. She tapped an umbrella against her ceiling, while I clunked around in my Crocs on the floor above her.

We didn't know Morse code—and anyone listening who did would've been utterly confused by our senseless dots and dashes. It was our own special system, just between us—Flipper Code. We probably could've come up with a more clever name, but we were young, and it just stuck.

Me:	(loud stomp, two soft stomps, three soft stomps) Are your parents making you go tonight?
Pepper:	(one soft thud, one loud thud, two loud thuds, four soft thuds) Yeah. You?
Me:	Yeah. It's gonna be so boring.
Pepper:	We'll make it fun. Promise.

We were both being dragged to an Astral Destiny company party, but I didn't mind—despite what I told Pepper. It was the first time my father was bringing me to one of his work events, and I was determined to prove I could act like an adult, as an adult would at an adult party. Very adult.

The party was for New Year's Eve. Everyone on Earth and Mars was speculating that it was the countdown to the apocalypse—that the worlds would end because our quantum computers couldn't handle changing the date from 2099 to 2100 and would subsequently explode. There wasn't a single person not attending a Y2K1H party.

At ten, all I knew about Astral Destiny was that some rich guy made dick-shaped rockets—not unlike every other billionaire on Earth—and I didn't pay attention to any other office politics.

Pepper's mom, Madison Chen, was the second-in-command on-the-ground executive directly beneath Buzz, which he loved casually bringing up in conversation. Back then, she was striking—athletic, doe-eyed, effortlessly composed, with long dark hair and light brown skin. The kind of enviably glowing skin that brand-name lotion promises but never delivers.

The Y2K1H party took place inside the Town Hall boardroom, where the Martian Astral Destiny executives spent most of their time.

It certainly wasn't made for New Year's Eve parties. Everything inside was a shade of brown with maroon accents, and there was only one window. The massive black conference table made the room feel even more cramped. There were only three festive banners—enough to mark the special occasion, but not enough to change the stuffy, suffocating atmosphere.

Not that it mattered to me. All I cared about was being at a party with Pepper. We grabbed a couple of party horns and chased each other around the table, blowing them as hard as we could in each other's ears.

Then I ran into Pepper's dad. Again. We were both scolded and told to stop horsing around.

Definitely not adult enough for an adult party.

"You're an embarrassment and a disappointment," my father said—his favorite catch phrase.

For the rest of the night, I was forced to stand by my parents' side and endure mind-numbingly boring adult conversation—mostly my father condescendingly talking *at* Pepper's mom. Some of my favorite bits were:

"Madison, you can handle those forms and contracts. My bandwidth is at its limit this week with some upper-level management tasks a little above your paygrade. Get me those deliverables ASAP."

And—"There's no way we have the budget for that project, Madison. It's not even worth looking into. Let's put it on the backburner, put a pin in it, and circle back in the new year."

Or—"Those quarterly reports were actually Madison's responsibility. I can jump in and put out the fire since it's more in my wheelhouse. Madison, per my last email, let's touch base offline so I can get you up to speed before we run the numbers."

That was my father making sure he stayed at the top—the Number One Guy on Mars.

For what felt like hours, Pepper and I made faces at each other while the responsible grown-ups chit-chatted about the CEO of Astral Destiny.

"Paul is really getting up there," Madison said.

"Must be some kind of record now," Pepper's dad said. "What is he—a hundred and thirty?"

"Something like that," my father said. "Who knows what experimental stuff he's pumping into his body? Probably harvesting organs from clones or injecting himself with his grandchildren's blood."

"He can't last much longer," my mother added. "He's gotta kick the bucket sometime."

"Who do you think is going to take his place?" Madison asked.

"I don't know," my father admitted. "I just hope it's not his second child . . . or third child . . . or sixth child . . . Definitely not his eighteenth! And let's pray it doesn't get handed down to the grandchildren." He smirked at my mother. "Iris knows what I'm talking about. Her ex-husband? What an absolute disaster."

My mother had been married to Duke Kingsley, grandson of Paul Kingsley. They met when she was celebrating her twentieth birthday going yacht bowling—a sport played by the richest, in which you sail your yacht into smaller abandoned boats, anchored into a triangular formation, and tally how many you sink. Duke Kingsley was yacht bowling one bay over.

After a few bottles of 1993 Dom Pérignon, the two of them hit it off. A few months later, he proposed during an exclusive Cameron estate excursion through the deepest part of the Mariana Trench. But their engagement wasn't without its troubles. Incredible amounts of cocaine consistently coursing through their bloodstreams often prompted cruel, unoriginal name-calling and twice-weekly wedding cancellations.

The marriage lasted three months. Duke hired the best divorce attorney in the world and took everything. Her inheritance. The house. The entire planet.

After the court approved a 12,451-mile restraining order, there wasn't a latitude or longitude on Earth where she could live—or even stand.

She was exiled to Mars.

It was fucked. Divorce was bad enough, but exile was malicious. Sociopathic. Hearing a story like that about my mother gave me my first real bout of debilitating indigestion. Iris never fully processed the abusive relationship and fell into the arms of the first powerful man she met on the Red Planet—my father, Buzz Buchanan.

Nobody should know this much about their mother, but Iris tended to overshare—using me as free therapy. Responsibility for her happiness weighed on my underdeveloped shoulders. All I ever wanted to do was make her laugh. And maybe I've just self-diagnosed the root of my flippant, detached sense of humor. But who knows. Therapy is too expensive.

Instead, I'm oversharing.

"I'm gonna get another drink," my mother announced.

"Oh, I'll join you," said Pepper's dad. "Actually, I don't think we've ever formally introduced ourselves. I'm Cliff."

"Iris."

They shook hands and wandered over to the punch bowl in the corner, where they stayed for the rest of the night—laughing, drinking, not-so-subtly grazing body parts.

* * *

Over the next seven years, I was allowed to see Pepper again—and I saw her more than ever. My mother and I were constantly heading downstairs for dinner with Cliff and Pepper, or they'd come upstairs to eat with us.

Every time we went to their place, I'd bring the snow globe and leave it with Pepper for safe keeping. Every time they came to ours, she'd pass it back to me.

Even though we'd spend our evenings together, Pepper and I would still stay up until the wee hours of the night, talking through Flipper Code.

> Me: I'm so full.
> Pepper: Me too. I'm never eating again.
> Me: SOS. Send help.
> Pepper: Help is not on the way. Too bloated to move.

Buzz and Madison were always stuck working late in the Town Hall boardroom, so it was nice to have what felt like real family dinners. My mother's drinking slowed, and she smiled more. Suddenly, the weight of her happiness—the burden I had been carrying alone for years—became a shared one. And it didn't feel so heavy.

Around that time, I started calling her Mom again. I liked calling her Mom—when she *was* a mom.

Cliff and Mom even let Pepper and me have sleepovers sometimes. As we got older, our sleepovers definitely crossed into slightly inappropriate territory—and borderline thoughtless parenting—but nothing ever happened between us when we were kids. It took me a while to realize that Cliff and Mom were having their own sleepovers too, and theirs were far less innocent. But I didn't mind. My relationship with my father was complicated, at best, and it was nice to see my mom happy for once, so I never said anything. I wasn't a snitch—the Catfish Trolls taught me well.

After a two-year sabbatical, Pepper and I reunited with the gang, but we left our cyber pickpocketing sols behind us. At least, until Paul Kingsley finally bit the dust at the ripe age of one hundred thirty-four. That's when Duke Kingsley—my mother's ex-husband—took over Astral Destiny, and things went to shit.

Duke tripled prices on all Martian Astral Destiny goods. A service fee, a cleaning fee, a delivery fee, and a hidden-fee-processing fee were slapped onto everything.

Duke gouged the colony for every last crimson he could. Stores closed. People were forced to squat in warehouses. The cost of living skyrocketed. The hard-earned savings of Martian colonists vanished. Civil unrest was brewing.

People were ready to throw hands.

CHAPTER FIVE

CAUGHT IN A FIERY GLAZE

Duke Kingsley was never an unknown—he was a constant presence in gossip tabloids and sensationalist rumor outlets. Paparazzi photos caught him dating supermodels, attending extravagant parties, getting arrested, trying to bribe the cops arresting him, mooning them when they wouldn't take the bribe, and so on. With Duke being a ne'er-do-well, the Catfish Trolls kind of looked up to him. That was before he ne'er-did-well to all of us on Mars.

He inherited Astral Destiny in 2106, when I was sixteen, announcing his reign with a highly televised press conference in Port Isabel, Texas—the company's primary launch site. Dozens of camera crews and hundreds of reporters crowded around a podium, on a stage hastily erected on top of a launchpad.

Duke Kingsley strutted barefoot onto the stage and up to the podium. Black leather jacket, no shirt, tight white jeans. Never once taking off his sunglasses. He pulled out a vape, took a massive drag, and proceeded to chuck fat clouds throughout his speech.

"Hey, I'm talking now," Duke announced.

The crowd quieted.

At the time, he must've been somewhere around mid-forties. Rail thin—like an uncooked spaghetti noodle—his curly brown hair bouncing atop his artificially-tanned skin. A prime example of "you're not ugly, you're just poor," the man wouldn't have been much to look at if not for his procurement of the family jewels—though only in one sense.

He read from a teleprompter—until he didn't.

"My grandfather, Paul Kingsley, built Astral Destiny into the multi-trillion-dollar beast that it is today and made humans an interplanetary species. He was a visionary ahead of his time, yada yada yada, blah blah blah. We've heard it all before. We all know who he is."

The personification of nepotism spoke in a higher pitch than most, yet boisterously and with disdain. He radiated entitlement, but much like Buzz and so many other "self-made" titans of industry, his success had far more to do with an auspicious birth than the overestimated talents he credited it to.

"Unfortunately," Duke continued, "as a way to rebel against *his* father, my father wants nothing to do with the family business. Fortunately, as a way to rebel against *my* father, I'm now running this shit. You're looking at the new CEO of Astral Destiny. Me."

He took one last puff of his vape and flicked the electronic into the front row, hitting a reporter directly in her eye. The woman was half-blinded for the rest of her life, according to the filed lawsuit.

Astral Destiny employees rushed onto the stage, enthusiastically spraying champagne. A team of aerial silk artists descended from the ceiling on flowing fabric curtains, twisting and spinning themselves midair while hip-hop blasted through refrigerator-sized speakers. Eight fire cannons erupted toward the sky.

All for an empty podium. Duke was already gone—vanishing off the launchpad before the champagne bottles had even emptied.

* * *

Needless to say, Duke Kingsley was a Category 5 hurricane of privileged debauchery, and his price hikes and hidden fees were ripping the Martian people apart. In response to the growing outrage in 2106, the Martian Astral Destiny executives held a public forum in the Town Hall auditorium, where colonists could air their grievances.

The building's still there. Everyone on Mars knows the iconic structure—the one at the center of the dome, right on the southeast edge of Lake Ares. It sits next to the main square and its restaurants, surrounded by a lawn lined with thick trees planted exactly equidistant apart.

Back then, a pole outside the entrance always flew the Astral Destiny flag—the A of Astral styled as a rocket ascending, exhaust trailing below, while the D was a half sunlit Earth.

Ever since my mom had stopped drinking, she had become more attentive, and after I started hanging out with the Catfish Trolls again, she made sure I was never unattended—dragging me to the public forum with her.

The night before, I had gotten a lecture from my father after getting one B—amidst a handful of A's—on my report card. So, hearing him speak condescendingly to a group of people was the last place I wanted to be.

I monitored the room for any opportunity for escape.

From the back wall of the auditorium, just a few meters behind our seats, a well-groomed Black British man in his forties held a mic and announced, "New news with Newt Newman is new at noon. I'm Newt Newman."

A catchy, alliterative tongue-twister—but misleading. Newt's reports almost never aired at noon. And rumor had it he'd had LASIK years ago but still wore glasses, thinking they made him look more credible. Yet even so, he remained the most trusted news anchor at the Martian Broadcasting Network.

MBN was established two years prior, running on a 24.65/7 cable news cycle. That was a problem, because there weren't nearly enough newsworthy events to fill the airtime. Journalists quickly ran out of things to report, turning instead to extremist opinion pieces from the most radical, outspoken individuals they could find. BREAKING NEWS banners dramatically overhyped everything, no matter how trivial.

Even so, every story ended with a bright, reassuring smile from the MBN news team, signing off with their slogan: "MBN News: Keeping You Well-Red."

The only other television station on Mars aired two shows: *NCIS: Mars* and *The Real Housewives of the Red Planet.* I denied ever watching the second one, but truthfully, my mom and I never missed an episode.

Like Earthlings, Martians got most of our content from UNAPAWD—Universal, Netflix, Amazon, Paramount, Apple, WarnerBros, Disney—the last surviving entertainment conglomerate, and its streaming platform—PLUS+.

At eight p.m., live on MBN, the Astral Destiny executives sat stiffly on a rug on stage in the Town Hall auditorium, like a corporate conference panel—attendance mandatory. My father, Buzz Buchanan, and Pepper's mother, Madison Chen, were front and center, flanked by the rest of the board.

As soon as my father started the forum with a patronizing speech, I tuned out. I stood and wandered to the back, grabbing coffee and browsing the donuts laid out on folding tables.

When the forum opened up to questions, both microphones near the stage were instantly mobbed. Dozens of people shoved their way forward, desperate to be heard. The room filled with angry shouting, baseless blaming, and malicious digs—all amplified by the auditorium's acoustics.

"These prices are outrageous! Absolutely out of control. I can't afford food for my baby anymore!" one colonist shouted at the front.

Pluto the donkey voiced her support with a hee-haw. Pluto's owner stroked her mane. "Shh, shh, it's okay, baby. Mama's gonna get you some Purina."

A younger colonist pushed forward next. "I've had to move back in with my parents because I can't afford my rent anymore!"

"Get a job, Gen Delta!" an older colonist heckled from the crowd.

"I have *two* jobs, Beta bitch!" the younger one shot back.

Another colonist wiggled through the mass of bodies. "I can't afford my medication anymore!"

Buzz raised his hands. "Everyone quiet! This is serious!" Looking at the colonist, he asked, "Is your condition life-threatening?"

The man hesitated. "Not exactly, but I get, like, super distracted without it."

The crowd erupted.

"*Freeze the fees! Freeze the fees!*" the people chanted.

Tension thickened in the room, and I couldn't help but laugh at the genuine concern on my father's face. It wasn't often he wasn't in complete control—at least, in our household.

"We hear your complaints," Madison reassured them. "We're all upset about these price increases. We have brought this to the attention of Earth, Astral Destiny, and Duke Kingsley."

Buzz cut in. "And we will continue to bring it to their attention until this is rectified. In the meantime, I think we need to lower the temperature and calm down."

The crowd ignored him.

"You're not my dad!"

"I'm not yelling—you're yelling!"

"You've changed!"

Madison raised her hands, trying to keep order. "Please! Everyone will have their chance to speak! Let's all be adults about this. Decorum, people! Decorum!"

Nothing good ever happens when someone shouts "decorum." Right beside me, someone leapt onto the concessions table with a clang, snatched a donut, and bellowed, "Freeze the fees!" before nailing my father on stage with a pastry.

The baked-good projectile shocked the crowd into silence.

"Who threw that?" Buzz barked, shielding his eyes from the stage lights, scanning for the culprit. I knew he couldn't see me from the back of the auditorium, and I saw an opportunity—a harmless, perfectly frosted chance to knock my father down a peg.

It's easy to rebel when you know you won't get caught.

I picked up a French cruller and tossed it in my hand a couple times. Then I let it fly. It was payback for everything he'd ever said to me. Every time he made me feel small. Every time I wasn't enough. All baked nicely into one airborne donut. The fluffy, sweet treat bounced off his chest and tumbled to the floor. The whole auditorium heard the pinwheel drop.

Sometimes, I really could be a little shit.

Frustrated colonists raided the confections, hurling fried dough at the unprepared executives as they joined the chant.

"*Freeze the fees! Freeze the fees!*"

It was one of those rare times when the second person matters more than the first. Without me, the food fight wouldn't have caught on. Some things just don't happen if a second person never joins in—like a conga line. Or sex.

What had started as a snoozefest spiraled into thrilling public disorder. Each executive on stage was pelted with missiles of puffy, icing-covered justice. They scattered, fleeing into the wings to escape the onslaught.

No one was hurt—except for a few donuts, their custard filling splattering the floor. It was a Boston Cream massacre. The roar of the commotion was like applause to my ears. I couldn't help but crack a smile, relishing what I had started.

It instantly faded when my mom snatched my arm and yanked me toward the exit.

Outside Town Hall, she abruptly stopped, whipped around, and got right in my face.

"What were you thinking?" she snapped.

All the air left my lungs. I let out a slight, uncomfortable laugh. "What do you mean?"

"I saw you."

"Okay . . . but *he* didn't," I promised. "He'll never know."

"Ugh, Flip." She exhaled sharply, exasperated, lifting her chin to the sky. "You've gotten away with too much for too long. I can't just let this slide. I can't keep this a secret." She started marching back to our apartment building. But I didn't move.

"I keep *your* secret," I said.

She stopped dead.

The sixtieth-of-a-minute it left my lips, I wanted to shove it back in and swallow it whole. I couldn't believe I had said it. Thinking it was one thing. Acting on it was something else entirely.

"I'm sorry," I blurted out, desperate to rewind. "I didn't mean that. I like Cliff."

Without turning around, she said, "You're grounded. I'll tell your father it's for some other reason. I don't know. I'll make something up." And with her back still to me, she walked away.

"I'm sorry!" I shouted again.

She didn't stop.

Sometimes, I really could be a little shit.

CHAPTER SIX

THE BIG HOUSE

My father's veins pulsed as he paced the living room.

"Mistake after mistake after mistake," he snapped. "You think life's easy? You think success just falls into your lap? That making a name for yourself is a cakewalk?"

I stood in front of him, trying to keep a brave face, but my skin was hot and my chest was tight. The water tension in my eyes was barely holding. The levees were going to break.

"You come from a long line of people history forgot," my father continued. "But I broke that curse. We're somebodies now. Our name *means* something. I've given you opportunities that generations before you never had, and you're just throwing it all away."

I swallowed hard. He was being especially harsh—clearly still pissed about the public forum. Whatever my mom had told him I did, it didn't matter.

"Do you care about your life?" He gestured wildly, infuriated. "Do you care about the world around you? Because this whole angsty, disrespectful teenage attitude is a little overdone, don't you think?"

He wiped his face from his forehead down, running his fingers over his furrowed brow like he was physically pulling himself together. "You don't realize how lucky you are. I'm building a legacy. What the hell are you doing with it?"

A lump, sharp and tender, wedged itself in my throat. I didn't want to be nothing, but I also didn't want to be like him. And it felt like I had to choose one or the other. So I rejected the whole thing, and—because I was a hormonal, stubborn whippersnapper—I blurted, "Oh yeah? What's your legacy? Leader of Mars, or the planet's biggest donut a-hole?"

I knew I shouldn't have said it. Talking back to my father was never a good idea. Worse, that comeback—if you can call it that—wasn't even clever. I was better than that. But my emotions were clouding my comedic judgment.

His face hardened, more confused than angry. "What?" He pointed down the hallway. "Room. Now. No phone. No friends. No fun. For the next two months, you're only allowed to see the four walls at school and the four walls in your room."

"Eight walls is plenty for me!" I shot back, as if that meant anything. Obviously, this was well before my rackethand injury. I hadn't yet learned the perils of walls and developed my phobia.

I stormed to my bedroom. As I grabbed my door handle, I turned back. "I threw the second donut!"

Then I slammed it shut.

"Five months!" he added. "Next time, you better be the one who throws it first!"

Finally alone in my room, the tears poured out. I paced in circles, sucking in short, stuttering breaths, choking on the mucus clogging my throat. My sinuses ached, and I wiped my eyes and nose with my sleeve, muttering nonsense under my breath.

Rebellion was a dangerous game.

A small part of me still wanted to make him proud. A larger part wanted to shake him—make him see me, accept me. The biggest part was furious that I cared at all.

Three soft thuds came from my floor.
I didn't respond, still recovering.
Thud, thud, thud.

Pepper:	You okay?
Me:	Yeah. I'm fine.
Pepper:	I heard yelling.
Me:	I got busted.
Pepper:	What are you in for?
Me:	Inciting a riot.
Pepper:	Badass.
Me:	Five months in the hole.
Pepper:	Rough. I'll still see you at school though, right?
Me:	Yeah.
Pepper:	Happy birthday.
Me:	Thanks. You too.

It wasn't what I envisioned for our seventeenth birthday.
But at least there were donuts.

* * *

Over the five months behind bars—locked away in solitary confinement—boredom became my worst enemy.

Like a retired empty nester, I spent most of my time online—I didn't have my phone, but I still had my tablet for schoolwork, and that was all I needed. I scrolled through pictures of friends from what felt like a lifetime ago and got into heated arguments with anonymous usernames over things that didn't matter.

At the start of my time in the slammer, fueled by spite, I created a pseudonymous Chattr account. At first, I started small—posting harmless rumors about my father like him wearing a toupee or eating soup with his hands.

To my surprise, I built quite a following. Over the next four months, my audience grew, and based on the comments, so did the colony's frustration with Duke Kingsley's price hikes and my father's seemingly submissive subordination. And as it goes with the social media machine, you gotta feed the beast—give the people what they want.

My Chattr posts became increasingly political. Eventually, I was posting unflattering and embarrassing holograms of Buzz with captions like:

IF THEY WORK FOR THE ENEMY, THEY ARE THE ENEMY

HOW MANY MARTIAN EXECUTIVES DOES IT TAKE TO SCREW YOU?

DRINKS THE BLOOD OF INNOCENTS, PERFORMS SATANIC CHANTS (DEFINITELY LATIN!), RUNS CHILD SEX TRAFFICKING RING

The likes and views flooded in. Soon, it seemed as if the whole biosphere was following my secret account. Then—just as quickly as I had gone viral—it was all shut down. My posts were flagged for misinformation. I was blocked from my account.

It didn't take long to connect the dots. Chattr was owned and operated by the same CEO as Astral Destiny—Duke Kingsley. Although I had made a point not to directly reference his company—sticking exclusively to personal attacks on Buzz—I had my suspicions that my father had called in a favor.

My Chattr audience might have been lost, but I was still connected—entrenched in the petty underworld of lonely, bored divorcees writing scathing reviews and feuding online with their neighbors.

Because of my mom's divorce and the legal precedents it created,

Mars had become a refuge for the dumped and disgruntled. In the years following the end of Iris's first marriage, there was a massive influx of recently divorced immigrants. By 2106, sexy singles pining for their second act made up thirty-two percent of the Martian population.

The moment I planted the idea that Duke had removed my Chattr account because Buzz had asked him to, the rumor spread like a California wildfire. They organized a march—protesting the additional fees and price hikes. But it was on the last sol of my grounding sentence. I was still trapped.

Pepper:	You going to the march?
Me:	Can't. Still grounded until tomorrow. Are you?
Pepper:	Yeah. Me, Cheese, Pockets, and Rizz are all going.
Me:	Wow. They're all going?
Pepper:	Everyone I know is going. You started something huge.
Me:	And no one will ever know.
Pepper:	You should at least see it.
Me:	If I get caught, I don't even know what he'll do.
Pepper:	He'll be too busy holding onto control of the dome. You have to see what you started.

Pepper was the only one I ever told about my pseudonymous Chattr account—I was too paranoid that word would get back to my father, and I'd never see the light of sol again.

I bit my lip, thinking—weighing my options. To sneak out my bedroom window, seventeen stories up, I'd need a bed sheet the size of the dome and the knot-tying skills of a seasoned sea captain. I had neither.

But the thought of letting it all happen without me got my stomach acid pumps churning.

My legs twitched, restless. It was my movement. My riot. My march. And I was stuck in my room.

Screw it—I'd walk out the front door. My father wouldn't notice anyway. And so what if he did.

I wasn't going to miss it.

Me:	The march starts at the exploration bay?
Pepper:	Yeah.
Me:	Fuck it. I'll see you there.

CHAPTER SEVEN

IT WAS A RIOT

Without wasting another moment, I grabbed a hoodie and slipped out of the apartment. Outside, I flipped my hood over my head and made my way toward the exploration bay. The streets were alive, buzzing with energy. People streamed toward the protest from every direction, their voices rising in a steady hum of frustration and unity.

I spotted Cheese, Pockets, and Rizz in the crowd. Shouldering my way through the crowd of colonists, I snuck up behind them.

"Hands up, degenerates," I muttered in a low, gravelly voice. "Your cyber crime spree is over."

For a second, they stiffened, but as soon as they recognized me under my hood, they nearly tackled me to the ground in a crushing hug.

"You'll never take me alive, copper!" Cheese riffed. She'd stretched out into a towering twig, all the extra weight from childhood vanishing during puberty. But she was still the funniest of the crew—so the nickname still played.

"You made it out of the joint!" Pockets cheered. Even in our teenage years, he was the smallest of us, but at least he'd finally grown into his baseball cap.

"Not technically," I admitted. "I decided to shorten my sentence by a sol for good behavior."

"Livin' dangerously." Rizz smirked. He threw his arm around me in the sort of one-shoulder, chokehold hug like he always did. After my growth spurt, he only had a couple centimeters on me—but he still felt so much taller. He always would.

"Sneaking out with only a sol to go? What's another five months?" Cheese quipped.

"No one's even going to notice I'm gone," I assured them.

Just then, Pepper found us in the pack. "Did I miss anything?"

Maybe it was the raging hormones tap dancing through me, but Pepper had somehow grown even more effortlessly cute and wildly attractive with each passing year. Her dark brown hair was longer and shinier, her golden-tan skin glowed without the help of cosmetics, and her deep brown eyes—the kind that made you want to sink into them like a warm, cozy blanket—were still her most unforgettable feature. Though, to be fair, at the time, I was focused on some of her more recently developed features.

"You're right on time," I said.

The crowd swelled around us, moving as one massive, undulating force. I couldn't see who was leading the charge, but we followed the people in front of us, who were following the people in front of them, winding through the streets of the warehouse district, past the laboratories, and looping around each apartment complex.

People watched from their balconies, cheering on the picketers below. All around us, banners and signs waved high:

UNITE UNDER THE DOME
PROTECT OUR HOME

KISS MY ASS-TRAL DESTINY

DEATH TO DEVIL-WORSHIPING VAMPIRIC SEX TRAFFICKERS! IT'S ALL TRUE. I READ IT ONLINE.

The final stretch of the march wove through the town square, around Town Hall, and ended along the shores of Lake Ares.

As the crowd gathered at the water's edge, a handful of colonists stepped forward, carrying dozens of bags of ground coffee—the product hit hardest by the price hikes. One by one, they tossed them into Lake Ares. While the rebellious act made a bold statement, polluting our only water supply with hazardous microplastics wasn't exactly a constructive act of defiance. Neither was what happened next.

One activist—amped by the raw energy of civil disobedience—ripped off his shirt and toppled a fire hydrant. Water spewed everywhere. The protesters scattered, and any fragile semblance of peaceful organization crumbled at once. Random, chaotic savagery ricocheted through the biosphere.

Pepper was knocked to the ground, and my pulse hammered. I threw myself over her, shielding her from getting trampled, terrified I'd somehow lose sight of her in the mayhem. When I helped her back to her feet, we became a pair of pinballs—bouncing between bodies, racking up triple bonus points.

We scanned the crowd, but the rest of the Catfish Trolls were nowhere to be found.

About a dozen meters away, I finally spotted Cheese and Rizz. Pockets was only a baseball cap, bobbing up and down on the sea of people.

"Hey Rizz!" I yelled. "You guys alright?"

"Yeah!" he confirmed.

"Don't worry about us, Flip-Flop!" Cheese hollered. "I got things under control! Save yourselves!"

She lifted Pockets onto her back and pushed forward. "Charge!"

Right in front of us, the pandemonium parted. People set fire to the Astral Destiny flag and hoisted the burning fabric back up the flagpole, a blazing signal that retribution was imminent.

I threw one half of my hoodie around Pepper, protecting her as best I could, and we fought our way home. On both sides of us, shops and restaurants were ransacked. Windows smashed. Glass shards flew. We ducked, covering ourselves from the incoming shrapnel.

Looters took whatever they could get their hands on—electronics, jewelry, even ketchup packets from In-N-Outer Space. It didn't matter, their vision blurred by greed and condiments.

A group of colonists burst out of Dome-ino's with an entire sack of pepperoni slices. They dragged the resisting cashier into the street, snapping his wrist in the struggle.

Madison Chen rushed out of Town Hall, shouting something neither of us could hear, and ran down the steps, trying to break apart a fistfight. Her efforts were fruitless. The unruly razing continued—until Buzz Buchanan emerged.

Standing at the top of the steps, he lifted an air horn into a megaphone and blasted it. The deafening screech ripped through the chaos. The frenzy came to a halt.

Buzz lowered the horn, turned to an executive behind him, and asked something inaudible. The woman nodded, holding up her phone, filming. Buzz gestured broadly to the frozen riot behind him. "Look at what you've done to us, Duke Kingsley! This simply can't go on. This must end. Now."

He turned to face the colonists frozen mid-riot. A woman in front of me twisted her head away, shielding her face from Buzz's eyeline. It was my mom. She was standing right next to Cliff. Pepper squeezed my arm when she saw them, knowing we'd both be in the biggest trouble of our lives if we were caught.

Buzz continued, "My people, I have been tirelessly fighting for change—fighting for relief, fighting for *you*." His voice boomed across the square, dripping with theatrical gravitas. "Thank you for showing Duke Kingsley what he has done to our home. I guarantee he will hear our protest. And if our shared agony fails to persuade him to end his wretched price gouging . . ." He paused for dramatic effect. "Then we will end his control over this colony! Together!"

The crowd murmured, energy and confusion crackling in the air.

Buzz lifted his chin, his voice swelling to a crescendo. "Mars—our colony, our home—is not a failsafe. We are not humanity's genetic backup drive. Mars will no longer be an afterthought! We come second to no planet! We are equal—*nay*, we are number one! We—Are—Mars!"

He thrust his fist into the air at the climax of his performance, which, by the end, felt like it was more about him than the colony. I didn't see who started it, but someone clapped. And like the tossing of donuts, I knew it wouldn't catch on unless a second person joined in.

I never meant to cause such carnage. It was supposed to be a peaceful protest. I needed the destruction to end. But if I clapped, Mom and Cliff would see me. I clenched my fists. I knew I would go down for it, but I didn't have a choice.

Rebellion was a dangerous game.

"Go," I told Pepper.

"What?" she asked.

"I have to finish this, and I don't want them to see you."

She held my gaze for a moment. Then let go of my arm, backed away, and turned to run. I exhaled sharply and slapped my hands together.

My mom's head whipped around. Her eyes met mine. I clapped again.

And again.

And again.

Soon enough, the whole crowd was applauding. Then cheering.

Everyone except my mother. I had never seen her move so fast. In the blink of an eye, she tore through the crowd, grabbed my hoodie, and ripped me away from the commotion.

She didn't say a word the entire way home. Not even a glance in my direction. Not until she slammed the door of our apartment behind us.

"I—"

"Don't." Her voice cut through the air like a whip.

Her jaw clenched. "Neither of us were there. You didn't see me there, and I didn't see you there. Because we were both right here." She grabbed the remote and clicked on MBN. "We only watched it on the news."

Newt Newman reported live from the edge of Lake Ares. The news banner read:

BREAKING NEWS: PROTEST IN THE STREETS, RAMPAGE IN THE SHEETS

"Sit," she demanded, pointing to the couch. I sat.

MBN cut to a commercial for rheumatoid arthritis medication.

CHAPTER EIGHT

MAKING IT OFFICIAL

A week later, I wandered into the kitchen and grabbed a bagel for breakfast.

"You aren't even going to toast it?"

I flinched. I had walked right past my parents sitting together at the table in our eating nook. I couldn't remember them ever sitting there. At least, together. At the same time.

Not once.

"Just raw?" my father pressed. "No cream cheese? Butter? Nut spread?"

"No," I confirmed, tearing off a bite of my plain, room-temperature bagel, digging in my heels whenever I had the chance, for no particular reason other than I had heels and I wanted to show my father they could do some digging.

"At least sit down," he said. "It's a big sol—it deserves a family breakfast."

Cautiously, I took the third seat. "Remind me why it had to wait until tosol?"

A bagel crumb fell from my cheek. My mother rolled her eyes, got up, got a plate, and set it under my bagel before sitting again.

"Well," my father explained, "the passengers on that ship will bring our population up to over a hundred thousand. That's the minimum number we need to keep the gene pool safely diversified."

I chewed, unimpressed. "And ninety-nine thousand wasn't enough? We needed over a hundred or else we'd all be kissing cousins?"

"I'm not a scientist, Flip. I have advisors who do the analysis."

I was all in on Martian independence—after all, I'd been championing the idea for months, secretly but obsessively. I was thrilled it was finally happening. What frustrated me was how long it had taken my father to catch up. It felt like he was only doing it because he had to—scared of losing control of the biosphere—and yet, he was still taking all the credit.

I gestured vaguely with my bagel, a few crumbs falling and missing my plate. "And you kept your plan secret from the Martian people for months—let them riot in the streets because . . . ?"

"It was all to justify our independence!" My father leaned forward, like this was the most obvious thing in the worlds. "You can't end a relationship with a calm, respectful discussion. That doesn't work. When both parties are getting something out of it? No reason to rock the boat." He sat back. "You'll understand when you're older."

He flicked a glance at my mom before turning to me. "Earth would've thought we were ungrateful brats, only taking without returning the favor. You need a little spark, a little fire—otherwise, there's no reason to get the extinguisher."

I looked at my mom, who met my eyes but didn't say anything.

Buzz smacked his thighs and stood. "I should get going. I would've loved to have you both by my side, but you know how cramped that room is. Only essential personnel, I'm afraid. And press. But you can watch everything on MBN."

He left his dirty breakfast plate on the table and walked out the door.

I struggled to swallow my dry bite of plain bagel and turned to my mom. "Do we have any cream cheese?"

* * *

An hour later, the two of us were on the couch, watching the news conference.

"New news with Newt Newman is new at noon. I'm Newt Newman," Newt began. He was packed into the boardroom with a swarm of MBN reporters, all crowded around the unwieldy, midnight-black table, the reflections of dozens of camera flashes bouncing off its surface.

At the head of the table, microphones stood poised toward two empty seats.

Madison Chen and Buzz Buchanan strode into the room, silently taking their seats to address the media, the Martian public, Duke Kingsley, and planet Earth.

"Thank you all for coming," my father began, straightening his cuffs. "I am Buzz Buchanan, former Martian Executive Officer of Astral Destiny. You probably know me better as the First Baby Born on Mars, the highest-grossing thespian on Mars, or the most followed and liked social media personality on the planet."

He gestured to Pepper's mom. "Sitting beside me—though you're probably less familiar with her—is the former MOO. Moo moo!" He laughed at his own joke. "Don't worry, she's not a cow—Madison Chen!"

My mother scoffed beside me.

"Thank you, Buzz," Madison said through gritted teeth.

She turned to the cameras, her expression sharpening. "Colonists of Mars, we have been through a tumultuous time together. But as one community, as a united people, we have risen up against the powers that be—because they have proven, time and again, that they do not have our best interests at heart." She took a deep breath.

"I'm speaking, specifically, of Astral Destiny and Duke Kingsley."

A pause, and then she cleared her throat. "Over the past few sols, we've gathered signatures from ninety-four percent of the colony. And it has become clear what is best for our people, for our colony, and for our planet."

In the week leading up to the press conference, the campaign for signatures had kicked off with a digital push. A hologram of a sinister-looking Duke Kingsley—shadowed under harsh lighting, his sunglasses reflecting an ominous glow—spread across Chattr. Bold white text below read: Free Mars from the clutches of Astral Destiny. Beneath it, a caption contained a link to an electronic petition allowing colonists to sign the document remotely.

Of course, Duke had the Chattr post removed almost as soon as it was uploaded.

The campaign was forced to pivot. A handful of colonists—including me, at my father's insistence—stationed ourselves outside the local Mars Mini Mart, tablets in hand, attempting to get shoppers to stop for "a quick moment to make history."

At first, we were wildly unsuccessful. We only managed to gather a dozen signatures—mostly from people who weren't paying attention to what it was for but were too polite to pretend they couldn't hear us beckoning them from a few meters away.

But as word spread about what we were actually doing, things shifted. Soon we were mobbed. People lined up, eager to sign what became known as The Martian Formal Notice of Autonomy.

Buzz continued his speech in the boardroom. "A spacecraft carrying the final supplies and passengers needed to secure our colony's population at over a hundred thousand—and maintain sufficient genetic diversity—is scheduled to arrive later this evening. Upon its successful landing, we will have more than enough colonists to be completely self-sustainable."

He smirked. "Duke Kingsley, your leadership is no longer needed. Astral Destiny, your services are no longer required. On behalf of the entire Mars colony—"

Madison joined in, and in perfect unison, they proclaimed, "We declare Mars an independent planet!"

A flurry of camera flashes exploded as they shook hands, then turned to shake a few more belonging to any vaguely important person within arm's reach.

Reporters yelled questions that went unanswered. The MBN banner updated in real-time:

BREAKING NEWS: MARS NOW INDEPENDENT AND THRIVING

On October+ 11+, 2106+, Mars became the first independent planet-state.

Over the rowdy crowd, Madison raised her voice. "For all those marginalized by the supposedly 'free' world on Earth, we welcome you. This is a new beginning—for the oppressed and persecuted, for global warming refugees, for those cheated by broken systems, widening wealth inequality, and corrupt leaders."

That last sentence was later inscribed on a plaque beneath a statue of Pluto in the middle of the biosphere's town square.

Buzz stood. "We are Mars! We are the future! And our doors—" He threw his arms wide. "—are open to all who can afford a spaceship ticket!"

That last sentence was *not* included in the inscribed quote.

He smiled for a photo op, then nudged Madison, urging her to follow suit. She reluctantly did. Then Buzz bent down toward the microphones and wrapped up the conference. "Uh, thanks for coming. That's pretty much it. Have a great weekend."

The MBN banner read:

BREAKING NEWS: BUCHANAN SARCASTICALLY WISHES KINGSLEY GREAT WEEKEND

As Buzz shuffled his way toward the exit, he waved for everyone to come along. "Now, if you'll follow us to the explo—"

"I would also like to announce . . ." Madison's voice cut through the room—she was still at the head of the table. Buzz froze mid-step. His shoulders stiffened. He turned, confusion and unease riddling his face—Madison was going off script.

"Buzz and I have agreed that, as we prepare to hold free and fair elections, I will be stepping into the role of Interim Director of Mars."

My jaw dropped. My mom's jaw was on the floor. The backstabbing twist was better than anything we'd seen on *Real Housewives of the Red Planet*. Still, Madison had to do it—she had to make sure Buzz didn't pull anything shady to secure his spot in charge before the people's voice was heard.

Once again, cameras flashed. Reporters shouted over one another, none of their questions discernible. Buzz was silent. Stunned.

I would've expected to relish his embarrassment. Instead, I felt a deep, aching pity watching my father endure a low blow on live television—stripped of power, publicly humiliated.

As the camera followed Madison making her way toward the door, she glanced at Buzz's dumbfounded expression—then quickly averted her eyes. Newt Newman and half the press scrambled to follow Madison, bumping into Buzz as they passed, going out the door and down the hallway.

The feed cut back to the boardroom, where Buzz stood alone, looking like he had been dumped in the rain on prom night.

Reporters pounced.

"What went into the decision to make Madison Chen the Interim Director?"

"Were you hoping to have the job of Interim Director?"

"What is the relationship between you and Madison Chen? Do you like her? Or do you like-like her?"

I should've been enjoying it. Every part of me should've loved watching him squirm. But something about the way he stood there, blinking at the flashing cameras, gave me anxious heartburn.

It didn't feel like a victory. It felt like a shellacking—like watching someone trip right before the finish line, only to get trampled by all the other runners.

Without answering a single question, my father turned and followed the flock of press at Madison's heels.

A pair of Crocs flopped down on my gut. I looked over—Mom was already standing by the front door, shoes on.

"Do we have to go?" I muttered.

She nodded toward the broadcast. "After that? Absolutely."

I groaned.

CHAPTER NINE

STICKING THE LANDING

Inside the exploration bay hangar, thousands of colonists suited up, preparing to step outside the biosphere. Technically, we were citizens at that point, but the shift from colonial pride to national patriotism was a gradual one.

When Madison and Buzz rushed in—still surrounded by camera crews and reporters—the crowd erupted into applause, cheering on the heroes who'd just declared our autonomy. But with suit gloves muffling our claps and our hurrahs dulled inside our helmets, the momentous occasion landed with an unintentionally underwhelming, muted enthusiasm.

As Buzz and Madison hurried into their spacesuits, I spied them exchanging a hushed, teeth-clenched conversation, all while maintaining perfect smiles for the cameras.

I knew my father was furious. Madison had outmaneuvered him, stolen the title of First Leader of Mars—even if it was just an interim position.

Again, they paused to pose for photos, holding their helmets at their sides. Madison secured hers over her head and strode off. Buzz twitched, like he wanted to storm after her but stopped himself before he could. I assumed it was because snapshots of his frustration would be a PR headache.

A portion of the crowd shuffled into the depressurization chamber—the airlock connecting the hangar to the Martian atmosphere. The inner door closed behind them, followed by the outer door opening, releasing them onto the surface.

The cycle repeated six times to get everyone outside.

My mom and I, along with Buzz and Madison, were in the last group.

As the inner door closed, my eyes landed on the man operating it from the control panel. He was the last one left inside. With no one else left to operate the door, he'd be stuck in the hangar, waiting, missing the historic event entirely. His sacrifice would not go unnoticed—I nodded to him with a quiet understanding and respect. He nodded back.

The crowd moseyed over to the projected landing site, gathering around a rickety stage with a single podium at its center.

Madison and Buzz took their seats on two flimsy folding chairs in the right corner of the stage. My mom and I had front-row seats reserved for us. Cliff and Pepper were already sitting in the two seats next to ours. We avoided conversation—all four of us unsure what to say, with Buzz and Madison locked in a gentlemen's duel.

The actor who played Special Agent O'Shea on *NCIS: Mars* stepped onto the stage from the right and walked to the podium. Underneath his spacesuit, his tan skin, full head of brunette hair, and lush beard made him instantly recognizable.

He adjusted his helmet and cleared his throat. "Welcome. I'm Special Agent O'Shea, and it is my honor to speak with you all here tosol."

A method actor, he insisted on being addressed only as Special

Agent O'Shea—and even changed both his legal name and online presence.

His voice swelled with well-rehearsed grandeur. "A community built from nothing. A culture we defined ourselves. Against impossible odds, we carved out a life on a barren planet. And earlier tosol . . ." He paused for effect. "We became our own nation."

The crowd burst into another muffled applause, dampened even more by the thin Martian atmosphere, where sound waves traveled at a fraction of their strength on Earth. Though, thanks to the earbuds handed out back in the hangar, we could still hear his speech loud and clear.

"For many—myself included—it has become our new home," he continued. "And now, we can finally call that home our own."

In every puff piece, he'd gloat about starring in every school production during his childhood in Syracuse, New York. His parents had told him he was special—a word headlined in his character's title, which I'm sure inflated his sense of destiny. Their unconditional encouragement, combined with his small-town achievements, convinced him he was bound for Hollywood greatness.

But he was merely a big fish in a small pond. Hundreds of auditions later, with nothing to show for it but a single background extra role, he was forced to confront his own mediocrity.

Instead of doing so, he swam to a different small pond—one millions of miles away from the Walk of Fame.

"To commemorate the occasion," Special Agent O'Shea continued, "I invite Ms. Anderson and the Armstrong High band up to the stage. They have prepared a very special performance for the ceremony."

Buzz shifted in his seat—he had never gotten over the high school being named after Naomi Armstrong. Neither Pepper nor I were in the band—once I knew I wasn't a saxophone prodigy, I chose not to put in the work of practicing—but Pockets was. Led by someone I assumed was Ms. Anderson, six high schoolers walked onto the stage.

I nudged Pepper and pointed at Pockets. We both pumped our fists up in the air, shrieking and hollering for him.

He definitely couldn't hear us. But he saw us. And nervously gave us a subtle wave and a strained smile.

Each band member wore a customized helmet, with a ridiculous protruding trumpet—partly inside the face shield, partly outside. The brass mouthpiece was positioned inside, allowing them to play, while the valves and bell extended outward.

I simply *needed* Pockets to snag one of them for me.

Ms. Anderson lifted her conductor's baton and counted them off. The band tapped their valves and buzzed into their instruments. Of course, only faint, pathetic sounds escaped into the thin air. But through our earbuds, we heard a pre-recorded performance of "Opening Fanfare."

Unfortunately, avoiding the live production did nothing to improve the band's sound. I had no doubt that, if I asked Pockets, he would've preferred the audience hear their horns on stage—less audible, and therefore much more enjoyable.

Ms. Anderson raised her hands for a dramatic final crescendo, and then, at last, the students were released from their public humiliation. She took one too many bows as the relieved musicians scurried back to the audience, their trumpets still jutting out of their helmets like brass snorkels.

Special Agent O'Shea returned to the podium. "Another round of applause for Ms. Anderson and the Armstrong High band!"

A half-hearted smattering of claps followed.

"I was absolutely humbled when I was asked to host this event," the actor continued. "And with an immense amount of pride and respect, I am pleased to introduce Interim Director Madison Chen! And our, er, Interim *Vice*? Interim Vice Director Buzz Buchanan!"

Madison and Buzz took their places at the podium. He reached for the mic first, but she slipped in a gentle elbow, nudging him aside—so subtle, no one beyond the front row would've caught it. All while smiling sweetly at the audience.

"Hello, and good evening," she said. "As I look at this crowd—"

"We," Buzz interrupted. "As *we* look at this crowd."

Madison cleared her throat but didn't acknowledge the correction. "As we look at this crowd, we see the faces of each and every person that made this colony possible. We've found a way to not only survive on this planet—but to thrive. And we'll continue to thrive."

She paused, letting the weight of the moment settle. "Tosol is a momentous sol for Mars. Tosol, a spacecraft will arrive carrying the final passengers and cargo needed to make our biosphere completely self-sufficient."

Buzz took over, his voice rising with practiced conviction. "We know some of you had your concerns. Some of you had doubts. But not I! Let us assure you, Mars no longer needs the aid or assistance of a planet two hundred twenty-five million kilometers away." His gaze swept the crowd. "With this newfound freedom, we will finally be able to *live*."

Madison stepped back in for the finishing touch. "And once that spaceship lands safely . . ." She let the moment hang. "We, as a unified Martian people, will no longer be a colony—but a free planet, independent of Earth!"

Madison and Buzz clasped hands and thrust them high into the air.

The crowd erupted—Martians leaping to their feet, fists pumping, voices silently roaring.

As the applause died down, a hologram flickered to life beside the podium, projected from a device on stage. It was a live feed inside the cockpit of the incoming spaceship.

With her co-astronaut by her side, the captain sat at the controls, making an announcement to the rest of the ship. "And as we make our final descent, please turn off all portable electronic devices and stow them away until we have arrived in the hangar."

She glanced at the camera, flashing a confident smile. "Oh—hi there, Mars!"

Buzz grinned. "Hello, captain! Sounds like you'll be landing any moment, and everything up there is going off without a hitch."

Suddenly alarms blared. Red lights flashed.

"Shit. There are so many hitches going off!" the co-astronaut said, eyes wide, looking all around the cockpit. "We've lost thrusters one and three!" His eyes landed on a monitor. "We're way off course! We won't hit our landing coordinates!"

"Adjust the critical boosters," the captain commanded. "Override the mainframe. Get this bird on the ground!"

The co-astronaut frantically slapped at buttons. "The mainframe isn't responding." Then flailed, flipping switches seemingly at random. "These ships are supposed to fly themselves—I've never actually had to do anything! I have zero control!"

The captain stared out the viewport, stoic, her face darkening. "May God help us all . . ."

Panicking, Madison whispered to stagehands around her, eventually getting a remote and lowering the volume of the feed.

Buzz turned to the crowd and whipped up a comforting smile. "Okay, they're obviously having a few technical difficulties." He forced a laugh. "But I'm sure there's absolutely nothing to worry about."

The hologram continued in eerie silence. Inside the cockpit, more warning lights flashed. The co-astronaut screamed soundlessly, closing his eyes and clutching his seatbelt straps like a toddler regretting their first Ferris wheel.

The captain slapped him across the face, yanked his spacesuit forward, and shouted something inaudible.

Madison tried to redirect everyone's focus. "The systems on these ships have been tested and retested, five times over. The likelihood of an accident is one in a billion."

In the hologram feed, the captain fastened her helmet, then noticed her co-astronaut was too distraught to put on his own. She secured his helmet for him—just as he vomited inside. Then fainted. His limp body jiggled in his seat as the ship experienced more-than-mild turbulence.

At that exact moment, the feed cut.

A hundred meters behind the stage, the spaceship plummeted into Mars. The ground shook. Momentum dragged the craft forward, carving a deep scar into the red terrain, sending kilotons of dust billowing into the sky.

And it was coming right for us.

"Everyone, please remain calm!" Madison shouted. "The drag will surely stop the ship before it reaches us."

It didn't. The ship barreled forward, burrowing its way toward its own welcome party.

Cliff shot to his feet and yanked Pepper up.

The first row followed suit. Like a wave, the second row stood. Then the third. Within seconds, the entire audience was on its feet, shoving each other backward, rippling out to the sides in a chaotic exodus.

My mom threw an arm around me, pulling me to the right.

Buzz cupped his hands to his mouth—or tried to, forgetting about his face shield. "Don't panic! Please flee in an orderly fashion!"

His smile had vanished. The color drained from his face.

The ship roared closer. The rickety stage ricketed. And then—

A thundering halt, directly behind the stage, the ship kissing it with its nose cone.

A long-delayed parachute puffed out, gently floating down on top.

For a moment, the crowd stood motionless.

A few brave souls rushed forward, eager to assist in any rescue operations, while the rest approached more leisurely—ambling toward the wreckage, trying to appear helpful without actually taking on the burden of any life-saving responsibilities.

An exit door popped open. A long, yellow, emergency slide inflated. Passengers desperately flung themselves down the chute.

I had always wanted to try one of those slides. But judging by the sheer terror on everyone's faces, it didn't seem as fun as I imagined.

The captain slid down the yellow chute—far more gracefully than anyone before her—and landed on her feet. She dusted herself off, held up her hands, and addressed the crowd.

"Nothing to worry about folks! Everyone is okay—I got us all down safely in one piece. We experienced a rapid unscheduled disassembly during landing, but I have no doubt that we'll all be generously compensated for any emotional or physical distress by Duke Kingsley and Astral Destiny."

"Generously" was a generous word to use—each passenger was gifted five hundred frequent flyer miles and one meal voucher.

The severely injured were transported to the hospital, while the unharmed new arrivals enjoyed light hors d'oeuvres and cocktails, watched the Paul Kingsley-hosted orientation video, and rode the roller coaster.

To this sol, one of the most popular true crime podcasts ever created investigates the crash, attempting to unravel its true cause. It's Pepper's favorite. Titled *Attempted Mass Murder: Crashing into Justice*, the ten hour-long episodes feature uncorroborated first-hand testimonies, compelling speculative clues, and wildly unsubstantiated evidence. Listeners are steered to believe that something sinister had transpired—that scandal was afoot. Although nothing was ever proven, the podcast suggests a deeper conspiracy—another layer to unpeel. In the final episode, the host implies, without explicitly stating it, that the crash was the result of sabotage—covertly executed by suspect numero uno.

Duke Kingsley.

CHAPTER TEN

DRUNK KIDS

With the safe arrival of all the passengers, the Mars colony was officially its own nation. Everyone was celebrating.

My father was occupied with Interim Vice Director duties—welcoming the newcomers and informing them that they had, in fact, been unwillingly dropped into a political revolution. My mother had to accompany him for optics, but she gave me permission to celebrate however I saw fit.

I wasted no time before meeting up with the gang at Rizz's place.

I had never met Rizz's parents, but they seemed to be around even less than mine, so we had the apartment to ourselves. And since Rizz was already over eighteen, he had successfully secured booze for the group—four six-packs of phyco.

Mars had beer, wine, and liquor like Earth, but their ingredients were typically reserved for more essential food production, making them rare and expensive. Phyco, on the other hand, was cheap and widely available—brewed and distilled from different types of algae, which was a staple of biosphere food systems.

Named after phycology—the study of algae—it was, essentially, fermented pond scum.

Ah, the stuff you drink when you're kids . . .

"I still don't know why you wanted this," Pockets said, giving me one of the space helmets with a trumpet jutting through the face shield, tossing it on my lap.

"Are you kidding me?" I said, dropping it over my head, leaning back on the floor, and pouring my phyco into the bell—trying to suck it through the mouthpiece . . . and getting nothing.

Pockets laughed. "Dude, it doesn't work like that."

I sat up, and phyco dumped from the trumpet, spilling all over my lap.

Sitting on the floor beside me, Pepper cackled as I flailed, trying to clean myself off, fumbling around while still wearing the helmet. Her laugh was the best sound in the world—wet pants were well worth it.

"I had to try," I said, taking off the trumpet helmet. "Toss me another Chlor."

Rizz threw me another bottle.

Pepper was still giggling as I cracked it open. I savored the ring of her laughter as I took a sip of the forest-green phyco. It had a distinctly earthy (Mars-y?) flavor. An acquired taste, but then comforting, almost nostalgic in a weird way.

"Be careful, Flip," Cheese warned from the couch. She smirked, lifting her bottle. "You know what they say—one Chlor, two Chlor, three Chlor, floor!"

Laughter rippled through the group.

"We all know Flip has never had a hard time holding his alcohol," Rizz said.

I wasn't sure if it was a compliment or a dig, but they always seemed impressed when I didn't grimace after throwing back a shot. I guess I had more practice than they did—gotta start 'em young.

"I like these Plankton Punches," Pepper said, watching the red phyco slosh around in her bottle.

"You would," Rizz teased. "Those are so sweet they taste like a headache."

Pockets burped, then grinned—already sinking into the couch, letting his kelp-brewed Seedy Weedy do its work.

I took another sip and leaned back against the couch. "Hey, do you think anyone else is going to run for director besides Madison and Buzz?"

"Who else would?" Pepper asked.

"Pluto's got my vote," Cheese declared. "I'd follow that donkey into battle. Sign me up for a plutocracy."

"Director Ass has a ring to it." Rizz laughed.

I turned to him. "What about you?"

"Me?" He cocked his head, raising an eyebrow. Genuine surprise. "Aren't I a little young?"

"You're old enough to buy us booze." I shrugged. "There aren't any age limits. No requirements or anything."

"I don't know how to run a biosphere," he said.

"Neither does my father."

Rizz hesitated, then half-smirked and tipped his drink toward me in acknowledgement before taking another sip. "Fair point."

"What's your platform?" Cheese asked. "It's all about platforms. Your status platform, your influence platform, your policy platform . . . People love platforms."

"Platforms platforms platforms," Pockets echoed, giggling.

"Pockets gets it." Cheese nudged him.

He giggled harder, then turned to her and slurred his words. "Hey . . . I luvoo."

"Shut up." Cheese smacked the bill of his cap downward, covering his eyes. "Love you too."

To Pockets, Cheese wasn't just a best friend—she was more like an older sister. The one who raises you if your mom isn't around. Come to think of it, I wasn't even sure if Pockets's mom *was* around. He never talked about his family. Or his background. And, I guess, I never thought to ask.

I should've.

"I don't know what my platform is." Rizz leaned toward me. "Ask my campaign manager."

My mouth opened but nothing came out at first. "Uh, youth? The future? Decisions made by the people who actually have to live with them. Why should a bunch of old people decide what's right when they won't be around long enough to deal with the consequences?"

"The experience of the inexperienced . . . " Cheese wondered aloud. She swirled her drink, thinking. "Needs a little zhuzh. But there's something there."

"Why don't *you* run?" Rizz asked me.

I shrugged. "What's the point? I wouldn't win. I'd just come in second." I blew a whistle into my bottle. "But you? You have a chance. Every kid in our school would vote for you. You're the coolest kid under the dome."

Rizz snorted. "Yeah, okay."

"I think it could work."

"I'd vote for him," Pepper said. She turned to me and smiled—soft, encouraging.

I wasn't sure if she was flirting with me or flirting with Rizz. Or just being nice to me. Or just being nice to Rizz. Or pitying me while also flirting with Rizz. I've been told women are better at multitasking than men—

A torn drink label hit my head, snapping me out of my spiral. Cheese rolled up another piece of her label and flicked it at me. "Someone's had too many phycos."

Rizz sat back in his chair, picking at his own bottle label, like he was lost in thought.

* * *

After we finished the six-packs of phyco, we found ourselves sprawled out on the roof of Rizz's apartment building, flopped onto a blanket—all five of us, our heads touching—gazing at the night sky. It was one of our favorite pastimes.

I haven't done anything like that in ages. Adults don't touch heads like they used to when they were drunk kids.

Back on the Blue Planet, Rizz and Cheese could barely see past the glow of streetlights—light pollution swallowed everything but the moon. But on Mars, the night sky stretched wide and endless—we could see billions of stars and planets. The Milky Way slashed across the panorama—a luminous, twirling reminder of just how small we are.

"I know I say it every time," Pepper murmured, eyes still locked on the stars, "but it really makes you understand why people on Earth lost their sense of wonder."

"And they aren't reminded of their insignificance every night," I added. "Which is why they're all so egotistical."

"Hey!" Rizz playfully hit my stomach, making me reflexively curl up.

"It makes you feel insignificant?" Pepper asked.

"Yeah. Doesn't it make you?" I tilted my head toward her.

"I guess a little. But it's always mixed in with, like, a sense of . . . I don't know, like . . . endless possibility."

"Flip, if you think it makes you insignificant, then it makes everyone insignificant," Cheese pointed out. "It sort of levels the playing field, right? Isn't that a little freeing? We're all just living a finite life in an infinite universe."

"There are more important people, though," I argued. "Celebrities, world leaders, historical figures—famous names etched in time, never to be forgotten."

"But zoom out," she told me.

"What do you mean?"

"You ever think about history lessons? You only have so many years in school to learn all of human history. As the timeline gets longer, there's more to cover, but no more time to teach it. So they cut the details for broad strokes. Names get tossed aside. Events slowly fade. People are forgotten."

"Where's the punchline, Cheese?" Rizz asked.

"That *is* the punchline," Cheese admitted.

"Jeez, that's dark."

"Maybe. But things aren't so scary when you can laugh at them."

Cheese had lost her parents when she was young and had to move to Mars with her uncle—already having experienced hardships most of us had yet to understand.

Tragedy and humor have a tragically humorous way of going hand in hand.

I propped myself up on my elbows, facing Cheese. "You think anyone is going to forget the name Paul Kingsley or Naomi Armstrong or Albert Einstein?" I asked.

"That quack?" Cheese jokingly scoffed. "But really, zoom out—a hundred years. A thousand years."

"Okay, I think people are still going to know those names."

"Keep zooming, Flip. Ten thousand years. A hundred thousand years." Cheese smiled at me. "I can do this all night."

I lay back down. "Okay, maybe some specifics would fall through the cracks at that point."

"If humans are even still around," Rizz added.

"And what's a hundred thousand years to a universe that's older than thirteen and a half billion?" Cheese asked. "We're all just blips. Here a blip. There a blip. Everywhere a blip blip."

"So, you're saying nothing matters, so why even bother trying?" I asked.

"No," Pepper countered. "It's not that nothing and no one matters—it's that everything and everyone matters equally. So there's no sense worrying about your profound importance to the human race. Stop comparing yourself to other people. You're free to live the life you want to live."

"That's my Two-Shoes." Cheese nudged Pepper. "All you can do is try to enjoy your life as much as possible before it's gone." She gazed back up at the stars. "Gone in a blip."

Rizz sat up. "Alright, that's enough existential, emo-teenager stargazing for one night. Let's go back inside. It's getting late." He glanced at the other side of the blanket. "You guys wanna stay over? I think Pockets has settled in for the night."

I twisted onto my elbow to see Pockets fast asleep, already drooling on the blanket. "Nah, I should probably head back before my parents get home. Don't need them seeing me drunk."

I pushed myself up and brushed the wrinkles off my shirt.

"You think they're still out?" Rizz asked.

"What time is it?"

"Like eleven."

"Shit . . . Shit, shit. I gotta go."

"I'll come too," Pepper said, popping up from the ground.

* * *

I walked her down to her apartment, where she leaned on the doorknob and swung the door open, still loose from the phyco.

"Hello? Hello?" Her voice echoed slightly in the empty space.

She turned back to me in the doorway, grinning, and whispered, "The coast is clear," then threw the door open wider and stepped inside, hinting at me to follow. "If my parents are still out, yours probably are too. You wanna come in for a bit?"

Tingles of excitable nerves ricocheted through my body, urging me inside. I gripped the doorframe, trying to physically pull myself into the room—but my feet stayed planted. I begged myself to just go inside. Take the invitation. Sit next to her. Do literally anything other than leave. Even stay standing in the doorway.

And yet . . .

"Nah, I should really get back before they do."

I still have no idea what the hell was going through my mind. My working theory is that, after living with my parents' loveless marriage, I figured I was destined to screw things up the same way. And I didn't want to do that. Not with someone like Pepper.

Or—I was just chicken shit.

I've replayed that moment inside my head countless times, hoping that somehow, someway, the words coming out of my mouth might change. But time travel involves expensive equipment and technical know-how—more than just a deep, yearning regret.

"Oh . . . Okay." She blinked, surprised. A flicker of disappointment.

"Not that I don't want to," I scrambled to explain. "I'm just kinda on thin ice lately."

"All good," she said, playing it off. "I'll see you tomorrow probably."

"Yeah. I'll see you tomorrow."

I let the door close—

"Wait!" Pepper stopped me. "Before you go . . ."

Disappearing down the hallway, she returned a sixtieth-of-a-minute later, lifting my arm and placing something in my hand.

Our snow globe.

She curled my fingers around it. "For safekeeping."

Then she smiled that perfect smile.

After the door closed, I stood there, motionless—already thinking of a thousand things I should've said instead. Things I still could say, if I just knocked on the door.

And yet . . .

CHAPTER ELEVEN

CAMPAIGN SEASON

A few months after the spacecraft crash-landed, an online survey link was circulated around the biosphere, allowing every citizen to nominate someone for the first official Director of Mars. Of the ten thousand people in the colony, only six thousand participated. Of the six thousand participants, only one thousand nominated someone other than themselves. Of the one thousand nominations, only four people got more than one vote.

Madison was one. Buzz was another. And so was Rizz.

The colony was immediately swept into an unrelenting campaign season. Political ads cluttered the airwaves, hijacking rackethand matches in between points. They were mostly harmless—except for Buzz's attack ads. He was the only candidate to stoop that low.

One of his ads interrupted MBN's *Searching for Mars with Special Agent O'Shea*—a culinary and cultural journey through the biosphere—and opened with a black-and-white, slow-motion video of him giving a thumbs up.

"I'm Buzz Buchanan, and I approve this message," his voiceover confirmed.

Then, in full color, the ad cut to a close-up of a famous book: *Men Are from Mars, Women Are from Venus.*

A deep, authoritative voice boomed, "This iconic work was published over a hundred years ago, but does it still hold true tosol?"

It cut to an interview with a female colonist answering, "The book is really about how each gender is different. The title isn't literal. And we're way past acknowledging only two gend—"

The ad abruptly cut to an interview with a male colonist grinning at the camera. "I guess I'm in my homeland, huh? Let's go, boys!"

The frame froze, draining of color, shifting back to black-and-white.

"Exactly," the voiceover stated. "*Men* are from Mars. *Women* are from Venus. Don't let a foreigner be in charge of your planet. A vote for Buzz Buchanan is a vote against Madison Chen."

After the ad, the feed cut back to Special Agent O'Shea, admiring the viscosity of a glass of phyco.

I grimaced. Not only was the ad offensive, but it barely made sense—though my father always preferred spectacle over sincerity.

* * *

In-person campaign events popped up around the biosphere as well—desperate attempts to sway the ever-elusive undecided voter. In the later stages of an election, those voters always seemed like mythical creatures to me, yet every cycle, they're studied, tracked, and hunted down like the chupacabra.

I couldn't stand the thought of my father winning—like he always did—but I was forced to fake my support and make an appearance at each of his events. As he always reminded me, I still lived under his roof, and I would do what I was told.

One took place outside Town Hall, where a flagpole—once adorned with the Astral Destiny banner—stood bare.

Music blasted from a set of speakers below it.

Buzz awkwardly danced in front of the crowd, slipping a sash over his shoulder that read: First Director Buzz Buchanan. Three expensive-looking women in bikinis and high heels took turns grinding on the flagpole and then on Buzz himself. All as my father handed out *I voted for Buzz* buttons to the men gawking at the performance—along with their embarrassed wives, who yanked them away.

Off to the side, my mom and I stood in the background, smiling and waving at the crowd—per Buzz's request. His attempt to appear like a family man.

"Why do we have to do this?" I muttered to my mom. "I don't want to be here. I only have a blip to live."

"A blip?" she asked, glancing at me. "What?"

"Just something Cheese said."

Though she kept her smile fixed in place, her voice was firm. "Listen, your father is the reason why we have the privileged lives we do. It's not too much to ask that you offer a little support in return."

I stopped waving. "I didn't ask for a privileged life. *You* made that deal."

"And I pay for it in more ways than you know." She turned to look at me, her smile gone. "Whether or not you asked for it, you got it. You're lucky. And I'm sure you'd be begging for this life if you were looking at it from the outside in. So put on a happy face, and wave like you want to be here."

I hated arguing with my mom. So I obliged.

* * *

Afterward, Buzz strutted over to Madison's event, where a much more understated gathering was underway.

"Madison," he greeted warmly, stretching out his hand. "I just wanted to say—best of luck in the race. You've done an incredible job as Interim Director and ran a great campaign."

Behind him, I subtly shook my head at Madison, warning her to proceed with caution.

Of course, she didn't notice me. She never did—especially when I was standing next to my father. Between them, two people with that much status, I just blended into the backdrop.

"Oh, uh, thanks. You too," Madison replied, tentatively taking his hand.

Buzz!

A sharp jolt zapped her palm, and she yelped, snatching her hand back.

Buzz cackled, revealing the cheap metal hand buzzer strapped to his hand.

"Just a little practical joke for you there! Here, you keep it."

He placed the buzzer in her hand and turned away, already moving on. "Marcus! Have you lost weight? You look fantastic! Get over here, you rascal."

As Madison rubbed her palm, she flipped the buzzer over in her hand.

A sticker plastered on the bottom read: Vote for BUZZZZZZ!!!

"Sorry," I mumbled as my mother and I hurried off, briskly tailing my father before he could notice us fraternizing with the enemy.

I wanted to help Rizz with his outreach, but as the directorial debate loomed, my father demanded more of my time. Cheese and Pockets took control, working together as Rizz's campaign managers.

Everything was set to culminate at the directorial debate in the Town Hall auditorium—home to not only political events, but also concerts, plays, and various other performances.

My father wasn't exaggerating when he claimed to be the highest-grossing thespian in Martian history. His talent was subpar at best, but he exploited his innate fame like many other celebrities—it wasn't his ability that landed him roles, it was his name.

As a boy, my father was cast as Kurt Von Trapp in *The Sound of Music*, and from the moment he took his first bow, he was addicted. His turn as the titular character in *Hamilton* garnered mixed reviews, ranging from "Decent rapping from a Caucasian" to "Maybe this isn't the greatest way to learn about history."

From there, he evolved into a multi-hyphenate: actor/writer/director/producer. A highly-coveted golden goose of entertainment.

A talent agent's wet dream.

Of course, his entire catalog consisted of only reboots. He never created anything, just rode the coattails of real artists with actually original ideas. To be fair, some of his adaptations were hits—like *Forrest Gump on Ice* and *The Godfather II: A Cappella.*

But his meteoric rise took a nosedive after he cast himself as the lead in an avant-garde production titled *The Ballet of the Planet of the Apes.* In it, prancing chimpanzees and twirling gorillas galloped on horseback, dance-fighting humans with spears that looked more like batons.

I have never once thought this about any other piece of theatrical work, but my father could have used more creative notes from the executive producers.

* * *

The night before the directorial debate, in the early hours of the morning, I woke to the sound of my father vomiting in the bathroom.

I knocked. "You okay?"

"Fine." His voice was muffled through the door. "Just a little food poisoning, I think. There was something fishy about that fish." He sounded like he was trying to convince himself, not me.

The toilet flushed. The faucet ran.

I hesitated. It's not like I wanted him to win—I wanted Madison Chen to beat him, anyone to beat him. But he clearly had a nervous stomach, and nobody likes puking in a toilet.

"It's okay if you're freaking out about tomorrow," I said.

The door opened. His face was damp—whether from sweat or from rinsing off in the sink, I wasn't sure.

"You think I have stage fright? Don't be ridiculous," he insisted. "I've spent my entire life in the spotlight."

"No, I know. It's just . . . This isn't acting."

He put a firm hand on my shoulder. "Flip, all politics *is* is acting. I'll feel right at home."

I was only trying to reassure him, but he mistook it for doubt. It was best to end the scene right there.

"Right. Of course. You're gonna be great. You got nothing to worry about."

We swapped places in the doorframe—he went back to bed, and I shut the bathroom door behind me.

CHAPTER TWELVE

MASTER DEBATERS

"New news with Newt Newman is new at noon," Newt announced—at eight p.m.

As he sat at a desk facing the stage in the Town Hall auditorium, he addressed the live audience behind him and the viewers at home. Isabella Jiménez—a Chattr news influencer—sat beside him, poised and professional.

On stage, four candidates stood behind sleek, identical podiums arranged in a straight line. Buzz, at center left, was slightly overdressed in a flashy velvet tuxedo. At center right, Interim Director Madison Chen wore a more appropriate yet commanding maroon pantsuit.

The front row of the auditorium had once again been reserved for family and friends. To the right of my mom and me sat Cliff and Pepper, while Cheese and Pockets sat on our left, directly in front of Rizz, who stood at the left-most podium.

"I'm Newt Newman. And I'm joined by Chattr news influencer Isabella Jimmy—uh—nease," Newt stammered, butchering Isabella Jiménez's name without acknowledging the mistake with so much as a wince, apology, or glance. For the remainder of the debate, he avoided addressing her entirely. She never spoke.

"Nine months ago, Mars declared its autonomy as a planet-state." Newt paused as the audience erupted in applause. "Now, standing before you are the four candidates who have received the most support in the polls. But only one will be elected the first Director of Mars."

He cleared his throat. "The rules of the debate are simple: each candidate will have one minute to answer questions pulled from the comment section of our live stream and thirty seconds for rebuttals. If a candidate exceeds the time limit, I will politely interject, and he or she will immediately cease their argument—obediently and respectfully."

He eyed the candidates with a raised brow. "Let's begin with the opening statements. Pastor Van Buren."

Pastor Van Buren—the leader of a niche, extremist religious sect worshipping the Greek god of war, Ares—stood behind the right-most podium.

Although my parents weren't religious, they believed I needed a religious education. We attended a few Aresian services, but they quickly decided that chaperoning me—and enduring the rituals themselves—was too great a sacrifice.

The Aresian Church had banded together to nominate the priest as their Holy Martian Director. Sweat drenched his long, dark cape—the traditional Aresian garb of leadership. And he barely managed to steady his red spear, the sacred weapon of Ares, in his clammy hands.

"As it is written in Aphrodite 3:16—'Praise be those who kneel before the almighty Prince of Olympus,'" he began. "My people, we all fear the righteous power of Ares, warlord of the heavens. We must make haste and form a theocracy, ruled by me, an enlightened priest, bequeathed with the divine word of Ares. Spoken through me and me alone, his virtuous teachings might appear convoluted and contradictory, but silence your questions, and you will be granted eternal paradise built upon the blood of the damned and the non-believers."

"Alright, great," Newt said hastily, rushing to move on. "Next up, Marco Rizzolo."

In order of least to most nominations, Rizz was next to deliver his opening statement. It was the most dressed up I had ever seen him—though, compared to the others on stage, still casual. Gray jeans. White button shirt—no tie. And a poorly fitted sports jacket.

"We don't need a government," he declared.

Rizz delivered the statement with such nonchalant confidence that the audience didn't know how to react—no laughter, no outrage, no applause, just an uncomfortable ambiance and two soft coughs.

"It's a restricting, controlling establishment created by power-hungry fascists and greedy capitalists. I say total anarchy. No more societal constructs. No more industrialist lobbyists. No more encroaching laws. Complete, unlimited freedom! I didn't even prepare for this debate. Fuck homework! Fuck bureaucracy! Fuck the system! Anarchy for life!"

A small but rowdy crowd of teenagers—right behind Cheese and Pockets—exploded in wild cheers. Pockets tossed Rizz a phyco on stage. Without hesitation, Rizz punctured the can with his thumb, shotgunned the drink, then crushed the empty can against his forehead, and punted it into the audience.

"Recycle!" he demanded.

The teen section lost their minds.

It was clear that Cheese and Pockets had refined my original message—maybe a little too much. But it definitely resonated with a certain demographic.

"As a reminder to the candidates," Newt said, "there is no food or drink permitted in this auditorium."

Rizz wiped his dripping mouth with his sport jacket sleeve.

Newt continued, "Now, with the second-most nominations—Interim Director Madison Chen. Your opening statement."

Madison's gaze shifted from the moderators to the audience, then to the candidates beside her. She took a deep breath and delivered her pitch.

"The most effective government will be an inclusive, ever-evolving system. A government that listens. One where every opinion—no matter how unpopular—is genuinely explored. In this system, each one of us will have the opportunity to vote on every law, bill, act, and decree, should we choose to participate.

"Our procedures will be built to adapt—easily amendable, capable of shifting alongside our needs and future circumstances. We must be prepared to evolve with the challenges of tomorrow. And we will be. Thank you."

As she finished, her proposal was met by a loud applause.

"Thank you, Madam Interim Director," Newt announced. "Lastly, Buzz Buchanan."

My father stepped out from behind his podium, flashing his signature grin.

"First of all, I'd like to just say—what an honor it is to be here, in the presence of such beautiful, inspiring, and intelligent people."

He worked the stage, moving from right to left. "Tosol, we're also joined by my esteemed guest—a warrior of this community—Peter Kowalski."

He gestured into the audience.

Directly behind my mom and me, the Dome-ino's cashier—the one dragged from his post during the riot—lifted his hand. The two fingers poking out of his wrist cast gave a stiff, mechanical, bunny-ear wave, like he'd never make a hand-tossed pie again.

No doubt his injury had healed by then, but my father needed the cast to heighten the theatrics.

"A patriot," my father continued. "Laying his life on the line to nourish the Martian people. Delivering justice within thirty minutes. Thank you for your service."

The audience rose in a respectful, earnest standing ovation. My mom had to pull me out of my seat to stand.

Buzz waited for them to settle before pressing on. "Now, my

colleagues have thrown around a lot of interesting ideas here tonight—but none of them quite capture the heart and soul of this community. But me?" He placed a hand over his heart. "I'm a man of the people. And when it comes to what kind of government we should have, I agree with *you*."

I winced at his ability to use so many words to say so little.

"I think you are absolutely right," he said. "Each and every one of you makes a great point. You've convinced me!"

He made his way back to center stage. "And I promise to do exactly what you hope I'll do. I will be the first-elected, first-chosen Director of Mars!"

He received even bigger applause than Madison.

My father was right. Politics wasn't about ideas—it was about performance. A charade. Hopelessness flooded my chest. I was ready to give up before the debate had even begun. I couldn't stand to think my father would somehow eke out another undeserved win, another undeserved title, another undeserved thing he could throw in my face.

My father's opening statement—void of any concrete ideas or actions—kicked off a raucous evening of back-and-forth quips and soundbites, all with the depth of a motivational poster:

"All men *and* women are created equal," Madison declared. "Women's rights have never been assumed—they need to be defined."

Applause rippled through the crowd.

"Not everyone is cis," Rizz chimed in. "Gender is a spectrum. Sexuality too."

"Of course," Madison agreed. "And to take it a step further, we may want to explicitly mention all races." Her eyes fell on her daughter Pepper in the front row. "As well as those of mixed race, which, in itself, could be considered a spectrum as well."

"Great! Another spectrum." Buzz clapped his hands together. "How about: 'All people on the spectrum are created equal'?"

Silence.

Heads in the audience tilted, brows furrowed. Candidates exchanged glances. All unsure if my father had just said something disgustingly offensive or transcendently tolerant.

"Our justice system cannot treat individuals differently based on their background or status," Buzz suggested, surprisingly. "We need a blanket solution—an eye for an eye," he added, unsurprisingly.

"'An eye for an eye would leave the whole world blind,'" Madison countered.

Buzz shrugged. "When's the last time you heard about a murderous blind person? Sounds pretty peaceful to me!"

"People should at least be presumed innocent until proven guilty," Rizz argued. "I've gotten into plenty of trouble for things I didn't do."

"All of us are guilty," Pastor Van Buren proclaimed ominously. "No one is innocent."

"Encouraging false accusations would take us right back to the Salem Witch Trials," Rizz pointed out.

Pastor Van Buren lifted his spear toward Rizz. "No one ever proved they *weren't* witches!"

"We can discourage false accusations by punishing the accuser if the defendant isn't guilty," Buzz proposed.

Madison sneered. "That's victim blaming."

Buzz shook his head. "No, in the case of a false accusation, the accused becomes the victim."

I blinked. I wasn't totally sure who was in the right or wrong at that point.

"We need to ban spades," Rizz urged. "Only contractors and exploration teams should have access to them. Nobody else needs a spade."

At that time, everyone had the right to purchase and operate a handheld spade—excavation drills that fired high-intensity laser bursts. Technically designed for boring through dense Martian bedrock, they were far more effective at dismembering a human body.

"What if I want to dig a hole?" Buzz asked.

"Use a shovel," Madison suggested. "You really want everyone walking around with a spade?"

"We'd have spades in spades." Rizz paused. "And let's call it what it is—a weapon."

"No, we're going to call a spade a spade," Buzz objected. "And if everyone has a spade, and a bad guy starts digging an unlawful hole, a good guy with a spade can blast a hole underneath the bad guy, making him fall in—thereby eliminating the threat of an unlawful hole."

"There would be no threat of an unlawful hole if the bad guy couldn't legally own a spade!" Rizz shouted.

Buzz leaned on his podium to look at Rizz directly. "What we really need to do is figure out why this mentally unstable maniac wants to dig such a big unlawful hole in the first place!"

Everyone left the debate having learned nothing at all.

* * *

That night, as soon as we got back to the apartment, my father poured himself a red malt, plopped into his sofa chair, and started scrolling through Chattr for debate coverage.

"I'm Isabella Jiménez, and this is *Jiménez Says*," Isabella announced at the start of her Chattr stream—correctly pronouncing her own name.

Since my father played it loud enough for the whole family to hear, I reluctantly watched over his shoulder.

"An hour ago, the candidates vying to become the first Director of Mars took the debate stage. But who won the night? Here to discuss is a trusted member of the Martian middle class."

The frame of Jiménez shrunk to cover only the left half of the feed, while the right half expanded to show a woman in her forties with a short haircut and an earth-tone cardigan. She looked like the type to file a noise complaint one minute after quiet hours started.

"I can't see how anyone other than Madison Chen wins this election," the woman said with certainty.

My father scoffed in his chair.

"I wouldn't trust anyone else to create the Martian government," she continued. "Half the people on that stage weren't serious candidates. Madison Chen was strong in her conviction and had a thoughtful answer for every question. She followed the debate rules and never spoke past her time. I wouldn't vote for anyone else."

"Pfft, Susan! Listen to yourself."

The left frame shrunk again, pushing Jiménez out of frame entirely to make room for another live feed—a middle-aged, overweight man in a wifebeater. He looked like the type to beat his wife.

"It's a fact: Buchanan won this debate. Buzz's buzzwords word things exactly the way people want to hear them. And he's famous! There's no way he's going to lose this election."

My mom scoffed more subtly from the kitchen. I might've scoffed too, but after paying attention to politics for the first time in my life, I was already disillusioned. It all felt like hollow pomp and circumstance. Just a big act.

I couldn't trust what politicians were saying. And I couldn't trust what the media was saying about what politicians were saying. And I couldn't trust what everyone else was saying about what the media was saying.

A lot of hearing people saying, but it was all just hearsay.

I wanted politics to be different. I wanted Mars to be different. And I wanted my father to be different.

CHAPTER THIRTEEN

WAREHOUSE FIVE

On the morning of the Election Results Reveal Party, I could barely get out of bed. I had no interest in witnessing our bureaucracy at work. I had already seen that performance.

It was mid-July, and I'd turned eighteen back in May. With Mars declaring its independence, it would be fitting for me to do the same—move out, set off on a coming-of-age journey, step into the world on my own.

But life rarely matches obvious, hokey storytelling devices.

And after graduating Armstrong High, I still had four more years at Kingsley Maximum School—Martian education was K-22.

So, there I was—still living under my father's roof. And somehow, despite everything else on his plate—Martian independence, his campaign, managing a biosphere on a barren planet—he still found time to lecture me about graduating as salutatorian of my class.

A huge achievement by any standard. Something that I was actually proud of. But to him, I wasn't the one giving the speech. I wasn't the one on stage, looking out at friends and family. I wasn't number one.

After being berated for my mediocrity for the thousandth time, I couldn't stand being a pawn in my father's campaign anymore—smiling and waving like the clean-cut, happy-go-lucky, well-behaved son who wants to grow up to be just like his personal hero, Daddy.

The election was almost over. But I was at my breaking point. All I wanted was to turn back the clock for a sol. Back to when I was younger—when there wasn't so much pressure. Back when I could run around with the Catfish Trolls and get up to who knows what.

That was it—the gang. That was exactly what I needed.

I stomped on my floor.

I could've messaged Pepper on Chattr, but Flipper Code meant so much more—every stomp and thud landed with the weight of our shared history.

I stomped again.

Me:	Crazy idea.
Pepper:	What? Just text me.
Me:	Wanna play hooky?
Pepper:	We can't. Our parents would kill us if we miss it.
Me:	We'll only miss the mingling beforehand. I promise.
Pepper:	Where are we going?
Me:	It's a secret.
Pepper:	Come on, Flip.
Me:	Meet me by the exploration bay. Tell the Catfish Trolls.

With the Election Results Reveal Party just hours away, everyone was out running last-minute errands before heading to the Town Hall lawn for the ceremony.

I waited outside the hangar—kicking pebbles and hocking loogies, reminiscing about my hobby when I was eight—before finally spotting Pepper making her way toward me.

"What took you so long?" I asked.

"It wasn't exactly easy to get away," she said. "I had to make something up."

"Where are Rizz and them?"

"Already at Town Hall—like we should be."

"That's where everyone will be," I said, pulling my hood up. "Which is exactly why we have to go now."

Pepper planted her feet. "Go where, Flip? What's going on?"

I put a finger to my lips, then reached into my pocket, pulled out our snow globe, and pressed it into her hand. I'm not exactly sure why I brought it. Or why I was giving it to her then.

Neither was she.

Her brow furrowed. She stared at the mini glass dome in her palm, eyes narrowing, then lifted her head, giving me a hard, uncomfortable look. Yes, I was acting weird. No, I couldn't explain why. Instead, I grabbed her arm and pulled her along.

Keeping the secret felt playful at first. Then playful turned into annoying. Then annoying turned into rude. By the time we reached our destination, Pepper was pissed.

"Seriously! Flip! Stop!" she screamed at me, screeching to a halt.

"We're here," I told her.

"Where?"

Warehouse Five stood before us. When we were kids, myths and tall tales surrounded the abandoned, run-down structure—like a neighborhood rumor about a twisted rock musician removing his own rib so he could go down on himself.

As the legend goes, years ago, a kooky, graying slave owner lived in the warehouse—manufacturing chocolate and other candies with the forced labor of miniature, orange men. One sol, the slave owner invited five children inside, killed four of them, and handed his candy empire to the sole survivor—an eleven-year-old boy with zero real-world business experience. After that, the candyman disappeared, rumored to have gone searching for new flavors all across Mars only to never return.

As for the boy, having limited knowledge of commerce, he ran the company into the ground—hence, the warehouse's decrepit state.

Over the years, several different groups of smug, sexy teens double-dog-dared each other to break in. But they never found a single trace of a sweet treat or a tiny orange man. They were always caught before they could even get inside.

"Warehouse Five?" Pepper asked. "Why?"

I gestured to the empty streets and alleys. "Everyone's at the Election Party."

"So?"

"So, there's no one around to catch us."

Pepper rolled her eyes and groaned. "Are you joking? This is stupid. Who cares?"

I deflated. "We promised each other—when we were kids. If there was ever a chance to see what's inside, we'd take it."

"We were kids!" Her expression hardened. "What's really going on with you, Flip?"

"Nothing."

I hesitated. For a second, I almost brushed it off. But instead, I took a deep breath.

"I can't watch him win again."

Pepper cocked her head.

"My father." I swallowed. "He always wins. And it always makes me feel like I'll never live up to his expectations. Like I'll always be stuck in second." My throat clenched. "I'll never make him proud. I'm not the best at anything. I'm just . . . normal. Average. Forgettable."

My voice cracked. A lump swelled in my throat. My vision blurred with a film of tears. All I could do was stare at the ground, trying to suck all my emotions back in, bottle them up, and push them deep down—right where they should be.

Pepper didn't say anything. Not right away. Then without a word, she pulled me into a fierce hug.

Her grip was tight. Unshakable.

"I'll never forget you," she whispered.

I didn't know what I wanted her to say. And I had even less of an idea of what I needed her to say. But that was the thing about Pepper—she had a knack for saying the exact right thing. Honestly, it didn't even matter what she said—all that mattered was that she was the one saying it.

After a moment, she pulled back. "Come on. Let's see what's in there."

After finding the fire escape ladder, I squatted against the wall, bracing myself.

"Climb on," I told Pepper.

She didn't hesitate, hoisting herself onto my shoulders and stretching upward, fingers grazing metal. She yanked the ladder down, and we climbed up.

We snuck in the same way we did when we slipped into the exploration bay and onto the orientation coaster—a maintenance entrance on the roof. Between our breaking and entering and my pebble kicking, I was having a lot of warm feelings of nostalgia for our younger years.

At the top, we found the door—its knob already jostled a little loose. All it needed was some encouragement.

We scanned the roof and Pepper found a fire extinguisher. She didn't bother to hand it to me—she just grabbed it and bashed the knob, snapping it clean off.

The door creaked open.

We exchanged glances. Then we stepped inside, creeping down a dark stairwell to the first floor.

Fluorescent lights flickered overhead, buzzing faintly. Mildew and mold clung to the walls and floors, formerly white tiles warped with decay. The air was stale and damp—like how I imagined a swamp might feel oozing over your skin.

"Spooky meter is at a four right now," I muttered.

Pepper didn't respond. She was peering into a small square window in the door, holding her hands around her face to see inside. She waved me over.

I pressed my forehead to the glass.

Inside, a glow cast jagged shadows of operating tables. Medical monitors. Toppled IV stands. Open cabinets, emptied.

A surgical theater, abandoned.

"Spooky meter is at a six," Pepper murmured, breath fogging the glass.

We kept moving, stepping deeper into the warehouse. At the end of the hallway, double doors loomed. We hesitated. Then together—we pushed our way in.

The stench hit us first. Thick. Sour.

It was even darker than the hallway. Dim lights illuminated the few meters around us, but then—pitch black. Like if we walked any further, we'd be sucked into a black hole. To our left, stairs. The metal groaned beneath our feet as we tiptoed up to another door, opening it into a compact control room.

"Oh my god!" we both shout-whispered at the same time.

In the corner of the room, a graying, bearded man was curled up on a filthy twin mattress, fast asleep.

"Candy slave owner?" I thought aloud.

"Do you think he lives here?" she asked, hushed, already slinking toward the panel of buttons, switches, and monitors. Then—

Alarms. Strobing lights.

We jumped as the old man bolted upright—eyes wild, arms lashing out—and in a flash, he grabbed Pepper.

"What have you done?" he bellowed in her face.

I don't know how she didn't soil herself. I nearly did.

"I didn't touch anything!" Pepper asserted.

Through the window above the control panel, more lights blinked on, revealing a giant hangar.

Cages. Towers of them, stacked on top of each other. And they weren't empty. Inside each one, dark figures stirred, roused from slumber by the sudden commotion.

That was when the cold sweat started.

A hangar jumbotron gradually brightened, glowing on the back wall. A face filled the screen—a familiar face. Curly brown hair.

Sharp, skinny features. A devilish smile.

"Hello, my friends," he said. "You may not know me, but I am Duke Kingsley—grandson of Paul Kingsley. You'll be happy to hear that my grandfather has passed—over a year ago at this point. Now, you may ask yourself, 'Then why am I still imprisoned here? For what purpose?'"

That was when the shiver went down my spine.

Duke paused, tilting his head, smiling wider. "To keep you secret. To keep you locked away where no one would ever find you. To keep Paul Kingsley's legacy intact." Duke's eyes glinted with mischief as he leaned in. "But no more! As soon as I discovered Warehouse Five, I knew what I had to do—set you free. Now, the only problem is, the Martian colonists who have kept you here? They might not feel the same way. They might not be so generous."

That was when the heartbeat thumped.

"Here is my proposition," he offered. "Eradicate the colonists. Take control of the biosphere. Claim the planet as your own. Then and only then, will you be free."

Someone seemed to say something to Duke off camera, and he checked his watch and held up a finger to give him a moment before turning back to the camera. "Sound good? Great. I'll leave the ways and means up to you. Looking forward to chatting when the job is done. Alright. Have a good one."

The video froze—Duke mid-reach, stopping the recording.

"What the fuck?" I blurted.

The disheveled squatter instinctively took a step back, away from the window. One by one, red lights turned green on the cages in the hangar and the locks released—*pop, pop, pop*.

And from the towers of enclosures, they crawled out. Hundreds. Maybe thousands. Dark figures clambering down the prison cell stacks like insects spilling from a busted nest.

A robotic voice crackled over the warehouse intercom. "Project Eternity aborted. Evacuate the building . . . Project Eternity aborted. Evacuate the building . . ."

The message repeated on a loop, mechanical and cold.

"Get out!" the scruffy stranger warned, "Now!" before bolting from the room.

He didn't make it far.

From the control room window, we watched a dark figure tackle the harried lunatic to the ground.

A swarm of the creatures descended on him.

"No . . . No! Please!" the man shrieked—begging. "I was just doing my job. I didn't mean to. I didn't want to. Please!"

The shadows engulfed him. His screams twisted into wet gurgles. Psychotic snickering rippled through the mob of monsters. They dipped their fingers into the man's remains, smearing his blood across their faces and bodies like war paint. A glimpse—two arms, two legs. They looked like they could be human. At one point, maybe. Long ago.

We needed to move.

I grabbed Pepper's wrist. "We gotta get out of here!"

We bolted from the control room, sprinting so fast we nearly tumbled down the stairs. Racing through the dim hallways that stretched out endlessly, trying every door we could.

Locked.

Locked.

Locked.

"Spooky meter is at a full eleven right now," Pepper muttered, forcing a joke. Maybe in shock. Denial.

Finally—*click*. One door gave way, and we threw ourselves inside, locking it behind us, collapsing to the floor, our backs against the adjacent wall, panting.

The room was no bigger than the compact kitchens in each Martian apartment—bare except for a long table and a few chairs facing the window above our heads.

I sucked in a breath, chest still heaving. Twisting onto my knees, I pressed my face to the bottom of the window to peer into the room next door. Several snickering, twitchy critters rushed inside, and I ducked back down without getting a good look. Pepper and I exchanged a wide-eyed glance before carefully rising just enough to watch over the window ledge.

We saw their hunched backs quivering as they raided the room, vaulting over an operating table like wild animals, grabbing what looked like surgical tools—bone saws, drills, needles.

"I think we're in a medical observation room," Pepper whispered. She hadn't noticed I'd impulsively started crawling backward. I hadn't noticed either—until my back bumped the table. And the long-abandoned coffee mug sitting at its edge . . .

Tipped.

Plummeted.

Shattered.

All of them turned at once, over a dozen pairs of eyes snapping toward the sound. Every single one—each and every one of them—Paul Kingsley. Late fifties, early sixties. Identical to the man in the orientation video.

The video might not have been a deepfake after all.

Torn, light-blue scrubs hung from their grotesquely scarred bodies, both fabric and skin slathered with bloodstains from the mangled old man. And there were hundreds more. Hundreds of crazed Paul Kingsleys running amok through Warehouse Five.

One of them released a slow, inhuman giggle.

Pepper's hand clamped onto my wrist. "We gotta go!"

We clambered to our feet and looked to our only two exits—the one we came in and another on the opposite wall. We had to decide fast.

I looked back through the window—

The Paul Kingsleys were gone.

We had to decide very fast.

They slammed themselves against the door we came in, rattling the frame. *Bash. Bash. Bash.*

Our decision was made for us. Pepper and I ran to the other door. No time to wonder what might be waiting for us on the other side.

We crashed through it, spilling into another hallway.

The walls shook with distant explosions, dust raining down from the ceiling.

I whipped my head around, desperate for an exit. Then—a sliver of natural light, leaking through a door at the far end of the impossibly-long hallway.

"Come on!" I gasped, sprinting toward our only hope of escape.

Thick, black smoke crawled along the ceiling. I yanked my shirt over my mouth, coughing against the sting in my throat. Pepper did the same.

Clang.

A door behind us burst open.

We froze. Turned.

A Paul Kingsley sauntered out, stretching, rolling his neck like he'd just woken up from a long nap.

My eyes burned. My lungs ached. My throat tickled. Every muscle in my body clenched, holding in a cough that desperately wanted out. Beside me, Pepper wheezed, then gripped my arm—tight—hoping she didn't give us away.

But she knew she did.

Paul Kingsley's head twisted. Locked onto us.

For a beat—nothing. Then he jolted, scampering toward us.

We didn't wait. Didn't dare look back. We bolted toward the exit, faster than I ever thought we could.

We charged through the door, staggering out of Warehouse Five, gasping, dragging ourselves twenty meters away before collapsing, chests still heaving, lungs begging for air. I dared to look back at the building. He was there, staring at us from the doorway. Still. Silent. Expression unreadable. Then he slinked backward into the shadows and let the door shut.

I would've preferred a whimsical slave owner obsessed with chocolate bars.

CHAPTER FOURTEEN

THE ELECTION RESULTS REVEAL PARTY

"The Pauls are coming! The Pauls are coming!"

Pepper and I galloped toward the ceremony on the Town Hall lawn.

"The Pauls are coming! The Pauls are coming!"

We gasped for air, pointing wildly behind us, toward Warehouse Five.

But nobody even looked at us.

Maybe no one heard us. More likely, we weren't making any sense. Most likely, no one cared what we were saying. It wasn't my first time being ignored. Still, we had to do something.

We ran toward the Election Results Reveal Party, which was already in full swing, like everything was hunky-dory. Citizens milled about, laughing, mingling, completely unaware.

"You have to get out of here!" we warned anyone who would listen.

No one did. They continued to meander from booth to booth—snacking on concessions while vendors hawked new businesses and peddled psychic readings. It felt like we sprinted out of a horror movie and straight into a small-town holiday special. Total whiplash.

We brushed past the thousands of chairs arranged in neat, orderly rows across the lawn, all facing a massive stage hidden by a thick red curtain—behind it, Lake Ares providing an idyllic backdrop.

It was obvious that we weren't going to convince anyone, so we searched for an authority figure people would listen to.

I spotted my father—shaking hands, still laying on the campaign charm. Madison stood next to him, rolling her eyes so hard I was surprised they didn't pop out. I nudged Pepper and pointed—they were our chance to evacuate everyone.

We scurried past local artists sketching caricatures, face painting, twisting balloon animals—mostly donkeys, since there were no other animals on Mars.

Without stopping to apologize, we walked through shots being filmed by MBN reporters and camera crews—B-roll of the extravaganza and interviews of celebrating citizens. Soft pop music played over loudspeakers—Ms. Anderson's high school band had not been asked to return.

The event was almost pleasant, if not for the incoming herd of crazed carbon copies of a dead billionaire.

"Flip!" My mom found us before we could reach Buzz or Madison. "Where have you been?" she demanded. "This started an hour ago. I can't keep covering for you."

"We were at Warehouse Five!" My words came out a kilometer a minute. "We broke in—there were cages—towers of them—fucking hundreds of Paul Kingsleys. But they were insane! They fucking killed a guy! We barely escaped. They're coming here—right now. We have to warn everyone. We have to get everyone out of here!"

Her brows knitted together. "Why are you so sweaty and dirty? Are you on drugs? What did you take?"

"We aren't on drugs!"

She looked at Pepper.

"We aren't!" Pepper confirmed.

The speakers sputtered, and an audio recording began. "Ladies, gentlemen, and everyone on the spectrum, we invite you to take your seats, as the ceremony will begin shortly."

My mom exhaled sharply. "We'll talk about this later."

"We might not have until later!" I pleaded. "Mom, I'm serious. No one is safe. We have to do something—right now."

"It is my pleasure to welcome you to the Election Results Reveal Party at our very own Town Hall. We do hope you enjoy the festivities."

She wasn't hearing me. She wasn't listening.

"Enough, Flip," she said flatly. "I know the past nine months haven't been easy on you, but this is no way to handle it. You're acting like a child."

"You don't understand—"

She grabbed my arm and turned to Pepper. "Go find your father." Then dragged me to the front row and shoved me into the aisle seat.

Pepper was pushed into the seat directly across—Cliff wouldn't be helping us either.

"Please take a moment to locate your nearest exit and turn off all electronic devices."

I twisted around, eyes scanning the horizon. They were nowhere to be seen. But I knew they were still coming. They were waiting for something.

"Without further ado, please welcome to the stage—from your favorite television program, *NCIS: Mars*, Special Agent O'Shea!"

The red curtain opened.

From the left wing, the actor emerged, wearing his uniform from the show—navy-blue suit, gray shirt, prop police badge around his neck, aviator sunglasses. He strode across the stage, stopping at downstage right. Then he whipped out a finger gun, mimicking his detective character.

I couldn't enjoy the show. My knee bounced like a piston, rattling the chair beneath me.

The applause died down.

"Before we get started," he announced, "it is my honor to unveil the brand new, official flag of Mars."

From the ceiling, a massive, fabric flag unfurled—a solid red circle on a black background.

It was met with sluggish, disappointed claps.

Though the flag design didn't receive much acclaim at the time, it was later hailed as one of the most influential designs in history—a minimalist masterpiece and a provocative, blatant plagiarism of the Japanese flag.

Volunteers wove through the rows, handing out miniature flags. One blocked my view, so I snatched a flag to get her to move. I didn't wave it—my mind was elsewhere.

"Mom, seriously—we have to get everyone out of here," I quietly muttered. "We're all in danger." Sweat dripped from my clothes like I had just taken a dip in Lake Ares.

She didn't even look at me. "Acting out like this isn't going to get you anywhere, Flip. Every sol with you is harder than the last. Please, just . . . Just make tosol a little easier."

That's what I got for being the *first* person to warn people of an imminent, life-threatening danger. That's why I had stopped trying so hard to be first.

But lives weren't usually on the line—at least, not so obviously.

"In addition to our flag," Special Agent O'Shea continued, "I am proud to announce the official sport of Mars. Invented in 2042+, right here on Mars, this sport quickly surpassed cricket and football to become the most popular in the solar system—watched by billions of people. You all know it. You all love it. Give it up for rackethand!"

Thunderous applause. Cheers. Whistles.

But I couldn't even clap for my favorite sport. My hands stayed locked in my lap, my head on a constant swivel, scouring the lawn.

At any moment, I expected to see a hundred Paul Kingsleys, sprinting toward us, raring to slice my head off with a bone saw.

"And it won't surprise any of you to hear—after years of serving as our unofficial mascot, bouncing around the biosphere and into all of our hearts . . . the official animal of Mars is . . . Pluto the donkey!"

The crowd erupted.

Pluto trotted onto the stage, ears twitching, making her way toward the carrot Special Agent O'Shea held out. The donkey got triple the cheers the actor had, and as soon as she ate the carrot, everyone leapt to their feet. Hats went flying. Strangers kissed. People sobbed. A woman fainted.

I ducked low, craning my neck around the celebrating colonists, searching for any sign of movement in the distance. Heart hammering.

No one was going to believe us. Not until they saw the Paul Kingsley horde for themselves. And I needed to give them as much warning as possible.

Special Agent O'Shea waited for the madness to settle. Then he grumbled, "I guess we'll have to offer Pluto a part on our planet's top television program, *NCIS: Mars*."

Unsure how to react, the crowd quieted, wondering if he was seriously jealous or just making a joke. Or both.

Everyone took their seats. The actor cleared his throat, moving on. "Please welcome to the stage, your candidates for the first Director of Mars: Pastor Van Buren, Marco Rizzolo, Interim Director Madison Chen, and Interim Vice Director Buzz Buchanan."

As each name was called, the candidates stepped onto the stage, receiving various levels of applause. Their outfits were coordinated, each featuring a distinct color: red, green, pink, and blue, respectively. I didn't know why. Not yet.

They all shook hands, except for Pastor Van Buren, who instead held out his hand, expecting each candidate to bow and kiss his ring.

No one did.

Once the pleasantries concluded, the candidates took specific spots on stage—two meters apart, forming a straight line. The lights cut out. Total darkness.

They took out the power grid—the attack had begun.

I jumped to my feet. Then four intense spotlights flashed on and tilted down from the stage ceiling, each zeroing in on one candidate.

The entire audience, everyone, remained seated, eyeing me. My mom pulled me back down. A deep, bass-heavy score rumbled through the speakers—laying on the suspense when my blood pressure wasn't in need of any more.

Special Agent O'Shea savored the attention, dragging out as many dramatic pauses as possible. "The candidate with the fewest votes is . . . Pastor Van Buren!"

The spotlight on the pastor snapped off—leaving only his shadow.

"The candidate with the second-fewest votes is . . . Marco Rizzolo!"

The beam on Rizz vanished. His silhouette threw up a double bird and everyone under twenty-five roared in approval of his civil disobedience.

I barely noticed.

I couldn't understand why the Paul Kingsleys hadn't shown themselves yet. They certainly seemed like they were in a hurry before. They had to be storming in at any moment, eager to serve a cold dish of revenge. There wasn't anything holding them up.

They were strategizing. They were patient. Preparing. They weren't just rage-fueled lunatics—they were organized.

My stomach dropped.

That was so much worse.

On stage, only two spotlights remained—one on Madison Chen and one on Buzz Buchanan. The other candidates were only outlines, barely lit by a dim backlight.

"Your first ever Director of Mars is . . ."

"There they are!" I hollered, pointing straight down the aisle. "The Pauls are coming!"

CHAPTER FIFTEEN

PAULS ON PAULS ON PAULS

Fifteen tank-sized rovers rolled in, filling the entire width of the streets. They had raided the exploration bay, outfitting themselves with vehicles and spades. An army of Pauls—armed, dangerous. At least a thousand of them. Maybe more. With Lake Ares at our backs, we were cornered, completely exposed.

My worst fears weren't even close. This wasn't a disaster—it was an extinction-level event.

We were fucked.

They marched across the Town Hall lawn, kicking up dust as they paraded forward in eerie unison. Then about fifty meters from the audience, they came to a halt.

"They ripped a man to shreds!" I yelled, stepping into the aisle—desperate for as many people as possible to see me. "And wiped his blood on their faces!"

"It's true!" Pepper shouted, standing on her seat, just as frantic. "Duke Kingsley set them loose to attack us!"

Some people stood, shielding their eyes and looking around, squinting. Mumbles rippled through the crowd—uncertainty, fear.

On stage, Madison and Buzz stepped out of their respective spotlights, disappearing into the shadows between. They turned their backs to the audience, whispering. After a tense moment, they strode toward Special Agent O'Shea. Madison muttered something to him. Buzz took Pluto's reins.

Special Agent O'Shea cleared his throat, adjusting his uniform. "Ladies, gentlemen, and everyone on the spectrum, I've just been told that there's absolutely nothing to worry about."

"They're gonna kill us!" I shouted, spinning around to tell everyone.

"Flip!" My mother's hand clamped around my arm, wrestling me back from the aisle.

Special Agent O'Shea hesitated—shifting on his feet, suddenly uneasy—before repeating what he'd clearly been instructed to say. "Our Interim Director and Interim VD are going to speak with our unexpected guests to, uh, iron out any misunderstandings."

Buzz swung his leg over Pluto. Madison mounted her behind him. They trotted off toward the Pauls.

Rizz hopped down from the stage, landing hard. "Flip, what the hell is going on?"

Cheese and Pockets rushed over. My mom and Cliff followed. The seven of us huddled together, voices low, urgent.

"It's Warehouse Five," I told them. "It's a cloning facility."

"There were thousands of Paul Kingsley clones locked up inside," Pepper added. "They were freed—and then told to kill every colonist they could."

"What the fuck?" Rizz muttered, shaking his head.

"Should we, uh . . . Should we head out then?" Pockets asked, voice tight.

I swallowed hard, glancing toward the stalled militia. Madison and Buzz had dismounted Pluto and were deep in conversation with the presumed leader of the Paul battalion.

"They haven't attacked yet," I said. "Maybe they're negotiating."

My mom and Cliff exchanged glances but remained silent. Figuring out a plan was supposed to be an adult's job—not ours. Yet, they stood there, just as scared as the rest of us. All I saw was my mom's hand slip into his.

From a distance, my father turned toward us. He raised his fist. And gave everyone a thumbs up.

Bang!

At that exact moment, six confetti cannons misfired, exploding behind us—spewing a storm of tiny pink strips of paper—the same shade of pink as Madison's suit.

"Open fire!" General Paul raised his spade and pointed it straight at us.

CHAPTER SIXTEEN

A BLIP

It all happened in a sixtieth-of-a-minute, yet time stretched, slowing to a glacial pace.

General Paul barked orders. Madison and Buzz scrambled onto Pluto, jerking the reins as they retreated. Spade bursts tore through the crowd, searing past my head. Terrified, everyone ducked and scattered—tripping over chairs, shoving past one another in blind, desperate panic, screaming, scurrying to protect loved ones, fleeing at all costs.

But it was too late.

The Pauls surged forward, mowing down countless unarmed civilians with mining equipment. Cliff threw his arms around us, tackling us to the ground. A barrage of spade fire zipped overhead, the heat of it kissing my cheeks.

When I lifted my head from the lawn, I saw her—

Cheese. Still standing.

Cliff's arms had just missed her.

Her wide eyes drifted downward. Multiple spade holes bloomed across her torso, dark and wet. Blood soaked through the fabric, spreading like brewing storm clouds.

Screams dulled to a muffled hum. Dust kicked up by spade fire floated weightlessly around me. I lay frozen, barely registering the frenzied feet stumbling over my body.

Cheese fell to her knees.

Then she collapsed.

I crawled to her, my gaze darting between her face and the gashes riddling her body.

"I don't know what to do," I whimpered. My shaking hands hovered uselessly over her wounds. "What do I do?"

She found my eyes. Even through the pain, she smiled.

"Look at me," she whispered. And with a small, exhausted chuckle, "I'm Swiss Cheese."

The light in her eyes faded. Her chest rose once more. In her last breath—

"Blip . . ."

Then she was gone.

My hands trembled. My lungs forgot how to breathe.

"Cheese?" Pockets crawled up beside me. His voice cracked. "Cheese?"

"Flip!" My mother yanked me to my feet. "Let's go!"

The crowd was breaking apart—running, searching for safety. There was no time to mourn. No time for anything at all.

Buzz galloped through the battlefield on Pluto, gripping the reins as she reared up on her stumpy hind legs and let out a resounding hee-haw.

"To Town Hall!" he bellowed, as the warm glow of spade blasts flickered across his face.

Maybe it was the drama of a warzone. Maybe it was him on donkeyback. But, for the first time, my father looked like a hero ripped straight from legend.

Everyone sprinted toward Town Hall, until I realized—

"Where's Pockets?"

Rizz and I whipped our heads around.

"There!" I pointed.

Pockets was still slumped next to Cheese's body, unmoving.

Before instinct could hit me, Rizz was already sprinting toward him—even with Town Hall just a dozen meters away from us—dodging spadefire before sliding onto the ground beside Pockets. He grabbed Pockets, pulling him away, hauling him back toward me, standing in the Town Hall door frame.

"Cheese! Cheese!" Pockets screamed, thrashing in Rizz's arms.

A half dozen Pauls were closing in. Fast.

Pockets went limp, his legs dragging uselessly across the lawn—*they weren't going to make it.*

"Come on, Rizz!" I shouted.

"Flip, we have to close the doors *now*!" my father barked. "Move!"

I didn't. I wasn't going to give up on them. He'd have to force me.

The Pauls were nearly on top of them.

"Flip!"

"Wait!" I shouted.

Just as my father grabbed me and threw me aside, Rizz hurled Pockets through the doorway and tumbled in after him.

In the narrow crack of the closing doors, I caught one last glimpse of the Pauls—wild-eyed, barreling straight for us.

Boom.

Buzz and Madison slammed the entrance shut and immediately barricaded it.

We were safe, if only for a moment.

CHAPTER SEVENTEEN

THE SIEGE OF TOWN HALL

As the sun dipped below the horizon, shadows of doom and gloom stretched across the colony.

Inside Town Hall, it was darker still.

The Pauls did end up shutting down the power grid. The only light came from the flickering beams of all our phone flashlights—but batteries were fading fast.

Injured citizens moaned in pain, some tended to by doctors, others by biology majors who couldn't get into medical school.

It was claustrophobic. Tens of thousands of people crammed into every available space—families pressed together in the hallways, bodies packed shoulder to shoulder, babies screaming.

Rizz, Pepper, Pockets, and I were squeezed into a corner.

"Stay here," my mom told us. "I'm going to find your father."

Down the hall, Newt Newman strutted toward the camera, his

voice dipped in rehearsed sorrow. "Reporting live, inside Town Hall, following a brutal assault on thousands of innocent, unarmed Martian civilians."

He walked at a measured pace, ensuring the cameraperson lingered on the most devastated citizens—gruesome injuries, soot-covered faces, raw grief.

"The motive behind the unrelenting aggression remains unclear. However, each of the assailants has been identified as the formerly-thought-to-be-deceased Paul Kingsley. It seems that because we've declared Mars an independent nation, he has returned with a vengeance unknown, raining down a fearsome hell upon our loved ones and neighbors. The hearts of the Martian people have been shattered and hope for our survival is dwindling. I, Newt Newman, will not rest, keeping you updated as this uncertain terror unfolds."

The moment the feed cut, Newt snapped his fingers at his cameraperson. "Get me a water before they're all gone. Gotta keep this voice fresh."

At the other end of the hall, Pastor Van Buren stood on a crate, two halves of a cardboard Dome-ino's box draped over his shoulders.

On the front:

THE END IS NIGH

And the back:

APOCALYPSE NOW

"We have all summoned the wrath of Ares, God of Mars!" he preached. "Submit to his power, and you shall be saved! As it is prophesied, during a time of war, Ares will shapeshift and reveal himself before teleporting his believers to Olympus."

He threw his arms to the sky, trembling with righteous fervor. "Join me now! For it is I who will transform into the God of Mars at any moment! His might can no longer be questioned! We were right! Ha ha! We were right!"

Honestly, that crackpot prophecy—the foundation of the entire Aresian dogma—made about as much sense as any other religion's beliefs.

I wasn't sure if the people surrounding him were potential followers listening to a ranting religious nutjob in a pizza box, or if they were just trapped with nowhere else to go.

In our corner, none of us knew what to say. There was nothing *to* say.

Pockets sat motionless, staring into space. I had never seen him without a hat before, but he peeled it off slowly, his jet-black hair matted flat. His fingers quivered as he gripped the brim, as if he was trying to hold himself together. We all loved Cheese—but she meant more to him than anyone.

My throat tightened. My tear ducts mixed a fresh batch.

"Hey . . ." I started, but my voice faltered. I wanted to find the right words, something—anything—to soothe his pain.

Nothing came to mind. I thought about what I needed someone to say to me after Cheese died, but I couldn't think of anything I wanted to hear. I just wanted her back.

But she was gone.

"Flip," Pepper nudged me, lifting her chin toward Buzz and Madison.

They moved through the crowd, handing out water bottles and blankets, helping wherever they could. Those that needed dry or untorn clothes were given backstage costumes from the last production of *Hamilton*—coats, ruffled shirts, knee-high braces—all from a bygone era.

Pepper stood, motioning for me to follow. I hesitated, looking back at Pockets. I didn't want to leave him.

Rizz caught my eye and gave me a small nod—*go, I've got him.*

I swallowed hard and pushed myself up, trailing after Pepper.

"Mom," she said, approaching Madison. I stopped behind her. "I think we might be able to help. Or at least . . . shed some light on what we're up against. We were in Warehouse Five—"

"Not here," Madison cut her off, her voice low but firm.

Her eyes flicked to the crowd around us. Too many ears. She wasn't about to let this turn into a full-blown panic . . . not that it wasn't there already.

Madison led us to the boardroom and typed 05-05-2089 into the keypad. It was easy for me to remember since it was my birthsol, though I assumed she picked the code for *Pepper's* birthsol, not mine.

Click. The door popped open.

She motioned us inside, and stepped in behind us, letting the door swing shut, but—

A foot blocked it.

"Buzz . . ." Madison groaned.

"The announcement was interrupted," Buzz argued, pulling the door open again. "Either of us could be the director, and I don't appreciate being excluded from a meeting the director should be a part of."

"You're not the director."

"It's impossible to know."

"The confetti cannons were pink." She gestured to her pink dress, which had since been dirtied and torn.

"That could be a complete coincidence! Totally unrelated to the election results."

Madison exhaled through her nose, steadying herself. "Buzz, how do I put this . . ." She studied him for a moment, searching for the right words. "Did you know that Pepper's grandmother was a history teacher?"

Buzz blinked, wondering where this was going.

"She used to tell me all the time: history is always better served by those who put the people before themselves. By those who shelve their ambition for the good of their country. By those willing to swallow their pride."

She leveled her gaze at him. "Swallow it."

Then she shut the door in his flummoxed face.

"Now," she said, turning to us. "Tell me everything."

She and Pepper took a seat at the table.

I stayed standing. Motionless. Stunned. I knew she and my father had quite a contentious past, but still. This felt so cold.

Finally, my feet moved, but not toward them—toward the door. I cracked it open to see my father, still there, dejected in the hallway. When his eyes lifted to meet mine, I stepped back, holding the door open in silent invitation.

He accepted.

"Fine," Madison muttered. "Just tell me what you saw."

It all came pouring out. Pepper and I didn't skip a single detail.

Buzz leaned back in his chair, exhaling sharply. "I knew he was harvesting organs!" He threw his arms up, and his hands landed behind his head. "Didn't even think about cloning being outlawed on Earth. Of course he had to do it on Mars."

Madison shook her head, still reeling. "Duke couldn't just let it go. He had to burn it all down."

"He must've known about Warehouse Five before tosol," Buzz added. "Why wait nine months after we declared independence?"

"The ceremony," I said.

They both looked at me.

"I made Pepper break into the warehouse with me because I knew everyone would be at Town Hall. No one would catch us." My throat felt tight. "He was waiting for the perfect time to release them. The Pauls could prepare, raid the exploration bay for weapons, and corner everyone. Kill us all in one fell swoop."

Buzz and Madison exchanged glances.

Madison straightened, snapping into action. "Go make sure your father and your mother are okay," she instructed Pepper and me. "Buzz and I need to talk."

Pepper stood, and I followed her to the door. As she pulled it open, my father said, "Sorry about your friend."

We both froze. The thought of Cheese crept back into my head—laughing, calling me Flip-Flop, slapping down Pockets's hat, rolling her eyes at something cocky Rizz said.

Those moments would never happen again.

"Thank you" didn't seem like the right response. Clearly Pepper felt the same way. Silently, we just walked out.

* * *

As the last light of dusk faded, we rejoined Rizz and Pockets.

Around us, people broke down furniture to fuel makeshift campfires, trying to keep warm—even though the temperature inside Town Hall hadn't budged from a comfortable twenty degrees Celsius due to the climate control within the biosphere.

My mom found some blankets and rolled one out for each of us, lying down next to me at the end of our little row. Cliff set himself up at our feet, completing the edges of our square in our cramped corner.

I don't think I slept the entire night. And it was the kind of night where morning never seemed to come. Every so often, I got hot and sweaty, pushing the blanket off, only to get too cold minutes later, pulling it back up. Over and over in an endless cycle. I didn't even care that I wasn't sleeping—I just wanted the night to end so I could stop trying to.

When morning miraculously arrived, there was movement—citizens shuffling about, helping Buzz retrieve remote-controlled stage horses from the auditorium's prop storage while others assisted Madison in gathering human-sized monkey costumes.

It didn't make any sense.

I squinted, recognizing both the horses and the costumes from my father's theatrical box office bomb *The Ballet of the Planet of the Apes*.

Pepper sat up. "What's going on?"

I could only shrug.

Word spread—everyone was to convene in the auditorium.

Nervous citizens piled in, thousands squeezing into the theater, the space so packed it was hard to breathe.

Madison stepped onto the stage.

Neither Madison nor Buzz had any tactical training or past experience coordinating military operations, but what they were about to propose was pure desperation. Utter madness. Their battle plan could only have been inspired by war movies—historical and fictional alike—of which Buzz had seen nearly all.

My grandparents, Penelope Aldrin and Eddie Buchanan, had worried that being born and raised on Mars might leave my father out of touch with his Earthling roots. Their solution was plopping him down in front of a screen for hours at a time—just like how most kids are raised these sols. Just like how I was raised.

He watched Earth's greatest stories. *Titanic. Saving Private Ryan. Paddington 2.* Every season of *The Kardashians.* And from his vast media knowledge, he and Madison had concocted an outlandish, cockamamie battle plan. A plan that was crazy—*so* crazy—that no one on Mars would think to say, "It just might work."

A plan so unrealistic, so unbelievable, that no self-respecting writer would ever risk their career by using such a contrived gimmick in their fictional storyline.

But truth is stranger than fiction.

CHAPTER EIGHTEEN

BATTLE PREPARATIONS

On the auditorium stage, Madison Chen looked out at thousands of frightened citizens. She took a deep breath. "Good morning. I—"

"Excuse me."

Buzz strode onto the stage beside her.

"Before we get started, I think we need to address something," he said, voice smooth, authoritative and patronizing—a noticeable shift from when he was standing outside the boardroom door. "As of right now, we are without a director. Without a leader. We'll never know the results of the election, and even if we did, they would no longer be viable after so many unfortunate deaths. Letting the dead vote is election fraud."

"They weren't dead when they voted!" Madison snapped.

Buzz ignored her. "I'm calling for an emergency election. Right now. With the survivors in this auditorium. All those in favor, raise your hands."

A small, well-positioned group shot their hands up, high and proud. Their quickness and confidence seemed to sway others to follow.

I knew he had been up to something. While handing out clothes and gathering supplies for the counterattack, Buzz shook a few too many hands, flashed his signature grin a little too often for a siege led by duplicates of his former boss. It wasn't kindness—it was insurgence. He was building support, quietly stacking the deck in his favor.

Buzz barely gave the momentum of hands time to settle.

"All those in favor of electing me as the Director of Mars, raise your hands."

Again, the lackeys' hands flew up immediately. And again, others followed suit.

I felt sick, like watching a boulder tumbling down a mountain toward a bus full of children. I couldn't stop a boulder—those children were done for.

This wasn't just an opportunistic power grab—it was mutiny. A coup. Buzz couldn't stand someone else being the most powerful person on the planet, the first Director of Mars. But even so, I'd never thought he would do something so slimy, so downright immoral.

Madison stood, frozen in disbelief. Buzz gestured for her to step aside.

"You—you can't just . . ." Her voice wavered. "You can't . . ."

Buzz smirked.

"History is best served by those who swallow their pride," he said, throwing her own words in her face. "Swallow it."

Madison scanned the room. The citizens who had once cheered her, backed her, fought for her, only stared back in uncertainty. Some avoided her gaze entirely.

Slowly, she stepped off the stage. In the stunned silence, Cliff muttered to my mom, "What the fuck did your husband just do?" She had no response. She was just as bewildered as the rest of us.

Pepper turned to me, eyes sharp with disgust.

I just stared back, caught between shame and shock, wishing I could offer an explanation—knowing there wasn't a good one.

On stage, Buzz stepped forward, seamlessly taking over Madison's speech.

"Good morning," he began, his voice steady, commanding. "I know you're scared. Terrified. I was too." He let the tension hang, surveying the faces in the crowd. "Scared we would surrender without standing alongside our neighbors—as a nation. Scared we wouldn't protect what's rightfully ours. Scared we would willfully hand over the home we've built together, letting the persecutors tear it away from us.

"But I'm not scared anymore." He paused, letting the moment hit. "We have a plan, and our plan will work. It *has* to work. And all of you brave Martians will go down in history as the valiant heroes who fearlessly defied the tyrants, the dictators, the imperial rule of corporate greed." His voice rose, gathering strength. "This sol, we are fighting for exactly that—the soul of this planet. And we *will* fight. We *will* survive. And we *will* take back our planet!"

The crowd erupted.

Rousing cheers crashed through the building, resonating in the auditorium acoustics, swelling into the sound of impassioned inspiration.

Then he described the plan. And whatever faith, whatever gusto he had galvanized immediately vanished.

But options were limited. And Buzz was the Director of Mars, after all, and surely a person in such power *must* know what they're doing.

But I knew better. The man standing on that stage, the man with the title and the status, hadn't earned it through skill, or cleverness, or hard work. He was standing there because he had been born at the right time, in the right place, with the right resources. In other words—luck.

But as much as I hated to admit it, luck was exactly what we needed. Without it, we didn't stand a chance.

After a rock-paper-scissors tournament, winning adults were assigned to stay behind and protect the children—"anyone under nineteen," according to the First Partner, my mom. It felt like targeted helicopter parenting.

Meanwhile, the rest of the colonists—many still in colonial garb from *Hamilton*—swarmed the entrances and exits of Town Hall, readying for battle. They sharpened broom handles into stakes, scavenged for curtain rods—anything that could pierce the skin or bash a skull. Others passed around tech crew theater headsets, repurposed for battlefield comms.

At every exit, we stationed artificial horses, securing one or two *Planet of the Apes* costumes on each to sit upright, as if someone were actually inside.

As I strapped an orangutan to a horse, I caught a glimpse of Pockets. He hadn't moved—still curled up in our corner, arms wrapped tightly around his knees, eyes vacant.

I walked over and squatted beside him. "Hey."

He lifted his head just enough to rest it on his knees but didn't look at me. "Hey."

"You okay?" I asked.

"Cheese is still out there."

My squat slid into a sit.

"Pockets . . ." I paused, unsure. "Cheese is gone."

He pressed his mouth against his knees, not responding. I wasn't going to rush him.

Finally—

"I know she's gone," Pockets murmured, his voice small. "But her body's just out there. In the cold. Alone." His grip tightened around his legs. "She shouldn't be alone. We were always together. She shouldn't be alone. I need to . . . If we could just . . ."

A tear dropped onto his jeans, darkening the fabric.

Watching him crumble—like something vital had been torn out of him—twisted my stomach with indigestion.

And then came the guilt. I hadn't had the instinct to rescue him on the battlefield—not before Rizz did, anyway. He was older, already in motion, so I let him handle it.

And then came the shame. Not for how I acted, but for how I didn't.

I swallowed hard. "I'll go get her."

His head snapped up. "What?"

"I'll go get her."

I stood up and scanned the crowd, spotting Pepper helping Rizz into a southern white-cheeked gibbon costume. He was over nineteen—he *had* to enlist, if you could even call it that.

"Rizz, I'm going with you," I said, grabbing a chimpanzee costume from the floor and sliding my legs into it.

"What?" Rizz looked up, confused.

"No, you aren't," Pepper said firmly.

"For Cheese," I told them. "We can't just leave her out there." I zipped up the ape suit. "Pockets needs this. I think we all do."

Rizz hesitated, furrowing his brow. Then after a beat, he sighed. "You don't leave my side and you do everything I say."

"Monkey see, monkey do," I promised.

Without another word, Rizz nodded. "Climb aboard."

I grabbed the back of the mechanical horse, threw my leg over, and hopped on.

"No," Pepper said, stepping closer. "You aren't going out there. You *can't*. You can't end up like Cheese."

"I won't be in the fight," I reassured her. "I'm just getting Cheese and coming right back."

Down the hall, I clocked my mom weaving through the crowd, searching the room. Before she could spot me, I pulled my chimpanzee mask over my face.

"Have you seen Flip?" she asked Pepper.

Pepper looked right through the eye holes in my mask, holding my gaze.

"No," she lied.

My mom exhaled sharply. "Come find me if you run into him."

Then she turned to Rizz. "Be careful out there."

She disappeared into the crowd.

Pepper turned back to me, eyes hard. "You get her, and you come right back." She shifted her glare to Rizz. "Protect each other. If anything happens to either of you, I'm gonna kill the other one."

"You got it, Two-Shoes," Rizz said, nodding sharply so the gibbon mask resting atop his head fell over his face.

The colonists braced themselves.

Over the headsets, Buzz's voice crackled through. "Release the monkeys."

The doors of Town Hall swung open.

The first wave of remote-controlled horses lurched forward, their empty ape costumes bouncing stiffly on their backs as they rolled toward the Paul perimeter.

The Pauls didn't hesitate. Spades lit up the battlefield. The hollow primates were shredded instantly, torn apart in a lightning storm of spadefire.

But we didn't stop. It was expected. It was part of the plan.

More mechanical horses charged forward. More empty ape suits endured an unrelenting shelling.

Wave after wave.

Then, our horse jolted, the wheels beneath us jerking forward. We were rolling.

And there would be no rolling back.

CHAPTER NINETEEN

GORILLA WARFARE

After tearing through the empty monkey costumes, the Pauls stopped firing, not wanting to waste ammo. Simply standing there, watching, confused.

Over the comms, Buzz commanded, "On my count . . ."

The mechanical equines at the front slowed to a halt, stopping just shy of the Paul perimeter.

One Paul prodded an ape costume with his spade. The empty suit slid from its mount and fell to the ground.

Paul exchanged glances with himself.

At that exact moment, Madison Chen—dressed in a gorilla costume atop Pluto—shimmied between two halted prop horses and drove a blade through a Paul trooper's chin, the tip bursting from the top of his skull.

Jeezus.

Madison doubled over, spewing vomit from the mouth of her gorilla mask. Fleeing from spadefire was one thing, close-up murder was another. And I knew I wasn't going to handle the brutal violence any better.

"Oh fuck. Fuck, fuck, fuck," I muttered under my mask.

It was as if the Greek gods of fear and panic, Phobos and Deimos—our two moons—had descended from Olympus to personally smite me. Terror consumed me. Only one feeling rivaled it—regret. The reality of my situation crashed down on me like a thousand kilograms of basalt.

This was a mistake. This was a huge fucking mistake. I have to get out of here. I have to—

"Don't you fucking move a muscle," Rizz hissed.

His voice was calm, but firm. He didn't dare turn around. We couldn't risk exposing ourselves. The real people hidden inside ape costumes were indistinguishable from the empties.

"We're going to be fine," Rizz assured me. "Calm down. Think of it like . . . Think of it like your dad's stupid ape ballet."

And with that, my brain completely dissociated.

My distress vanished. Dread dissolved into nothing. My emotions detached. The battlefield sharpened—colors deepened, shadows stretched. Everything brightened with surreal contrast, like a lucid dream.

Over the theater comms, my father's voice rang out, calm, steady.

"And a five . . . six . . . five, six, seven, eight."

Orangutans, gorillas, and chimpanzees launched themselves over their horses, leaping through the air like ballerinas, executing flawless jetés, landing gracefully on top of the Pauls.

From behind the Town Hall walls, reinforcements emerged—spinning, pirouetting into battle.

Spade fire cracked around us in sharp, percussive staccato—its deafening blasts booming like a pulsing bassline.

The battlefield became a matinee.

Pauls and apes moved in unison, wrestling in synchronized duet, pulling each other back and forth in perfect counterbalance.

Red ribbons spiraled through the air, unraveling from the torsos of injured colonists and pierced Pauls, who all danced en pointe, clutching their sides, collapsing in elegant finales.

In front of me, the southern white-cheeked gibbon dismounted in one fluid motion. I followed, both of us holding our horse as we bent our knees in a soft plié.

We glided toward the fray, where Paul Kingsley copies were already being overwhelmed by a flurry of dancing colonists and apes. The gibbon twirled into a Paul, kicking him to the ground.

I stood there, helpless. Surrounded by orchestrated fistfights, staged chokeholds, and produced point-blank kill shots with red ribbon projectiles, my eyes darted through the swirling chaos.

A bloodied bonobo fell at my feet.

Every performer froze, pausing for my solo as I tip-toed backward, threw the back of my hand to my forehead, and crumbled to the ground. Distraught.

The southern white-cheeked gibbon broke away from the tableau, tapping my head.

I looked up.

The gibbon waved for me to follow.

As soon as I rose, the dance company resumed their choreography. The apes and colonists pirouetted and dispersed, chasing retreating Pauls.

We chasséd toward the lawn stage—toward the spot where Cheese had been killed.

But her body was gone. All the bodies were gone.

The gibbon lifted a hand above his eyes, miming a search. Then shrugged.

Dramatically, I rested my chin on my thumb, tapping my index finger to my jaw, deep in theatrical contemplation.

The bodies must have been cleared from the battlefield. Carried away—maybe for burial outside the dome after the war.

I stretched out my hairy chimp arm, pointing toward the exploration bay while rotating my other arm in a slow circle, signaling the gibbon—*that way*.

We glissaded through the pandemonium, weaving between dueling ballerinas, pirouetting past bodies, dodging spadefire bursts.

Not all of the Pauls were part of the siege of Town Hall—smaller platoons had been raiding the colony, sweeping from building to building, hunting down fleeing colonists. Apartments flashed with pulsing red and yellow stage backlights, flames devouring homes around me. Storefront set pieces were splintered, doors swinging from one hinge.

Gorillas and chimps spun past me, running rampant through the biosphere—a primate diversion meant to distract the Pauls. The rest of our ballerina revolutionaries took advantage of the monkey business, striking from cover with hit-and-run ambushes.

The balance shifted. Once armed with stolen spades, citizens easily picked off the Pauls one by one.

As we hustled toward the exploration bay, I watched them drop like flies—crumbling mid-scream, convulsing, collapsing.

Despite their heavy firepower, the Pauls seemed shockingly easy for people to kill. It made sense. Years of organ harvesting and experimental atrocities had left the majority of them disfigured, disabled, or suffering from chronic and degenerative conditions. In a state of unending pain, some barely put up a fight. Some even stood perfectly still, waiting for death's embrace, welcoming the tranquil relief at long last.

Not exactly the indomitable, unstoppable force of vengeance Duke Kingsley had hoped.

A chimpanzee bounded past us, whirling down a street. Every Paul within eyesight stopped—blinking in confusion, lowering their weapons—and the colonists struck.

A colonist stabbed a Paul in his back.

Another Paul stabbed *that* colonist in *her* back.

Another colonist stabbed *that* Paul in *his* back.

Another Paul stabbed *that* colonist in *his* back.

Another colonist stabbed *that* Paul in *his* back.

The first stabbed Paul stabbed *that* colonist in *her* back, completing a circle of the stabbed and the stabbing.

Still gripping their weapons, they all swayed side to side, then clockwise, then counterclockwise—before finishing with a manège, performing pas de bourrées as they all simultaneously collapsed to the ground.

A gorilla twirled a hoolock gibbon, who spun en pointe—arms stretched outward—firing a spade from each hand with a dramatic flourish.

A cardboard cutout of a hijacked Martian rover was pulled by an offstage rope into an ensemble of Pauls. An orangutan popped its head up over the top of the rover as if driving it, while the rover trampled them—each one tumbling, then flinching and spasming as the wheels rolled over their bodies.

Another troupe of dancers skipped through the streets, wielding pikes adorned with papier-mâché Paul Kingsley heads, red strings trailing from their severed necks. The dancers tossed the pikes between each other in a macabre game of catch.

Orange lights rippled over blue fabric, simulating shimmering flames in the reflection off Lake Ares.

The Pauls' numbers dwindled. Fearing inevitable defeat, the remaining soldiers twirled batons with white flags on each end, signaling their surrender.

But the percussive music thundered on. The spades kept firing. It wasn't clear if interplanetary humanitarian law applied to *all* Great Apes—or just to homo sapiens.

Only when one Paul remained did the apes and colonists finally relent.

The lone survivor raised his hands. Then after one final pirouette, he spread his arms wide, slid his leg back, and fell into a deep, theatrical bow.

The curtain closed on my fever dream coping mechanism. The music cut out. My brain chemicals rebalanced. The performance came to an abrupt halt when my eyes landed on Cheese's body, laid in a line of the dead outside the exploration bay. The reality of her death—of all their deaths—came crashing back down to Mars.

It wasn't a ballet. The bloodied props, the choreographed violence, the destroyed set pieces—not theater effects. All of it, real. But I wasn't ready to confront what I had seen. I'm still not.

And I never will be.

PART II

CHAPTER TWENTY

DOPPELGÄNGERS

Over the next two years, after Duke Kingsley was quietly demoted by the Astral Destiny board, tensions with Earth began to ease. Trade routes reopened. And all efforts turned to rebuilding the biosphere after the war. When it was finished, another massive celebration—bigger than the Election Results Reveal Party—took place on the Town Hall lawn.

Rizz had to work the event. I'd stopped asking Pockets to come to anything—he always said no. I wasn't even sure if he left his apartment those sols. I still asked Pepper, though—even if she turned me down just as often. She said she was going with other people. We weren't her only three friends—at least, not anymore.

That left me stuck attending with my mom. At least we had front row privileges again.

Speakers crackled on. "Please welcome to the stage, for the worlds premiere of our national anthem, the talented, the revolutionary . . . Jizzy!"

The crowd roared, already on their feet. Cheers swelled, a deafening wave of catharsis and pride. Getting into it, I let out a whoop.

My mom joined in with a whoop whoop of her own.

Fog machines kicked into overdrive, pumping out dense mist that blanketed the stage, swirling around the DJ deck at the center, spilling over the edge, and kissing the front row with an icy vapor.

An earnest voice came over the speakers. "When I was composing our national anthem, I wanted to create something classic, traditional. Something that sounded like a musical resurrection of a genre long-dead a hundred years ago. Something that wasn't just inspirational . . . but transcendent."

A black light flickered on, illuminating the fog along with multi-colored lasers dancing on the stage.

From beneath the DJ deck, Jizzy rose through the mist, fist in the air. "Whaddup Mars!"

The sound of a thousand panties dropping ruptured my eardrums.

Jizzy wore a black jumpsuit with red polka dots—an homage to the Martian flag. Reflective ski goggles gleamed behind the clear face shield of an astronaut helmet, which bobbled loosely, unattached to the jumpsuit.

"Bwow bwow bwow!"

The crowd erupted. Electricity crackled through the air, moving through shared currents among the masses. Jizzy placed his hands on the deck. A spacey, ambient drone faded in, morphing into a hypnotic four-four beat. A NASA recording, aged and distorted, counted down.

"Ten . . . nine . . . eight . . ."

Rocket engines rumbled, slowly crescendoing, charging the intro's build.

"Seven . . . six . . . five . . . four . . ."

A brief, rhythmic motif repeated itself, each time layering on new sounds—expanding, evolving, growing more dynamic and robust.

"Three . . . two . . . one . . ."

The music cut out.

"Liftoff."

Bwoom—fzizizipzip—bwoom.

The bass dropped—a seismic pulse vibrated through every chest in the crowd, rattling ribs, scintillating dopamine receptors. The main melody surged forward, euphoria gushing through the masses, lifting the hairs on the backs of thousands of necks.

Smoke blasted from the DJ deck. Neon lasers sliced through the fog.

Jizzy jumped up and down to the beat, one hand on the mixer, pretending to create the pre-recorded music in real-time—just like the DJs of old.

Between drops, a female vocalist drifted through the speakers, her voice slightly autotuned, haunting yet uplifting:

Sowing the seeds, breaking the ground,
Roots running deep where once nothing was found.
No air to breathe, nothing alive,
Yet we planted our future, watched it thrive.
We staked our claim, forged our name,
From a whisper, became a flame.
We are the red, we rose from dust,
We are the people—in us we trust.

Arms wrapped around shoulders. The entire audience swayed left and right—even my mom and I.

The music built again. Anticipation rippled through the crowd. Kids were lifted onto shoulders. Rows of people leaned forward, almost crushing me, but I didn't care.

Then—the second drop. Pure, collective ecstasy. Unified, all-encompassing, sheer patriotism.

As the anthem faded, a familiar recording crackled through the speakers—Neil Armstrong's famous words. "That's one small step for man, one giant leap for mankind."

My mom and I exchanged a smirk, knowing that line would make my father's skin crawl.

Jizzy raised his fist again. "They're gonna shit themselves when they play this at the Olympics!"

The crowd lost their minds. The song, titled "March of the Sowers," hit number one on *Billboard's Hot 100* and stayed there for thirty-eight weeks—doubling the all-time record, which had previously belonged to something called "Old Town Road." To this sol, no song has broken its record.

I wish I could've shared the moment with the Catfish Trolls. But those two years after Cheese's death had been difficult. We drifted apart. Rizz was appointed to the Ministry of Mars—a move by Buzz to maintain the support of the youth—along with Madison Chen, who had earned war hero status after being the first to stab a Paul Kingsley, and Pastor Van Buren, to keep the religious sector in check. With his new political career, Rizz became harder and harder to pin down.

Pockets withdrew from everyone after Cheese died, retreating into himself. I hadn't seen him in months.

Pepper pulled away too.

Even when we did manage to get together, there was always something missing. Every hangout felt heavy, laced with grief. Having fun together only made us feel guilty. At every dinner, there was only the unshakeable reminder that Cheese wasn't there.

So we saw each other less and less.

I didn't want to have any energy left to stew on what had happened to Cheese, what had happened to us, so I threw myself into rackethand—training every sol, leaving me too exhausted to think about anything else.

That all changed when my mom and I were leaving the concert. I thought I saw her in the crowd. I thought I saw Cheese.

I did a double-take. *Impossible. A trick of the mind.*

But I couldn't help it. My body moved on its own—shouldering through the mob, chasing the back of a head I hadn't seen in what felt like a lifetime.

"Flip?" my mom called, confused.

I didn't have time to explain.

"Cheese!" I yelled out.

The rabble parted just enough for me to catch one last glimpse of her before she disappeared around the corner of a building.

I knew I should've turned back—brush off the tasteless joke my brain was playing on me and move on with my sol. Still, I followed my hallucination. I had to make sure it *was* one.

My walk turned into a jog. My jog became a sprint. But by the time I rounded the corner, she was already gone.

Telling my friends only made things worse between us. The more I insisted it wasn't just a delusion, the more upset they became. I thought they would believe me—if they didn't, no one would.

And no one did.

Nights spent talking to Pepper through Flipper Code, stomping and thudding on our floor-ceiling, grew fewer and fewer, until they stopped altogether.

And still, I couldn't let it go.

I had pushed through all five stages of grief. Finally reached acceptance. And then, just like that, I was back at denial.

Worried about my mental health, my mom sent me to a psychiatrist—despite my father fighting tooth and nail against it. He ranted about the "exorbitant price of a fake doctor who shifts all the blame to the parents and rewards whining and complaining with pills."

But apparently, I wasn't the only one seeing ghosts.

Dozens of civilians were reporting the same thing—visions of people they had lost. At first, it was dismissed as chronic déjà vu, a symptom of collective trauma. But the so-called Doppelgänger Phenomenon stumped even the best mental health professionals.

Until a whistleblower blew his whistle.

* * *

One afternoon, my mom and I watched the lone episode of *Survivor: Mars*—turns out, you can't outwit, outplay, or outlast an uninhabitable atmosphere, but it did make for one incredible broadcast, however brief. The news autoplayed afterward. We were both slumped on the couch, far too sunken in to even consider reaching for the remote, making it impossible to watch anything else. My father was in his usual spot—his worn-out sofa chair—sipping red malt, oblivious.

"After hundreds of reports of body doubles and deceased loved ones seemingly rising from the dead, MBN has received evidence from an undisclosed source that this is not simply a case of mass hysteria," Newt Newman reported from behind his anchor desk.

I jolted upright, scrambling to crank the volume.

Beside me, my father's glass froze midway to his lips.

Newt continued. "ChromosoME—a genetic testing company that provides family tree breakdowns and informs you whether you like cilantro or not—was hacked. The genetic codes of many Martians were compromised. And, using Warehouse Five, our government created clones of our most able-bodied citizens—not as an unsettling crutch for distraught widows, but for cheap labor to rebuild the colony after the devastation of the war."

The news banner below read:

BREAKING NEWS: CHANGE YOUR PASSWORDS

My mom and I turned our heads toward my father and stared.

"It's not a big deal!" my father snapped.

"Not a big deal?" My mom scoffed, incredulous. "Buzz, you let our son believe he was seeing his dead friend!"

"I told you he didn't need therapy!" my father shot back, like that was a good explanation. "The project was classified. I had to keep my mouth shut."

"I'm not even upset about that part," I cut in, my voice sharp. "How could you do something like this?"

Hundreds of unsuspecting Martians were victims. He had stolen their genetic codes—quite possibly the most personal, most unique possession of any human being. And on top of that, he bred people for the sole purpose of an extra set of hands, forced labor.

I couldn't look at him. But I also couldn't look away.

My father leaned forward, eyes locked on me. "Would you rather I not have done it, Flip?" He spoke like he had already practiced his defense a thousand times in his head. "I saved your life. I save all our lives. You think Mars was rebuilt in a sol?"

He shook his head, taking a long, measured sip of red malt. "Ninety-five percent chance. Ninety-five percent chance we were all going to suffocate, starve, or die of thirst before we repaired the life support systems. I made sure that didn't happen."

A sip. Another sip. Suddenly, he needed a refill.

He pushed himself up, retreating to the kitchen, pouring another drink as he continued, "I should be getting a fucking medal instead of being dragged through the mud by the media and chastised by my own flesh and blood."

I shifted on the couch to face him in the kitchen behind me. He wasn't going to run away from this.

"They're human beings! They have rights!" I yelled.

He exhaled through his nose, shaking his head. "All *people* on the spectrum are created equal. There's no mention of clones."

"They have thoughts and feelings! Just like you. Just like me."

"Yeah, you sure have a lot of those," he grumbled under his breath.

I clenched my fists. "They are genetically and scientifically human!"

My father's eyes darkened. "I will not apologize for saving all of our lives." His grip tightened around his glass. "I'm not the villain here. I'm the *hero* who saved the Mars colony. The *hero* who saved every single Martian on this planet. Without me, we'd all be dead."

"Don't act like you didn't have a choice!"

"Enough!" My mom's voice cut through the room, raw and shaking. "Both of you!"

She turned to me first. "Flip, it's been done. You've said your piece—just go to bed."

Then to my father. "Buzz, I'm sure you'll get a much better night's sleep on the couch tonight."

She stormed off to their bedroom, slamming the door behind her.

I glared at my father over the back of the couch, then stood to walk away without a word. Anything I said would've been lost on deaf ears. Behind me, he sighed. "I had to do it, Flip. You know I had to do it. Just be glad it's not on *your* conscience!"

I didn't turn around.

In my room, I paced in a tight circle—one of my favorite pastimes as a teenager, a hobby I thought I would outgrow by age twenty, but I guess not. It wasn't just that my father had cloned Cheese and forced her into hard labor—though that was bad enough. Cloning her didn't bring her back. It brought back her body, not *her*. I couldn't be happy that my friend was suddenly alive again—because she wasn't.

The clone wouldn't have her memories, her humor, smarts—nothing. Only her face. She was still dead. Just replaced by a knock-off. Warped into a fraud. An imitation. A hollow echo.

And that was worse. It tainted my relationship with the real Cheese. Spoiled it, like something left out to mold.

I exhaled a quiet chuckle, shaking my head. "Blue Cheese."

It was a joke she would've made.

Maybe my friends would finally understand. Maybe I could fix everything. Or at least, I could try. It was time for a reunion.

I stomped on my floor.

Silence.

Another stomp.

Nothing.

One more time—louder. A desperate, echoing *stomp*.

Pepper: Just stop, Flip. Please.

CHAPTER TWENTY-ONE

UNEXPECTED GUESTS

Since Pepper wouldn't talk to me, I turned to Rizz.

As soon as I messaged him, a realization hit me—he could be a part of it. He was in the ministry, the ministry was part of the government, and the government was responsible for the ChromosoME hack—who was to say that Rizz wasn't a part of the illegal replication of compromised genetic codes. Someone I looked up to more than anyone, like an older brother, helping cook up clones for cheap labor.

He could've even been the one who suggested using Cheese's DNA.

Rizz had seemed just as upset as Pockets and Pepper when I told them I had seen Cheese. But that could've all been an act.

He wouldn't tell me anything in writing. Instead, he asked me to meet him at the edge of the dome that night—where the new expansion construction was breaking ground. There, he'd explain everything.

A bright light flashed in my face. I threw up a hand to shield my eyes.

"Ugh, what the fuck, Flip."

The beam dropped. Pepper stood in front of me, scowling. "You seriously made Rizz ask me to come here for you?"

"No," I said. "He told me to come here too."

Two more lights cut through the dark, as a couple shadowy figures approached.

Tilting his light upward, Rizz cast exaggerated shadows across his face and spoke in a deep, Eastern European accent. "Velcome to a night of terror you could only imagine in your nightmares . . ."

Rizz certainly wasn't acting guilty. Maybe he was hiding behind the joke.

Pockets stepped out from behind him.

"Hey," he said sheepishly.

"Hey," Pepper and I responded.

"Ve vill show you a hell unknown vhile ve suck your blood . . . and uh . . . Vhat's another good 'w' vord?" Rizz giggled.

"Quit it," Pepper snapped. "Seriously. What are we doing here?"

My suspicions were growing—maybe he'd brought all of us there to silence us.

On the other hand, at least he'd brought all of us there. It had been too long since we were all together. It was nice, regardless of the circumstances.

"Relax, Two-Shoes," Rizz said. "Had to talk to you all in private, where no one else would be listening."

"Why?" I needled. "What is it?"

"I'm the whistleblower." He whistled the typical tone when someone reveals something huge. "Figured it out about a week ago. It just clicked—why Flip was so convinced that he saw Cheese, how the biosphere was rebuilt so fast, how we survived against all odds. Warehouse Five. Clones. Your dad did it all under our noses."

Phew. It wasn't Rizz.

He turned to me. "I've learned quite a lot about him over the last two years."

My body relaxed, and I let out a chuckle. "Nothing good, I bet."

Rizz smirked but didn't confirm either way. "I gathered all the evidence I could and went straight to MBN."

I caught Pepper glancing at me, ashamed.

"Not that it'll change much," Rizz added. "It's not like we have a law against it yet—we're still working out the kinks of our whole justice system. Cloning people is more . . . just like . . . frowned upon."

"You can't make a law?" I asked.

Rizz shrugged. "Your dad's the director. And he's the one who did it. So not a whole lot of motivation there. We're gonna try, but . . ."

"So you dragged us all the way out here for that?" Pepper asked.

Rizz grinned. "I know I've been busy. We haven't gotten a chance just to hang out again, and I wanted to see you guys. I miss you."

"Me too," I admitted, not that they would be surprised.

"Miss you too," Pepper said, quieter.

"Likewise," Pockets choked, clearing his throat—trying to hide the fact he was about to cry. "I'm sorry I haven't . . . I'm sorry I've been . . ."

"It's okay," I said, hitting the bill of his hat down like Cheese used to.

"And I have a little surprise for you," Rizz said in a singsong voice. "Thought we could get into a little mischief. Like old times." He strolled past Pepper and me and stopped, putting his fists on his hips and puffing out his chest. "Follow me." Then he lifted a strand of yellow caution tape and ducked under.

Pepper and I exchanged glances, hesitant. Before either of us made a move, Pockets squeezed between us, trailing Rizz. I shrugged at Pepper, grinned, and followed. After a beat, she sighed and walked in after us—into a sealed-off construction site.

"As a distinguished member of the Ministry of Mars," Rizz said, his voice dripping with mock grandeur, "I'm privy to some confidential information."

He flicked his flashlight downward, illuminating a massive ravine in front of us.

Pockets abruptly stopped at the edge, and I nearly slammed into him.

"The expansion project has required a lot of excavation," Rizz explained, tossing each of us a harness and rope from a nearby pile of supplies. "This whole site collapsed during digging and opened up a giant cavern. Cool, huh?"

After the biosphere was rebuilt, efforts had shifted toward expanding the dome to accommodate immigration and natural population growth. How they actually enlarged the glass was lost on me—I only knew it involved intense heat and a lot of blowing.

"Do you know what's down there?" I asked.

"Nobody does," Rizz said, tightening the harness around his waist.

We rappelled down the pit, landing on uneven ground. Once we detached from our ropes, we fanned out, exploring the cavity.

Shallow pools filled the craters in the rocky floor, and the damp walls glistened under our flashlights.

"Rizz, you could've mentioned we might need shoes for wet bouldering," Pepper huffed, frowning at her feet.

"It's called spelunking," Pockets corrected.

"Spelunking—sounds like what I did to Flip's mom last night!" Rizz quipped.

I groaned. "Seriously? That shit hasn't been funny since we were kids."

"That's what makes it so funny *now*."

My right foot slipped into a puddle. A shock of cold shot up my leg. "Jeezus H. That's freezing."

"There's nothing like exploring a shadowy, foreboding tunnel before someone—or some *thing*—pops out at us," Pockets mused, leaning into the spooky. "Right as the background music swells into a crescendo of clashing tones—*dun dun*!"

"We don't even know what's down here," Pepper cautioned.

"Don't worry," Rizz said, smirking. "I'll protect you from the scary cave spikes."

"They're called stalactites and stalagmites," Pockets corrected again.

We all paused, staring at him.

"What?" he said, shrugging. "I like rocks."

Rizz grinned. "Stalactites and stalagmites—"

"Don't," I warned.

"—Sounds like what I put inside Flip's mom last night!"

We followed the natural curve of the cavern, our flashlights bouncing off rough rock. Ahead, a narrow tunnel stretched forward, a small creek trickling through.

"Shall we investigate?" Rizz waggled his eyebrows.

We followed the stream's flow, stepping carefully over the slick, jagged rocks. The tunnel narrowed, forcing us into a tight single-file line.

"Guys, seriously. We've had our fun. Let's just go home," Pepper pleaded.

"I promise you, nothing is down here except the four of us," Rizz assured her.

A shrill, glottal shriek echoed through the passage.

We stiffened.

No one dared to breathe.

"What the hell was that?" Rizz whispered.

"You tell me," I whispered back.

Our flashlights whipped around the tunnel like an amateur basement rave, frantic beams bouncing off damp stone, trying to find whatever made the sound. At the edge of a fading light, something scurried past—a shadow, a blur.

All four of us focused our beams forward, eyes locked on the passage ahead.

We squinted.

A head—bald, smooth . . . translucent?—popped into the light, staring at us.

Staring at us *without eyes.*

A screech rang out behind us. We spun around.

Six more of them stood on two legs, close enough to touch us with either of their two arms, their clear skin glistening faintly blue in our flashlight beams.

A chorus of wailing cries grew louder, multiplying, closing in, bouncing off the walls in a maddening cacophony.

"Ahhhhh!"

That wailing cry was us.

"Let's get the hell out of here!" I yelled.

Pepper bolted first, barreling through the creatures blocking our exit. Rizz was right behind her. I took off next, and Pockets brought up the rear.

"Guys!" Pockets hollered.

We turned.

One of the creatures had stepped between us, cutting off his escape.

"Pockets!" I shouted.

Why was it always Pockets?

This time, the rescue instinct was there, but my feet wouldn't move. Cemented to the cave floor, I stood there, terrified to go back for him. Once again, he needed me. Once again, I couldn't do it.

My mind raced for excuses.

There would be no point in trying to save him. They were already on him—he'd be dead before I even got there. And then they'd kill me.

"Flip!" Pockets called.

Rizz shoved me aside, shooting me a look of pure disappointment as he ran past—rushing to attempt the rescue I wouldn't. The rescue he expected *me* to make since I was closer.

And there it was again—the guilt, the shame.

Before he reached Pockets, I thought it was already too late. The creature bent forward—low, poised, ready to strike. I braced myself, already picturing it tackling Pockets, slamming him into a stalagmite, impaling him on a cave icicle. My hesitation was going to get Pockets killed.

But it didn't.

Instead, the being gestured for Pockets to bend forward and mirror its own movement. As Pockets bowed, their heads touched, the being's forehead glowing ever so slightly.

Rizz stood beside them, watching in stunned silence just like Pepper and me.

A greeting, not an attack. When they straightened, Rizz reached for Pockets's arm, gently pulling him away, still afraid to make any sudden movements. It looked like Pockets almost resisted, like he wanted to stay.

"Come on, come on, come on!" Pepper urged.

As Pockets passed me, guilt rose like acid in my throat—there didn't seem to be an emotion that *didn't* give me stomach problems.

"I'm sorry . . ." I mumbled. "I—I just couldn't . . ."

He didn't look at me. Didn't say a word.

Maybe he didn't hear me. Maybe he did. Maybe he was preoccupied, processing his otherworldly experience, becoming the first human to make contact with an alien.

I trailed behind him as we made it to the bottom of the cavern opening. While the three of us hurriedly attached ourselves to our ropes and climbed to safety, Pockets took his time.

He wasn't in a rush anymore.

CHAPTER TWENTY-TWO

THE DOWNSTAIRS NEIGHBORS

In late 2109, UFO scholars and tinfoil hat enthusiasts rejoiced: humans weren't alone in the universe. The Aresian church was less enthused, scrambling to explain the beings as (literally) underworld souls given another chance by Hades. Religions on Earth chalked up the aliens on Mars as God's rough draft—a lost text that predated the Book of Genesis—prompting many religious leaders to hurriedly write a prequel.

Alongside a military escort, a specialized team of biologists and linguists rappelled down the same collapsed pit we had. But the beings refused to engage with anyone—except for one person.

Pockets.

When a squad of government officials armed with spades strongly suggested he volunteer his assistance, he joined the team. Over a few months, Pockets and the linguists decoded their language—using nothing but a tape recorder and a dry erase board. Eventually, our two species were able to have detailed conversations.

After developing a deep bond with the beings, Pockets became their fiercest advocate—accusing the on-site scientists of speciesism and leaking excerpts from their non-peer-reviewed reports:

The species exhibits anatomical features nearly identical to those of Homo sapiens, including bilateral symmetry, two upper and lower limbs, a nasal and oral cavity, and both internal and external reproductive structures. The most immediately observable difference is the epidermal layer, which is translucent and possesses a faint bluish hue.

The probability of such anatomical congruence arising independently is statistically improbable, indicating the possibility of a shared progenitor species or common point of cosmic origin. Nevertheless, due to current evidentiary limitations, such hypotheses remain speculative and are not recommended for further scientific pursuit at this time.

The vocal communication system employed by the species comprises low-frequency glottal resonances, high-frequency click consonants, and tonal modulations which at times extend beyond the upper and lower thresholds of typical human auditory range.

Harping on their skin tone, denying our identical genetic code, and claiming their accents were incomprehensible—human supremacy at its finest, according to Pockets. The scientists, he said, refused to accept that *we* were the aliens in this scenario. And rather than using the proper term Native Martians, most called them Cavernese, simply because they were found in what were thought to be caverns.

It was official. The Catfish Trolls had discovered alien life.

Officially-officially, Hector "Pockets" Martinez got all the credit. He was the one who made first contact, and he'd go on to spend the next four years living underground with them, learning from them. To me, it just seemed like another way to retreat—another excuse to isolate himself after losing Cheese, all neatly wrapped in a "cultural immersion" bow.

As for me, rather than being celebrated for a society-altering, science-defining, religion-challenging discovery with far-reaching consequences for our understanding of the universe and life itself, I was punished.

"Think of it like a boot camp," my father said, leaning against my bedroom door frame.

I'd been grounded for the past three months for sneaking out and night spelunking without permission—while Pockets was kicking back, cracking phycos with E.T. As I sat on my bed, I looked to my mom—whose head was poking out above my father's shoulder—pleading for backup.

I didn't get any.

"You've proven time and again that your mother can't control you," my father said, speaking for her.

I huffed. "So you're sending me away?"

"I need you to stop fucking around and get serious with your life."

"I'm the second-ranked rackethand player on Mars!" I shot back.

"Exactly. *Second*-ranked. And you can't count on a career in sports—one injury and it's over." It was almost like he foreshadowed me dislocating my shoulder on the rackethand court years later.

"I'm not gonna get injured!" I promised. "Don't punish me just because you were bad at sports!"

My father tutted. "Kid, I was ranked number one in my sol."

"Yeah, back when there were only four people who played!"

He held out his hands, egging me on. "Give me all the attitude you want—you're going. As long as I pay for your school and you sleep under my roof, you do as I say."

"I'm twenty years old!"

"And you're still living at home."

"Wait . . ." I paused, realizing. "What about school? I still have two years left."

"I've arranged for you to have a little gap year."

"What?" My stomach dropped. "What about my friends?" My

voice cracked slightly, and I hoped he didn't notice. "I'll be a grade behind them! They'll graduate without me!"

"Hmm, let's see." He counted on his fingers, listing my greatest hits of misbehavior. "Throwing donuts at respected authority figures, sneaking out to go to a riot, breaking into Warehouse Five, dancing around a battlefield, cave diving at night with no experience or professional guidance—need I go on?"

I clenched my jaw.

"Maybe if you actually gave a shit, you *would* be the top-ranked rackethand player. Maybe you would've graduated high school at the top of your class. Where's your ambition? Your drive?" He crossed his arms. "We are a family of champions. You gotta learn how to act like it. You gotta learn what it takes—determination, initiative."

"Oh my god! None of that stuff matters. It means nothing. We're all just blips!"

My father narrowed his eyes. "I have no idea what 'blip' is slang for, but that attitude is exactly why you're in this position." He put his hand on my doorknob. "And I hope after this trip, that attitude changes."

And with that, he shut my door.

* * *

The next sol, I crammed my entire life into a single backpack. Clothes, essentials—shoved in haphazardly. I stood in the room I was leaving behind, eyes scanning the space, knowing I wouldn't see it again for a long time—knowing I wouldn't see *anyone* again for a long time.

I knocked on Pepper's door. Cliff answered instead.

"Oh, is Pepper around?" I asked.

"She's out with her mother, but they'll be back soon. You wanna come in?"

I hesitated, then shook my head. "No, that's okay. Thanks. I gotta go. I'll text her—I just wanted to give her this."

I handed him the snow globe.

CHAPTER TWENTY-THREE

BOOT CAMP

The walls of the Native Martian tunnels were smooth, rich mahogany-colored rock stretching endlessly in either direction, the floors leveled by generations of passage.

Hiking through, carrying all my baggage—literal and otherwise—felt like an on-the-nose metaphor for an arduous journey of self-discovery. My father probably pictured the punishment as a grand, humbling experience—his aimless son trekking into the unknown to learn discipline and hard work. The whole thing reeked of heavy-handed storytelling.

And I wasn't having any of it. I pinky-promised myself I wouldn't mature or evolve as a person during the trip.

"You sure packed a lot," the Native girl walking beside me remarked.

Through heavy breathing, I managed to sputter, "Wasn't . . . sure . . . what to . . . bring."

She made a few high-pitched squeaks, which I had to repeatedly remind myself was her cute version of a giggle.

At first, the translucent skin of the Natives had been unsettling.

Seeing all of their insides pulsing and pumping was like staring at a living, breathing biology poster pasted on the wall of Armstrong High.

On the Martian surface, I only ever saw them clothed from head to toe, shielding their organs from pesky UV rays that would otherwise cause irreparable damage to their internal organs—and quite an unforgiving sunburn. Most humans incorrectly assumed the garb was religious or cultural.

In the darkness of the tunnels, however, they had no such need for clothing. Which meant the girl walking next to me was, unmistakably, naked. And once my penis registered that fact, it scampered to adapt.

It happened gradually, my discomfort morphing into something else entirely. Our anatomies were identical—the differences purely aesthetic—and my hormones quickly got on board. Before long, I found myself stealing peeps.

When I caught a glimpse of her left kidney, with an adorable little freckle—or maybe a cyst?—it was over. I was smitten.

She was a couple years older, and her name was [glottal shriek, two clicks, four glottal shrieks, harrumph]—which, despite my best efforts, I never managed to pronounce correctly. After a dozen failed attempts where I unintentionally insulted both her and her entire bloodline, I surrendered to calling her Freckle.

A nickname, as if she was part of the Catfish Trolls too.

"Need a hand?" Freckle asked.

"No, no . . . I got this . . . No problem," I wheezed, trying and failing to appear unfazed.

As it turned out, Freckle was a masterful linguist, capable of speaking several dialects of Eekungh—the Native language—and swiftly picking up conversational English, without offending me or my bloodline.

She also happened to be of royal descent.

Her family had inherited ancient texts which spoke of a lost treasure, one that had long been dismissed as a myth. For generations, the Native Martian royal family had attempted to locate the fabled fortune, even pinpointing a possible site. But despite their best efforts, they had never been able to reach it—the bedrock blocking their path was simply too dense to bore through.

After witnessing the destructive power of the surface dwellers' excavation tools, they hoped spades could break through what they couldn't.

An agreement was made. Freckle's mother and my father shook hands—a custom the Natives have always found bafflingly rude. Living underground, they think of hands as the filthiest part of the body, covered in dirt and someone else's grime.

Hard to disagree.

Regardless, the humans and the Native Martians agreed to work together, planning to share the legendary riches that might lay in wait. Freckle was the expedition's designated translator and guide.

We walked alongside a mixed group of humans and Natives, all of whom carried provisions, operated heavy equipment, handled logistics, and lit the shadowy tunnels with headlamps and portable floodlights. Meanwhile, the two humans managing the expedition carried nothing, couldn't read the map, and didn't understand a word of Eekungh.

Yet, when history was written, only their two names would be remembered.

After the first sol of our journey, we set up camp for the night, gathering around a portable electric stove—building a fire underground had its ventilation difficulties. As soon as I set my backpack down, I nearly collapsed onto a nearby rock next to Freckle.

Across from us, our cook shaped what looked like ground meat in his hands before pressing it onto the stove. The patty sizzled, filling the cavern with an unfamiliar but mouthwatering aroma.

"What is that?" I asked, eyeing it warily.

"Gnukka meat," Freckle answered.

"Gnukka?"

"That's the easiest way for humans to pronounce it." She hesitated, as if choosing her words carefully. "It's, uh, kind of like what you would call an insect?"

I grimaced. "We're eating bugs?"

"It's our main food source. Not too many options underground."

"Gross."

She looked at me—at least, I thought she did. The Native Martians didn't have eyes, relying instead on echolocation, which was why their tunnels lacked ornate, crystal light fixtures.

"Don't knock it till you try it," she said.

A moment later, the cook handed me a plate with a gnukka burger and a side of fried roots—some kind of moss-like plant that could be cultivated without sunlight. I wasn't about to offend Freckle any more than my mispronunciations had already, so I took a cautious bite.

My eyes widened.

It was possibly the best meat I had ever tasted—melt-in-your-mouth tender, perfectly salty, and juicier than a premium lab-grown sirloin.

"Oh my god," I mumbled, my mouth still full, not even waiting to swallow before sharing my five-star review.

"Right?" Freckle giggled, a few high-pitched squeaks bouncing off the cavern walls. The way her lungs pulsed and her heart palpitated when she flirted always sent me into a giddy tizzy—a dizzying rush I could never get enough of.

After everyone had eaten their fill, we retreated into our individual Spurt Yurts—portable, self-inflating, pressurized shelters designed for use outside the glass dome. While we were already protected by the Martian atmosphere underground, the yurts were far easier to pitch than traditional tents—though still just as much of a pain to fold the next morning.

* * *

The next sol, my entire body was stiff and sore. Every muscle ached. My pack felt heavier than ever, and I knew I couldn't keep carrying all the weight. So, I made some sacrifices—ditching my brand-name clothes, camping chair, and sleeping pad. But I held onto the bottle of vodka for a special occasion.

"Wise choice," Freckle said, as I lightened my load.

"I'm a wise guy." I winced as I slung the pack over my shoulders. "Not like that . . . Well . . . I guess kind of like that . . . sometimes."

She squeaked out a giggle.

We walked side by side the entire sol.

"So, uh, do you like living underground?" I asked, trying to make conversation.

She shrugged. "I don't know anything different. Mars lost its magnetic field and the atmosphere was stripped away three and a half billion years ago. We couldn't exactly vacation above ground."

"Wait—" I furrowed my brow. "You guys used to live on the surface?"

"Yep. Had advanced technology, knowledge beyond what we can even imagine. Or so the legend goes." She gave me a sideways glance. "Kind of like what humans have now. But we had to go underground and abandon everything."

"You couldn't bring anything with you?" I asked, hoping that wasn't a question that made me sound stupid.

"We did—almost as much as you brought with you."

I smiled. I loved her playful ribbing. And I loved her ribs.

"But after the tunnels were built, kingdoms across Mars battled over cave space and limited supplies," she explained. "So much was destroyed and forgotten that we lost the ability to harness electricity and spent billions of years in dirt and darkness."

"Oh, so is that the reason for the . . . ?" I trailed off, gesturing vaguely to her two empty eye sockets and translucent skin.

She smirked. "Not much use for biological cameras in pitch-black burrows."

"Evolution is funny like that," I said, then quickly clarified, "Not like 'ha-ha' funny but, you know . . . "

Freckle suddenly stopped walking. "Are you making fun of my echolocation?"

I froze. "What? No. Sorry. I didn't mean to . . ."

And there were those few high-pitched squeaks again—she was messing with me.

"Flip, it was billions of years ago," she said. "I don't exactly remember having eyes!" She waved a hand in front of her face. "And they're only stories at this point. Who knows if any of it's even true."

"Hah . . . Right."

We only took a few more steps before another question popped into my head. "But you guys are good now, right? Like, you have . . . stuff."

"It's all happened relatively recently in the grand scheme of things," she said. "On the timeline of space and everything, it's all really just been a blip."

I stiffened, while she kept walking forward.

"A blip?" I repeated.

She turned back around. "Yeah. What? Did I not use the right word?"

I blinked. "No, you did."

* * *

For months, Freckle and I hiked beside each other every sol. And every night, we shared a gnukka-based meal together.

She never hid anything from me, never pretended to be someone she wasn't. She was who she was. No secrets, completely transparent—physically and otherwise. Take it or leave it. It reminded me of Rizz—Freckle never wasted time worrying about being cool, which was exactly what made her the coolest person I'd ever met.

Honestly, I had no idea why she liked hanging out with me. Maybe it was just the lack of options in a ragged crew of dirt-covered expeditioners.

On the night of my twenty-first birthday, I pulled out the bottle of vodka I had been saving. We passed it back and forth, sitting around the electric stove, giggling and squeaking.

Eventually, she retired to her yurt, and I, in my drunken haze, tripped over a rock and collapsed onto mine. The flimsy structure deflated under my weight. Instead of dealing with the hassle of pitching it again, I resigned myself to sleeping right on top of it for the night.

Then I heard the same unzipping and zipping of yurts that echoed through the camp every night. No one ever spoke about it, but we all knew. The two men managing the expedition hadn't volunteered for this grueling trek because they had a passion for backpacking. They had volunteered to escape their crumbling marriages—disappearing into the romantic backcountry to have an affair.

It wasn't the vodka. It was the sound of someone else taking a risk—and probably the vodka—inspiring me not to make the same mistake again. This time, I wouldn't lose my nerve when a beautiful girl expressed interest.

I sat up from my deflated yurt and tiptoed over to Freckle's.

"Hey," I whispered. "You up?"

A pause.

Then came the soft hiss of her yurt unzipping.

CHAPTER TWENTY-FOUR

BOOTY CAMP

"So, uh, was that good for you?" I asked Freckle, lying beside her in her yurt, post-coital.

She tilted her head. "Do you want me to rate you or something?"

"No, no . . . Not unless it was really good, like a ten out of ten or something."

She paused. "Okay . . ."

The silence stretched between us. The flip side of her never spewing bullshit was that she never tolerated it from anyone else. I couldn't lic to hcr.

"Sorry, I just—uh—I've never done that before." I blurted it out before I could stop myself and immediately wanted to unblurt it. I swallowed hard, as if I was trying to pull the words back down my throat.

Freckle propped herself on her elbow. "Seriously? I had no idea. Didn't you just turn twenty-one?"

Embarrassed, I couldn't meet her eye sockets. "Yeah, I don't know. It just never happened. Not that there weren't opportunities.

I'm picky, I guess. I think—I think I just built it up too much in my head."

I crouch-crawled around the cramped yurt, fumbling to get my clothes on as fast as possible. "It's okay. I didn't want you to know. I'll just get out of your hair."

"I don't have any hair to get out of."

Her classic Freckle humor made me trip on the tent floor and fall to the ground, flailing with one leg in my pants and an arm stuck in my shirt. "Right. Yeah. Sorry. I'll just . . . I'll let you get some sleep."

Squatting, pants still undone, I reached for the yurt flap in a desperate bid for dignity.

"If yours is broken like you said, you can stay here for the night," she offered.

I lingered, my hand still on the zipper.

"Please," she added. "Let's get that 8.5 to a ten." She stretched her arms out like a starfish and flopped back down.

I twisted to look at her. "8.5?"

Freckle let out a few amused squeaks and patted the floor beside her. Before she could change her mind, I dove back into her sleeping bag and wrapped my arms around her, pulling her into a cuddle.

We spent the rest of the night talking and canoodling. My body relaxed, sinking into sleep, until Freckle's voice stirred me awake.

"Why did you come on this trip?"

"What?" I murmured, half-asleep.

"Most people here are running away from something, or were hired as a translator, like yours truly. Royal duties and all. But you're the youngest one here. Don't you have school or something?" Her head readjusted on my chest as she spoke.

I exhaled, unsure how honest I wanted to be.

But I was never a great liar.

"My father made me. Said I was getting into too much trouble, misbehaving. I don't know. I don't think I was doing anything that bad, but he has these insane, unrealistic standards I can never meet. He wants me to be someone important, someone who means something, a household name like he is. But no matter what I do, no matter how hard I try, I always seem to just barely miss whatever asinine goal he's set in his head for me."

She let that sink in, dragging her fingers over my torso. "That's a lot of pressure to put on someone."

"My family has a real problem with being second."

Freckle lifted and tilted her head—whenever she did that, I knew it was her way of focusing her echolocation eyes on me. "You don't have to be first to matter."

I stared up at the curved ceiling of the yurt, tracing patterns in the fabric in my mind. "Honestly, I'm starting to think this whole thing wasn't even about character-building at all. I think my father just wanted someone on the inside. Someone to report back to him about whatever we find."

"Whatever he only gets half of," Freckle reminded me.

"If it was up to me, you'd get all of it." I squeezed her tight. "And hard life lesson or not, I think this might be the best thing he's ever done for me."

She squeaked out a laugh. I kissed her forehead, and we nuzzled each other. A tinge of guilt hit me when my mind drifted to Pepper—I had always imagined her being my first.

Though to be fair, when I was a teenager, I imagined a lot of people being my first. But still. I hadn't heard from Pepper since I left. I hadn't heard from anyone—reception underground was less-than-spotty, which was also why remote learning wasn't an option.

No messages, no calls, no school. Nothing but the caves and Freckle.

Which wasn't too bad at all.

* * *

For the next few months, life in the Native Martian tunnels, underground and inside Freckle—wink, wink, nudge, nudge, wink, nudge—was a dream. Every night, every morning, and sometimes even during our lunch break, we were spurting our yurts, docking the rocket, bumping, blowing, and blasting. I never wanted it to end.

Unfortunately, we eventually got to the x that marked the spot.

Using spades, the crew penetrated the bedrock—*oh, that's another good one*—of the once-impenetrable stone. And after six months of hiking, we broke through the wall of a lost cavern, arriving at the exact coordinates on the ancient Native Martian map.

Freckle pushed her way to the front of the crew, scanning the empty chamber with her high-pitched sonar, her translucent skin practically glowing with anticipation.

Her voice faltered. "I don't understand . . ."

I stepped up beside her. "What is it?"

"It should be here. It should be right here!"

A dozen flood light beams whipped around the cave but only illuminated its emptiness.

"Could it be somewhere else?" I asked. "Maybe the interpretation of the texts was off?"

"No." She shook her head, adamant. "No, I've spent my whole life studying those. There are no other coordinates. It has to be right here."

But there was nothing. No treasure chest. No forgotten city. No ancient artifacts.

I put my arm around her. "I'm sorry."

She wiggled free, grabbed a spade from another crew member, and furiously fired at the wall of stone opposite us, screaming as vaporized rock and sediment filled the air.

After a long moment of rage-filled drilling, the spade ran out of juice.

Panting, Freckle threw it into the red dust cloud and stepped forward to the rock wall, pressing her forehead against the cold stone, her body slumping in defeat.

The dust settled. Something caught my eye—something shiny embedded in the rock. A patch of silver. Metallic.

I squinted. "What's that?" I pointed to the glistening streak beside Freckle.

"What?" she asked, her auditory radar unable to differentiate between the dull bedrock and the sparkling ore.

I walked up to the wall, pried out a chunk, and caught it in my palm. Before I could react, one of the human expedition leaders snatched it from me, turning it over in his hands as he examined it.

"Lithium," he muttered, eyes wide. "It's lithium!"

The other man gasped. "We found lithium!"

They grabbed each other. "We did it! We're going to be heroes . . . The two of us!"

Then one of them kissed the other. They both froze, knowing their not-so-secret secret was out. Then they fully made out, not holding back any longer, trying to swallow each other's faces.

The ancient texts had marked something far more valuable than a lost treasure—massive deposits of lithium, the rare metal essential for batteries and electronic devices. Reserves had been rapidly depleting on Mars, and even more so on Earth. The discovery was beyond significant. It would change the trajectory of Mars forever.

But only the names of the two gay explorers would be remembered.

That night, the crew threw a massive party inside the cavern—drinking, dancing . . . and penetrating the bedrock.

* * *

Our six-month trip back was just as incredible as the first six of our journey. In only one year, I had gone from a late bloomer to an overachiever. But it was more than that. Every sol, Freckle and I hiked side by side. Every night, we fell asleep tangled in each other. I couldn't remember a time when I was happier.

Then on our last night, my fantasy came to a screeching halt, and the walls of the tunnel felt like they were caving in.

"We haven't talked about what happens after," Freckle murmured, snuggled in the crook of my shoulder.

"I haven't wanted to think about it." I exhaled. "I'm going to miss those gnukka burgers too much."

Freckle gave me a playful shove. "Stop! I'm being serious."

"Me too."

"Flip!"

I sighed. "Sorry, I, uh . . . I don't know what to say." I paused, thinking. "I'm gonna have to go back to school. I'll have to live on the surface."

"I know. And my parents will force me to—" She cleared her throat and dropped her voice in a mocking tone. "—continue with my royal duties." Then she added, "I'm so sick of bowing and waving. Figureheads are so pointless. I never actually do anything! And why do people care? Just because of who my ancestors were?"

"I don't know."

"But you can visit, right?"

"Of course." I pulled her closer. "And we'll get you a bunch of clothes to wrap you in so you can come up and visit me too."

She let out a soft squeak, but it faded quickly. "How much school do you have left?"

"Two years."

"Two years . . ." She trailed off.

The two of us snuggled, but reality had snuck in between us, pushing us apart. I tightened my grip around her. "Hey, I love you."

Pepper had been my first love, but I had never dropped the L-bomb before. Not like this. Not out loud.

Freckle shifted in my arms. "I love you too." She paused, then whispered, "I love you to the two moons and back."

I kissed the top of her head. "I love you to the two moons and back."

Neither of us slept well that night, tossing and turning until morning came. When it finally did, we packed up camp without a word. We still walked side by side, but neither of us tried to make meaningless conversation, ending our erotic backpacking sex odyssey in awkward silence.

The last leg of our trek was the longest.

Once we were back below the biosphere, the humans boarded the brand-new elevator to the surface and waved goodbye to their

Native crew members.

I lingered on the platform, then I hugged Freckle as tight as I could. "Have fun bowing and waving."

"You know I won't," she said into my chest.

"We'll figure this out. I promise."

"We will," she echoed.

I stepped into the elevator and didn't break eye socket contact as the doors slid shut. Even though we were only a few meters apart, we were already alone.

We did not figure it out.

CHAPTER TWENTY-FIVE

THE BREAKUP

"Lithium, you say?" my father wondered aloud, sitting at the head of the black conference table in the stale Town Hall boardroom. "How much?"

I stood with the two human leaders of the expedition, who had just finished reporting our findings. Madison sat to Buzz's right, with Rizz beside her, then Pastor Van Buren, and the last remaining Paul Kingsley clone on the far end. Across the table were Special Agent O'Shea, Jizzy, and Newt Newman—all handpicked for the Ministry of Mars by Buzz, presumably for their fame rather than their qualifications. A few others filled out the remaining seats.

"Enough that sharing the deposits with the Native Martians would basically go unnoticed," I said, reminding my father of the deal he'd made with Freckle's royal family.

"Of course! Of course." Buzz slapped both palms against the table. "And I'm sure that will ease some of the tension."

My brow furrowed. "What tension?"

"Flip . . ." Rizz's voice was serious—unusually so. "You've been gone a long time."

And apparently, all Rizz had been doing during that time was lifting weights—his arms thicker, his chest broader, his jawline sharp enough to cut the glass dome.

"Hardly any tension, really." Buzz backpedaled. "With the expansion, a few of the foundations compromised the structural integrity of some of their tunnels. We didn't want to put any of them in danger, so we politely asked them to relocate."

I imagined humans storming into the tunnels with spades, demanding that the Natives pack up everything and move like they didn't belong in their own homes.

My internal temperature spiked more than a few degrees Celsius. My face flushed, the redness creeping into my peripheral vision.

"You can't do that. Those catacombs have historical significance."

"I know," he said, as if that made it better. "And as soon as we realized, we adjusted our plans and moved the construction to avoid the unstable areas."

"You're kidding me," I said through gritted teeth, barely keeping my voice steady.

"No joke!" he said—entirely sincere—unaware that I was upset, bragging about his self-perceived selflessness and generosity. "And we graciously dug brand-new holes—*homes*—for those affected. Free of charge, of course, out of the goodness of our hearts."

Suddenly, my rage turned to worry. My mind went to Freckle—had her home been one of the ones destroyed? She certainly wouldn't leave without putting up a fight. A fight I prayed she'd win.

I needed to know if she was safe.

"I can't believe you," I spat. My stomach twisted.

"Believe it!" Again, completely sincere. "And we've also welcomed all Cavernese who wish to live amongst humans on the surface—as long as they make a point to learn our language and customs, and don't demand additional street signs in Cavernese." Buzz grinned, as if expecting applause.

I surveyed the room, my eyes landing on Rizz. "You allowed this?"

"We had to compromise," Rizz admitted. "There are other

issues at play."

I didn't want to hear excuses. I shouldered past the expedition leaders and made my way to the door.

"Now, hold on a minute, Flip," my father insisted. I stopped, my hand on the doorknob. "We still need to discuss this lithium," he said. "Sounds like Mars is about to be a very wealthy nation."

"Wealthy enough for you to retroactively pay the clones you bred for forced labor," Madison interjected.

Buzz's smile vanished. He shot her a dirty look. "That agenda item has already been wrapped up, Madison. We've moved on to the next agenda item. We have to follow the agenda. That's what agendas are for."

"I don't care about the goddamn agendas!" Rizz slammed his hands on the table, gripping the edge like he might flip it over. "Buzz, we conceded the Native Martian relocation so you'd free the clones and pay them for the work they've done. Along with one hell of an apology."

"That would tank the economy!" Buzz countered. "And I'm not apologizing."

"The apology is the least important part of this," Madison added.

"I do think you should say you're sorry, though," the Paul Kingsley clone noted.

Buzz gestured toward him. "Why is he even in the ministry?"

"He's a genius!" Madison said. "We needed his brain."

"He's the *clone* of a genius," Buzz corrected.

"That still makes him a genius!" Rizz shot back.

"Fine!" Buzz threw his hands up. "Here's an apology: I'm sorry for saving all our lives. I'm sorry for doing what needed to be done in order to survive. I'm sorry Mars is thriving!"

I still hadn't taken my hand off the doorknob. Part of me wanted to stay, to watch the ministry attack my father. Maybe they'd finally get through to him, convince him. Maybe I could chime in with something that would change his mind.

Not that he ever listened to me. I couldn't say anything that I hadn't already said a hundred times before. I was just his disappointing kid. Always would be.

I stayed quiet.

Madison sighed, trying a different approach. "You're right. You saved us," she admitted. "But we're not in danger anymore. The expansion project is finished. We don't need them to work for free anymore."

Buzz didn't respond right away. The room fell into an uneasy stillness.

"I'm sorry," he said finally, his voice softer. "But I won't do it. I can't. If it stays legal, then I never did anything wrong. If we free the clones, then I'll always be known as the guy who criminally enslaved them in the first place."

Madison shook her head. "Buzz, that *is* who you are."

With his brow furrowed and lips pursed, my father glared daggers at Madison. Then without a word, he abruptly swiveled in his chair to face the expedition leaders.

"How much lithium did you say?"

"Haven't we moved on from that agenda item, Buzz?" Rizz taunted.

One of the men cleared his throat. "It's just an estimate, but roughly ten million metric tons."

Buzz tilted his head, eyes drifting to the ceiling as he mumbled calculations. "Ten million. Lithium's around two million crimsons per . . . Shit, how many zeroes is . . . Twenty trillion?"

His expression changed. The tension in his jaw loosened. He smiled, swiveling back—slower this time—to face Madison.

"How about this? Here's a little compromise for you." He stood, planting his hands on the table, leaning forward. "You can do whatever you want in *this* biosphere. Declare clones are free. Declare clones are people. Hell, declare clones are gods among men, for all I care!" He straightened, throwing up his arms. "I'm taking the clones east. I'm building a new dome."

Madison's face darkened. "Buzz, calm down. You can't do this."

"I'm still the Director of Mars, Madison. I'm the leader of this planet. I can do whatever I want." He smirked. "And, soon enough, I'll be the director of a new biosphere. A better biosphere. I'll be the Director of . . . *Better* Mars."

Madison shot up, her chair flying backward, crashing against the wall behind her. Regardless of the silly name, my father was dead serious. He was really going to do it. Madison stepped next to him, meeting him at eye level.

"History is better served by those who swallow their pride," she warned. "Swallow it."

Buzz huffed. "You must have this power dynamic confused. I'm the one in charge. I'm not the one on my knees. I don't have to swallow anything." Buzz stormed toward the exit. I barely had time to step aside before he yanked the door open. "Pack your things, Flip. We're moving."

And then he was gone.

It didn't register at first, my father's words bouncing around my skull like the sound of the slamming door around the hushed boardroom.

Moving away from the biosphere. Away from Pepper. Away from Rizz and Pockets. Away from Freckle.

And right as I'd finally made it—

"Welcome home, Flip," Rizz grumbled.

CHAPTER TWENTY-SIX

TWO WORLDS

There was no point in unpacking—I'd just have to shove everything back in again. But I was used to carrying the weight of everything I owned, living out of a backpack, never settling in one place for long.

And I didn't have much time. I needed to say my goodbyes. And my hellos too—since I had been gone for almost a year.

That night, Rizz and Pepper met me on the roof of our apartment building, where we had gazed at stars so many times before.

Pepper pulled me into a long hug. I nearly forgot how she smelled—maple and almonds. She was more beautiful than I remembered.

"I can't believe I have to say goodbye—right as you finally come back," she mumbled into my shirt, her head resting on my shoulder.

I took a deep breath, saving the memory of her smell for when I needed it. "It sucks."

She clung to me tighter. "I missed you so much."

"We both did," Rizz added softly.

"I missed you too," I said, letting go of Pepper so I could see her face—rosy, a little puffy, eyes shimmering in the starlight.

"Do you have to move with your dad?" she asked.

"He isn't exactly giving me a choice."

"You could live with me," she said, hopeful.

"My father would never allow it," I told her. "Buzz's son living under the same roof as Madison Chen? No way."

"You could live with me," Rizz offered.

"I don't have any money of my own. I can't make you feed another mouth on a ministry salary." I forced a half-smile. "For now, it's whatever the old man says. I won't be able to get a job before I finish school—my father made sure to tell me twice. And he's probably right."

"Authority figures don't have as much wisdom as you think," Rizz said. "Or as much authority."

I sighed. "What can I do? He's still my father." They didn't argue with that. "It's just two more years," I said, trying to convince myself as much as them. "At least we'll be able to talk to each other this time, since I won't be underground."

Pepper gasped, suddenly realizing. "Wait—we haven't even heard about your trip! Was it awful? I can't imagine being underground for so long."

"It was actually pretty great," I admitted, cracking a smirk.

"Really? Underground?" She wrinkled her button nose. "Wasn't it just a bunch of lugging stuff around? I thought your dad sent you as a punishment."

"Yeah, it was. And he did. But I gotta do it with some pretty great people."

Right on cue, as if she had been waiting for the perfect moment to make a grand entrance, Freckle pushed open the rooftop door. Since the sun was shining on the other half of the planet, she didn't have to bundle herself up in protective layers like she usually did on the surface. Her translucent skin shimmered under the night sky, the soft glow of her lungs breathing faintly beneath.

"Hey," Freckle greeted, walking up beside me.

"Oh, uh, hi," Pepper responded, caught off guard.

I chuckled uncomfortably—I had hoped Rizz and Pepper would be gone before she came. Instead, I had to introduce them. "Rizz, Pepper, this is [glottal shriek, two clicks, four glottal shrieks, harrumph]." After a year together, I had finally learned how to pronounce her real name.

But I knew they didn't have a year.

"You can call her Freckle," I told them before they even tried.

"Nice to meet you." Pepper, wary, took a moment to extend her hand.

"Oh, uh, we don't . . ." Instead of shaking Pepper's hand, Freckle leaned her head forward.

Pepper blinked. "Oh, uh . . ." She chuckled awkwardly and shot me a glance, asking for guidance.

I leaned forward and tapped my forehead, demonstrating.

Pepper mimicked the greeting, bowing and touching heads with Freckle—just like Pockets had when we first discovered the Native Martians.

Rizz followed suit, more naturally after seeing it done.

"So this is the famous Pepper and Rizz," Freckle said, tilting her head slightly, examining them.

"That's us!" Pepper confirmed, a little too enthusiastically.

"Where's Pockets?" Freckle asked.

Rizz scratched the back of his neck. "He couldn't make it. He's actually in the tunnels. Dropped out of school. Fully moved underground to live among the—with your—uh—be with—um—" He exhaled. "He lives underground now."

Freckle giggled—squeaked—at his verbal flailing.

"Thanks for coming to the surface," I told her.

"I was happy to," she said. "I've never seen the stars—still haven't! What, with all the . . ." She gestured vaguely to her empty eye sockets and ears.

Rizz and Pepper shifted anxiously, unsure how to respond.

I laughed, already familiar with Freckle's sense of humor.

"We can, uh . . . We can let you two have a moment," Pepper said suddenly, making an excuse to escape her discomfort. She reached into her pocket. "I just wanted to make sure to give you this."

Pepper pulled out our snow globe and held it out to me. "I made sure to keep it safe while you were gone."

I hesitated. "Oh. Thanks." I took it, careful not to make a big deal about it in front of Freckle. It weirdly felt like Pepper was defending her claim on me—not that she had a claim to defend. I had never seen her jealous, if that's what it was.

"What is it?" Freckle asked.

"Oh, it's a snow globe. Just kind of this thing we've done for a little while." I kept my tone casual, trying to walk a fine line—trying to make it seem unimportant to Freckle without disrespecting what it meant to Pepper and me.

"More than a little while," Pepper corrected. "We've been trading it back and forth for forever. It's our thing."

She smiled at me.

Freckle's head tilt darted between Pepper and me.

"Your thing . . ." Freckle echoed, her voice trailing off, picking up on exactly what I had been trying to avoid. Her posture tensed. "Is *she* why you couldn't come say goodbye to me underground? I know you only have one night, but I wanted you to meet my family."

I had also never seen Freckle jealous, if that's what it was. It felt like a slight overreaction when I had already told her that Pepper and I were just friends, but Pepper was definitely acting a little weird.

I shook my head, keeping my voice steady. "I had to say goodbye to everyone—"

"But Pockets is underground," she cut in.

I half-smiled, uncomfortable, shrugging with my hands in my pockets. "But I didn't know that until now. I thought he was going to be here. I thought I'd be able to see everyone this way."

"You just had to say goodbye to Pepper up here," she continued, her tone sharpening. "Romantically. Under the so-called stars I've heard so much about. Under the *two moons*."

"Oh, it's not like that," Pepper insisted.

"What's it like then?"

"Flip and I, we're just old friends."

"Old friends with a *thing*."

"They're not together," Rizz asserted.

"And how would you know?" Freckle asked.

"I'm with someone else," Pepper explained.

"You are?" I asked, unable to hide my shock.

"I . . . We . . ." She glanced at Rizz.

"Whoa." Rizz held up his hands, backing away. "I thought we weren't going to get into this tonight."

That time, it was *my* head tilt darting between Pepper and Rizz.

The air felt thinner. My brain scrambled to catch up. My two best friends. Someone who was like an older brother and someone who was like . . . whatever my relationship with Pepper was like.

"Wait—what?" was all I could muster.

"Why do you care?" Freckle challenged, watching my reaction.

"I don't—I just—It's a surprise!" I stammered. "I don't know. I didn't know!"

Pepper looked down. "Sorry, I didn't know how to tell you."

Instead of getting angrier, Freckle seemed to back off, soften, which was all the scarier. "And why would she have trouble telling you, Flip?"

"I don't know!" I yelled, not matching her tone, making me look like the aggressor. I backed down. "I don't know anything about this. I don't even know how long it's been going on."

I said it as a statement, but Rizz knew I was really asking.

"It was one time," he explained. "The night of independence. We drank all those phycos . . ."

My chest tightened. The night of independence. The night Pepper's parents were out. The night she invited me in. The night I chickened out.

Pepper swallowed. "And then, more recently, it wasn't."

Rizz met my eyes. "You've been gone a long time, Flip."

"Yeah, and that whole time, he was with me," Freckle reminded them.

"We'll leave you two to, uh—yeah," Pepper muttered, grabbing Rizz's arm and pulling him toward the door.

As they stepped through, she turned back. "Text us."

The door swung shut.

"Text us?" Freckle needled, fixing me with a look.

I exhaled. "She's just a friend."

"That wasn't really the vibe, Flip." She said it like she wasn't bothered, like she was already over it—too mature to deal with such childish love triangles. Or squares. Or whatever shape we were.

I turned to her, reaching for her hands. "It's nothing. I'm with *you*. I love *you*. I love you to the two moons and back."

"I can't even fucking see the two moons, Flip." She pulled away, retreating backward toward the door. Her voice fell quieter. "I don't know. I think I need some time to think about all this."

As she stepped through, she turned back. "*Don't* text me."

The door swung shut. It wasn't exactly how I'd wanted my last night to end.

When I plodded back to the apartment, my parents were busy packing up the kitchen. I walked past them without a word, straight to my room, collapsing on my bed.

Thud. Thud. Thud.

Pepper:	You okay?
Me:	What was that, Pepper?
Pepper:	I'm sorry. I didn't want you to find out that way.
Me:	Why did I need to find out a certain way?
Pepper:	You know . . . We have . . . I thought your feelings would be hurt.
Me:	We were never together.
Pepper:	We weren't . . . I just . . .
Me:	You just wanted to keep me around as a backup. In case things with Rizz didn't work out.

Pepper: It's not like that.
Me: Looks like I'm second again.

It was silent for a long while. So long, I wasn't sure if she was going to respond or if that's where we were leaving things.

Pepper: We'll be waiting here for you when you get back.
Me: For two whole years? You won't forget me?

I was saying it with an attitude, still pissed, but making sarcastic stomps was tricky. I figured she would still get the picture.

Pepper: I'll never forget you.

If I wasn't so irritated, maybe I would've realized that was the last time we'd ever use Flipper Code on our floor-ceiling.

I should've taken a moment to savor it.

CHAPTER TWENTY-SEVEN

BETTER MARS

After our fight, I gave Freckle some space. A lot of it—the lithium deposit was on the other side of Olympus Mons, the largest mountain in the solar system.

With a team of clones and a fleet of rovers, my parents and I arrived at the site far faster than any Native Martians could have through the winding tunnels below. My father wasted no time. Detonations rocked the red landscape, cracking open the ground, exposing veins of lithium. But the blasts didn't just unearth—unmars?—the rare metals. They also collapsed the newly-burrowed tunnel leading to the deposit, cutting off all Native access.

My father claimed it was an accident. Said it was necessary for mining operations. Swore up and down he wasn't reneging on his "deal with the Cavernese"—the agreement that had been cemented with a handshake. But the Natives soon learned their repulsion to the human convention was warranted, and the deal was just as dirty as Buzz Buchanan's hands.

Freckle stopped speaking to me altogether after that. I tried to apologize for my father. I told her how pissed I was at him. But there was nothing I could do, nothing I could say to fix it—even though it wasn't really my fault.

After thirty-four unread messages, she blocked me. That was it. No explanation. No closure. Just the coldest of shoulders.

I had never felt so alone—not just without a girlfriend, but without any friend. With nothing else to occupy my time, I threw myself into rackethand training again, getting back into shape after a year underground. I sweated out my frustration on the court—which I built myself—channeling everything into the game, filling my empty hours with sport, leaving me too exhausted to dwell on Freckle.

While the second biosphere was being built, I shared a Spurt Yurt with my parents. Thankfully, it was only for a year—with an endless cash flow from lithium exports and an unpaid workforce of clones, the dome was constructed in record time. By early 2112+, we were living inside another biosphere.

My father actually named it Better Mars, true to his word—or, more likely, doubling down on his frazzled, off-the-cuff comment. Madison Chen promptly renamed the old biosphere First Mars, purely to get under his skin—and it worked.

Better Mars was practically a replica of the old dome. A man-made lake took up a quarter. Life support systems filled another. The living quarters were more compact to make room for the lithium mine swallowing the remaining third of the dome.

At its center—instead of a version of Town Hall—a gaudy mansion sprawled across an obnoxiously large estate. The home of Director of Better Mars Buzz Buchanan and his family—including me.

It was sickening to live in a palace built by clones, enjoying a life of luxury while others toiled. The thought made me nauseous every time a butler took my jacket, every time a maid folded my laundry, every time a personal chef plated a gourmet dinner.

And yet, I still ate the meals. I still wore the freshly pressed clothes.

Like always, I didn't have much of a choice.

The only thing I could do was accelerate my remote-learning education—or try to. Graduate early, get a job, and move back to First Mars. Maybe then I could patch things up with Freckle.

I was one assignment away from finishing maximum school. All I had to do was write a report on an educational virtual reality video game about crossing the treacherous trail between domes.

My family and I had it easy. Everyone that came to Better Mars after us didn't have the luxury of rovers—the exploratory vessels weren't authorized for personal transport. They had to make the trek on foot. A months-long hike over Olympus Mons.

And I experienced it all through the safety of a headset.

The game gave me two options—I could play as a family of four or a filthy gang of aspiring prospectors. A few classmates told me the report was easier if I chose the family, so I reluctantly passed on the rowdy miners—even though they looked like a way better time.

Text faded onto my headset:

> *In 2111, thousands of Martians traveled nine hundred kilometers between biospheres, lured by the promise of lithium and striking it rich.*
>
> *Attempting the brutal journey was deadly . . .*

My audio and visual surroundings faded in, and suddenly, I was outside the Mars Mini Mart.

A prompt appeared:

BEFORE LEAVING ON YOUR JOURNEY, BUY EQUIPMENT AND SUPPLIES.

YOU HAVE FIVE THOUSAND CRIMSONS TO SPEND.

Naturally, my first instinct in the virtual world was to steal everything. I punched the digital cashier, chucked supplies out the window for my family to catch, and knocked over entire shelves in the process. But the game didn't react to any of my shenanigans.

In the end, I was forced to cough up my hard-earned, simulated crimsons for spacesuits, food, a janky carriage, and other supplies.

Finally, we set off on our trek. As my virtual family and I trudged over Olympus Mons, the educational game peppered in real journal entries from a twelve-year-old boy named Ravi Singh—my character's POV.

April 31, 2111
Tosol, we're leaving for Better Mars. I don't want to leave my friends for some stupid shiny rock we have to dig for, but my parents are making me. Mama told me to pack light and ripped out my Pluto stuffed animal that I've slept with since I was a baby. I know I'm too old for stuffed animals, but I can't sleep without something under my arm. Papa came in afterward and told me I could pack it, and he wouldn't tell Mama.
-Ravi

At the end of the sol, I had to cook a stew for my family of four—grabbing ingredients, throwing them in a pot, and boiling them over a virtual camping stove. A warning flashed across my screen, reminding me that if I didn't strictly ration our provisions, we'd starve before the journey was over.

I sat beside my pixelated parents and sister, watching them eat and wondering why the hell the young boy was the one responsible for cooking and rationing—probably because he was the one with the journal entries.

The rest of my virtual family would have to start pulling their weight or I would cut the fat—though, the game probably wouldn't let me.

May 16, 2111
My legs are killing me. We walked for the whole sol and barely

took any breaks. I tried to hop on the wagon for a ride, but Priya snitched. Mama said if I wasn't walking, I wasn't getting dinner. I was already starving so I got off. Priya is such a bitch.
-Ravi

We stopped at a massive oxygen container at the base of the mountain, a rare opportunity to refill our tanks—for a price. Unfortunately, I had spent too many crimsons at the Mars Mini Mart and could only partially fill our levels.

Feeling strangely guilty, I apologized to my video game family, assuring them we'd have enough to make the trip. Though, I wasn't entirely sure.

August 3, 2111
Papa died tosol. We had to cross a crater. Going around would take too long, and we didn't have enough oxygen. We threw our stuff across the hole, using the low gravity, but some of it didn't make it. Mama jumped over first, then Priya. Papa gave me a bit of a boost to help me across. When he jumped, he slipped and cracked his helmet on the edge. We grabbed his arms and pulled him up, but his helmet was leaking. He hugged me and told me to listen to Mama and be nice to Priya. Then he died.

That night, I had to bury Papa. I shoveled heaps of Martian soil and dumped it over his grave, as Mama and Priya just stood there and watched.

The game was much darker than I expected—making me question the target audience, and our school curriculum.

December 25, 2111
Priya is sick. Mama said it's something called decompression sickness. It's like when soda bubbles up after you open it, but in your bloodstream. Something happened to her suit, and she got sick really fast.

For the rest of Christmas, I monitored Priya's oxygen levels and cranked a virtual handle whenever they dipped too low. My palms had never been so sweaty.

January+ 01+, 2112+
Priya was too sick. She died. I have to help Mama pull the wagon now. We were both crying today. We've run out of food because we lost some in the crater. I don't know if we're going to make it.

I was given a choice: eat the last bit of food or give it to Mama. I tried to hand it over, but the NPC refused, shaking her head—the sacrifices virtual parents make for their virtual kids. The food reappeared in my hand, no matter how many times I threw it at her.

You can lead a donkey to water, but you can't make Pluto drink.

Then just as we got our first glimpse of the dome, Mama collapsed. Right at the finish line. I finally understood why I had been playing as the twelve-year-old—he was the only one who survived.

The next sol, another family found me and brought me the rest of the way to Better Mars. Peppy music played. Sparkling text appeared on the headset:

CONGRATULATIONS! YOU'VE MADE IT ACROSS OLYMPUS MONS! PLAY AGAIN?

Jeezus H. No thanks.

The dirty prospector storyline was supposedly about how the miners failed to strike it rich, while the ones who sold spades raked it in. A simple economics lesson, nowhere near as grim as the family of four narrative, which was about . . . camping preparedness? Either way, after turning in my report, I graduated maximum school at twenty-three.

It was time to get a job.

CHAPTER TWENTY-EIGHT

A TALKING TO

Every job I applied for was stationed in First Mars. Moving back was all I wanted. I didn't care what kind of work it was—I'd stack shelves, I'd do paperwork, I'd scrub toilets. Okay, maybe not toilets.

But the thing about always being the second-choice candidate is you still don't get hired. I applied to hundreds of jobs, interviewed for dozens, but the runner-up remains just as unemployed as every other applicant.

I couldn't get a job to save my life—even after swallowing my pride and applying in Better Mars. Which meant I was stuck. Stuck living with my parents. Stuck in a gaudy, oversized mansion with a full help staff. Stuck with no way out.

"Look who decided to get up," my father said, sitting at the kitchen island as I shuffled in still in my pajamas, my hair sticking out in different directions.

"It's nine o'clock," I muttered, grabbing a mug from the cupboard.

All of our mugs—every last one—had the official flag of Better Mars plastered across the ceramic. The flag itself featured a shirtless Buzz Buchanan riding on Pluto, spades in both hands, explosions and fireworks behind him. It was on everything. Mugs, shot glasses, hats, T-shirts, pillows, blankets, bikinis—every product imaginable.

I poured myself a cup of coffee—brewed earlier by one of the Directorial Estate servants—and leaned against the counter. "Nine o'clock isn't that late."

"Flip, you're gonna have to start paying us rent," my father said, setting his own mug down like it was a final decree.

I looked around at the massive marble kitchen where a chef was plating crab cake eggs benedict for each member of the family. "Are we struggling?"

He sighed. "You have to learn that nothing in life is free."

"Lesson learned. Things cost crimsons. Job well done." I lifted my coffee cup in a mock toast and took a sip.

My father pounced. "I'm glad you brought up a job, because you're going to have to get one."

I paused mid-sip. "Wait, what? You don't think I've been trying?"

"Your mother and I agreed that for you to really understand the value of a crimson, you have to earn your stay."

I exhaled sharply. "Iris?"

My mother sat across the island, swirling her third glass of white wine, lost in its viscosity. She had started drinking again after we left First Mars—after we left Cliff. And for whatever reason, it hurt even more this time. I had gotten a taste of her motherly love only to have it taken away again.

Just like before, calling her "Mom" felt like a stretch, so I was using her first name again in some desperate attempt to get her to notice me. But she didn't.

And she didn't react then either.

Time to deflect. I turned back to my father. "Have *you* earned your stay?"

My father leaned back, inviting the challenge.

I spread my arms, mug in hand. "We have all this because you stole lithium from the Native Martians and forced clones to do free labor. You don't actually do anything. You just point and tell others to do the work."

His jaw tensed. "I spent my whole life working my way up to where I am now. Kept my head down, nose to the grindstone. I paid my dues. And being an elected delegate is *delegating*. It's management. It's not as easy as it looks. I'm under an immense amount of pressure. At the end of the sol, I'm the one getting the heat. I'm the one they blame."

"Or the one who steals the credit," I mumbled into my coffee.

My father drummed his fingers against the island. "It's easy to ridicule from the sidelines while still enjoying all the spoils of my hard work." He stretched his arms out, gesturing at our glistening, marble-and-gold castle.

I glanced at my mother again, searching for backup. But I wasn't going to get any.

Her attention was fixated on one of the three projectors in the kitchen that was tuned into IBS (Interplanetary Better Mars System). This morning, the cooking competition *Gourmet O'Shea* was on—it was better than Special Agent O'Shea's dating show *Love Under the Dome* or his home improvement program *Sweat Equity*. After *NCIS: Mars* finished its last season, the actor had been forced to move on to other projects—projects that only had an audience in Better Mars.

I sighed. "I don't know what you want me to do. I've applied to hundreds of jobs. Every time I get to the final round of interviews, they hire someone else."

Job hunting in 2112+ was brutal. In the online worlds where everyone is so connected, no one really is.

My father shrugged. "Life's unfair."

"Life's unfair. Life's not free. I feel like I'm getting the picture." I set my mug down. "Look, I can't get hired. It's not my fault—it's the family curse."

He shook his head, chuckling. "I broke that curse when I was born. You can't blame everything on something else. You have to take matters into your own hands."

"I don't know what you want me to do."

"Figure it out."

"If I had a prescription . . ." I muttered without thinking.

It was a local Better Mars colloquialism, a reference to the lithium used in mental health drugs—shorthand for "wouldn't it be nice if things came so easily." But the phrase ignored the fact that the lithium in mood stabilizers was insignificant, relatively worthless—and that having a prescription also meant struggling with a severe mental health illness.

First Martians called the phrase offensive. Better Martians called First Martians overly sensitive. I hadn't done a deep dive into either perspective—but I still caught myself saying it anyway.

My father sighed theatrically. "Do you want me to ask around for you?" Not generous—smug.

I stared into my coffee. The last thing I wanted was to ask my father for help. I sputtered into my cup, "I mean . . . yeah . . . Whatever . . . I guess so."

"What was that?"

I groaned, rolling my eyes. "Yeah. Thank you. Jeez." Coffee in hand, I plodded upstairs and put on *Love Under the Dome.*

CHAPTER TWENTY-NINE

THE WORKFORCE

Like a chef's-kiss cliché, my narcissistic father got his disappointing son a job in the mines. Of course, since clones did most of the manual labor, I wasn't subjected to the backbreaking work of extracting the lithium from the sediment. Instead, I was hired as a supervisor.

I spent my shifts pacing the pits—man-made caverns carved deep into the Martian crust—scanning for lithium with a surveying device. My monitor marked where the deposits were. I pointed; they did the work. They did the digging.

Managing clones re-aggravated my chronic indigestion. It made me sick—like finding several pieces of hair on your plate after you've already finished eating, wondering how many more you might have swallowed.

But as always, I didn't have much of a choice. So there I was—a participant and benefactor of the very system I hated. I was opposed to clone indentured servitude, but I lived in a place where it was legal, and I needed money to move somewhere it wasn't.

At least, that's what I told myself to sleep at night.

During my lunch break, halfway through my second week, I

nearly dropped my sandwich when I saw someone I never expected to see again—Cheese.

Thinner. More chiseled. But unmistakably her.

As she wiped sweat off her forehead with her sleeve, her eyes flicked toward me before quickly looking away. Then a moment later, they shifted back. Then away again.

She recognized me—maybe. Maybe, somehow, the copy of Cheese remembered me on a deeper level, beyond human understanding, something science could never explain. And maybe—if I spoke to her—the rest of Cheese's memories would come rushing back, all at once, and we'd run into each other's arms, and I'd hug my best friend who I thought I'd lost forever.

But it wasn't that. She was looking at me because I was staring at her—a weird, unblinking guy, frozen in place, holding a gnukka sandwich mid-air. I quickly lowered my head and buried my face into my lunch, pretending I hadn't just been eyeing her like a lunatic. But for the rest of the sol, as I surveyed the rock walls for lithium, I found myself trailing her. Just . . . following. Every time she glanced over her shoulder, I darted behind a stone column.

Completely normal behavior.

"Alright, seven o'clock—time to pack it in for the night," the lithium mine foreman called out.

The clones obeyed, falling into line as they shuffled toward the mineshaft exit, their silhouettes swallowed by the dim glow of floodlights and the flickering bulbs strung along the rock walls. But I didn't see Cheese's clone leave. I scanned the cavern, searching for her everywhere, but I didn't find her until—

She popped out from behind a stone pillar.

I dove behind a boulder before she saw me. Peeking over the edge, I saw her fire up a spade and aim it at the cavern wall. But according to my monitor, she wasn't in a designated drill zone. She wasn't supposed to be drilling there. To keep quiet, she'd set her spade to its lowest setting—small, controlled pulses of energy barely chipping away at the solid rock. Slow. Quiet. But chipping away still.

I stayed crouched, watching her work. After about an hour, she stopped—it was time to get back for evening roll call—and checked to make sure the coast was clear. She knelt to spread out the loose waste sediment, pulled a mine cart in front of the hole to conceal it, set the spade back in its place, and slipped out of the mine.

I walked over to the hole. The tip of it poked out above the cart. Someone would notice her secret project—a project that would get her killed.

The cart wouldn't do. The next sol, Cheese's clone returned to find the mine cart moved. In its place, a Better Mars flag—plucked from my family's closet of endless paraphernalia—hung from the cavern wall, draped over her extracurricular digging. The other workers rolled their eyes and went back to work, dismissing it as more propaganda. But Cheese's clone stiffened. Her eyes scoured the mine, darting from clone to clone. Searching. Wondering who had done it. Then they landed on me.

I was staring at her again.

I nodded. She hesitated, then nodded back.

That night, and every night after, we both stayed late. In the depths of the mine, she would look to me, I would look to my monitor, and my monitor would look to the weakest bedrock surrounding the hole. Then I'd point in the direction she should dig that evening.

Once the cavern was empty, she would lift the Better Mars flag and slip into the growing tunnel behind it.

At the end of each night, we scattered the evidence—fistfuls of debris casually dropped into mine carts, blending in with the rest of the dust of the sol's labor. The pile never built up, and no one ever noticed.

We never spoke. Maybe she was afraid that breaking the silence would break our unspoken deal. And maybe I didn't *want* to hear her voice—it would sound like Cheese, but it wouldn't be something Cheese would say. It wouldn't be her.

But in a way, she was the second-edition Cheese. Which meant, in a weird sort of way, we had something in common.

Then one night, she crawled out of the hole, dusted herself off, and looked at me. She nodded. It was finished. She had burrowed her way to the Native Martian tunnel I had been leading her to. The final layer had crumbled. She had broken through.

Escape was within reach, but she didn't know the tunnels like I did. She didn't know Eekungh.

I would have to go with her.

* * *

Over those seven months, I had saved almost enough to support myself in First Mars for a little while. Almost. I was still a little short.

So as I packed my bag that night, I swiped a few lithium trinkets around the Directorial Estate—decorative knickknacks my parents wouldn't even notice were gone.

At dinner, I sat across from them, cutting into a slice of beef wellington.

"I think I might be ready to move out," I said.

My father chewed loudly, barely glancing up. "You saved up that fast, huh? Guess we should've been charging you more rent."

"It might not be as much as I was hoping, but an opportunity has presented itself, and I'm not sure how long it'll be an option."

"Good boy. Take it first—before someone else steals it from you," he said through a mouthful of beef.

I turned to my mother. "Maybe once I'm settled, you can come visit."

She looked up from her wine, smiling vacantly. "I'd love that."

And that was the only goodbye they were going to get.

* * *

The next night, after the foreman called everyone away for the sol, I slung my backpack over my shoulders and met Cheese's clone by the Better Mars flag.

We clicked on our headlamps.

She lifted the image of bare-chested Buzz riding Pluto and we scurried into the tunnel, crawling to freedom—her freedom, not mine. She was escaping; I was just . . . leaving. Sometimes I felt like a prisoner in my own home, but I would never equate that to the plight of clones. This was her tunnel, her brilliant, dangerous escape. I only pointed where to dig and hung a flag. I was just tagging along, making sure she made it to First Mars.

I'm not claiming to be some human savior in this story either, just to be clear. I apologize if anything comes across as offensive or out of touch. That is not my intention. Please be kind on Chattr. I'm not a bigot—I have one clone friend!

Once we dropped into the tunnel, I pointed left, and we started walking.

We didn't make it far. After turning a corner, we came face-to-face with a Native Martian patrol, baffled to run into surface dwellers so deep in their territory. They grabbed us and escorted us away. I grinned—we might've been captured, but Cheese's clone was finally free.

With only our two headlamps, it was hard to see where they were taking us. The tunnels twisted and sloped downward before opening into a massive chamber.

They let go of us, and we whipped our lights around, trying to figure out where we were, until our beams landed on a Native Martian leader. He sat in front of us, reclined in a carved rock chair covered in shag rugs. Six guards flanked him—three on each side, standing at attention.

"Hello," I greeted, using the little Eekungh I knew.

The clone's headlamp swung toward me, blinding me with a flash of light. No doubt she was surprised—to hear me speaking Eekungh, and to hear me speaking at all.

I hadn't practiced the language much since my breakup with Freckle, so my vocabulary was embarrassingly limited.

I could only understand a few words when the Native leader perked up and responded. "Oh! You— — —language— —good."

And I could speak far fewer. "Uh . . . I . . . Flip. Yes."

His chest pulsed in what I hoped was approval. "How— —you— — — — —here? How— —you— — —come?"

I hesitated, racking my brain for any usable words. None came. But the social discomfort was too much—the pause in conversation had to be filled. "One. Two. Three. Four . . . Five?"

The leader tilted his head, studying me with his echolocation like how Freckle would, then turned to the guards on either side, as if checking whether they understood something he didn't.

Cheese's clone nudged me.

I cleared my throat, desperately reaching for another phrase. "Uh . . . how are you tosol?"

The leader blinked his empty eye sockets.

"Good morning. Excuse me." I rattled off every beginner phrase I could remember. "Welcome to my house. What do you like to do? Where is the library? Oh! Where . . . where . . . [Freckle]?"

The leader straightened. "Where is [Freckle]?"

"Yes!" I nodded aggressively.

He thought for a long moment, then gestured to two of the guards, said something, and they left. As I watched them go, I hoped I had asked for Freckle, but worried that I had accidentally gotten her into some kind of trouble.

"— —you— — —food— — —?" the leader offered.

"Yes. Gnukka."

We scarfed down the meal they brought us. Starving, Cheese's clone didn't hesitate with the unfamiliar gnukka meat, tearing into it without a second thought. I savored every bite, delighted to be reunited with my favorite food from the expedition.

Halfway through our meal, Freckle entered the chamber.

I choked on my bite. As I coughed, I wiped my face with my sleeve and stood. It had been more than two and a half years since I last saw her. And she still had the cute extra growth on her kidney.

"Hi!" I blurted out, my brain scrambling for anything better to say.

She stood there, hesitating—not exactly happy to see me there but not upset either. More confused.

"Hi," she echoed, equally at a loss. "Why . . . Who . . . How are you here?"

I nodded my head toward Cheese. "She dug a pretty big hole." After a beat, I added, "Wait—how are *you* here? Don't you live under First Mars?"

"Yeah, but I work here. There's a train now." She kept her distance. "We built a direct tunnel instead of taking a million detours through the pre-existing system. We've still been trying to break through to the lithium."

"Well, you should have access now," I said, grinning, gloating. Though, I wasn't sure how useful our tunnel would be—it was only wide enough for one person at a time.

Cheese's clone nudged me again, and I shot her a look. She clearly wasn't picking up on the seven-novel saga of subtext in my conversation with Freckle.

"Listen," I said, getting back to business. "We need your help."

CHAPTER THIRTY

REUNIONS

That night, the Natives under Better Mars hosted us, giving each of us our own room.

They only had a handful of lights lying around—they weren't used to having human guests—so each room was dimly lit with small lanterns that flickered on and off. I still had my headlamp, so I made do. And after my previous experience in the tunnels, I quickly fell back into the rhythm of operating with limited vision.

Next door, I heard Cheese's clone stumbling around, cursing under her breath—for the first time, I heard her voice. And for a moment, I forgot. The way she swore, it sounded just like Cheese. It was comforting. And at the same time, uncomfortably eerie. Unsettling.

My anxiety mixed with the gnukka, burning together into a deep, acidic pit. I knew I wasn't going to sleep. And at that point, I figured I should probably see a gastroenterologist.

I got out of bed and tiptoed to Freckle's door. Before I could knock, the door swung open.

"I heard you coming," Freckle said as she left the door open and walked back into her room.

I stood there, still frozen mid-knock, my fist hovering in the air. After shaking it off, I followed her inside and shut the door behind me.

"I thought I was being pretty quiet," I bragged.

"No human is quiet," she said simply, settling onto her bed.

"Right. The whole . . ." I gestured to my ears and the space around me, hoping she'd squeak-giggle at the callback to one of her jokes. She didn't. "So you work under Better Mars now? Important figurehead business?"

"I work everywhere. Even the surface. After your father screwed us over, I couldn't stand the meaningless spectacle. I told my parents I was done, and I got to work uniting all the different clans—I figured we'd have more leverage against humans if we stood together. And I guess I've sort of become the unofficial ambassador."

"That's amazing!" I said, still standing in the empty space of the room without having moved any closer to her. "Wow, I'm so proud of you. That's perfect for you."

"Thanks."

She meant it, but she didn't offer anything else.

"Your parents were cool with it?" I asked.

"It didn't really matter how they felt about it—I was doing it." Then she added, "But yeah, they were cool with it."

She gave a tight smile, then looked past me—at the wall, at the ceiling, anywhere but at me. I didn't exactly feel welcome.

"Do you want me to go?"

"I assume you came here to say something, so say it."

"Yeah . . . Yeah . . . I came here to say something." I stalled, realizing too late that I should've actually thought of what to say before I came. "Not seeing you, not talking to you . . . That clean break was—" I exhaled, a sigh of relief, finally talking about it. "It was hard."

Her voice softened. "Yeah . . . it was."

"And it happened after one fight—not even a fight. More like . . . a disagreement. Or a misunderstanding." I paused. "I'm gonna go with a misunderstanding."

For the first time, I realized that I was upset with her too.

She gave me a look. "You never told me that you and Pepper had a thing."

"We didn't have a thing!"

Freckle tilted her head. "Fine—an unspoken thing. There were still feelings there."

I didn't try to weasel my way out of it—she didn't tolerate bullshit. "Yeah," I admitted. "There were still feelings there."

Maybe I was maturing. At twenty-four years old, I always looked back on my twenty-year-old self and thought, What an idiot.

Freckle sighed. "Look, I get it. You've been friends your whole life—there were bound to be some complicated feelings. But I don't know . . . The whole snow globe thing. It seemed like it meant more than an old friend getting you a knickknack. I just expected a little heads-up."

"You deserved a heads-up," I acknowledged.

I took a step closer. She didn't flinch backward, so I sat beside her on the bed.

"I'm sorry."

"I'm sorry too," she said. "For my reaction. For cutting you out. I was angry."

I braved a chuckle. "Yeah, when you cut someone out, you really cut them out."

She exhaled. "I've just been down that road before. I didn't want to do it again. And then everything with your dad . . . It just pushed me over the line."

I lay back on the bed, staring at the uneven, textured ceiling. "So where do we go from here?"

Freckle lay down beside me. "I don't know."

I twiddled my thumbs, bit my lip, then turned toward her. Slowly, I leaned in.

She pushed me away. "Flip, *no*. Come on." She sat up.

Now, at twenty-eight, looking back on my twenty-four-year-old self, I still think I was an idiot. Which probably means that, four years from now, I'll look back on this book and think it's a stupid piece of shit.

I sprang off the bed. "Sorry. I must have gotten my wires crossed."

"I'm seeing someone," she babbled. "It's been two and a half years."

"What?" My voice rocketed from a baritone to an undignified tenor as I retreated. "That's amazing. I'm so happy for you. I simply must meet this lucky man. Maybe we'll set up a double date."

"Oh, are you seeing someone?"

I opened the door. "Nope. No idea why I said that. I'll see you tomorrow on the train."

"Okay. Good night." She sighed. "I'm sorry."

"No, *I'm* sorry."

I shut the door behind me, then muttered under my breath, "Jeezus H. Fuck. What the fuck was that?" After remembering her acute sense of hearing, I added, "Shit. She can hear me. She can totally hear me. Fuck. Shut the fuck up."

I hustled down the hallway, shut off my headlamp, and embraced the growing intensity of my indigestion.

* * *

In the morning, I met Cheese's clone outside our rooms, where we were greeted by two Native Martian guards.

"—you— — — —go?" one of them asked.

"Yes," I replied in Eekungh.

Down the hallway, Freckle stepped out of her room and headed toward us.

I picked up my backpack and threw it around my shoulder. In what felt like slow motion, the snow globe slipped out of the side pocket, hit the ground, and rolled along the circumference of the miniature dome—landing perfectly at Freckle's feet.

She picked it up, shook it around in her hand, and tossed it to me. "You dropped something." Turning to the guards, she said in

Eekungh, "We— — —go. Fast."

On the train to First Mars, none of us spoke. The three of us sat in separate rows of an otherwise empty train car.

For the entire ride, I stared out the window at a repeating, endless rock wall. I didn't know why the train even *had* windows. Echolocation would just bounce off the glass—they wouldn't be able to see out. Maybe they were installed to appease human tourists. But there still wasn't anything to look at. Maybe the Natives wanted humans to feel more comfortable? Provide them with familiarities. Yet still, it didn't seem like the Native Martians entirely grasped the purpose of windows. Or maybe the engineer was just having a laugh at my expense.

I thought about it the whole ride. I *still* think about it.

When we arrived, it was night. The train dropped us off at a platform below First Mars—the same one with the elevator to the surface.

"I remember this place," I said. "It was where you and I—"

Freckle cut me off. "We don't need to make this a thing."

"No. Right."

The cavern had been expanded—wider platform, more room for passengers to board and exit. Large light fixtures hung from the high ceilings, accommodating any human travelers.

Though the three of us were the only ones on the platform.

"It's changed a little," I noted.

"You've been gone a long time, Flip," Freckle reminded me—it wasn't the first time I had heard someone say that to me.

"Cheese?"

I turned my head.

Pockets stood on the platform a few meters away. His hair was long, pulled into a bun that poked out through the gap in the back of his baseball cap. A well-kept beard rested on his chin.

I hadn't seen him in four years.

And he hadn't seen *her* in six.

Slowly, he stepped forward, his eyes locked on the clone of

Cheese, studying her face. Unsure who he was, she took a step back, glancing between me and Pockets, looking for help or an explanation for the weird stranger approaching.

"This isn't . . ." I struggled to find the words. "Pockets, she's not . . . She's . . ."

Before I could finish, he surged forward and pulled her into a hug as tight as he could. She stiffened—arms hovering awkwardly around him—before hesitantly patting him on the back.

Pockets finally let go, wiping a tear from his cheek.

"I haven't seen you in so long," he choked.

"But she's not Cheese." I wasn't sure if I was trying to convince him or myself. "She looks like her. She sounds like her. But she's not, Pockets. She's not Cheese. This is . . ."

I turned to the clone. "I just realized, I never asked your name."

"I never got one," she said.

"Do you want one?"

She paused, thinking. "Your friend—the one who looked like me—her name was Cheese?"

Pockets nodded.

She considered it for a moment. "How about you call me Cheddar?"

I repeated the name out loud, taking it for a spin. "Cheddar . . ."

"It's perfect." Pockets beamed. "It's very nice to meet you, Cheddar."

He leaned his head forward in a Native Martian greeting. I nudged Cheddar and mimed returning the bow, tapping my own forehead to show her what to do—just like I had with Pepper when she first met Freckle years prior.

Cheddar pressed her forehead to Pockets's.

After their greeting, Pockets turned to me and yanked me into a hug. "I missed you, man."

"I missed you too," I told him. "I'm glad you could meet us." As we pulled apart, I added, "Cheddar is actually the person I told you about."

Communication cables had been installed in the tunnels—Freckle's doing—so I was able to get in touch with him beforehand. It enabled the Natives to communicate with the surface dwellers as well.

"She needs help getting all the other clones out of Better Mars," I explained.

Pockets nodded. "I can do that."

"Sounds like we got everything squared away," Freckle said, clapping her hands lightly. "I'll leave everyone to it."

"Oh," I uttered, rocking slightly on the balls of my feet—I hadn't expected her to leave so soon. "I guess I'll . . . Maybe I'll see you—"

"Like I said," she interrupted. "We don't need to make this a thing."

That stung.

She turned to the other two instead. "Pockets, Cheddar—good luck. I'm sure I'll see you guys around. I'm here if you need anything."

With that, she backed away, turned, and walked down the platform. I wanted to say something more, but the odds of making things worse were far too high. Staying silent was a safer bet.

"You heading up to the surface?" Pockets asked.

"Yeah, I guess so . . . " My voice trailed off, my eyes still on Freckle as she disappeared into the darkness. "I got some things to figure out."

"Keep us updated," Cheddar said. "And thank you . . . for everything."

"No thanks necessary," I told her. "I'm sorry for everything."

I pressed the elevator button and waved as the doors slid shut.

* * *

On the surface, in First Mars, I only had one place I could go.

I knocked.

A moment later, Pepper opened her apartment door, the slight breeze catching a lock of her dark hair, magically tossing it onto her shoulder in slow motion, the sunlight bouncing off her skin like a cloud of glitter. A fantastical display for our long-awaited reunion.

She smiled. A slow, warm smile. “Hi.”

I smiled back. “Hi.”

My fingers brushed against the snow globe in my pocket—our cherished, sentimental symbol of our bond—ready to give it back to her and pick up our friendship right where we left it.

Then the door swung open the rest of the way.

“Hi,” Rizz said, grinning as he threw his arm around Pepper. “Come on in, Flip-Flop!”

CHAPTER THIRTY-ONE

ROOMIES

I was out. Out of school. Out of Better Mars. Out from underneath my father.

Yet, I still found myself in a prison of my own making.

Living with Pepper and Rizz was excruciating. Comfortable, sure—they had a spare bedroom across from theirs, and the apartment was nearly identical to my family's old place—but watching them leave for work together every morning and curl up on the couch together every night was a constant, gnawing ache. A dull, unrelenting throb in the pit of my stomach that never took a break. And another in the back of my throat.

It wasn't that I still had feelings for Pepper. That ship had sailed a long time ago. By then, that ship was in a completely different sea. But I still remembered that ship being docked in my harbor at some point . . . I'm losing the metaphor a bit.

A part of me—an old part of me—was still hurt. They were both my best friends, my family. Not that I was still harboring—*oh, maybe the metaphor is back on*—harboring romantic feelings for someone who had become more like a sister. It was more like watching my older brother date the girl I once thought I'd end up with. Every sol. Every night.

And they were happy. And I wanted them to be happy. And I also didn't want them to be happy.

Eventually, I gave Pepper the snow globe. But since we lived together, it didn't make sense to trade it back and forth anymore. Instead, we placed it on a decorative bookshelf—one filled with tchotchkes rather than books. And as it goes with all things you see every sol, we stopped noticing it altogether. Its meaning gradually faded.

For three long, grueling months, I looked for work. Nothing. Even after pawning the lithium in my stolen trinkets, my savings dried up faster than I expected.

Rizz and Pepper refused to accept rent, but I couldn't live off their charity. Paying my parents room and board had actually strengthened my sense of pride—though I'd never admit it to my father—and I wasn't willing to let that go.

Although I still asked Pepper to ask her mother, Madison Chen, to get me a job, like my father had done for me. Life is just a series of trade-offs—and hoping you choose the ones that don't cost you too much of your self-worth.

All three of us worked in Town Hall—Rizz continued his position in the Ministry of Mars, Pepper worked as an aide in the boardroom, and I spent my sols in the administration office. Sorting red tape, filing red tape, and taping red tape. A mind-numbing job, but a job. I was grateful for the paycheck.

Plus, I got to—*had to*, sometimes—eat lunch with Rizz and Pepper in the mess hall every sol.

One afternoon, Pepper and I set down our lunches at a table.

"How was your morning?" she asked.

"Eh, it was fine. How was yours?"

"It was ridiculous. Oh my god, Pastor Van Buren is insane."

Rizz slid onto the bench next to her. "Flip, you should've heard him."

"We were talking about the two domes," Pepper continued. "And—wait—what did the pastor say?"

"Well, first—Flip—your dad called us," Rizz said, taking a bite of his sandwich. "And he still can't figure out how the clones are escaping. He's baffled—says they vanish as quickly as they're making them. He knows they're coming to First Mars—he just doesn't know how."

"I'm not surprised," I said. "His ego's so big, it would never even occur to him that clones might not want to proudly hang the flag of a country that enslaved them—just because he's shirtless on the front."

We chuckled.

"He thinks we're smuggling them out," Rizz added. "And he's threatened to attack if we don't extradite them. I think he's bluffing, but we're still making preparations in case there's an escalation."

"And the pastor said—oh, how did it go?" Pepper tapped Rizz's shoulder. "'Thou must not—wait, something about the promise of war . . .'"

Rizz picked up a carrot and held it like a staff, clearing his throat before dropping into a deep octave. "'Thou must not twiddle thy thumbs with the promise of war on the horizon, for the meek will be the first to die while the reckless will inherit Mars.'"

He snapped off a bite of his carrot. "Zeus 5:5."

They giggled together as I sat there, watching from the outside of an inside joke.

"I really hope we're not making our foreign policy decisions based on an old book written by a cult tripping on Martian spores," I said, more serious than joking.

"Blasphemy!" Rizz gasped in mock outrage, waving another carrot around. I had no idea what he was mimicking. It was like I was playing a game of charades and the answer was a word I didn't know. I didn't laugh.

But they never stopped.

"Do you really think things will escalate?" I asked.

"I don't know. You tell me," Rizz said. "You know him best. What's he been saying?"

"I haven't talked to him."

"For how long?" Pepper asked.

"Since I left."

"You haven't talked to your dad in three months?"

I shrugged. "He hasn't tried to call me either."

Pepper gave me a look of pity. Rizz dropped his head, staring at his food. "Huh . . ."

"What about your mom?" Pepper asked.

"She's been kind of distraught since we left First Mars—since we left Cliff, really," I admitted.

"Yeah, he misses her too," Pepper said. "Especially now that he's an empty nester, and my mom's work hours have only gotten longer."

"What's the deal with those two?" Rizz asked. "Aren't they, you know, married to other people?"

I pursed my lips together, tilting my head side to side, then turned to Pepper to answer.

"You know how my mom is," she said. "It's always been this unspoken arrangement. All four of them know what's going on. It's not like they're real marriages. Buzz and my mom are politicians."

Unsurprisingly, the downer of a conversation stalled.

"So what else did the pastor say?" I asked, wanting to lighten the mood, even if it meant watching them share something I couldn't.

"What was it he said the other sol?" Rizz asked.

Pepper touched his arm. "Oh, uh . . ." She did her own impression, dropping into an overly dramatic alto. "'Not the promise, but the display of power is required for all others to quiver with willful respect and bow lovingly.'"

"Poseidon 7:29," Rizz finished, with a swish of his carrot.

They howled with laughter.

"Stop—I can't breathe," Pepper wheezed, grabbing Rizz's leg for support.

I hadn't even started eating yet, but I suddenly felt the urgent need to be finished with lunch as quickly as possible. Without a word, I began shoveling food into my mouth at an alarming rate.

They asked me a few questions here and there, but my mouth was always too full to answer or ask anything in return. I kept pointing to my face as I chewed, as if I desperately wanted to answer but I had simply taken a bite at the exact wrong moment.

As soon as I shoved in the last bite, I stood, tapped my wrist, pointed to the door, and waved goodbye—still chewing, unable to say a word.

I had to get a different job. Or at least my own place.

I needed space.

CHAPTER THIRTY-TWO

IS THERE A DRAFT IN HERE?

That night, I went back to the apartment, parked myself on the couch, and put old Earth movies on in the background. Then I started the apartment hunt.

The pickings were slim.

Pepper came home by herself.

"Where's Rizz?" I asked.

"He had to work late," she said, heading into the kitchen and grabbing a phyco.

She plopped down next to me and absentmindedly picked at the bottle label, not looking at me. "Hey, are you okay?"

"Yeah, I'm fine," I lied. Then, exhaling, I let my head fall back against the couch.

One thing I learned from Freckle was that honesty was relief. I didn't want to keep hiding behind unspoken understandings, subtext, or body language. That wasn't communicating. Nobody could read minds.

And it was time I stopped thinking they could. It was time I grew some balls and said how I felt.

"Sometimes it can be a little hard with you and Ri—"

Crash.

The apartment windows exploded. Shards of glass disappeared into the night as a violent gust tore through the room. Kitchen appliances ripped from their plugs and shot out onto the street.

The crushing force made me feel like a feather in a leaf blower—like I was weightless, while at the same time, getting slammed by a speeding rover.

We were airborne. Getting sucked toward the shattered windows.

Pepper barely managed to grab the column between the living room and kitchen, her legs flailing wildly like one of those inflatable men outside a car dealership.

"*Flip!*" she cried.

The couch had tipped, throwing me back against the side of the kitchen counter, flipping over me and out the window. I was clutching onto the edges of the counter as the air rushed around me, pushing me into it, trying to pull me away.

"*Pepper!*" I shouted back.

Her fingers were slipping—she wouldn't hang on much longer.

It felt like the entire apartment had been turned sideways, the relentless wind pulling me like a gravitational force, dragging me toward the gaping, broken windows. I rolled over on my stomach and crawled toward her.

"*Take my hand!*" I screamed, reaching for Pepper as far as I could.

She tried, but as soon as she stretched toward me, her grip on the column skidded, and she had to grab it again with both hands. "*I can't!*"

I hopped to my feet, gripping the counter for balance as I reached as much as I could without losing my own footing.

"*You can!*" I braced myself, shifting my weight, stretching farther.

Her fingertips were sliding—she only had seconds left. She reached again.

And then she slipped.

The wind wrenched her away, carrying her toward the window, on her way to fly out and slam against the building next door.

I wanted to catch her at the last moment—like heroes did in the movies—but real life had no patience for tropes. Once she lost her grip, I couldn't suddenly stretch farther than I could before. If I lunged for her, we'd both be airborne, sailing into the open abyss.

Part of me wishes I had done it anyway. But I didn't. Survival instincts locked me in place, and instead, I watched her as she flew away from me—on the verge of being whisked out the window and vanishing altogether.

Then—

Thump.

We both crashed to the floor, right before she was sucked out the window. As quickly as it started, the wind stopped.

We lay there, stunned, just breathing. My ears rang. My hands trembled. My mind tried to catch up to what had just happened. After a few groans and some rolling around, I finally asked, "Are you okay?"

"Yeah . . . You?"

"Yeah . . ." I exhaled, checking my body for any wounds. "What was that?"

"I don't know."

I paused.

"I'm sorry," I muttered. "I couldn't—"

"It's okay," she interrupted. "You did everything you could."

But I wasn't sure I did. Then silence was only filled by the sound of our unsteady breaths and panicked noise from the street.

As I sat up, my eyes landed on the only thing still inexplicably inside our toppled bookshelf—the snow globe. It had been knocked around—many times over—but somehow, it survived. Seemingly unbreakable, save for a few fresh cracks in the glass.

I lifted the shelf back into place and set the miniature dome where it belonged. Inside, the glitter whooshed around—like it knew what we'd just been through.

MBN flickered on in our living room.

"New news with Newt Newman is new at noon. I'm Newt Newman," the anchor reported, his usual enthusiasm replaced by grim urgency. Pepper slowly got up, brushing broken glass off her shirt, and we turned toward the broadcast. "Three simultaneous explosions have decimated the First Mars exploration bay, causing a catastrophic pressure differential and instant, destructive winds. In one swift moment, buildings, homes, and Martian citizens were swept away in gusts reaching over four hundred kilometers an hour. The destruction only ended when a heroic team of first responders secured a tarp over the breach. Authorities have linked five individuals to this targeted act of terror, but they have escaped capture."

The MBN banner read:

BREAKING NEWS: DID YOU FEEL IT? FIRST MARS BLOWN BY SNEAKY COMMANDOS

"Oh my god . . . Rizz . . . My mom!" Pepper gasped, bolting out the door.

I hurried after her.

* * *

The streets of First Mars were chaos. Fires blazed, ruptured power lines sparked, and rubble blanketed the roads. The dome that had once been rebuilt once again looked like a war zone.

We sprinted through the destruction in record time, reaching Town Hall just as Rizz came rushing out the door.

"Pepper!" he yelled, his eyes wide with panic.

They collided into each other's arms.

"Thank god," he breathed. "I would've gotten to you sooner, but there were so many people here—"

"It's okay," she cut him off. "Where's my mom? Is she alright?"

"She's fine. She's in the boardroom."

Pepper didn't wait. She shoved past him and disappeared down the hallway.

Rizz turned to me and pulled me into a tight hug. "You were with her?" Rizz asked, his voice raw. "When it happened?"

"Yeah," I answered.

Rizz exhaled, squeezing my shoulder. "Thank you."

I flinched—I certainly didn't deserve a thank you.

We hurried after Pepper, stepping over chunks of debris, our shoes crunching on broken glass. Inside the boardroom, the entire ministry was already at work—lifting overturned chairs, rehanging wall art. Everyone was moving slowly, still dazed.

Pepper was already hugging her mother. "What happened?" she asked her.

Madison's voice was stoic, matter-of-fact. "From what we know now, we believe this was an orchestrated attack by Better Mars."

My heart sank. Nerves shot through my stomach. Tingles crawled up the back of my neck. Madison kept talking, but I'd already stopped listening. Without a word, I slipped into the hallway. After months of silence, I finally called my father.

His smug hologram flickered to life above my phone.

"Oh, so nice of you to make the time to call your father," he greeted, his voice dripping with condescension.

I glanced down the hallway to make sure no one could hear—I didn't want anyone knowing I was talking to him. "What the fuck did you do?"

His smile didn't waver. "What are you talking about?"

"First Mars. It's destroyed."

That got his attention. His tone shifted immediately, laced with something that almost sounded like concern. "Is that where you are?"

"Yes!" I shouted, flinging my free hand in the air.

"Are you okay? Are you hurt?"

"I'm fine, but people died. *I* could've died."

His response was immediate. "Well, I didn't know you were there!

We haven't heard from you. I assumed you were still somewhere in Better Mars."

"So it *was* you."

He paused, switching gears into defense. "What was me? I have no idea what you're talking about. What happened in First Mars?"

"Fuck you."

A beat of silence. Then softer—

"People died?" he asked.

"Yes."

"How many?"

"I don't know."

His hologram turned slightly, gaze shifting to something off in the distance. Then under his breath, almost to himself—

"I didn't think . . . It wasn't supposed to . . ."

I didn't wait for whatever excuse was coming next. I hung up.

With my head down, ashamed, I tapped on the boardroom door. Pepper answered. I raised my eyes to meet hers.

"It was him."

CHAPTER THIRTY-THREE

BLANKET SOLUTION

"Four sols and seven hours ago, we were attacked," Madison Chen addressed a crowd of thousands from a small stage in the center of the town square.

I stood just behind her and to the right, wearing a First Mars Battalion uniform alongside three others. A sea of people from across the biosphere surrounded us. I spotted Pepper, Rizz, and Cliff near the front of the crowd.

"Not by an oppressive corporation. Not by another country. Not by another planet. But by our own," she continued. "Simply because we stand for freedom—freedom for all. Because all people on the spectrum are created equal. Now, we must fight together to protect this right, defend our friends, our family, and our neighbors under the dome. To the First Martians who will be joining me on the battlefield, I thank you."

Applause erupted, waves of appreciation for everyone in uniform.

For four sols, First Mars had ground to a halt. Everyone had come together to repair the damage, care for the injured, and prepare for the counterattack. At the heart of the battle plan lay a weapon of mass destruction—known only to Madison Chen and the few who had built it.

As the cheers quieted, Madison pressed on. "If everything goes according to plan, no more Martian blood will be spilled. We will return safely. And we will be victorious. When that sol comes, I ask that you forgive those of Better Mars. We may have our differences, but we are all Martians. Be gracious. Welcome them back to our nation—one nation of Mars."

A final roar of approval rose from the crowd. As we exited the stage, we were met by the rest of the First Mars Battalion—marching through the streets in full spacesuits, waving with their helmets in one hand. Flags flapped, "March of the Sowers" played, and citizens blew kisses to the departing troops.

Almost lost in the mass of people, Rizz caught my eye and jokingly blew me a kiss. Pepper did not. She wasn't smiling—she was pissed. Pepper didn't want me to enlist, afraid of what might happen to me.

But I had to.

It was mostly out of guilt, I think. My father was the one who attacked First Mars, and even though we were two different people—*very* different—I couldn't shake the sense of responsibility by association. But worse than that was the shame of letting Pepper slip away in the wind without doing more. I told myself it would've only gotten us both killed. I told myself I couldn't have reached her. But I should've tried. I should've done more.

Enlisting was the only thing I could do that felt like doing more. And I did so without worry—Madison assured us that the secret weapon would guarantee no one would get hurt. It couldn't be any worse than the battle with the Paul Kingsleys.

Thankfully, we were able to take rovers, since it was for government use. So we didn't have to make the trek over Olympus Mons on foot like poor Ravi Singh.

At the base of the mountain, we could just make out the outline of the Better Mars dome on the horizon. With the attack scheduled for the next morning, we set up base camp in Spurt Yurts and settled in for the night.

As I tossed and turned, I realized I had been lying to myself. Not about feeling guilty—but about why. Well . . . those other reasons were still very much applicable, so maybe it wasn't *exactly* a lie. But the main cause of my guilt wasn't my father. It wasn't Pepper.

It was my mother.

I had left her behind in Better Mars. Not just physically—but emotionally too. When she'd fallen back into her old ways, I'd given up on her. I couldn't handle it again. But after I had seen her clean herself up, after she had proven to me that she could, I should've tried harder. I should've been there.

I couldn't let anything worse happen to her. She didn't deserve it. As for my father, he certainly deserved what was coming to him. I was angry with him. Furious. But I still didn't wish him dead.

I needed to know they would both make it out alive.

* * *

Early in the morning, I slipped out of my yurt and set off for the dome before anyone else was awake—the attack wasn't planned for another few hours. The stars were still vibrant in the night sky as I walked. As the first light of dawn crested over the horizon, they faded, swallowed by the sun—rising perfectly behind the dome, making it seem as if Better Mars and the sun had become one.

(Some reader, somewhere, is stretching, reaching, desperately searching for some hidden metaphor to prove their intelligence—some grand, poetic symbolism about my journey or the fate of Mars. But nope. Just a sunrise.)

I made it to the exterior door of the Better Mars exploration bay and stood, pausing. It occurred to me that I had no idea how to get in. There was no friendly doormat on a front porch, no doorbell for the neighbors to ring when they wanted to drop off a pie. There were cameras, I imagined, but I had no idea if anyone was watching them that early.

I only had one idea.

Clang. Clang. Clang. I knocked. The outer door ascended, and I stepped inside. After it lowered back into place, the chamber pressurized with a familiar hiss, and the inner door rose.

The hangar was empty—except for the lone worker stationed at the control panel. I recognized them immediately. It was the same person who had operated the doors when the new ship arrived, right after Mars declared independence seven years prior. I wondered if they ever left their post. And I wondered why I would remember such an insignificant person in my life.

I waved. They nodded. That was the extent of our deep, meaningful connection.

After shedding my cumbersome spacesuit, I left the hangar and headed straight for the Directorial Estate.

I pressed my fingertip to the scanner—nothing. They had changed the locks. So I rang the bell. Surprisingly, instead of a butler, my father answered the door. It seemed that even the estate clones had managed to escape through the lithium mine.

He was in his robe—hair mussed, eyes tired—standing in the doorway, unmoving. "The prodigal son returns."

I squinted. "Do you know what that means?"

He thought for a moment. "No. Do you?"

I thought for a moment. "No."

We both stood there, considering it.

He wondered aloud, "Prodigal . . . Prodigal . . . Huh . . ."

"We can look it up later. Where's Iris?"

"She's still sleeping."

"Wake her up. I need to tell you something."

We went upstairs to her bedroom—they slept separately—and I shook my groggy mother awake before warning them both about the incoming First Mars Battalion.

My mother blinked up at me. The words weren't registering. Either she was still too hungover or still too drunk from the night before.

My father adjusted his robe, as if it would protect him. "What's this weapon of mass destruction?"

"I don't know," I admitted.

"You don't know?"

"All I know is Madison seemed hopeful that no one would die."

His lip curled. "Doesn't sound very destructive."

"I don't know what to tell you," I said flatly. "But I think you two need to get out of here. Leave the biosphere."

A sixtieth-of-a-minute later, sirens blared through the dome.

They moved up the attack.

Someone must've seen me. I was too late. They were coming.

My father's gaze flicked to mine, his brow furrowed. Straightening, exhaling sharply through his nose, he re-tied his robe tighter. "Come with me."

* * *

My father led me to the edge of the dome—still in his slippers and robe—stepping right up to the perimeter to meet Madison Chen, waiting for us on the other side of the glass. Fifty meters behind her, the First Martian Battalion stood in formation.

Buzz and Madison locked eyes. I stood off to the side, unsure what my role was at that point. They couldn't speak to each other—not through Madison's helmet, the Martian atmosphere, and the thick glass of the Better Mars dome.

Naturally, my father resorted to pantomiming.

He tapped his finger to his chin in exaggerated contemplation, then pointed at Madison, punched his fists downward, and stomped his feet—he was attempting pre-battle negotiations through interpretive dance.

Madison shook her head and shrugged.

Buzz frowned, thinking, then stepped closer to the glass and exhaled, creating a circle of fog. His finger squeaked as he traced a message:

YOU MAD?

Madison's expression didn't change. She calmly pulled out a tablet, typed in bold letters, then flipped it around:

89 PEOPLE DEAD

Buzz frantically wiped the condensation off the glass, then breathed again to write a new message:

SORRY
TRULY

Madison's glare hardened. She typed again, her fingers hitting the screen with force.

SURRENDER AND NO MORE WILL DIE

Buzz hesitated. Then he breathed on the glass once more—

NOT SCARED OF YOUR

—then sidestepped and breathed again to expand the circle—

WEAPON OF

—then sidestepped and breathed again:

"MASS DESTRUCTION"

Below it, he added:

STEP ONE CENTIMETER IN HERE AND
YOU'LL REGRET IT

At the mention of the weapon, Madison's eyes snapped to me—like sunlight through a magnifying glass, they could've set me on fire.

She fiercely typed on her tablet:

WE'RE NOT GOING IN. YOU'RE COMING OUT.

Madison lifted her right arm. Behind her, a line of soldiers stepped forward from the legion, each one pushing a cannon into place. One by one, they loaded the barrels with massive steel balls. Another set of troopers adjusted the cannons' angles, cranking them upward.

I tensed. My stomach dropped.

They were going to shatter the glass dome.

If they fired, everyone inside Better Mars would perish instantly—either freezing to death or suffocating, whichever came first. Unlike the First Mars attack, this pressure differential would balance out in less than a second. There would be no hope for survival.

My father and I exchanged looks—fear in our eyes.

Then my father smiled, like he knew exactly how all of it would end. He wiped away the leftover condensation on the glass, exhaled another foggy circle, and wrote:

NICE BLUFF

Madison barely read the message before she was typing on her tablet.

NOT A BLUFF

Buzz swallowed hard, writing with shaking fingers.

LET'S TALK ABOUT THIS

And then Madison was the one laughing as she wrote.

THAT TIME HAS COME AND GONE

She lifted her right arm again.

Buzz's breath quickened. He was huffing. Puffing. Panicking. His fingertip quivered as he scrawled out one last message.

YOU'LL KILL US ALL

Without another word, Madison chopped her arm down.

The signal was given. The soldiers fired their cannons.

And that was it. I was about to die. My blip was coming to an end.

At twenty-four, having accomplished next to nothing with my life, the air would be sucked from my lungs and the blood in my veins would ice over. I would never see Rizz or Pockets or my mother again. I would never see Pepper. I would never see Freckle.

The last thing I would see was my sixty-two-year-old, hairy, overweight father in a bathrobe and slippers, sweating and rubbing bathroom mirror messages onto the glass dome.

I thought of Cheese—the original. When faced with death, bleeding out from multiple spade wounds, she'd still seen the humor, she'd found a joke.

I closed my eyes, and suddenly the Better Mars dome transformed into one big snow globe. Once the cannons hit, the glass splinters would fall like shaken-up glitter. The temperature would drop, and the frozen shards would snow down on us like the first flurry of the season, a Christmas-morning miracle. But instead of jolly snowmen on the front lawn, it would be us—frosted corpses, frozen right where we stood.

I couldn't find the joke. Or at least, it wasn't very funny.

A dozen balls headed straight toward us, arcing in the sky, sailing to their target.

All missed.

They soared over our heads, over the dome, and landed on the far side of Better Mars.

My father and I exchanged a look before turning back to Madison. Her eyes shifted between the two of us, and then . . . she grinned. She raised her left arm this time and snapped it down.

I braced for the next volley of cannonballs—but nothing came.

The tiniest shimmer in the sky caught my eye. Then another. Then three more.

Cables jerked and twisted taut against the glass dome, like fishing lines finding their prey. I tracked the lines to the other side of the biosphere, where the cannonballs had landed. At the front of the First Mars battalion, covering the entire width of the army, something massive unfurled.

A thick, black sheet.

The giant bedspread billowed as it lifted, sailing over the dome. A colossal shadow swallowed us whole as the enormous black pocket square took flight. The sun vanished. The dome darkened. And as the giant napkin gently glided to settle over the Better Mars dome like a black hole engulfing a star, Madison's secret weapon became as clear as Native Martian skin.

It wasn't a weapon of mass destruction—it was a weapon of *mass*. Both domes ran entirely on solar power. Without the sun, we were thrust back into the dark ages, metaphorically and literally.

Buzz stared at Madison with charged, weighted eye contact that only broke as the final corner of the black, titanic tablecloth fell between them.

Then—movement. The folds in the sheet twitched.

Madison sliced a flap in the oversized handkerchief, lifting it for one last message:

LEAVE AND YOU WILL BE SHOT
KNOCK IF YOU WANT TO TALK

CHAPTER THIRTY-FOUR

BLACKOUT

Street lights automatically blinked on under the blanket, triggered by the sudden darkness.

Buzz took off, hustling back to the Directorial Estate, and I leapt to catch up. As we rushed through the biosphere, confused citizens stepped outside, staring up at the eerie black sky, wondering if there was some unexpected solar eclipse.

"Everything's fine!" Buzz called out, waving his hands. "Nothing to worry about! Go on with your sol!"

Unconvincing. Especially coming from a man sprinting through the streets in slippers and a robe.

When we reached the estate, Buzz finally changed into real clothes before calling an emergency meeting of the Ministry of Better Mars.

Everyone gathered in the south wing of the mansion. There was a real boardroom in the east wing, but the south wing had a fully stocked bar. The situation called for it—despite the fact that it was the crack of dawn. It was still pitch-black outside, so who can judge.

The bar stretched across the entire right-hand wall, with an absurd selection of top-shelf alcohol. Two sets of long couches facing each other in the center of the room, separated by a sleek, skinny coffee table. Floor-to-ceiling windows lined the back wall, offering a breathtaking view across the lake to the Martian surface beyond. It was stunning—the clones had excellent taste in interior design.

Of course, that sol, the view left much to be desired.

"They built a blanket-shaped EMP bomb!" Special Agent O'Shea cried.

"I'd give it two, maybe three sols, assuming we ration our stored solar power," another member estimated grimly.

"Calm down," Buzz said, reassuringly. He stepped behind the bar, casually pouring drinks for everyone. "No one's been hurt yet."

"Yet!" Iris slurred from the couch against the wall. She burst into laughter before taking a long swig from her wine glass.

"Sorry," I whispered to the ministry members, sinking into the couch beside her. My mother wasn't a part of the ministry, but since they were meeting in my parents' house, nobody was going to kick us out. As long as my mother didn't keep interrupting.

"Why don't we fight our way out?" Jizzy proposed. "We have more spades and more rovers."

"We'd be mowed down," Special Agent O'Shea countered. "Only a certain number of soldiers can go through the airlock at once, and there's an entire army waiting for them on the other side."

Buzz sighed. "It was a clever trick," he admitted, pacing the room as he distributed the first round of drinks. "But that's all it was. We haven't lost anybody. The lights are still on. This is a siege. They have to starve us out. And I would bet a million crimsons we can outlast them."

He gestured vaguely toward the dome's edge. "They're stuck outside in their yurts. They need food, water, and oxygen for all those soldiers. How much could they really have brought? We just have to wait them out."

I wanted to object, but I was only a soldier—I wasn't privy to the logistics. I didn't know everything they had, or how long it would last. Just like the weapon of mass, the battle plan was strictly need-to-know.

Buzz brushed his palms together, dusting off imaginary dirt. "Then when they're forced to retreat, we stroll outside, yank the blanket off, and . . . " He grabbed his own drink and took a victorious sip. "Done deal."

And that was the plan—if you can call it that. Wait it out.

And so we did. Almost entirely in the south wing bar.

* * *

Thankfully, instead of the estimated three sols, the remaining solar power lasted eight sols and eight nights—a miraculous event still commemorated and celebrated once a year by the descendants of Better Martians.

By the ninth night, even essential utilities—water purification, food production, air recycling, WiFi—were on their last legs.

Lit only by the glow of my phone, my father, my mother, and I huddled together on a couch along the wall, watching a Chattr stream for the final pieces of news before our batteries died.

"I'm Isabella Jiménez, and this is *Jiménez Says.*" The news influencer took a deep breath. "Nine sols ago, the Better Mars solar power grid was attacked by the irrational, emotional leadership of Madison Chen and First Mars, and unfortunately, this will be our final night of power and my last broadcast."

She barely blinked as she delivered the news. "Based on reports from the Directorial Estate, because all clones have selfishly abandoned this great state, there is now a surplus of food, purified water, and oxygen—enough to last weeks, even months. So with nothing to worry about, the ministry suggests we use this time as an opportunity to unplug, unwind, and reconnect with family and friends."

A link flashed across her news banner, reading:

BREAKING NEWS: TOP TEN PLACES TO STAY-CATION IN BETTER MARS

"This is Isabella Jiménez saying goodnight, goodbye, and have a good time."

The feed cut.

Everything went dark.

All before we were able to see the best places to stay-cation.

* * *

For a week, all of Better Mars lived by candlelight.

Chattr was inaccessible—scrolling junkies, notification dependents, and validation seekers experienced communal dopamine withdrawal, cut off from their personal IV drip of unlimited screen time. Feeds wouldn't refresh, daily streaks came to an abrupt halt, and pop culture gossip became obsolete overnight. Desperate thumbs mindlessly rubbed blank phones out of sheer muscle memory.

My parents struggled to adjust to living in the shadows—suffering countless stubbed toes and the occasional jump scare of mistaking a shirt on a doorknob for a lurking intruder. But once again, after spending so much time in the Native tunnels, I felt right at home. And I knew I could make a grand escape through the lithium mine—it crossed my mind more than once—but I couldn't abandon my mother again.

I couldn't abandon every Better Martian, trapped in darkness under the black dome. It would take weeks to evacuate everyone through Cheddar's hole—and some probably wouldn't even fit.

Every sol, I tried to convince my father to surrender.

"Don't you want to end everyone's suffering?" I asked him one evening in the south wing bar. At least, I thought it was evening—it was always hard to tell. I sipped on a glass of vodka, skipping the phyco and going straight to the hard stuff.

Across from me, my father drained his glass of red malt and poured himself another.

"I think 'suffering' is a pretty misleading word choice, Flip," he said. "It's a slight inconvenience. One we can all muscle through in order to maintain our way of life. Madison Chen and all those people brainwashed by MBN and the media can't take away our culture."

I took a sip. "I think 'culture' is a pretty misleading word choice for clone servitude."

He refilled my glass of vodka before I had even finished.

"It's part of our traditions and customs," he said.

"It doesn't have to be."

"This family can't be remembered as the people who illegally enslaved thousands."

"There are more important things than legacy."

Buzz swirled his drink, watching the candlelight reflections ripple across the liquor. "Legacy is everything, Flip. And history is written by the winners. We have to win."

"This doesn't feel like winning."

"To negotiate favorable terms, you have to be in a position of power. We just have to wait them out a little longer. A few more sols. Tops."

"If I had a prescription . . ."

We finished our drinks.

After a moment of silence, my father shifted in his chair, still avoiding eye contact. "Listen." He exhaled, drumming his fingers against his glass. "I never thanked you for warning us." He cleared his throat.

"I'm not sure it was much of a warning," I admitted.

He waved it off. "You showed a lot of character. Those years in the tunnels and mines must've served you well."

There it was.

A thank you. From my father.

And a subtle, built-in self-compliment at the end, sure. But still. A genuine thank you. For a brief moment, the longstanding barrier between us cracked. A mix of emotions surged through me, swirling, colliding, impossible to process all at once. The muscles I hadn't realized were tense suddenly released, sending shockwaves of relief crashing through me.

If I hadn't already been sitting, my knees would've buckled.

Then came the warmth—a long-awaited, stirring pride. Then sweeping joy, overwhelming and unbearable. A lump throbbed in my throat. The pit of my stomach twitched—but it wasn't indigestion.

At the peak of my volatile, debilitating, all-the-feels sensation, I could only push out one thing—

"Yeah . . . No problem."

Then we were just two men, sitting at a bar in silence, each trying not to express an amount of emotion that would make the other uncomfortable.

I couldn't repress the profound catharsis any longer. I pushed back from the bar and stood. "Alright, well . . . I guess I'll probably see you tomorrow."

"Probably will," he muttered, turning his head slightly away, tilting it up—making sure his tears stayed in his eyes instead of spilling over.

* * *

I left the estate after bundling up in a few extra layers. With no working climate control, each sol was chillier than the last. The dome was only warmed by the collective body heat of the hundred thousand people under the dome, insulated by the enormous blanket covering the glass.

Going more than a little stir-crazy, I had made a habit of walking the biosphere at least once a sol. Every time, I passed Isabella Jiménez outside the Fourth Hard Rock Café from the Sun, where she had taken her live streaming show from digital to in-person.

At first, only a few people stopped to listen—I assumed most didn't recognize her without a ring light or through a camera lens. But every sol, her audience grew.

That night, after a full week of disconnection from cyberspace, she stood before hundreds.

"Some people are saying that biosphere cooling is a hoax," she declared to the sea of anxious faces. "But the evidence is as clear as sol. You can feel it in the air. This morning, I swear I could see my breath. Candles won't do anymore. We need something with more heat."

Her assistant handed out *Jiménez Says*-branded torches—fifty crimsons a pop.

The next night, the gathering had doubled in size. More terrified citizens packed the square, shoulder to shoulder, hanging on her every word.

"Are we just supposed to blindly believe the ministry when they tell us there's plenty of oxygen, water, and food?" she asked, her voice thick with righteous indignation. "I don't know about you, but I've been feeling a little short of breath as of late. I'm starting to think that we need to take matters into our own hands. We can no longer afford to sit idly by, living on trust and hope. We need to purify our *own* water. We need to farm our *own* food."

Her assistant handed out *Jiménez Says*-branded pitchforks—sixty crimsons a pop.

The sol after that, the crowd was even larger. Angrier. More frightened. And far more willing to make unjustified purchases.

I was starting to worry. Of course, my father dismissed me when I warned him what was happening outside the estate. But I wasn't going to stop monitoring the situation.

The next night, there wasn't any room in the square. Jiménez had to scream just to be heard. "Where is the ministry now?" she barked. "There have been no announcements, no bulletins, no newsletters—nothing!"

In fairness, the ministry wasn't exactly equipped to handle such archaic methods of communication. But technicalities rarely matter to an angry mob.

"They're holed up, safe in their high towers, while the good, hard-working folks of Better Mars are in agony!" Jiménez preached.

In fairness, they weren't exactly high towers either. Most apartment buildings were much taller than the third level of the Directorial Estate. And the people around me didn't seem to be screaming in agony. But again—technicalities, angry mobs.

"We need to make them listen!" she urged. "We need to make them see! We will not be ignored! Together, we will show them!"

A torch flew through the air. It crashed into the side of a nearby building, flames licking up the walls.

And that was all it took.

The frenzied horde surged forward, looting storefronts, shattering windows, vandalizing the streets. From Jiménez's terrified face, it seemed like the riot wasn't part of her regularly scheduled program.

I was out of time. My mother was in danger, and I wouldn't leave her behind. Not again.

I bolted home.

* * *

"Iris!" I shouted, bursting into the mansion. "Iris!"

No response.

I sprinted to her bedroom—empty. She was really only ever in one of two places in the house, so I dashed to the south wing.

There she was, sitting in the dim candlelight with a glass of wine.

"We have to leave," I gasped. "They're coming."

Next to her, my father frowned. "Who's coming?"

"Those people I warned you about," I said, heaving, hands on my knees. "There's more of them now. They're coming here."

"It'll be fine." Buzz took a sip of his drink. "I'll talk to them."

"They aren't exactly in a calm, rational conversation kind of headspace," I snapped. Then I turned to my mother. "Iris, come on. We're leaving."

She looked at my father.

"You don't need to go anywhere," he said evenly. "I'll handle it."

"*You* can stay," I said to him. "Do whatever you like. *We* are leaving."

My mother looked back at me—and finally, she stood. My father scoffed and finished his drink. I grabbed my mother's hand and pulled her out of the south wing.

"Should I pack a bag or . . . ?" she asked as we hustled through the halls.

"No time."

"Where are we going?"

"The lithium mine," I said.

We reached the foyer, and I helped her into a few extra layers before swinging the front door open and—

Isabel Jiménez stood on our porch, smirking. Behind her, thousands of people brandished torches, casting ominous shadows of their pitchforks.

"Oh," she said. "I didn't even have to knock."

CHAPTER THIRTY-FIVE

MUTINY

Standing face to face with an angry mob at our door, my mother and I instinctively stepped backward. Isabel Jiménez matched our pace, creeping inside the house, some of her followers close behind.

"Where is he?" she asked.

"Who?" I feigned ignorance.

She rolled her eyes. "You know who."

My mother leaned in, whispering in my ear. "Run."

We bolted, scrambling through the foyer and into the maze of hallways, hoping to lose them in the winding corridors.

Behind us, I heard Jiménez bark, "Search every room!"

We rounded a corner near bathroom number twelve, and I slammed into a lithium vase. It toppled and shattered into a thousand sparkling fragments, which twinkled like searchlights as the crash echoed like a blaring siren.

We reached the south wing bar, out of breath, and I threw the door shut behind us.

"I knew you'd be back," my father said, completely oblivious.

"Buzz, we need to go. Right now."

"He's serious, Buzz," my mother added, panic snapping her out of her haze of detachment. "They're going to kill us."

That got his attention.

"Okay," he said, setting his glass down. "Let's go."

We rushed toward the back exit, but the second my fingers touched the handle, dozens of crazed faces swarmed the windows along the back wall. One of them grinned—wild-eyed and demented—and tapped on the glass.

We staggered backward.

"We'll find another way," my father said.

We rushed back the way we came in. When my father cracked open the door, flickering torchlight illuminated the hallway, growing brighter. Voices echoed, growing louder.

"Get behind the bar," my father ordered.

For the first time, I heard true fear in his voice. True concern for my well-being—and for my mother's.

But it was too late. The mob was already on us. Two people grabbed me, hauling me backward into the room.

"Tie them up," a voice ordered from the hallway.

A moment later, Isabel Jiménez rounded the corner.

Someone yanked my arms behind my back, zip-tying my wrists together before throwing me on the couch. Another set of hands forced my ankles together, binding them just as tight. My mother landed beside me with a sharp grunt.

"I'll talk to you," my father said steadily, his expression unreadable. "But only you."

Jiménez considered this, never breaking eye contact with Buzz. Then, with an almost lazy flick of her wrist, she lifted the spade in her right hand and waved the mob away. "Leave us."

There was a brief hesitation, but her loyal followers obeyed.

Buzz took a breath, straightening his shoulders. "Care for a drink?" His shaky voice couldn't quite hide his tremors.

"Martini. Vodka. Bone dry with a twist," Jiménez replied smoothly.

As the last of her people exited, the room dimmed, lit only by the torches of the seething mob outside the windows, their reflections dancing in the mirror backsplash of the bar.

The door shut and Jiménez immediately deflated.

"Oh thank god," she whispered as she frantically exhaled. "Oh my god, oh my god." She ran a hand through her hair, then pointed to the windows and asked, "They can see us but not hear us, right?"

"Right," my father confirmed, looking confused as he handed her a martini.

"Oh my god." She gulped the entire thing in one go. "I am so sorry. I am so, so sorry." She held her empty glass and her spade, rolling them both in a circle, begging us to—

"Just keep acting scared, like I'm being super intimidating."

"What's going on?" my father asked, his voice careful.

She exhaled sharply, rubbing her forehead. "Okay, okay—so after the power went out, my show ended." She shoved her empty glass toward my father, silently demanding a refill. "I couldn't stream. I couldn't post. I couldn't even fucking thumbs-up a fan's comment. I was completely cut off from my consistent, unwavering flood of support and adoration. Do you know what that's like?" She gestured toward my father with her spade.

He flinched.

Her eyes darted between me and my mother. "Do you?" She pointed the spade at us.

We recoiled into the couch.

"So I shouted whatever bullshit on the streets like a fucking town crier, looking for any kind of attention. I was really losing it. And everyone else was too—bored, lost, adrift without Chattr, without their connection to people they don't even really know. So they stopped. They listened." She leaned forward, her voice lowering, like she was letting us in on a secret. "Do you know how much more intense an in-person connection is? Not some fleeting username, but a face—real eyes on you, from someone who truly cares." She let out a manic laugh. "I didn't. I had no idea. And then I was hooked. Like . . . junkie-level hooked."

My father handed her another martini. Jiménez took a few deep gulps before continuing. "I needed more. More praise. More devotion. More viewers. So I gave the people what they wanted. And nothing sells like fear! Fear, fear, fear!" She waved her arms around, spilling a little of her martini. She shrunk. "But then I couldn't stop. You can't just keep feeding them the same stuff over and over—law of diminishing returns. They get *used* to it. It stops being scary." After another long sip, she wiped her mouth. "So I had to keep upping it. Raising the stakes. And suddenly—I was leading a fucking mob. Terrorizing the entire dome." She waved her hands, crossing them over each other. "Listen, I never wanted to hurt anyone—I just wanted some attention. Is that so selfish?" We were too afraid to answer. "And now I think they're going to hurt *me* if I don't give them what they want."

She swallowed. "And what they want is to hurt *you*."

"Kill his kid!" a muffled voice shrieked from outside, followed by a maniacal giggle. "You won't!" It was the man with the demented grin, the one who had tapped on the glass.

"See?" Jiménez twirled her spade absentmindedly in her grip. "So where do we go from here?"

"Are you really going to kill us?" Buzz asked, his tone oddly level.

Jiménez paused. "No."

A deep, rhythmic thumping echoed through the room. All four of us flinched, tense. The same crazed, overexcited ruffian outside was pounding on the glass like a drum. Then—one by one—the others joined in.

"I don't want to," Jiménez admitted. "But right now, it's either you or me."

Whomp. Whomp. Whomp. Every pound on the glass made her spin and aim her spade at a different person.

Whomp. Buzz.

Whomp. Iris.

Whomp. Buzz.

Whomp.

Me.

I stopped squirming. Stopped breathing. Stopped blinking. Staring death down the barrel of a spade.

The drubbing on the windows grew louder, hammering the heightening tension.

A cold sweat dripped from her temples. Her finger quivered over the trigger.

"Alright!" Buzz blurted out. He raised his arms. "I'll surrender. Just don't kill Flip."

For my entire life, I never thought my father cared whether I lived or died. And yet, here he was—yielding for me. It's what any father would do. It should've been expected. It should've been obvious. It shouldn't have mattered this much. But it did. And all it took was a tiny murder threat.

"Do it anyway!" the same lunatic howled from outside.

"I'm surrendering!" Buzz bellowed, still with his hands up.

Jiménez let out a long, shaky breath, then dropped her spade.

"However"—*of course my father had conditions*—"I can't be seen as someone who negotiates with terrorists. I'd lose respect."

He lowered his hands and straightened his shirt, walking out from behind the bar. "As far as the people are concerned, this was all my idea—all part of my master plan. I needed everyone to come together, united, to show that we won't back down to the First Martians. And because of this powerful display of fierce loyalty and solidarity, in addition to my unparalleled negotiation skills, Madison Chen surrendered to *me*."

And not a sixtieth-of-a-minute later—there was the old Buzz.

Jiménez wiped a trembling hand down her face. "Fine!" she blubbered. "I don't care. Just make it end." She turned to her followers outside the mansion and held her fist into the air, victorious. The mob erupted, hollering and drumming on the glass harder—forgetting any rhythm.

After Jiménez and Buzz cut our restraints, we all made our way to the front of the house. Buzz stepped onto the porch, arms open wide, beaming at the mob. "My people! Thank you for joining me here tonight and illuminating our beautiful biosphere with the brightness and warmth . . . of your spirit! Our enemies have tried to tear us down. Tormented us for too long. But I will put a stop to it. I, Buzz Buchanan, your fearless First Director of Better Mars, will end this terrible crusade against our people once and for all! I will defeat Madison Chen and her band of fringe extremists. We *will* see the light again!"

His short speech was met by silence, uncertainty and confusion. But then I did something I hadn't done before—I clapped. I had never taken the first-clapper initiative—too afraid the second clapper would never come.

And my fear—much like what Jiménez was selling—was realized. No one joined in.

I stopped clapping.

But at least we weren't killed.

The mob herded us to the edge of the dome where Madison had cut a flap in the black fabric.

Buzz knocked.

CHAPTER THIRTY-SIX

NEGOTIATIONS

To avoid an intense, extensive discussion through hastily scribbled messages on a tablet and condensation-fogged glass, Buzz and Madison agreed to meet in neutral territory—the airlock chamber attached to the exploration bay.

The mob escorted us to the hangar, pressing close, ensuring Buzz followed through on his promise. My mother and I stood outside the airlock, surrounded by restless, torch-wielding pyromaniacs and pitchfork enthusiasts, watching Buzz through a thin horizontal slit in the door.

Buzz secured his helmet onto his suit and readied himself. Through the skinny window, I saw the outer door open, revealing nothing but the black curtain draped over the dome. Then the sheet was lifted in the center and a sudden, searing brightness stabbed my eyes. A sharp pain shot through my skull—my vision overwhelmed by the light of sol, having not seen it in weeks—and I jerked backward.

Once my vision adjusted, I saw Buzz kneel down, placing his hands behind his head. A squad of shadowy figures charged in, forming two lines on either side of the chamber. They stood at rigid attention, flanking the space like an honor guard.

Then, from the opening, a single silhouette emerged.

The black curtain dropped, plunging the space back into darkness. Once again, my vision had to adjust. A dull headache grew. Finally, I saw Madison Chen, standing tall before a groveling Buzz.

The outer door closed. The airlock sealed.

We couldn't hear anything through the thick chamber walls, but we could see them. Buzz slowly rose from his knees. They removed their helmets. A conversation began, silent to us, but full of movement. Madison's posture was firm, unwavering. Buzz, on the other hand, was full of theatrical hand gestures—shrugging, throwing his hands up, pointing back toward everyone watching behind the door.

The ten-minute conversation felt like an agonizing hour. When they finished, Buzz gave us a thumbs up, and the inner wall of the airlock rose. He strolled out, head held high, beaming like a conquering hero. The mob of Better Martians watched him expectantly.

He put his hands on his hips and puffed out his chest. "Talks with First Mars couldn't be going any better. You asked, and I delivered! The bedspread of damnation is no more. The lights will be back on momentarily. This nightmare is over!"

A roar of cheers echoed through the hangar.

Buzz threw his arm around my shoulder. Then, glancing at my mother, he said, "Iris, we'll be back in no time."

"Wait—what?" Before I realized what was happening, he brought me into the airlock as the inner wall descended. "Where are we going?"

"Just taking a little trip to First Mars to iron out all the details," he said breezily.

I narrowed my eyes. "But why am I going with you?"

"Well," Buzz exhaled, adjusting his spacesuit, "we had to make some initial concessions—a symbolic gesture of goodwill. But don't worry, I'll handle it. We'll figure it out when we get there."

I stopped in my tracks. "Handle what?"

As Buzz secured his helmet over his head, he said, "You're being extradited for some light treason."

A beat. "What?"

He pointed to his ears in his helmet and shrugged, acting like he couldn't hear me anymore. The soldiers in the chamber forced me into a spacesuit. I didn't have a choice.

When we stepped out onto the Martian surface, only one rover was waiting for us. Just one rover. No fleet. No army. The entire First Martian Battalion was gone. They had only been there for the opening act, a show of strength to prove they were a legitimate threat. But once the blanket had been thrown over the dome, there was no point in keeping an army stationed outside. It would only drain resources. And everyone in Better Mars would be none the wiser.

That was how they outlasted us. They had all the provisions of a full army, but only a handful of people to sustain.

Buzz and I were shoved into the back of the rover, and then came the longest, most uncomfortable, dead-silent road trip of my life. I had all the time in the world to spiral about what might happen to me. Best-case scenario: My father would somehow get me exonerated. Not-as-good scenario: I'd be thrown in prison for the rest of my life. Worst-case scenario: Exile—forced to wander the barren landscape of Mars in a spacesuit until my oxygen ran out.

A shiver ran through me. I knew people would disapprove of alerting my parents to impending doom, but I never thought it'd be considered full-blown treason. Had I known, maybe I wouldn't have snuck off to warn them.

I'd never gotten the sense that Madison Chen liked me all that much. Not that she hated me—she was just kind of indifferent. And she definitely knew about my mother's relationship with her husband. She certainly wasn't a fan of my father.

I worried I was about to become collateral damage.

Then again, she also knew I was her daughter's best friend. Maybe she'd be lenient.

* * *

The moment Madison and her soldiers stepped inside First Mars, they were met with a hero's welcome—hurrahs, hoorays, yahoos, yippees, yeehaws, and yays. Loved ones ran into each other's arms, dipping one another for dramatic kisses. "March of the Sowers" rang out in the streets, playing on repeat, the familiar anthem swelling around us.

My father and I, on the other hand, were paraded through the dome to a very different kind of reception. Booed, jeered, spat on—though, I wasn't sure if it was because of my treason, or hatred by association. Guilt by genetics. Born to the wrong man and punished for it.

As we passed through the biosphere, I noticed nearly all of the destruction from the attack had already been cleaned up, with only a few noticeable dings that still needed to be buffed out.

Outside the boardroom, I watched as Madison typed in the door code. It was still the same—Pepper's birthsol. My birthsol. The door unlocked, and Buzz and I were pushed inside. We were forced into two seats at the far end of the long conference table. Every member of the ministry was present, their expressions unreadable.

I met Rizz's eyes, then looked at Pepper. She furrowed her brow, shaking her head slightly as she twisted her palms up, silently demanding an explanation. All I could do was purse my lips and shrug.

Madison's voice cut through the silence. "Give us a minute."

With some hesitation and quiet objection, the entire room gathered their things and filed out.

Then it was just the three of us. Madison sat at the head of the table, on the complete opposite side—so far away, we'd have to project.

Logistically, it made no sense. Strategically, it must have been an intimidation tactic. Realistically, I was less intimidated by her, and more by the logistics.

Madison leaned back in her chair, squinting at me. "Why is it always you, Flip? Why are you always . . . around?"

"I don't know," I answered. Because I didn't.

She tapped her fingers against the tabletop. "So here's the deal: Buzz, you have caused a great deal of pain—you have blood on your hands. You're also responsible for the oppression of thousands of clones. You tried to fight, and you lost."

He took a breath to speak, but Madison cut him off. "But you've already surrendered. And I'm more interested in moving forward as a united Mars—quickly and efficiently—rather than focusing on retribution." Buzz sat stiffly, uncharacteristically listening to everything before opening his mouth again. "It's the same thinking that stopped me from disputing your insurrection during the battle with the Paul Kingsleys," Madison revealed. "We didn't need infighting. We wouldn't have survived. We needed unity. So I stepped aside. *I* swallowed my pride to better serve history. And now, I'm hoping you can do the same."

Buzz gulped, then gave a slow, reluctant nod.

"Better Mars is no more," Madison declared. "Both entities are now part of one Mars. The original biosphere will be called Spirit, and the biosphere formerly known as Better Mars will be called Opportunity—named in honor of the twin rovers that landed here together at the start of the twenty-first century."

Instinctively, Buzz stirred, wanting to argue—but Madison's piercing glare silenced him.

"You will no longer hold the title of director, and the Ministry of Better Mars is hereby dissolved," she continued. "I will serve as the Director of Mars for both domes, and my current ministry will retain their positions. All Better Mars trade agreements with Earth will be absorbed, along with its treasury."

Buzz nodded, offering no resistance.

Not that I wasn't interested in the details of Better Mars' demise, but I was a little eager to move on to my impending treason charge.

"Finally," Madison went on, "all clones and all children of clones in Spirit and Opportunity, and any future Martian territories, are hereby free and granted full Martian citizenship under the law." She held her finger up, signaling one last point. "Oh, and one more thing. I've been asked that Pluto the donkey receive retroactive compensation for the use of her likeness on the Better Mars flag. How does all that sound?"

Buzz exhaled, shaking his head. "That's a lot to take in."

"You aren't in a great position to negotiate," Madison added. "But I want to wrap this up ASAP, so in exchange for your timely cooperation, I am open to accepting a few of your terms."

After taking a deep breath, Buzz glanced at me. My pulse quickened. This was it—he was going to have my treason acquitted.

"I want a seat in the ministry," he said instead. "And I want my involvement in manufacturing and owning clones to be stricken from any and all historical records, publications, and media."

Prick.

Madison folded her hands, tilting her head. "Is that everything?"

"No." He paused. "I want Flip's treason to be pardoned." I must not have been breathing, because I gasped. Relief flooded my chest.

Madison considered it. "You can have two of the three."

My chest tensed right back up.

For a painfully long moment, Buzz deliberated. "The seat in the ministry . . ." he said slowly. "I can lose that one."

"Deal," Madison agreed.

I was absolved. No prison. No exile. No public execution.

"Now, one last thing." She leaned forward over the table, her voice lowering just slightly. "There is a full ministry outside that would love nothing more than to rip you a new one. The terms of surrender will remain what we have agreed upon, but I think it would help everyone move on if they feel like they really gave it to you." Buzz raised an eyebrow, intrigued. "I'd like to invite them back in under the guise that we haven't landed on anything. Come out swinging. Make outrageous demands. Let them feel like they're bending you over a barrel."

Buzz Buchanan, ever the thespian, wasn't about to refuse a role of a lifetime. Without hesitation, he nodded. "I can do that."

It was a negotiation, not a trial, but what followed was like a live courtroom drama—seven grueling hours of objections, sidebars, hearsay, witness tampering, cross-examinations, and an egregious amount of perjury.

When all was said and done, we stood to exit.

Madison caught my arm. "Flip, hold on a second."

I stopped, watching everyone else leave the room.

"Just between you and me, I was never going to try you for treason," she confessed. I blinked. "I know you were only trying to protect your parents. And you've done a lot for the cause—sneaking the clones out through the mine. I just wanted some extra leverage."

I let that settle for a second, then shook my head. "I wouldn't think I'd be much leverage in my father's eyes."

A small, knowing smile crossed her face. "More than you know," she said.

And with that, she turned and walked out the door, leaving me alone in the empty boardroom with nothing but my thoughts, low blood sugar, and a painfully full bladder after a seven-hour meeting.

CHAPTER THIRTY-SEVEN

DRUNK YOUNG ADULTS

The real unification celebration didn't happen for another two months, postponed to coincide with the grand opening of the new rail stations. While Spirit already had an elevator to the underground Native Martian train platform, additional elevators and escalators were installed in a new surface-level transportation center attached to the exploration bay. A matching station was built in Opportunity, and with the launch of the high-speed rail, the two domes were permanently connected.

Pepper, Rizz, Cliff, and I watched the event on MBN from our apartment. By then, we had cleaned up the broken glass and replaced the kitchen appliances that had flown the coop through the living room windows.

On the broadcast, Newt Newman reported live from outside the Spirit transportation center. Behind him, Madison Chen stood beside a man completely wrapped in layers of protective clothing, only recognizable by the nametag on his chest. He was one of the Native Martian leaders—Freckle's father. To Madison's other side stood Pluto the donkey.

A thick red ribbon with a massive bow hung stretched across the entrance, and Madison held an equally giant pair of scissors, ready to cut it.

"And I'm told the feed from the Opportunity station is now live," Newt said. "Let's listen in."

The feed split in two. On one side, Madison stood poised in Spirit. On the other, Buzz stood in front of another red ribbon hung at the Opportunity transportation center entrance, holding his own oversized scissors.

We stopped chit-chatting, and I turned up the volume.

Madison spoke first. "It is my great pleasure to signify the unification of Mars with the official opening of these two train stations. In partnership with the Native Martian peoples, we have forever established a connection between Spirit and Opportunity." She paused for a brief applause. "So, on the count of three, Buzz Buchanan and I will cut these ribbons together—"

"Oh, what was that, Madison?" Buzz interrupted, cocking his head. "I think there's a bit of a delay."

Madison blinked, confused. "It seems fine on our end."

Buzz made a show of pausing, acting as if he were waiting for her to say something, then nodded. "Yeah, there's definitely a delay. Just go ahead with the countdown, and I'll try to time it right."

"Okay." Madison readied her scissors. "One, two—"

Snip.

Buzz cut his ribbon before she finished counting. "Oh, shoot! I may have jumped the gun a bit. Looks like I cut my ribbon first." He chuckled as if it were an honest mistake. "Hey, we'll get it next time!" Madison stared at the camera, dead-eyed, before begrudgingly snipping her own ribbon.

Confetti and balloons rained down around her, fanfare

blaring—none of which matched the scowl on her face. The MBN news banner read:

BREAKING NEWS: OPEN WIDE, HERE COMES THE CHOO CHOO

Of course, the prior two months hadn't been all rainbows and butterflies—not that I would know much about either, having never seen them in person.

While I had stayed in Spirit, Buzz had returned to Opportunity and promptly commissioned sculptors to erect statues of himself—as if he were some great war hero. After substantial backlash, some of the statues were removed. But many remained standing, following backlash against the backlash—claims of historical significance. That, of course, sparked backlash against the backlash against the backlash, insisting the statues commemorated a history unworthy of celebration. And so the cycle continued.

Society remained divided. Clones were freed, granted full citizenship under the law—but that didn't mean they were treated as equals. And the intolerance wasn't just contained to Opportunity. Spirit wasn't exactly a beacon of progress either.

In many public places, signs labeled spaces for "ORIGINALS" and "CLONES," pushing the divide further. Though Mars had never had public water fountains before, they were constructed for the singular purpose of hosting the labels—despite the fact that no one ever used the bacteria-infested spouts.

I never understood it. A hundred generations from now, everyone will be mixed, and no one will be able to tell the difference. No one ever could. But people are still judged for how they're born—like they had some say in it. Still, freeing the clones and uniting Mars was progress. And progress was worth celebrating.

We turned off the news, cracked open a few six packs of phycos, and got to work doing exactly that.

Living with Rizz and Pepper got easier over time. Like

everything else in my life, I accepted that I would always be second in Pepper's heart. And that was okay—Rizz was the kind of guy who would've reached for Pepper's hand before she blew away. A hero. She deserved that. And I wasn't that. At least, not for her. At least, not then.

We sat around and had a drink together before there was a knock at the door.

"It's open!" Rizz yelled.

Pockets and Cheddar strolled in, arms raised triumphantly, holding up more phyco. Behind them, lingering in the doorway, was Freckle.

Like a spring-loaded idiot, I shot up from the couch as soon as I saw her.

"Freckle?"

"I hope you don't mind," Pockets said, twisting the cap off a Seedy Weedy. "The three of us have been working together a lot—freeing the clones, building relations between humans and Native Martians. Freckle's kind of my boss now, so I invited her."

Obviously, I didn't mind. It was also great to see Pockets above ground again. Ever since he started working with Cheddar and Freckle, his walls had slowly begun to crumble. He wasn't a recluse anymore. He wasn't hiding.

"I'll let you kids have fun," Cliff said, sliding into his Crocs.

"You can stay," Pepper offered.

"Nah. With the opening, your mom has a few other obligations to attend tosol. And what is she without her arm candy?" Cliff waved goodbye and shut the door.

But I barely noticed him leave. My focus was entirely on Freckle.

"I'm glad you came," I said.

"Sounded like a good time," she replied, nonchalantly.

"Can I get you anything?"

"I'll take a Chlor if you have any."

I headed into the kitchen, grabbed two Chlors from the fridge, and cracked them open before handing one to her.

I clinked my bottle against hers, took a sip, and blurted, "So is your partner coming too, or . . . ?"

"Nope."

"Cool, cool, cool," I said, very coolly.

Freckle generously offered me an escape from my uncomfortable line of questioning. "I heard you've had an eventful few months."

I let out a laugh. "Nah, not really. Almost died only once or twice. Narrowly escaped treason charges. The usual routine."

"Seems to be," she said, smiling.

"Do you guys want to play Pluto?" Pockets asked. "The drinking game, not the donkey."

"Is this the one where you play pong and build a stack of cups into a rocket ship?" Pepper asked.

"That's the one!" Pockets started setting it up on the table. "Once the rocketship is built, you play flip cup to get to the next planet. You start at Mercury, so nine flip cups later, when you make it to Pluto, you have to finish a phyco that's been icing over in the freezer the whole time."

"Simple enough." Rizz said, hopping off the couch. "I'm in for a drinking game."

"The Martian ministry at its finest," Cheddar quipped.

We all froze. Every Catfish Troll stared at Cheddar.

"What? Was that too far?" she asked.

"No," Pockets said. "It was funny. Really funny." Then he added, "Oh, did we tell you they're making a movie about Cheddar? The clone who escaped and rescued thousands. It's already got awards buzz."

"It's kind of embarrassing," Cheddar admitted.

"Don't be," I said. "It's an important part of history and everyone should know about it." I secretly wondered if my character was cut from the story.

We played a game of Pluto. And got properly wasted.

Pepper and Rizz retired to drunken snuggling on the couch, but Pockets wanted to play another drinking game. That left Freckle and me squaring off against Pockets and Cheddar in a game of pong, each team at opposite ends of the table.

Our vision and reflexes weren't what they used to be—earlier that evening—so the game dragged on. Lots of rim shots, bounce-offs, and air balls.

But that meant spending extra time beside Freckle.

"I'm glad we're hanging out again," I told her.

"Me too," she said, catching a ball as it bounced off the table.

"I mean, it's not the kind of hanging out we used to do, but it's still fun."

She took her shot—missed. "Far fewer balls going into holes with the way we're playing."

I smiled. My shot hit a rim and bounced away.

"Are you okay?" she asked. "You've had a lot going on."

I took a beat, wanting to be honest. "I'm doing better," I admitted. "It feels like I have more of a handle on things? I don't know. Growing up, I thought I already had it all figured out—everything was black and white. As I've gotten older, I've realized I never did, and probably still don't."

I fumbled an incoming pong ball and didn't even aim before tossing my next shot. "Have you ever thought about how life speeds up as you get older?"

She furrowed her brow. "How do you mean?"

"Like a year to a five-year-old is a fifth of their life, but a year to someone who's fifty is a fiftieth of their life. There's a huge difference between a ten-year-old and a fifteen-year old, but barely any between fifty and fifty-five." Freckle took her next shot and sank it. I kept yammering on. "Like, I'm twenty-five, and I know way more than a toddler, but I'm starting to realize that I don't think someone my parents' age knows that much more than me. They've only lived one twenty-sixth, plus one-twenty-seventh, plus one-twenty-eighth—and so on for however many years difference—they've only lived *that* much more life than me." I leaned forward, arms crossed on the edge of the table. "If I don't know what I'm doing, I'm not sure someone older than me knows that much better. So that means *nobody* knows what they're doing, and we're all just floating around on a giant space rock, hurtling through a vacuum of nothingness, all trying to figure it out . . ."

I blinked. "Am I still talking? What was the question?"

Freckle giggled—those squeaks I missed so much. "I forgot I even asked one."

Pockets sank one of our cups, and Freckle grabbed the drink and swallowed it all in one go. I watched her esophagus push the liquid down to her stomach. "But I get it," she said, wiping her mouth. "Older people, the people in charge, the people you thought had infinitely more wisdom than you—they might not."

"Exactly. It's scary . . . but also kind of comforting?"

For once in my life, I actually made a pong shot. "So are you still dating someone, or did you just not want to invite them?"

Freckle hesitated. "We broke it off a few months ago."

"Oh, I'm sorry."

"It's okay . . . It never felt right."

Freckle hit another cup.

"Hey, there we go!" I clapped my hands. "Balls back!"

"Finally. Things are looking up," she teased, nudging me lightly with her elbow.

Pockets and Cheddar groaned, rolling their eyes, but surrendered the pong balls.

Then—a sharp rap at the door. We weren't expecting anyone else.

Then another, louder, more impatient.

Pockets turned down the music. Pepper squeezed out from underneath a drunk and dozing Rizz, stumbling toward the door. When she opened it, her body tensed. "Dad?"

Cliff stood in the doorway, disheveled—eyes puffy, red-rimmed, his face pale. His hair was an absolute mess.

For a moment, he just stood there, staring at his daughter.

Then his voice cracked.

"It's your mother," he said. "She's been shot."

PART III

CHAPTER THIRTY-EIGHT

BAD ACTORS

In 2114+, while attending a celebratory event commemorating Martian unification, Madison Chen was assassinated. The murderer was none other than Special Agent O'Shea.

Once the nation united, the IBS television station looked to grow its viewership in Spirit, no longer catering exclusively to one dome. IBS pivoted its programming to appeal to a broader audience. As a result, *Gourmet O'Shea*, *Sweat Equity*, and *Love Under the Dome* were all cancelled. Special Agent O'Shea suddenly found himself out of work.

And there's nothing more dangerous than a method actor without a part to play.

With too much free time and an apparent deep dive into every conspiracy theory on Chattr, the actor radicalized himself, outlining increasingly anti-clone rhetoric in his manifesto. He claimed they didn't deserve the same rights as originals and that eliminating the "evil tyrant" Madison Chen would reignite the Better Mars cause and restore original supremacy.

So, he legally acquired a spade, and illegally fired it at Madison

Chen. Before he could take a second shot, Special Agent O'Shea was gunned down by *actual* special agents. The man who had solved so many homicides on *NCIS: Mars* had no trouble solving his own—all the while bleeding out on the ground in front of hundreds of credible, cooperative witnesses.

For the following three sols, I didn't see Pepper or Rizz—they stayed with Cliff. The next time I saw them was at Director Madison Chen's state funeral.

People from both Spirit and Opportunity gathered on the lawn outside Town Hall—clones and originals alike. Even respected members of the Native Martian administration attended, with Freckle among them. Seating had been arranged for ten thousand, but hundreds of thousands more filled the standing room, dressed in formal attire—mostly in black and gray.

As my family made our way to our seats in the second row, I spotted Pepper and Cliff in the first, seated directly in front of us. When they noticed us, they stood. Pepper and I embraced, holding on for a long time. I wanted to say something—anything—to comfort her, but I didn't know what she wanted to hear. So I just held her in silence.

My mother hugged Cliff—for too long, judging by my father's expression. He stood beside them, shifting stiffly, awkwardly offering his hand for a shake to hurry the hug along. When it went ignored, he pulled the hand back, then hesitated and tried again. After they finally separated, Cliff shook Buzz's hand, and we all took our seats.

Cheddar sat beside me. A moment later, Rizz and the other ministry members solemnly walked down the aisle, carrying Madison's casket. They set it on a raised platform at the front of the stage before unfurling a Martian flag and draping it carefully over the casket. Then they took their reserved seats in the front row.

As Rizz sat next to Pepper, he reached to put a comforting hand on her leg. But she jerked her leg away.

On stage, Pastor Van Buren stood at the podium, his expression somber. Beside the casket, Pockets and three other trumpet players stepped forward, raising their instruments. Together, they played a brass instrumental rendition of the EDM Martian national anthem—slow, melancholic, and reverent. Their performance was surprisingly moving.

I hadn't been close with Madison personally, but she had always struck me as a wise, reasonable, and compassionate leader—especially in contrast to my father. I knew Pepper had a complicated relationship with her mother. She had always craved more of her mother's time, more of her attention—something beyond her strict-but-fair parenting. I couldn't imagine what Pepper was going through. I hoped I would never have to experience it myself.

It seemed like Pockets had been practicing his trumpet quite a bit—perhaps making use of the incredible acoustics in the Native tunnel system. The band, too, had made significant improvements since Ms. Anderson's high school music class, sans Ms. Anderson.

As the final notes faded, Pockets lowered his trumpet and quietly took his seat beside Cheddar.

The pastor cleared his throat. "The Aresian scripture states, 'It is never with malicious delight, but always with great benevolent sorrow that I welcome another soul to the underworld.' Hades 6:14. I knew Madison Chen well, having worked closely with her for the past six years. She had a fierce heart—one the Aresian church holds in high regard—yet a calm mind, ever vigilant and prepared while remaining prudent and compassionate . . ."

I stopped listening. All I wanted to do was comfort Pepper, but sitting in the seat behind her, the only thing I could do was place a hand on her shoulder. Maybe two hands—one on each?

No, that would feel weird.

My better judgement won out, knowing that would only be incredibly awkward for her, for me, and for everyone who saw it. Especially if she shook me off the way she did Rizz.

Instead, I did nothing.

"Of course, no one knew her quite as well as her daughter, who has prepared a few words for us tosol," Pastor Van Buren concluded, nodding toward Pepper.

Cliff and Rizz whispered what I assumed were words of encouragement, but she responded with nothing but determined silence. Without further hesitation, she stood and made her way onto the stage.

The pastor stepped aside as Pepper replaced him at the podium, stoic.

"I loved my mother," she began. "She could be controlling and stubborn—we had our fair share of arguments, loud ones. But I loved her. She wasn't always there—sacrificing more than a few family dinners for the good of the Martian people. But I loved her. I didn't always like her. But I loved her."

I didn't know how she was holding it together, standing before a hundred thousand people, speaking about something so deeply personal. And she did it with such eloquence, such elegance. Behind that podium, Pepper was a spitting image of her mother.

"She will be remembered for her contributions to Martian independence, for her leadership on the battlefield, and for brokering the unification of our great nation," she continued. "But she will also be remembered as a mother, as a wife, and as a woman I will look up to for the rest of my life."

Half the audience must have been swallowing a lump in their throat—including me—but Pepper remained unflappable, her voice steady, her eyes dry.

"My mother gave Mars a beacon of hope. And despite her passing, that beacon will not be extinguished. That light remains. In every reflection off Lake Ares. In every refraction through the dome glass. In every burn of thrusters descending home." She paused—just for a moment. The tears were about to come.

But they didn't. "Thank you, Madam Director. Thank you, Madison Chen. Thank you, Mom."

Her words hung in the air, heavy.

Then all at once, we rose to our feet, a standing ovation swelling through the crowd.

Pepper stepped away from the podium and walked down the steps—but she didn't come back to her seat. I poked my head above the crowd, but I still couldn't see where she went.

The ministry members returned to the stage, lifting Madison's casket once more.

"Ready . . ."

On the lawn to the right of the stage, five former First Martian Battalion soldiers stood in formation, aligning themselves precisely.

"Aim . . ."

Instead of raising their spades, they lowered them, pointing toward the ground to avoid firing at the glass dome overhead.

"Fire!"

Five bursts rang out in unison. The sequence repeated three more times—four volleys total: one for each planet before Mars, and a final one for Mars itself—as the casket was carried past us and down the aisle. Above us, twenty drones streaked across the sky, releasing thick plumes of black and red smoke, the colors of our flag.

After the ceremony, we filed out. Soft, mournful murmurs drifted through the crowd, spreading across the biosphere. By the time I got back to the apartment, Rizz was already there, still dressed in his suit, slumped on the couch.

"Where's Pepper?" I asked.

"In our room," he said, rubbing his face. "She won't come out."

"Give her time."

Pepper didn't leave her room for two weeks.

CHAPTER THIRTY-NINE

TWO GIRLS, A GUY, AND A HARD PLACE

"Have you seen her cry?" I asked Rizz one morning as we sat in the apartment's eating nook.

"Not once," he answered. "Have you?"

"No. Is that weird?"

"I don't know." Rizz shrugged, his usual confident charm drained. "I guess everyone grieves in their own way?"

"It doesn't feel like she's grieving."

Before Rizz could respond, we heard the bedroom door click open. Both of us tensed, caught off guard, scrambling for a new conversation subject—

"Yeah, totally," I said, responding to nothing. "That was crazy when that . . . Did you see that thing where . . . ?" I laughed uncomfortably. "Oh, hey, Pepper."

Pepper shuffled into the kitchen in sweats, her usually perfect hair a tangled mess, her typically glowing skin dull and pale. She didn't look at us as she poured herself a bowl of cereal.

"No, *please*," she said dryly. "Keep talking about me behind my back. I didn't mean to interrupt."

"Can I make you some coffee?" Rizz asked quickly. "Tea?"

"No," she said, clipped.

"I can make you some eggs? Toast? Something more substantial?"

"No."

"What about some orange juice or something?"

"Marco! I'm fine! Just stop!"

The room went still. I rarely heard Pepper use Rizz's real name. Without another word, she grabbed her bowl and disappeared back into her bedroom, throwing the door shut behind her.

I exhaled, breaking the silence. "Well, it *was* rude of her to interrupt."

Rizz gave a weak smile but didn't laugh. "I don't know what to do, Flip. Everything I try is wrong."

"I wish I knew." I leaned forward, elbows on my thighs. "It was hard on all of us when we lost Cheese, but I've never lost a parent. And it's not like I have the best relationship with either of them anyway."

Rizz slid further in his seat. He was the kind of person who never had to struggle to have a handle on anything, floating through life with ease. But for the first time, he was at a loss. And I was at a loss of what to say.

The silence lingered. I had to go to work, and I desperately wanted to escape the uncomfortable stillness. But walking out on him during an emotional moment would be uncomfortable too. Maybe more so.

I stayed, hoping I'd picked the lesser of the two discomforts.

* * *

For another two weeks, Rizz and I tiptoed around the apartment, careful not to set Pepper off. I escaped whenever I could, heading down to the Native tunnels to hang out with Pockets, Cheddar, and Freckle—then, eventually, just Freckle.

Nothing romantic happened between us, but I could feel her walls beginning to crumble. Not that I was necessarily trying to get back together with her, but I wasn't *not* trying to either. I wasn't sure. It didn't seem like she was sure either. It was just nice to spend time with each other again.

Meanwhile, after Madison's death, an emergency directorial election was scheduled, giving candidates a month to campaign. Unfortunately, my father was one of them. And one month wasn't enough time for anyone else to build as strong a following—he still had ardent supporters in Opportunity—but I held onto hope that someone would catch up to him in the polls.

Instead of another Election Results Reveal Party—since the optics would have been insensitive at best, given that the last one ended in a massacre—the results were announced live on MBN.

That night, Freckle and I had a date to watch the coverage together. Not wanting to seem overeager and arrive at her place at exactly the agreed-upon time, I stalled in the apartment, sipping a phyco on the couch, half-listening to MBN in the background.

"It's decision sol on Mars," Newt Newman reported from behind his anchor desk. "Earlier tosol, Martians hit the digital voting booths to cast their ballot for the new Director of Mars. The votes were tallied instantly, but the official announcement won't be released for another hour, as scheduled. Until then, we can only postulate based on prior polling and our past election.

"So let's pivot to our projection pal Paige, presenting polling percentages from our particular populace to paint a political panorama of our planet. Paige, please propose your precise prognosis of the people's preferred party."

The feed cut to Paige, standing in front of a digital map of our nation—which, essentially, was just two circles side by side.

"Thank you, Newt," she said, stiffly. "As you can see here, with votes for Buzz Buchanan in orange and votes for the incumbent political party in green, you can see just how close this race is by this shade of yellowish brown."

She tapped on the digital projection, zooming into the left circle, which was divided into four equal quadrants. "If we take a closer look, this quadrant is a darker brown, meaning strong support for Buzz Buchanan, but other quadrants are more of an olive color. So it's looking like a dead heat, Newt."

The feed cut back to Newt. "We still have almost an hour before the results are announced, Paige, so no need to be brief. Spare no detail."

When the feed returned to Paige, she looked terrified, visibly gulping as she realized she had to stretch to fill more time.

"Of course . . ." She tapped on one of the four sections in the circle, zooming in even further. "When we split up each quadrant into quadrants—"

Slam.

The bedroom door down the hall sounded like it had flown off its hinges.

"Stop fucking saying you're sorry!" Pepper screamed, stomping into the living room.

Rizz hustled after her, his face flushed. "I'm sorry!"

"What did I just say?" she snapped, stomping into the kitchen. "Do you know how many times people have said that to me? What is everyone so fucking sorry for? Did they kill my mom? No. If I hear enough sorries, is my mother going to be resurrected and rise from the dead? No. She's fucking not."

Hearing cabinets being yanked open and thrown shut, I was reluctant to turn around. I was afraid to make eye contact with the raging monster inhabiting Pepper's body.

"I don't know what else to say!" Rizz said, desperate. He stopped at the kitchen threshold like it was a force field, keeping his distance for safety purposes.

"Anything but that!"

"Okay! I'll stop saying it. What else can I do to help you feel better?"

Pepper froze mid-motion. "You're not fucking hearing me, Marco." She turned, venom in her voice. "I don't *want* to feel better.

My mom *died.* I *shouldn't* feel better."

Rizz took a breath. "Your mom wouldn't want you to be sad the rest of your life."

Her entire body went rigid. "Don't you *dare* fucking tell me what my mom would or wouldn't want."

"You're right. I'm sorry."

"Fucking *oh my god*, Marco!"

"That was an accident! Let me—let me make you some tea. Or ice cream. Or—"

"Just stop." She threw up her hands. "Can you do that? Stop. Stop looking at me with pity. Stop waiting on me every minute of every sol. And stop being so nice when I'm being an *absolute fucking bitch* to you!"

Rizz stood stiff in the eating nook, his face a mess of helplessness. "Pepper, I love you. All I want to do is help. All I want to do is be here for you."

Pepper stepped right up to his face. "Maybe the best way to help is to *not fucking be here*. Maybe *I* don't love *you.*" Her voice wavered for a second. "Just give me some space. Just leave me the fuck alone."

Rizz went still. His throat bobbed.

"You don't mean that." He turned, went to the front door, and slipped on his Crocs. "You can call me when you realize that."

"Don't wait by the phone," Pepper said.

And then, Rizz left.

Halfway through storming back to her bedroom, Pepper pivoted on her heel and pointed at me. "Don't say one fucking word."

Then—*slam.*

I messaged Freckle that I wasn't going to make it to her place that night—I couldn't leave Pepper alone in the state she was in. I stood outside Pepper's door, hesitant, and opened my mouth to ask if she was alright but stopped myself. Not one fucking word, as requested. Instead, I leaned my back against the wall and slid down to sit on the floor, thinking.

I still wanted her to know she wasn't alone, but I had to do it without speaking a word. With my elbow, I rapped against the wall. *Thud thud thud.*

Me: You okay?

For a while, there was nothing. Which was fine. I didn't need a response—I just needed her to know I was there.

Much like Rizz, Pepper made everything look easy. She was born a celebrity. She was our high school valedictorian. Her mother ran Mars. Both her parents adored her. But only then did I realize: just because someone's never struggled doesn't mean they never will. On some level, I already knew that—we all do—but sometimes, we have to be reminded. We have to see it.

Thud thud.

Pepper: No.

My phone buzzed.

Freckle: No worries. What came up?

I answered Pepper first.

Me: It's okay to not be okay.

Then I answered Freckle. I didn't want to lie to her, so I told her the truth.

Me: I'm still home. Pepper is having a rough night.

Freckle: Oh okay. I totally understand. You need to be there for your friend.

Me: I promise I'll make it up to you. This was just the worst I've seen her.

Freckle: No worries. What happened?

Me: She lost it on Rizz. He left. She's holed up in her bedroom. I'm just sitting outside her wall.
I think they might've broken up?

Freckle: Oh so that's why.
Me: No it's not like that.

More thuds behind me.

Pepper: I want to be alone.
But I don't want to be alone.
Me: I'll be right here.

A pause. Then—

Pepper: Thanks.

More messages from Freckle.

Freckle: I get that her mom died and you're just trying to be a good friend, but this feels like more than that. It's starting to feel like I'll always be the second most important woman in your life.
That's not going to work for me.
You of all people should understand.

I clenched my jaw.

Me: You're not!
This isn't that.
It's a bad night for her and I'm only sitting by myself in the hallway.
Freckle: It's not just this one time. You know that.
Me: I want to be with you.
Freckle: Then why aren't you with me?

More thuds.

Pepper: You've always been there for me.

More texts.

Freckle: You know how I feel about you, Flip.
And I think you feel the same way about me.

Thuds.

Pepper: There's no one else in the worlds like you.

Text.

Freckle: Tell me I'm wrong.

Me: I love you to the two moons and back.

For a sixtieth-of-a-minute, my thumbs hovered over my keyboard. A chill flowed through my veins—I wasn't sure if I had texted Freckle or used Flipper Code.

I glanced at my messages. Freckle's challenge sat there, unanswered.

My thumbs couldn't move. My lungs couldn't breathe.

Then Pepper's door creaked open. She stepped out, wordless, and slid down the wall beside me, resting her head on my shoulder. "I love you too," she whispered.

There was no way I could text Freckle back, not with Pepper crying on my arm.

More notifications buzzed—I ignored them. Freckle would understand once I explained. I knew she would. She had to.

We sat in silence on the floor of the hallway for a long time.

In the background, MBN crackled from the living room, but I heard Newt Newman's voice crystal clear. "The people of Mars have spoken. Buzz Buchanan has won the election. He is, once again, the Director of Mars."

CHAPTER FORTY

HEE-HAW

Freckle did *not* understand once I explained.

After I told her everything that happened that night—why I stopped texting her back, why I stayed with Pepper—she still wanted to end things.

That's what didn't make sense to me. We hadn't even technically gotten back together. There was nothing to end. And yet, it still felt like a breakup. I still replayed and regretted everything I said, everything I did. I still missed texting her goodnight at the end of every sol.

And I still ate the same amount of ice cream.

Pepper and Rizz did really break up. He moved out of the apartment and got his own place. I didn't exactly have the funds to move out on my own, and there wasn't necessarily a reason to—even though it felt like there was.

It was a confusing time full of things that were only sort of things, but not technically things, yet still felt like things.

Gradually, Pepper transitioned out of anger and straight into the depression stage. And since I was also recovering from a breakup—one that was only sort of a breakup, but not technically a breakup, yet still felt like a breakup—we were miserable together.

We spent most of our sols on the couch in sweats, rewatching our favorite old movies, binge eating In-N-Outer Space burgers, and wallowing in our respective wallows.

Having someone to commiserate with helped us both—especially Pepper. It seemed like a relief to her, taking care of someone else instead of everyone trying to take care of her.

I still hadn't seen her cry, though. Three months later, I finally did—after the death of another beloved, respected Martian hero: Pluto.

Pepper and I stood among thousands of grieving citizens in the middle of Spirit's town square. It was nighttime, but the center of the dome still glowed—hundreds of candles flickered among bouquets of carrots and turnips, crayon-drawn pictures of Pluto leaping over Phobos, and bottles of anti-anxiety medication. It was a worthy tribute to the therapy animal.

At the heart of the display—a five-meter tall, cloth-draped figure. The official reveal hadn't happened yet but based on the donkey-shaped profile of the fabric, I had a solid guess.

My father stepped onto the platform beside the covered statue. His voice carried across the square, smoothing over the hushed sorrow of the crowd.

"Pluto was a Martian icon. A pillar of this community. In many ways, a symbol of our planet." He paused, letting his words hang in the air. "She represented our Martian values—companionship, freedom, and compassion. Every sol, as she trotted through our streets, greeting each Martian along the way, she reminded us that no matter how lonely we felt, we knew we had the companionship of a loving donkey—a friendship shared by all. Whenever we watched her weightlessly bounce around the dome, she reminded us of our freedom, unbound by the laws of gravity, forever leaping toward a better future. And when we were down, she was there to lift us up with the power of understanding and compassion—reminding us that it's okay to have a bad sol, as we all do now and then." Buzz cleared his throat, genuinely choked up. "We will miss you, Pluto."

A heavy silence settled over the square. The candle flames danced—not from wind, but from the current of collective, restrained breathing of a mourning colony holding back tears.

Pepper grabbed my hand and squeezed it tight, trembling.

My father was actually giving a beautiful eulogy, and I wondered if he had somehow become more in tune with his emotions, or if it was one of his classic politician performances, and he was simply reading his speechwriter's words.

"A planetary sol of remembrance will henceforth be recognized every leap sol added to the calendar each year to stay in sync with Earth," Buzz declared. "A tribute to Pluto's spirit—her endless leaps around the biosphere, and her eternal leap into the heart of Mars itself."

He reached for the draped fabric beside him. "It is my honor to unveil this statue of Pluto, a monument to the donkey who was so much more. Forever memorializing the national treasure, the most human of us all."

With a firm tug, he pulled the sheet away, revealing the statue of Pluto—bronzed mid-leap, ears perked, eyes full of warmth—that still stands at the center of the town square tosol.

As Buzz stepped down, the composer of the Martian national anthem, Jizzy, climbed onto the platform. With a guitar slung around his shoulder, he strummed a slow, melancholy chord progression.

"As you learn the lyrics," he said, over the opening of his song. "I'd love for you all to join in during the chorus."

The entire square swayed together and sang:

Not eight planets, no, there are nine
Though this one ain't ice, it's equine
Goodbye, old friend Pluto, goodbye
Forever you'll sparkle in our sky
One last time, a final yeehaw
Hee-haw, hee-haw
Hee-haw, hee-haw

As the song neared its end, Pepper broke down. Not just crying—bawling. The kind of sobbing that sounded dangerously close to choking, if not for the whines and wails in between gasps for air.

The people around us stopped swaying and singing, their focus shifting to her—probably wondering what the asshole next to her had said.

I had no idea what to do. I wrapped an arm around her and tried to keep us moving with the music, but we were hopelessly out of sync. The memorial was sad, sure, and I had teared up more than once, but I couldn't understand why Pepper was *so* upset—especially when I hadn't even seen her cry over her own mother.

The silence that followed the final note of the song made everything worse. Pepper clung to me, burying her face in my shoulder, as if she could will herself invisible. But there was no hiding. Everyone was watching.

As I glanced around, desperate for someone to step in and help, my eyes landed on Pockets in the crowd. Next to him—Rizz. And he wasn't looking at me with pity or concern like everyone else—he was looking at me with piercing eyes, flared nostrils. He was pissed.

I hoped he didn't think that Pepper and I had gotten together after their breakup. We hadn't. We were just two friends leaning on each other. There was nothing wrong with that. But it was one of those things that was only sort of a thing, but not technically a thing, yet still felt like a thing.

I was getting really sick of those things.

The only move was to bail. Make a run for it. I started leading Pepper away, and the swarm of prying eyes parted for us, their stares never breaking.

While walking Pepper back to our apartment, it took me an embarrassingly long time to realize her emotional outburst wasn't about Pluto at all—it was about her mom. After her mother's death, Pepper must have felt forced to bottle up her grief, to stay strong not just for her father, but for all of Mars. The weight of an entire planet's expectations had been an impossible burden, one she had carried alone. Pluto's candlelight vigil was the final straw in her hay bale. The quake that sent a tsunami of repressed emotions crashing through the dam.

When we finally reached the couch, she cried until she was all dried out. Not long after Pluto's death, Mars found itself entangled in interplanetary conflict. Because Pluto hadn't died of natural causes.

Pluto was killed.

Neither Pepper nor I knew exactly what was happening—we'd spent months isolating ourselves in our pit of pity—but we caught snippets. We watched it all from the safety of our couch.

The war on Earth was at a stalemate, neither side willing to surrender. Whether or not the conflict would reach Mars was unclear, but after the devastation of past battles, most Martians wanted nothing to do with foreign affairs. That all changed when one of the warring Earth nations fired a missile.

Alongside a public relations team, Pluto had been en route to Earth for a publicity tour—trotting down red carpets, biting ceremonial ribbons at restaurant openings, and answering every question on a late-night talk show with a well-timed *hee-haw.* The donkey-centric PR blitz was meant to promote the development of two new Mars biospheres, attracting migrants and boosting tourism.

But when their spaceship entered Earth's upper orbit for an innocent press junket, it was mistaken for an enemy vessel. Taken out before it even touched the atmosphere, leaving nothing behind but space debris and outrage.

Though the press tour never happened, the PR team pulled off the most effective campaign of their careers—unknowingly, and at the cost of their own lives. The death of Pluto triggered the greatest shift in public opinion in Martian history. Suddenly, nearly every citizen wanted war.

We allied against Pluto's killers. Though, looking back, the broader war was a tangled mess of old treaties, economic interests, and historic grudges—less good guys versus bad guys. Still, we buddied up with some guys. Obviously, the non-Pluto-killing guys.

In 2114+, just months into his directorship, Buzz declared war on Earth. And almost as quickly as we entered the war, it ended. As soon as Mars joined one side, the even stalemate teetered—and the other side folded. A clean, effortless victory—one that catapulted our nation onto the worlds stage and inflated my father's reputation to undeserved heights.

My mother wasted no time. Seizing the media distraction, she filed for divorce.

CHAPTER FORTY-ONE

DOME-WARMING PARTY

Construction of the two new biospheres accelerated, funded by war reparations. Buzz named them after two other historical Martian rovers, Curiosity and Perseverance, to honor the late Madison Chen—without actually naming one after her. Curiosity sat directly south of Spirit, and Perseverance south of Curiosity, forming a straight line of biospheres. Two additional high-speed rails connected the three domes, and since the new tracks didn't have to burrow under Olympus Mons, they were built above ground. From a satellite's eye view, Opportunity looked isolated but was still connected via the underground train.

At the start of 2115, my mother moved to Curiosity. Cliff joined her—finally, they could be together, openly and freely.

Of course, there were obviously some mixed feelings. Especially for Pepper. It hadn't even been a full year since her mother was shot. But we were both on the train to Curiosity anyway, on our way to see their new place.

"I know this is probably going to be weird for you," I said, glancing at Pepper in the window seat beside me.

"Yeah, maybe," she said, staring out the window at a much better view than the underground train had. "It's not like it won't be weird for you too."

"I guess. But my father is still alive. It was just their marriage that died."

"Both of our parents' marriages died a long time ago."

"Still . . ." My voice trailed off. "Kind of weird that our parents are officially together now. But that doesn't make us brother and sister, right?"

"What? No. They're not even married," she said, like that alone settled it. "And we were friends before they even knew each other, so our relationship trumps theirs."

"Right. Not like relationship-relationship though, right? You just mean relationship as in the general umbrella term—the connection between any two people. Like I have a *relationship* with my father."

"Right. Yeah. Right?" She turned to me, suddenly uncertain, as if she'd confused herself, genuinely wanting to know what my answer would be.

"Right. Yeah. Right?" Not even on purpose, I echoed her exact question.

"Right."

"Yeah."

"Right?"

I changed the subject. "I'm excited to see their new place."

"Me too. Curiosity as a whole, really," Pepper said.

The train ride wasn't long, and we arrived about an hour later. Curiosity's layout was similar to the other domes, but the housing sector wasn't all apartment units. There was an actual neighborhood—rows of houses, mostly reserved for families. But Iris and Cliff had connections. Divorced or widowed, having previous ties to powerful political figures still had its perks.

Their house sat near the edge of the dome where the shorter

housing units were built. The taller apartment buildings clustered toward the center, where the glass ceiling arched higher. Their place was a light gray, two-story building—narrow but functional, probably with three bedrooms at most. The front door was painted solid red. I couldn't tell if it was a patriotic statement or just an attempt to add an accent color.

I knocked.

"Oh shit, we should have brought something," Pepper said. "I totally forgot."

"What? Like wine or something?"

"Yeah. It's basically a housewarming party."

"Are we at the age when we're expected to do that?"

"It's not like there's a specific age. It's just polite."

I shrugged. "But they're our parents. I doubt they're expecting a fancy bottle from their kids."

"If their kids are adults, they might be."

Iris answered the door with a bright smile. "Flip! Pepper! Come in, come in."

"Sorry, we were going to bring a bottle of wine—" I started as we stepped inside.

My mother waved me off. "Oh, don't be silly. I stopped drinking that stuff anyway."

"And I knew that!" I lied. "That's why we didn't bring any."

"Haven't had a drop since you rescued me and Better Mars."

I paused, taken aback, not having realized it when I saw her during the state funeral.

My mother had sobered up on her own. Not with Cliff's help. Not for Cliff. For herself.

"Oh—I—I didn't know it had been that long," I stuttered, as she ushered us through the foyer. "Wow. Good for you."

Immediately, I could tell that she had stopped drinking—at fifty-four, she looked younger than she had at forty-eight.

She led us into the kitchen, where a few platters of finger foods sat on the island counter.

"Can I get you two anything?" Cliff asked us, dumping ice into a cooler full of phycos between the open kitchen and living room. Before either of us could answer, he was already tossing a Plankton Punch to Pepper and a Chlor to me—our favorites.

"Let's give you a tour!" Iris squealed, more excited than I'd seen her in years. "This is obviously the kitchen and living room." She pointed at a door on the far side of the kitchen. "And that's just a little storage space."

She touched my arms, guiding me along the tour. "Let's go upstairs. We have two bedrooms, all set up."

We followed her back through the foyer and up the stairs. At the end of the hallway, a full bathroom sat between two bedrooms—one on each side.

"The one on the left is our guest room, where you two can stay," she said. "There's only one bed, but we have a futon we can lay out. You two don't mind sharing a room, right?"

"Oh, no, we weren't planning on staying the night," I said, laughing a little too quickly. "The train is only an hour or so—we were just gonna head back."

"Oh, okay. No big deal," she said, though I could tell it was a little bit of a big deal. "And in here, we have the primary bedroom."

Iris opened the door to her right and led us into a spacious room with a king-sized bed, white walls, and a few pieces of abstract art. A digital picture frame on the dresser shuffled through a collection of photos—mostly of Pepper and me.

"Wow, it's beautiful," Pepper said. "You really know how to decorate, Mrs.—uh—Ms.—"

"Call me Iris," she offered smoothly. "And thank you."

She hesitated for a beat before turning to Pepper. "Listen, Pepper, um . . . I know this might be difficult for you . . ."

All I wanted to do was get out of there and avoid the conversation entirely, but I was the farthest from the door, and they were blocking my only exit. No room to sneak around. I was trapped.

"Oh, no, it's okay, we don't have to—" Pepper started, eyeing me for help. But I was too concerned with my own survival.

"No, I need to say this," Iris pressed on. "I am in no way trying to replace your mother."

"No, I know—" Pepper tried again, but there was no way out.

"You don't need to call me Mom. You're both adults now, and Cliff and I are adults—two consenting adults—and we've had feelings for each other for some time—"

"We don't need to get into all this, Iris," I cut in, throwing everyone a lifeline. "We get it. We're happy for you two."

My mother smiled, relieved. "Okay then! Let's go back downstairs."

We sat around the kitchen table, eating, laughing, and reminiscing about our faux-family dinners when Pepper and I were kids. I hadn't seen Pepper smile this much in what felt like an eternity.

I had never been in the house before, but the whole evening felt like I'd somehow gone back home.

The doorbell rang.

Cliff stood to answer it.

"Sorry I'm late," a voice said.

Pepper's smile vanished. Her wide eyes locked onto mine, filled with panic.

"I brought some wine," Rizz said as he walked into the kitchen, holding a bottle of Double Red. Pockets followed behind.

At the table, Pepper's back was to Rizz, but I was sitting across from her, in full view. Completely exposed. And I could only gawk at him.

"Oh, thank you!" Iris said, standing from the table to greet him, accepting their only housewarming gift.

Without turning around to acknowledge Rizz, Pepper asked, "Dad, can I talk to you for a second?" Then, through gritted teeth, added, "I didn't realize the invite list had gotten so big."

"You two were so good together," Cliff said. "And you all have always been such good friends."

She grabbed his arm and pulled him into the living room—far

enough that we couldn't make out their words, but not far enough that we couldn't hear them whispering.

Pockets looked at me, then at Rizz. Wanting no part of the tense reunion, he veered into the kitchen. "How can I help, Iris? Put me to work."

Rizz slid into Pepper's seat. "How's it going, Flip?"

"Good . . . Good . . ." I answered. "How are you?"

"Good." He smiled. I couldn't tell if it was friendly or malicious. "It's been a while." He tilted his head slightly, as if waiting for me to say something wrong. *Definitely malicious.*

"Yeah, it has," I admitted. "Sorry, I meant to reach out."

"It's alright. I get it." *Friendly?*

"It just felt so weird, with Pepper, with our history."

"I mean, we were best friends. We lived together." That felt sharper. *Malicious?*

"Yeah, I know," I said. "But Pepper and I were best friends too. And we were still living together. I didn't want to have to pick sides or anything."

"But you did." *Getting more malicious.*

"I only ever said good things about you," I told him. "I might not have reached out, but I wasn't saying anything behind your back. And I missed you. I really did."

"Dad!" Pepper's voice cut through the tension, louder than a whisper, snapping our attention toward them. A much-needed breather from our standoff.

But Rizz wasn't done. "Are you and her together?"

"No," I answered him honestly. "After you two dated . . . You were so happy together . . . It just never felt right. Neither of us even tried, really." I hadn't realized why nothing ever happened until I said it out loud. "I couldn't do that to you. And she couldn't either. Not that we ever really talked about it. It was always just this . . . unspoken thing."

"Here you are," Iris said, suddenly appearing with a glass of wine for Rizz before sitting back down at the table. "Oh, Flip, how are you and Freckle?"

Mothers and their perfect timing.

"We're not really talking anymore," I admitted. "Haven't been for some time."

"That's a shame," she said. "I know I never met her—and that was my fault, admittedly—but you two always sounded like you were good for each other."

I shrugged and took a sip of my phyco.

Pepper and Cliff returned to the kitchen.

"Rizz, can we talk?" Pepper asked.

"Sure," Rizz said, standing from the table and following her to take Cliff's place in the whispered living room conversation.

Cliff lingered, long enough to realize this was his cue to leave Iris and me alone.

"It looks like Pockets needs some . . . I have to . . . Over here," he muttered as he made a hasty exit.

I wished I had used the "I have to over here" excuse earlier to flee Pepper's conversation with my mother.

"Uh, Flip," Iris said, turning to me. "I need to say . . ."

Before she could get another word out, she was already crying, dabbing her eyes. "I'm sorry, Flip."

It was hard to tell if this was the best or worst housewarming party—it was definitely the hardest.

When I was young, my mother wasn't there for me. And then, when she met Cliff, cleaned herself up, and abruptly decided to be a mother, she was. And then, after we moved to Better Mars, and she started drinking again, she wasn't.

And then, here she was.

Before I could get another word out, I was already crying, dabbing my eyes.

Like mother, like son.

I always wanted an apology from my mother, but I never expected one. And suddenly, in a single moment, I had to process it, accept it, confront my own guilt, and bear the immediate pressure to return the favor—all without the emotional preparation such a moment required.

At least it wasn't too many words.

"I forgive you." Whether I meant it yet, I wasn't sure, but I *was* sure that I would mean it one sol. And there was no point in holding onto my anger or delaying her redemption until then. It would only prolong the pain for both of us.

I just hoped she would feel the same way.

"I'm sorry too," I said.

"For what?" she asked. "I was the terrible mother. Even after I cleaned myself up, I got lost again. And I was so ashamed of falling back into that place, I completely gave up on myself. I left you to fend for yourself. I abandoned you."

"I abandoned *you*. I left you in Better Mars. I left you with *him*. I shouldn't have done that. What kind of son does that?"

We both gave up on our tear dabs and graduated to full sleeve wipes.

"That's exactly what you should've done," she said. She stood, pulling me into a hug. "I love you, Flip."

I hugged her back.

"I love you too, Mom."

CHAPTER FORTY-TWO

BLUDGEON BALL

"Match point," the chair umpire warned.

It was the 2116+ Summer Olympics. Sweat poured down my face as I stared across the rackethand court at my opponent, who was preparing to serve.

Rackethand is played in the deathbox—an enclosed court forty-six meters tall, forty-six meters long, and sixteen meters wide. Each athlete removes their weighted Crocs to take full advantage of Mars's low gravity and straps a snowshoe-sized racket to their dominant hand as they take opposing sides. The court is separated by a long net stretching from wall to wall—similar to tennis, but it's raised halfway between the floor and ceiling, allowing balls to pass over or under.

The sport can be played in singles, doubles, and triples. But only singles players are respected.

I was in the semifinal match, in the third game of three. The score: twenty to nineteen. My opponent was one point away from advancing to the final.

They tossed the ball up and smacked it down, bouncing it under the net before the ball launched back up. I hurled myself toward the ceiling and whacked it into the back corner of my opponent's court, placing it perfectly for three quick bounces and a rebound.

Out of my opponent's reach, the ball hit the floor for a fourth time without a return.

"Deuce," the chair umpire announced.

I let out a long, shaky breath of relief.

We were playing on Earth, and the advanced anti-gravity tech used to simulate Mars's lower gravity had only been developed two years prior. No doubt, the groundbreaking, revolutionary technology had far grander applications, but instead, it was primarily used to convert every pickleball court on Earth into a deathbox. Only then did rackethand become an official Olympic sport. But it was still relatively new to Earthlings and not many played it, which is how I qualified, even at twenty-seven.

My opponent served again, this time aiming over the net, bouncing the ball off the ceiling. I hammered it downward with as much spin as possible. The ball twisted left—exactly as I had planned—but my opponent was too quick.

I faked another power shot but, at the last second, simply tapped it. The ball floated gently over the net, descending in a slow, graceful arc. My opponent let it bounce a few times before priming for a counter, then fired it back like a spade pulse.

The point was lost . . . until the line judge ran over to the chair umpire and whispered.

My lob had barely kissed the ceiling, making it a four-bounce play.

The point was mine.

"Advantage—Mars."

Even after a long career and countless matches, this was the toughest of my life—my opponent was an artificially intelligent robot.

The first advanced AI robots replaced doctors with the easiest professions. The podiatrist bot could only suggest better shoes. The gastrobot simply shrugged and prescribed an unnecessary colonoscopy. And the dentist bot strolled in after the hygienist had done all the work, glanced inside the patient's mouth, and sent them on their way.

In the early 2100s, AI took a massive leap forward, fully replacing *real* medical professionals. Eventually, robots formed a society of their own—complete with an economy, a legal system, and armed borders.

Before the Summer Games kicked off, the robots touted their mechanical superiority, claiming human biology was obsolete, flawed. No nuts and bolts. Inferior.

It wasn't hard to see through their posturing—they were using the Olympics as a propaganda campaign, masking their anti-human agenda under the guise of sportsmanship. Tensions were palpable—I was in the middle of the most astro-politically charged competition in decades.

Smash.

The robot's serve blasted off the ceiling and ricocheted into my bottom left corner, bouncing three more times before I could react.

"Deuce."

I glanced at my mom in the stands, cheering me on with Cliff, Pepper, and Pockets. In the section over, my father sat with Rizz and the rest of the Ministry of Mars, all relying on me to take down the bot across from me.

Though I knew my father had another reason for wanting me to bring home the gold. I could feel his eyes on me. Judging. Expecting. Waiting.

It was my serve.

I was exhausted. I wouldn't last much longer. I had to finish it.

I tossed the ball, and we volleyed—neither of us yielding. After the robot launched into a high jump for a smash, it floated downward in the low gravity, slowly descending.

I pounced.

Striking the ball below the net, I sent it straight toward the bot. Helpless in midair, its only option was to dodge the incoming ball—but the bot was too close to the back wall.

As the robot spun around, the ball rebounded off the wall and thwacked the robot square in its metallic face.

A bludgeon ball—worth two points.

"Game and match—Mars."

My muscles gave out, and I collapsed to the floor, drenched in sweat, overcome with relief.

A human—me—had triumphed over alleged mechanical superiority and claimed victory over the robots.

They won gold in every other event, of course. But they would at least lose this one.

Even so, the head-to-head had only been the rackethand semifinal—I hadn't officially won anything yet. The gold medal match came two days later, and my opponent was another Martian—Ravi Singh, the boy who had journeyed across Olympus Mons to Better Mars. The boy whose entire family died. The boy whose journal entries had been exploited for a subpar educational video game.

He wasn't a boy anymore.

Ravi's biological family hadn't been big on athletics, but the family who rescued him were die-hard rackethand fans. The moment they adopted him, his training began. They didn't just save him. They raised one of the greatest rackethand athletes of our time. For nearly a decade, he and I had been the top two ranked players in the solar system. But he always found a way to be number one.

Leaving me, of course, second-best.

* * *

"New news with Newt Newman is new at noon. I'm Newt Newman," Newt began, launching into his MBN Olympic primetime coverage from an open studio—no desk, just a chair and a spotlight.

"Ladies, gentlemen, and everyone on the spectrum, earlier tosol—excuse me, *today*—we're on Earth, Newt!" He laughed to himself. "Earlier today, robots swept the podium in the hundred-meter dash, breaking the world record by five full seconds. Today was also the first day in the pool, where robots claimed the gold in the freestyle relay—though officials are still debating whether involuntarily short-circuiting and electrocuting the competing swimmers warrants a disqualification."

With the Martian flag draped around my shoulders, I sat across from Newt.

"Before we dive into tonight's primetime coverage," Newt continued, "I'm sitting down with rackethand player Flip Buchanan to discuss his victory over the robots and his performance in the rackethand final last night. Flip, thank you for joining us."

"Of course. Thanks for having me," I said, trying to keep my expression neutral.

"First of all, congratulations on your semifinal win and your triumph over artificial intelligence. You've had quite a legendary run at these Summer Games."

"It was the toughest win of my life," I admitted.

"We could see your struggle in the court. That bludgeon-ball finish was something special. How did it feel entering the final match after such a huge semifinal win?"

"I was feeling pretty good. Confident." I sat up in my chair. "I knew I was going to take home the gold."

Newt cleared his throat. "But then, you didn't. Ravi Singh took home the gold."

I sighed. "Ravi is an amazing athlete, an incredible player. He didn't beat an AI robot—some people would say that's a bigger deal than any medal—but he played a great game."

I cleared my throat. "Of course, my injury had a lot to do with his win."

I let the Martian flag slip from my shoulder, unveiling my right arm in a sling.

"Yes, it was late in the third game of the match," Newt recalled. "Take us through what happened."

"I was up by a few points, and it was match point. I didn't need to risk it, but I could taste the gold. He returned my hit, and I saw the chance for a four-bounce play—if I could just get to the ball. I dove for it . . . a little too hard."

I exhaled sharply. "I slammed my shoulder against the deathbox wall. Dislocated my collarbone from my joint."

"You were screaming in pain. Medics hustled into the deathbox, but you waved them off."

"I wanted to finish what I started. I was winning. I just needed one more point, so I took my racket off my left hand and strapped it to my right."

"You thought you still had a chance with your non-dominant hand?"

I shrugged, then immediately winced at the stinging pain in my shoulder. "If I pulled it off, it would've been the greatest moment in sports history. If I didn't, I figured everyone would understand. Low risk, high reward."

"And then, in a heroic display of sportsmanship, Ravi lobbed every serve, every return, handing you the win. But you couldn't do it. Anytime the ball got close to a wall, you let it go."

"Whenever I looked at a wall, I froze . . . And walls are everywhere you look inside a deathbox."

My eyes shifted around the studio. Four walls. My heartbeat accelerated. A cold sweat formed on my skin.

"And Ravi won every point after that, however unintentionally, taking the gold," Newt said, as if I needed a reminder.

"Silver is still a huge accomplishment," I offered, desperate for validation, trying to convince myself it still meant something.

"Sure."

No doubt my father was watching. Disappointed. Embarrassed. Critical.

Newt turned to the camera. "Let's take a look at the rackethand medal ceremony that transpired just one hour ago."

Beside the camera, a hologram projection flickered to life, playing a recording of the ceremony, allowing Newt and me to watch along with the audience at home.

Ravi stood on the top spot of the podium while I was one step down to the left. Still in excruciating pain, I tried to fake a smile—but with my post-sobbing bloodshot eyes, it made me look less like a decorated athlete and more like a psychotic clown.

I leaned forward as someone placed the silver medal around my neck. As I straightened, the heavy pendant swung into my injured arm. I gritted my teeth, holding in a yelp.

Above us, two Martian flags and a robot flag lowered from the ceiling, and our planetary anthem began to play. Jizzy was right—everyone did shit themselves when they played it at the Olympics.

I couldn't face my father after failing to take home the gold, so I avoided him at all costs. But a few months later, a rocket would be hurtling through space, locked onto Mars, heading straight for one of the four domes.

And he'd soon be the only family I had left.

CHAPTER FORTY-THREE

IN PIECES

After shoulder surgery, I returned to Mars. And by 2116+, interplanetary travel had improved so much that the trip only took a month or two.

Once healed, I reentered the rackethand circuit, competing in a Perseverance tournament—my first event since my Olympic failure.

Still terrified of walls, I never performed at the same level again. I was eliminated during the round robin portion, and before the tournament even ended, I was already riding the train home in shame.

Since Curiosity was between Perseverance and Spirit, I had promised my mom I'd stop by on my way back. As I stared out the window, drifting off to sleep, I was startled by a flurry of alerts and notifications pouring in. Headlines read:

MARS ATTACKED, MISSILE SHATTERS GLASS DOME

CURIOSITY DESTROYED, CATS AVENGED

LADIES, BREAKING THROUGH GLASS CEILING NOT SUCH A GOOD THING AFTER ALL

That was when I saw the shroud of smoke billowing over Curiosity. The train slowed but continued toward the mushroom cloud ahead.

Biting fear. Sheer panic. Then—like two cancelling frequencies—they disappeared, leaving only a chilling numbness.

I called my mom. I called Cliff. I called my mom again.

Again.

Again.

Again.

I called Cliff. I called my mom.

No one answered.

When the train arrived in Curiosity, the haze was still thick, a hovering cloud of smoke clinging to the air. Passengers were instructed to stay on board and return to Perseverance, or suit up to transfer trains and head to Spirit. No one was permitted to leave the station. I deboarded with half of the passengers, all of us filing down the platform toward the station lobby to reach the connecting train track on the opposite side.

"Keep it moving," barked the station attendants, lined up against the wall like a blockade.

Through the station windows, I caught a glimpse of what remained of Curiosity—a fractured dome, glass shards blanketing kilometers of wreckage, everything glazed in frost from the subzero Martian atmosphere.

It had been reduced to a pile of rubble.

The missile appeared to have struck the far edge of the biosphere, and my mom's house was as far from the blast site as it could've been. Maybe they were still alive.

I had to know.

Just as I stepped off the platform and into the lobby, I bolted—breaking from the herd, sprinting toward the front entrance. A few others joined me.

"Hey! Stop!" one of the attendants shouted.

We didn't. We ran as fast as we could—which, in a spacesuit, wasn't all that fast. But the attendants were bogged down just the same, and they couldn't chase all of us. I managed to slip away.

As I stumbled through the ruins of Curiosity, I realized the explosion itself hadn't caused the worst of the damage. When the missile shattered the dome, a pressure imbalance corrected in an instant—just like what happened in the original biosphere. Just like what I'd thought Madison was doing to Better Mars when she fired those cannons.

Two hundred thousand people. A quarter of the Martian population. Gone in an instant.

When I finally reached my mom's house, it was like walking into a nightmare. Half the house was blackened, charred by the blast. The other half was frozen solid. The red door hung open, barely attached, creaking on a single hinge.

Uneasy, I stepped inside. Glass crunched beneath my boots as I moved from the foyer toward the kitchen.

The table where we'd shared their housewarming dinner was toppled over. Chairs were scattered across the floor. The couch had been knocked out of place.

But the first floor was empty.

No Mom. No Cliff.

I climbed the stairs to the second floor. At the end of the hallway, the bathroom light flickered. On my left, the guest bedroom door was blown off. I peered inside.

No Mom. No Cliff.

I even checked the closet. No one would be there, but I was delaying the inevitable. Delaying finding what I knew I'd find. Delaying seeing what I knew I'd see. I stood outside my mom's bedroom, the door still closed. Just stood there.

I took a deep breath.

Then I pushed it open.

No Mom. No Cliff.

Maybe they hadn't been home when the attack happened. Maybe they were somewhere else. Maybe that was good? Maybe it was worse.

There was one more place to check.

I went back downstairs into the kitchen and stared at the storage room door—the last place they could've been.

When I opened the door—

Mom. Cliff.

My mom was in a spacesuit. Cliff was holding her helmet just above her head. Both of them were frozen solid, their bodies locked in place, coated in frost. Cliff hadn't put on his own suit yet—making sure my mom was safe before he was. They were cemented in the most beautiful display of love I had ever seen.

I waited for the tears.

None came.

The second I saw them, it was like my tear ducts dried up before they had a chance to fill. They didn't look like themselves. Frozen. Dead. The uncanny sight jolted my body, triggering a fight-or-flight response I'd never felt before.

Maybe that's what happened to Pepper. Maybe that's why I never saw her cry.

And I felt guilty that I didn't cry. Which almost made me cry but didn't. Then I felt guilty that I didn't cry about my guilt. Which almost made me cry but didn't. The cycle spiraled until I didn't even understand what I was feeling—just that it wasn't what I was supposed to feel. It wasn't what other people felt.

I was grieving wrong.

My knees buckled. I collapsed onto the scorched floor, a cloud of ash rising around me before settling like dust in a forgotten place.

It was as if the air had been sucked from my lungs.

For a long time, I sat there in a daze. Unmoving. Staring.

Piercing alerts screamed inside my suit—my oxygen levels were depleted. And yet I didn't move from the soot. I didn't leave my mom. The sharp tones blared in my helmet, warning me I was about to suffocate.

But it felt like I already had.

CHAPTER FORTY-FOUR

ENLISTING

I took an empty seat in the Town Hall auditorium, surrounded by hundreds of other young Martians. Conversations buzzed around me, but I didn't recognize a single familiar face.

I hoped my friends would understand why I was there.

But I knew they wouldn't approve.

As the lights dimmed, the audience quieted.

On stage, a hologram projection sparked to life, playing an enlistment video. The image panned over a row of young adults in military uniforms, standing at attention on a wide, concrete airstrip.

A soft, solemn piano melody drifted in. Then a deep, folksy voice—the kind that's innately trustworthy—narrated:

"These are Martian Space Force cadets."

In slow motion, the soldiers dropped to the ground for pushups in unison, their sweat and grime glistening under intensified color contrast.

The music swelled, layering strings atop the piano.

"Not long ago, they too were below-average young Martians from below-average Martian families, yearning to be something more. Something better. Now, they are."

The video cut to the interior of a massive spaceship bridge, sleek and futuristic—like something inspired by the reboots of the reboots of the reboots of *Star Trek*.

A captain barked orders, his voice muted beneath the brass and percussion entering the score. Around him, young cadets rushed to press buttons, flip switches, and spin dials, moving with synchronized precision as the music crescendoed, climbing to its peak.

"Now, they're capable men. Inspiring women. Accomplished people on the spectrum. Essential Space Force personnel."

Cutting back to the airstrip, the frame locked onto one soldier, pushing himself up from the ground, marching forward with newfound purpose. As he turned and snapped into attention, the music climaxed—then abruptly pulled back into the soft, solemn piano.

"These are the adventurers. These are the patriots. These . . . are the heroes."

The frame zoomed out, revealing the soldier had stepped onto a space elevator.

Over the image, bold maroon text faded in:

Your greatest triumphs . . .

The view expanded, revealing dozens of elevators, each carrying a single soldier, ascending toward orbit.

. . . are forged together.

Side by side, the elevators rose into the darkness of space, lifting the soldiers toward a monstrous military spaceship waiting above Mars.

Rise to your full potential.

It cut to black.

The Martian Space Force logo faded into the hologram.

The auditorium lights slowly brightened, revealing two recruiters stationed at the ends of the aisles, standing beside tablets on sleek metal stands.

Before I even processed that the presentation was over, commotion exploded. Kids younger than me sprang from their seats, scrambling to sign up first. Some even hopped over my lap to get in line.

I had expected something a little more than a minute-long ad when I showed up for a recruitment presentation—we were all volunteering our lives for the cause, after all. But I guess the military didn't see the point in spending more when people would eagerly enlist after the targeted attack on Curiosity.

I stepped into line.

For too long, I had waited on the sidelines, assuming my role as a secondary character in other people's stories. I never took action. Couldn't save Cheese. Couldn't save Pockets. Couldn't save Pepper. I told myself I was nobody, so there was no point in trying to be somebody.

But that excuse had worn thin.

I didn't even really know what the war was about. All I knew was that it had killed thousands. It killed Cliff. It killed my mom. And I was done doing nothing.

"No, you aren't."

A voice rudely interrupted my engaging internal dialogue.

My head whipped around. Rizz stood there, his expression matter-of-fact. Before I could react, he grabbed me and yanked me out of line, pulling me toward the side of the auditorium.

"You're lucky Pepper didn't see you here." Rizz's voice was low, steady, and cut like a knife. "Or you'd be handcuffed to a pipe with a bag over your head before you even became a prisoner of war."

He and Pepper had gotten back together after their whispered conversation at my mom's housewarming. She apologized for sending him away. He apologized for leaving. They both apologized for being too stubborn to apologize sooner. Those were all the specifics I knew.

"I'm going," I shot back.

"Don't you remember how you froze when Pockets needed you?" His tone was flat, dismissive. "What about the battle with the Pauls?" He paused—but not for an answer. "I won't be there to step in this time. I won't be there to protect you."

"That was almost ten years ago." My hands curled into fists. "I don't need your help. I don't need your protection. I'm going. I have to."

"So this is about getting revenge for your mom?" I opened my mouth, but he didn't give me a second to answer. "What's getting yourself killed going to do for your dead mom? Nothing. She's dead." Harsh. Heat climbed up my neck. My face flushed. "And you know that." Rizz didn't let up. "Fuck you, Flip. You're running away."

Really harsh. My face flushed more, hot. "Fuck you!" I snapped. "I'm not running away. I'm running toward something. I have to do this."

"Why?"

My face flushed most, on fire. I wasn't expecting that question. It should have been obvious, but I somehow couldn't find the answer.

"I have to because, you know, all this . . ." I waved my arms around vaguely, gesturing to the auditorium, the recruits, the war propaganda hanging from the ceiling.

"I'm not talking about this." Rizz didn't take his eyes off me as he stepped forward. "I'm talking about you."

"I have to because what else am I supposed to do?" The words slipped out before I fully understood them myself. "I lost my mom. I don't talk to my father. My rackethand career is over. I'm not in a relationship. You and Pepper are back together."

It was just a grocery list of boohoo produce. Life sucked. I didn't need to tell Rizz that. I needed to circle back to a point. Before I could—

"Sounds like you're running away," Rizz repeated.

I paused. If I couldn't find my point, the next best option was deflection, a twist of the knife. "I can't handle watching her grieve another parent. I did one. Maybe you can take this one."

Rizz's jaw tensed. "That's not fair."

"I don't care, Rizz." This time, it was my voice that was sharp. Final. "You're not my older brother. Never were."

"You're abandoning her when she needs you most."

"I'm not dating her. You are." I stared him down. "You don't care that I'm enlisting—you just care that I won't be here as the backup boyfriend."

I turned and walked away, heading back toward the line of recruits.

"I care because you're my friend," Rizz said. "I need my friend."

I stopped. Twisted around. Faced him. "You don't need me. I'm not someone people need. Never was."

Without taking my eyes off him, I stepped backward, letting my words sink in. He had no response. When I turned around, my fellow countrymen wouldn't let me squeeze back in.

Fine. I'd lost my mom. I'd lost my friends. And I'd lost my spot in line. Time to go lose my life.

And I didn't mind waiting in the back for it.

* * *

Before I left Mars, I sent Freckle a text.

I didn't think she would want to see me. Or maybe I was just too chicken shit to go see her. Probably both.

I wanted to tell her I was sorry. I wanted to tell her I had been young and confused. That, on paper, my relationship with Pepper only *seemed* like the epitome of a perfect love story—childhood friends, first love, that underlying will-they-won't-they dynamic from romance movies and half-hour comedies that last more than three seasons.

I wanted to tell her that *first* love isn't the same as *real* love. That it might feel like it hits the hardest—the most enchanting, the most passionate, the most heartbreaking—because there's nothing else to compare it to. That I had been fumbling through emotions, trying to figure out what any of them meant—and most of the time, I'd been wrong.

I wanted to tell her I was enlisting. That if anything happened to me, she needed to know how I felt about her. That she wasn't my first love—she was my *second* love. My *real* love. That it had taken me seven years to figure out, but I finally had. That I loved her to the two moons and back.

I wanted to tell her all of it.

So I cracked my fingers, psyching myself up to type the most articulate, romantic text of my life.

Me: Hey

CHAPTER FORTY-FIVE

ACTUAL BOOT CAMP

The bleach-white corridor of the spaceship hummed with movement—soldiers hustling back and forth, voices echoing, boots hammering against the floor.

With a small backpack of personal belongings on my shoulders and my assigned uniform in my arms, I followed the signage to my designated sleeping quarters.

Inside, six bunks lined the right wall—three on top, three below. Same on the left wall. All the bunks looked claimed, except for the two at the far end of the right wall, where the only other person in the room was unpacking his things.

"Are you a top or a bottom?" he asked me.

I paused. "Uh—"

"Bunk," he clarified. "Top bunk or bottom bunk? I was taking the top—"

His voice cut off when he turned and saw me.

I returned his gaping stare. "Bottom works."

Without breaking eye contact, I stepped forward and set my things down on the thin mattress.

"Hey, man," Ravi Singh said.

"Hey," I responded flatly to the gold-medal thief beside me.

Ravi was eighteen then—a brown-skinned kid with short, dark hair that wasn't styled in any way. A patchy beard—mostly peach fuzz—was just starting to come in.

I couldn't believe I had to share a bunk with the kid who beat me in rackethand at the Olympics. Who beat me every time, in every final, taking every title. We had never been this close, never actually talked to each other, only stared one another down across dozens of deathboxes. Neither of us tried to make small talk as we unpacked. I didn't want to boil over. He didn't want to touch the hot pot.

I felt a bump in my bag—something I didn't remember packing. I reached in the pocket, my fingers closed around smooth glass with a few scratches, and I smiled.

The snow globe.

Pepper must have snuck it in. Maybe Rizz did it. Even after our blowup, not exactly on speaking terms, they didn't want me to leave without it.

I slipped the miniature biosphere into the cargo chest pocket of my Space Force uniform. And for the duration of my service, I never took it out.

* * *

From that point on, I couldn't seem to avoid Ravi, no matter how hard I tried. We shared a bunk. We were in the same unit. We had the same schedule—orientation, fitness training, drills, meal breaks. Everywhere I went, he was there.

"You have one job, maggots." The astro officer's voice was thick with gravel and spit as he paced the front of the lecture hall, hands clasped behind his back, veins pulsing wherever skin was showing. "One job. And that's killin' 'bots."

After the Olympics, the robot regime had been sweeping across territories, annexing one after another, rounding up humans like cattle—shipping them off to work camps only to be systematically killed. It was genocide. No human was safe.

"The AI is powered by nothing but pure, goddamn evil and geothermal energy," the astro officer continued. "And that energy is produced by a volcano in the central hub of the mechanical ecosystem."

He stopped pacing and gestured toward a hologram map, floating in the air beside him. He tapped a space on the map, zooming in, highlighting a massive volcanic structure, its nerves of lava firing like circuitry.

"Destroy the volcano, destroy the AI."

"Can you blow up a volcano?" Ravi asked, sitting a couple rows in front of me.

Whoosh. The officer lunged across the room, getting right in Ravi's face, almost headbutting him.

"*I can blow up whatever I goddamn please!*" he yelled, spit spewing from his mouth. "*Is that goddamn clear? Is that clear, soldier?*"

Without receiving anything more than a mumble, the officer resumed his pacing at the front. "Firepower, people. With enough firepower, we can wipe that volcano off the face of the planet."

I was pretty sure blowing up a volcano would only expand the vent in the Earth's crust, releasing more magma and geothermal energy. Maybe they were trying to collapse the mountain, bury the lava vents in a rockslide.

But I wasn't about to be the next dumbass to ask a question.

* * *

Each afternoon, we ran for kilometers through the endless corridors of the spaceship. The artificial gravity was unforgiving. During our second week of training, Ravi stumbled to the wall of the hallway and puked, dropping to his knees.

Our unit kept running without a second glance.

I slowed my pace, jogging up behind him.

He was my bunkmate, and there's something about sleeping in

the same space—being that vulnerable—that creates an immediate bond. A silent trust that you won't put their hand in warm water or fart bare-ass in their face while they sleep. And that trust had been building for two weeks, even if we hadn't said a word to each other.

I stopped beside him. "Slacking on the rackethand cardio?"

He chuckled, wiping his mouth with the back of his arm. "I've always been the one hitting the bludgeon balls, not getting bludgeoned."

I patted his back. "Come on."

Before our astro officer could catch him struggling, I hauled Ravi back to his feet. When I saw him down the last drop of his canteen, I gave him whatever water was left in mine.

* * *

In our final week of training, just a few sols before the invasion, our unit performed a combat drill in the spaceship's command center. The room looked almost identical to the one in the recruitment video, which surprised me—the shiny set piece and lens flares weren't just a marketing gimmick.

My job was simple—fire our payload as soon as we were close enough to the volcano that the robot missile defense system wouldn't have time to react.

I sat at the front of the command center, directly below the viewport, monitoring our distance to the target. Crosshairs locked onto the volcano vent. All I had to do was keep my hand steady on the joystick and press a button.

Ravi sat beside me, toggling our plasma shield, which couldn't remain on while I fired. The missile would explode on impact against the inside of our shield—the plasma wasn't a one-way mirror. So Ravi had to drop the shield, let the warhead through, and raise the shield back up before enemy fire shredded us.

Behind us, other cadets sat at complex control panels of the utmost importance, overseeing vital ship systems—though I had no clue what any of them actually did.

"Approaching our target," our astro officer called from his oversized chair at the center of the room. "Shields up."

Ravi pressed a few buttons and pushed a handle forward. "Shields up!"

"Ready the weapon."

On my monitor, the crosshairs hovered over a mock volcano, waiting for my cue.

"Incoming fire from starboard!" the officer barked.

The viewport screen flashed red as simulated enemy fire lit up the right side of our ship.

"We'll have to time this perfectly, cadets! On my order—shields down, fire, and get those goddamn shields back up as soon as that goddamn bomb leaves this goddamn ship. Is that clear?"

"Yes, sir!" Ravi and I shouted in unison.

"Ready . . ." The officer eyed the enemy barrage, vigilant, waiting for a gap in the attack. "Shields down!"

Ravi jerked his handle back. "Shields down!"

"Fire!"

I pressed the only button I was responsible for. "Missile away!"

"Shields up!"

Ravi's hands flew over his controls—

"Shit."

He tried again, fumbling the sequence of buttons—

"Shit."

"Shields!" the officer roared.

Ravi's hands quivered. His forehead dripped with sweat.

Boom. We were bombarded by simulated enemy fire. Red lights flashed. Sirens blared. We were dead.

A second later, our astro officer was on us.

I swiveled around in my chair and stood at attention. Ravi didn't move. Too terrified. Staying seated, still facing away. I nudged him, and he reluctantly stood.

"We're all dead," our officer said. "You just got yourself and every goddamn one of your comrades killed."

Ravi's throat bobbed. "Sorry, sir."

"Sorry? *'Sorry' can't revive anyone, goddammit!*" the officer spat.

Pepper had once said something very similar.

The officer's voice climbed. "Your performance is goddamn unacceptable, cadet! I want your sorry ass at this goddamn station every goddamn waking moment—practicing until your goddamn fingers bleed! I want you to see this goddamn sequence in your goddamn sleep! Sleep you *will not* have tonight because you are on night patrol for the next three goddamn nights! *Dismissed!*"

Night patrol—the go-to disciplinary action for mistakes and insubordination. There was no real reason to patrol the sterile corridors of the ship—military personnel were the only passengers aboard and we were space. Nobody was sneaking inside without us knowing. It was pointless, which was exactly the point.

* * *

That night, I couldn't sleep.

In my mind, Ravi was always at the top. The best rackethand player in the worlds. A force of perfection that kept me pinned below him, stuck in second place.

But I only ever saw him on the court. I never saw him practice. I never saw him try. I never saw him struggle.

That didn't mean he never did—on the court or off. I didn't know what his home life was like. I didn't know if he had friends. I didn't know if he had a family.

And then, I remembered—he didn't. I'm sure I had made the connection before, but I'd forgotten, distracted by all the disappointments he kept serving me. Ravi Singh was the character in that VR video game I had to do a report on for maximum school graduation. I watched his whole family die. It was virtual for me, but he actually lived it. He endured the tragedy before he even stepped foot on the rackethand court.

Before he was somebody, he was nobody—alone on Olympus Mons, with nothing to his name.

Firsts didn't always have it easy. You see them at their finest, but that doesn't mean they were never at the bottom. Ravi struggled before the top. Pepper struggled after. It could happen on either side of the peak. Firsts were human, too—more accomplished, more celebrated, but human nonetheless.

I snuck out of my bunk and found Ravi walking the white halls of the ship. I strolled up behind him and tapped his arm. "Come on," I said. "Let's just sit."

Ravi hesitated. "But . . . if they catch me slacking . . ." His voice was small, like he had already failed enough for one sol.

"It's the middle of the night." I leaned my back against the wall and slid down to sit. "No one's checking on us."

After a moment, Ravi sank down next to me. For a while, we just sat in silence.

Ravi broke it. "I'm sorry about the Olympics, man. I really tried to—"

I waved him off.

"That was my fault, not yours." And I meant it, I had never admitted it to myself, much less anybody else, but I meant it. "You were just trying to help me out."

"How's your shoulder?" he asked.

"Totally fine. Back to normal. It's this vendetta with walls that made me retire." I turned to him. "What about you? Shouldn't you be on the court?"

"My sister enlisted." He sighed. "I was just trying to keep her safe, but we got put on different assignments."

"Damn." I paused. "I can't imagine what it must feel like—to be worried about losing more family. I know what happened when you were young. That must've been awful."

He unexpectedly chuckled lightly. "You played, huh?"

"Yeah. How could they make a game of that? I'm sure it was terrible for you—reliving it all again."

Ravi shrugged. "It was a long time ago. And the royalties weren't bad. I was happy to pay my family back for saving me."

"That's big of you."

After a moment, Ravi asked, "Why did you enlist?"

I nibbled the inside of my lip. "My mom was killed in Curiosity."

Ravi stiffened. "Oh, shit. I'm sorry."

I hadn't given myself a chance to really mull on it—purposefully. And, like usual, I hid behind a joke, imitating our astro officer. "'Sorry' can't revive anyone, goddammit!"

Ravi bowed his head, unsure of what to say.

"It's okay." I picked at my fingers. "I'm not even sure bloodthirsty vengeance was the reason I joined."

"I guess it doesn't really matter. You're here." He tilted his head back against the wall. His voice was lighter, almost teasing. "I'll try not to kill us all."

I nudged him with my elbow. "You'll be fine. We'll all be fine. And then we'll go back to Mars and . . ."

I had no idea what I was going to do if we made it back to Mars. Which might have been the *real* reason I left.

"A diner," Ravi murmured.

"What?"

"A restaurant." He didn't look at me, just stared down at the floor. "I'm gonna open up a restaurant. Just a small, hole-in-the-wall kitchen."

"No rackethand?"

Ravi shook his head. "Nah. I never even really liked it all that much."

That stung. The kid who stole my gold didn't even care about it.

"It was my family," Ravi admitted. "They sorta forced it on me."

If Ravi hadn't been adopted by a rackethand-loving family—if his entire biological family hadn't died on Olympus Mons—maybe I would've done better than silver. I'm not saying my loss was my father's fault for throwing a tantrum and building Better Mars, but it kind of was.

The sting faded as I realized the only reason I cared about the gold as much as I did was because of *my* family.

"Family can be hard," I said.

"Sometimes I feel like I get swallowed by them."

Swallowed. It was an interesting word choice. Not one I was expecting. One that made me think of Madison Chen—and what she always said about people swallowing their pride.

"Speaking of swallowing, what kind of food would you serve at this restaurant of yours?" I asked.

Ravi turned to me, curious. "You ever have gnukka?"

"Dude. It's the best."

"The best!" Ravi grinned. "Ever since I tried it, I've wanted to open a gnukka kitchen. Call it The Gnukka Nook."

"I'll make sure you get back to Mars so you can open that kitchen."

"I'll make sure you get back so you can be my first customer."

"Either of us die, deal's off."

Ravi chuckled, leaning his head against the wall again. "We both die?"

"We both die . . ." I flicked a piece of dead skin from my finger. "And I guess it's like the deal never happened in the first place."

CHAPTER FORTY-SIX

S-SOL

The sol of the invasion had arrived. I strapped in at the weapons system station. Ravi took his seat next to me. The Martian Space Force and an armada of allies stormed into Earth's atmosphere. The invasion consisted of two phases—the initial attack, with spaceships designed to eliminate anti-spacecraft and missile defenses; and the bomb squadrons, smaller units equipped with payloads reserved for the volcano.

We were in the second phase.

Through the viewport, Earth's edges glowed with a vibrant, aquamarine hue—a stark contrast to the dull, matte haze of Mars. The planet looked alive. And yet, we were flying straight into a battle that only promised death.

The first wave of allied ships streaked toward the Blue Planet.

When they reached low Earth orbit, they fired—and the robot defenses countered simultaneously. Hundreds of thousands of weapons shot off at once, like extending tentacles of two sea anemones trying to catch their prey.

An allied ship exploded.

Then another.

Then ten more.

The first wave was annihilated before our eyes. I swallowed hard, the weight of it hitting me.

After so many years, it became clear: I had been *hiding* behind second. And all it took was the decimation of half an army for me to finally understand.

Firsts led the charge and took the hit. Seconds followed safely behind. Firsts carried the weight of expectations. Seconds loitered in obscurity. Firsts were relied on. Seconds were overlooked.

In second, I could watch the chaos without facing it. I could criticize from the sidelines without taking action. No one expected anything from me. I didn't have to fight. Didn't have to lead. Didn't have to pay the price.

I was just a self-righteous Chattr post, typed from the comfort of my bed.

Second was safe. Second was easy. Second never had to make the hard choice. There was no accountability in second—just great excuses.

Maybe there was a family curse, but I was just a coward.

"Advance!" our astro officer barked, gripping the armrests of his oversized chair.

The ship lurched forward, accelerating toward Earth.

The first wave had successfully neutralized many of the robot defenses, but not all. The fight still raged—a blizzard of laser bursts whipped back and forth. Ships were torn apart, leaving metric tons of debris to dodge.

"Steer clear!" our officer ordered. "But hold our pace."

On Earth's surface below, explosions lit up the runway for our incoming squadrons. We plunged straight into the inferno welcoming our approach.

The curvature of the Earth disappeared as we rocketed downward. The volcano came into sight—still tiny from our altitude but growing fast.

"Shields up," the officer spat.

Ravi's fingers danced over the controls—a few buttons, a handle push forward. "Shields up!"

I tightened my grip around the joystick, watching my crosshairs float over the volcano vent. One button. That was it. But we had to get closer first.

"Incoming fire—port side!"

Alarms shrieked. Warning lights flashed.

Our plasma shell absorbed the barrage, protecting our hull, but the enemy had us in their sights—they were locked on.

"We've done this before," our astro officer growled. "You know what to do. On my order—shields down, fire, and get those goddamn shields up as soon as that goddamn bomb leaves this goddamn ship!"

"Yes, sir!" Ravi and I roared in unison.

My hand slipped slightly on the joystick. Ravi's hands trembled, hovering over his panel.

"You got this, Ravi," I told him. "I trust you."

He snapped his head toward me, wide-eyed, and nodded slowly—his Adam's apple bobbing.

Boom.

A deafening explosion shuddered the ship. Enemy lasers zipped past like an unsynchronized light show, crisscrossing over the volcano's jagged rim, expanding as we neared.

"Approaching target," our astro officer trumpeted, voice taut as the enemy fire intensified. "Ready . . . "

The bombardment paused for half a second—

"Shields down!"

Ravi yanked the handle back. "Shields down!"

"Fire!"

I slammed my one button. "Missile away!"

"Shields up!"

Ravi's hands flew over his controls. No hesitation. No mistakes. His sequence was flawless.

"Shields up!" Ravi yelled, his voice cracking with relief.

It didn't matter.

As if the entire robot defense force had locked onto our ship alone, a wall of anti-spacecraft fire battered us. Relentless. Continuous. Unending. The ship convulsed as if it was having a seizure.

"Evasive maneuvers!" our officer barked. But it was too late. We lost control. My stomach shot into my throat as we spiraled into freefall—pulled in by Earth's gravity, plummeting toward the surface.

I yanked my seat belt straps tighter, my knuckles white as I gripped the armrests.

Through the viewport, clouds ripped apart, unveiling Earth's surface hurtling toward us. A vast, blue ocean—our final resting place—grew bigger and bigger.

"Brace for impact!" our officer bellowed.

The ship whined, rattling like it was coming apart panel by panel, bolt by bolt.

And then—black.

CHAPTER FORTY-SEVEN

DOWN WHERE IT'S WETTER

When I came to, I was still strapped in my seat, my head throbbing, warm blood trickling down my temple. The entire command center was filling with water.

"Hey, Ravi . . . know how to swim?" I croaked, groggy.

Ravi's body was limp in the seat beside me, head slumped forward, arms hanging lifelessly at his sides.

"Me either," I muttered.

Most people on Mars never learned to swim—no reason to. The only bodies of water were artificial, strictly used for irrigation, drinking supply, and indoor plumbing.

I blinked through my daze, searching the bridge.

Nothing. No one. Everyone else was gone.

The reality of our situation sank in—probably at the same speed as our ship.

We'd been left for dead.

I fumbled with my seat belt, my arms weak, fingers clumsy. When the buckle finally gave way, I collapsed into the meter-deep pool below, my uniform heavy with water, dragging me down like an anchor.

I fought to my feet, gasping.

"Ravi!" My voice was hoarse. I grabbed his shoulders and shook him hard. "Ravi!"

No response.

I slapped him once. Twice. Thrice. His head just flopped to the side.

No. No way.

I unfastened his seat belt and hauled him up, every muscle straining under his dead weight—not *dead*, just unconscious. Unconscious weight.

The water was climbing higher, sloshing at my waist. My pulse pounded in my skull like a subwoofer. I twisted around, desperate for something—anything—that could help us escape. But the emergency evacuation pods lining the walls had all been ejected. Gone, leaving us stranded, sinking to the bottom of the sea.

We were going to drown.

On Mars, I never had to worry about drowning—only suffocating.

Suffocating.

I lugged Ravi through the rising water, heaving both of us toward the locker of emergency evacuation spacesuits. They had been left behind—no reason to take them in the escape pods when we weren't in space.

I wrestled Ravi's unconscious body into a suit, working as fast as I could before the water devoured us completely. My breath came in frenetic bursts, my fingers bumbling with the fastenings.

I thought about my mom and Cliff frantically scrambling into their suits before the Martian atmosphere froze them solid. I wasn't going to let Ravi and I meet the same fate.

With a grunt, I flung his body over the locker. He stayed atop, partially supported by the chest-high ocean water, as I took a deep breath and dipped below the surface to pull out a suit for myself.

Water flooded into my suit as I climbed in, gripping the locker to keep myself from being dragged under. As soon as I secured my helmet, I took a deep breath, relief hitting me in full.

We were safe.

Then I saw the waves lapping at Ravi's face—his bare face.

No helmet.

Fuck.

I went back under. The salt water stung and my vision blurred. I blindly searched for the helmet inside the locker, lit only by the occasional flashing alarm light. No luck.

I surfaced, water lapping at the chin of my helmet, my eyes darting wildly, searching.

Then I saw it—floating away on the waves.

The helmet.

I reached as far as I could without letting go of the locker, my fingers just brushing the edge, making it wobble atop the surf. I stretched and I stretched—

The water crept up Ravi's body, his nose and mouth just barely breaking the surface.

I stretched and I stretched—

Somehow, in every situation, I could never reach far enough.

I had a helmet—I could try to paddle for it, but I didn't know how to swim. Even if I managed to grab it, I probably wouldn't make it back to him in time.

Ravi would drown, get swallowed by the ocean. And I would watch. Helpless.

No. There was one other thing I could do.

I lifted Ravi as much as I could, practically shoving his face into the ceiling, letting water pour out of his suit. Then I wrenched off my helmet and locked it into place over his head, sealing him inside. I let go of his body—too heavy to keep holding—and it sank to the floor.

But he could breathe. Soon, I wouldn't be able to.

My eyes locked onto the other helmet, bobbing away, farther and farther.

I had one shot at this.

Planting both my feet against the locker, I launched myself toward the drifting helmet—lunging headfirst into the opening. Water sloshed against my face as I twisted it on just before it filled. And just before the water reached the ceiling of the command center.

I hit the floor, my body fully submerged. And spat out salt water.

Clang. The entire ship vibrated with a deep, metallic thud, then settled in eerie silence. We had hit the ocean floor.

For a moment, I didn't move. Just took slow, measured breaths—my lungs burning, muscles shaking, adrenaline still buzzing in my ears.

A well-deserved break.

"Flip?"

I turned to my right. Ravi was waking up from his nap—casually coming to, only to find himself completely underwater at the bottom of the ocean.

"Hey, man," I said through our comms, pushing myself to my feet. "Come on. You've got a Gnukka Nook to open."

I helped him up and we stumbled to the emergency hatch. It took a few tries to pry it open—our strength already spent—but eventually, it gave. We stepped out into the abyss.

Neither of us could swim—not that it would've helped. Even if we were Olympic swimmers instead of rackethand athletes, we couldn't make it to the surface, weighed down by a waterlogged spacesuit.

"I guess we walk," Ravi said.

I looked around, hoping for a better idea. My helmet lights found nothing. "I guess we walk."

Step by step, we hiked along the ocean floor, trudging through the sand and silt, over toothed rocks, climbing underwater cliffs. Hours passed. We figured we couldn't have crashed far from shore—we'd been shot down right after flying over the volcano. But we had no clue if we were even heading in the right direction.

Still, we were moving up an incline, and that was good enough for us.

With each step, the salt water swished in my helmet, splashing against my face.

"We're going to be shriveled up like raisins by the time we make it up," I said.

If we made it up.

We let out a nervous laugh.

We were probably going to die. But at least I found the joke.

"Hey . . . thanks for saving me," Ravi said. "Not a lot of people would've done that."

I looked up at the endless blue expanse, the surface not even in sight. "I haven't saved anyone yet."

For nearly an entire sol, we tromped along the ocean floor—or maybe it was a lake, a sea, a gulf, or whatever else Earthlings call their bodies of water. From the bottom, we couldn't tell. When I wanted to call it a sol, Ravi forced me to keep going. When Ravi wanted to call it a wash, I forced him.

Finally, we dragged ourselves onto the beach, peeling off our spacesuits as we crawled away from the waves. Then we collapsed in the sand, in no rush to keep trekking forward on land, first letting ourselves dry out in the sun.

Maybe I was dreaming. Maybe I was hallucinating. But when I turned my head, I saw a gorilla a dozen meters away, just standing there, watching me.

For a long moment, we just stared at each other.

Then, without a sound, the great ape turned and slipped into the jungle brush at the edge of the beach.

Whatever metaphor the universe was shoving down my throat could wait for some English professor to analyze. Instead, I just rolled over.

And puked up a mouthful of salt water.

CHAPTER FORTY-EIGHT

SPACE LASER

A unit of the NEC (Nations of Earth Collective) army found Ravi and me before our wrinkly skin had even finished drying in the sun. According to the Martian allies, our mission had been a success—several ships managed to drop their payload into the volcano, reducing it to a pile of rubble. By the time we washed ashore, the battle was already won.

But the war was still ongoing.

I explained what had happened to our ship and pointed them toward where I thought it had gone down. The rest of our crew was found alive, drifting in the middle of the ocean, floating aimlessly in their escape pods—with no hope for rescue, had it not been for the two comrades they'd left to die. Though, I guess if they hadn't, we *all* would've been stranded at sea.

Ravi and I were both discharged and put on the next return flight to Mars. Upon landing, I was immediately escorted to the Town Hall boardroom to receive a commendation for my "heroic acts on the battlefield"—their words, not mine.

But I didn't hate it.

When I walked in, the entire Ministry of Mars was seated

around the conference table. My father was there, of course. But to my surprise, so was Pepper—sitting in her mother's old seat.

After the attack on Curiosity, Pepper had been just as determined as I was to act. But instead of enlisting in the army, she chose a different battlefield. Politics. Change things from the inside. Her composure at her mother's state funeral—so reminiscent of Madison Chen—had caught the public's attention. It caught Buzz's too. Soon after, he appointed her to the ministry.

Buzz's relationship with Madison had always been contentious, but he respected her. In fact, that deep respect was probably the very reason it *was* so contentious.

"Flip!" my father called, rising from his chair as I entered. He strode over, extending his hand, giving mine a firm shake, and slapping my shoulder with his other hand. "We heard the tales of your bravery—the stuff of legends. Please, take a seat."

He ushered me into a chair beside him at the head of the table.

"Because of your acts of heroism," he continued, pulling his seat closer to the table, "we wanted to honor you by showing you a little something we've been cooking up."

I sat back, wary. My brow furrowed as I glanced at Pepper—who immediately looked away. Then at Rizz—who met my stare with pursed lips.

At the far end of the table, Paul Kingsley's clone stood stiffly, hands clasped behind his back, silent.

Buzz leaned in, his voice dropping to a conspiratorial tone. "Now, as you know, we kneecapped the robot regime when we destroyed their geothermal energy source. But they have yet to surrender. We think one final blow might force their hand."

It wasn't exactly glee—more like a nervous energy coming from him. "While you've been serving, a classified, top-secret team of covert scientists has been working on a confidential project—discreetly, behind closed doors, surreptitiously."

I raised an eyebrow. "Sounds pretty under wraps."

"Extremely." Buzz couldn't sit anymore. He stood and paced,

gesturing animatedly. "The program was launched several months before S-Sol, and its mission was twofold." He lifted a finger. "First: to push the boundaries of knowledge, science, and human understanding. To unlock the true potential of humankind in our ever-expanding universe by exploring the relationship between matter and antimatter. And second—" He strutted to the far end of the table and stopped behind Paul. "Find out if it could blow things up." Buzz clapped his hands onto Paul's shoulders. "And what did we learn, Paul?"

Paul nodded, expression flat. "It can."

"It can!" Buzz's grin widened.

Pastor Van Buren was nearly out of his seat, salivating. "How big of an explosion are we talking about?"

"The biggest humanity has ever seen," Paul warned solemnly.

Buzz meandered back to his chair and plopped down, beaming. "So, we built one of these antimatter hyper beams—AHB, as we call it—on Earth's moon. Y'know, just in case we needed it." He leaned forward, elbows on the table, scanning the room. "What do we think? Do we need it?"

After a long moment of silence, Buzz leaned back, waiting for a healthy dialogue, swiveling right and left. Right and left. Right and left.

Nobody uttered a word. Mumbles, shrugs, and cocked heads signaled a collective, resounding, "*Maybe?*"

I wasn't sure why I was there. Just for show? Or was I being asked for my opinion? I didn't know which one was worse: being a prop or being part of the decision.

Paul Kingsley's clone gestured to a red countdown timer projected on the back wall—one I hadn't noticed before. "The timer counts down to the moment the weapon is in position to fire at a specific target—in this case, the second-largest robot metropolis. With the moon revolving around the Earth, and the Earth rotating on its axis, there is only a brief window—roughly five minutes—when the laser is properly aligned."

I almost laughed. For such a powerful weapon, it was a rather absurd restriction.

The timer counted down its last ten minutes.

"We can't use it," Rizz blurted. "We'd kill millions in an instant."

"We'd kill millions of *robots*," Buzz corrected.

"Use it!" Pastor Van Buren urged, nearly salivating. "As the teachings preach, 'Rejoice in the fiery rain of peace through power.' Athena, 4:14."

"The AI is sentient," Rizz shot back. "They feel pain. They have emotions. It would be like murdering an entire city of people."

Buzz groaned, rolling his eyes. "Clones are people. Cavernese are people. Robots are people. Where is the line with you radicals?"

Pepper inhaled deeply, as if preparing to confess a dark secret. "It's clear they'll never surrender, even though they're fighting a losing battle. And if they refuse to stand down, we'll have to consider another full-scale invasion. Tens of millions would die—robots and humans." She glanced at the countdown clock. "If they surrender after we fire the AHB, analysts have estimated that fewer lives would be lost in the long run."

She sounded just like her mother—calm, calculating, weighing every option with precision. It made her seem older. More mature. Maybe she was seeing me in a similar light—a veteran, newly acquired nerves of steel, confident-ish.

We were both grown up. A far cry from the eight-year-olds running around with the Catfish Trolls. It made me proud. And a little sad. With just a sprinkle of yearning for the old sols.

"Pepper, you're justifying murder with murder," Rizz argued.

"I'm not saying it's the right thing to do, Rizz," Pepper clarified. "Just presenting all the information we have."

Buzz pursed his lips. "And it's more like justifying a smaller amount of murder with much more murder."

"It's the trolley problem," Pepper said.

Buzz swiveled away. "Eh, I've never been much of a train person."

"I think it's a little more complicated than that, Pepper," Rizz said.

"It is complicated. There's no perfect solution," Pepper explained. "It's a thought experiment."

She exhaled sharply, stood, and grabbed a tablet linked to the hologram monitor in the middle of the table. As she sketched, her finger-drawn diagram appeared before us—a train track running beneath a bridge.

"There are a few different versions of it, but basically, you're on a bridge and see a train coming down the track below." She added a cluster of stick figures. "Fifteen people are tied to the rails, unable to move. However, a man and his son are standing next to you. If you push them off the bridge and onto the track, their combined weight would stop the train, saving the other fifteen people."

Buzz rubbed his chin. "So, we either let the train run over the people on the tracks or drop a fat man and a little boy to stop it—killing two to save fifteen." He shrugged. "Math checks out, no?"

"It's not a math problem," Rizz asserted.

Paul placed a detonator at the head of the table in front of Buzz—a large gray cube with a big, red button sitting atop, protected by a plexiglass shield. Then he pressed a white, coin-shaped key fob into a fitting indent on the front of the device.

Slowly, the key turned—rotating a full three hundred sixty degrees as a white light brightened around its edges.

Click. The glass shield fractured into four perfect diagonal quarters, each retracting smoothly into the cube's interior, leaving the big, red button fully exposed—vulnerable to pushing, punching, and pressing.

The ministry stared at Buzz. He met every gaze.

Then, without a word, he plucked the key from the detonator. The white light vanished. The shield slid back into place, covering the button once more.

A collective held breath released—relief, uncertainty, unease. Buzz was locking up the detonator and throwing away the key.

Then he lifted the round key into the air.

"This side: Use it," he announced. He flipped it around. "This side: Don't."

CHAPTER FORTY-NINE

AND THEN THERE WERE TWO

Buzz flicked the detonator key upward with his thumb. It twisted in the air for what felt like hours—partly because of the heart-stopping tension in the room, but mostly because of Mars's low gravity.

When it finally hit the black table, the coin bounced three times, spun thirteen-and-a-half times, and then fell still.

Everyone leaned in.

"You can't do this." Rizz shot up from his seat.

Buzz gestured vaguely at the room, looking around at everyone. "But the powers that be—the coin flip of truth—say that we must."

"I won't be a part of it," Rizz confirmed. "If you go through with this, that's it. I'm done. I won't continue to be a member of a ministry that okayed this."

Buzz glared at him. "Fine. Have your resignation on this table tomorrow."

Rizz paused, scanning the room for support. "Pepper?"

She looked away.

He exhaled sharply, and then strode toward the door, hesitating and then turning around for one final plea. "Think about the destruction. Think about the loss. Just . . . don't do it."

And then—he was gone.

"We're doing the sensible thing," my father assured. "We're saving lives."

The red countdown timer on the wall hit zero. Immediately, it turned green and reset to five minutes, signaling the AHB was in position to fire at its target—but only for the next three hundred sixtieths-of-a-minute.

The green timer ticked away.

My father turned to me. "Now, here's where you come in." He slid the detonator in front of me. "As a token of our gratitude for your acts of bravery on the battlefield, we'd like to give you the honor of firing the AHB."

My stomach dropped. The chronic indigestion I thought I had under control returned with a vengeance.

"What?"

I had only been a silent observer—until, suddenly, my father wanted me to push the button. Obliterate millions of robots just like that. Who was I to make that call?

There had to be another way. I didn't have a better solution to the trolley problem—but there had to be one. Why were those stick figures tied to a track in the first place? Had they done something wrong, or were they victims? And who were the man and the boy on the bridge? Did they tie the others to the track? Or were they just innocent bystanders?

There wasn't enough information. The trolley problem was an overly simplified depiction of something much more complex. And I knew one thing for sure—

"You can't seriously fire this thing because of a coin flip," I said.

"Don't be naive, Flip," my father scolded, just like he used to, in front of everyone. "We were going to fire it no matter which way the coin landed. That was only to get everyone to make up their minds. And now that it's landed—" he gestured around the room, "—can we all agree this is the right call?"

No one objected.

"I shouldn't be the one to do this," I said, leaning back, hands waving in protest.

"Come on, Flip," my father pressed. "You'd be the *first* person ever to use it."

Every eye in the room was locked on me—some eager, some terrified, most uncertain. Lots of raised eyebrows. A few lips being chewed. Some tongues pressed against cheeks.

The green timer sped through its final minutes.

I don't know why I hesitated. This was my chance—my opportunity to make my father proud. My redemption from all the disappointment. I would finally be someone in his eyes. A man of action. A man of importance. A *man*.

All I had to do was press a button. It's not like I hadn't done it before—I blew up an entire volcano.

But that wasn't a solo operation. I was part of a Space Force unit, and that unit was one of dozens with the same objective. It wasn't all on me. And that wasn't good enough for my father. I wasn't good enough for him. Never was.

If I slammed my hand down on the big red button in front of me, that would all change.

Then again, if I didn't press the button, if I stood up to my father, I would be my own man. That's what he wanted—at least partly, I think—just not how he wanted it. Then again, not pressing it might make me a coward, once again. Then again, pressing it under pressure might too.

Two Flip sides to every detonator coin.

One minute left.

"I can't . . ."

"Yes, you can, Flip," my father urged—his tone more stern than supportive. His hand landed on my back—firm, heavy, guiding me toward the detonator, almost pushing. I glanced around the room, hoping someone would say something, but no one did. My father physically moved my chair closer to the table. Closer to the button. I gripped the edges of my seat, pulling myself deeper into the cushions.

"We're going to use it with or without you," he promised.

My heart raced. Sweat trickled down my temples.

The green digits plunged.

I looked at Pepper, but I couldn't read her face. I didn't know if she wanted me to press it or not. I didn't know if *I* wanted to press it or not.

I was an adult. A war hero. Yet, in front of my father, I still felt like a little boy. When it came to him, it was always two steps forward, one step back.

I had to decide. Push the button. Don't. Just do something. Anything. My father had me immobilized. Unmoving. Undeciding. Unbreathing.

Just make a decision, Flip.

The detonator beeped.

My gaze lowered. A hand was on the button. A much hairier and more wrinkled hand than my own.

I exhaled sharply.

"Goddamn it, Flip," my father huffed, lifting his hand from the detonator.

* * *

Thirty minutes after my father fired the AHB, news coverage from Earth flooded in. Notification pings lit up our feeds:

MAN ON THE MOON NOT TO BLAME, LASER FIRED BY MARS

LASER KILLS MILLIONS IN AN INSTANT—LASER TAG FACILITIES RESPECTFULLY HALT OPERATIONS

23 THINGS TO KNOW ABOUT THE AHB. YOU WON'T BELIEVE #17!

And just like that, the robots surrendered.

Thirty *sols* after my father fired the AHB, more headlines poured in:

NATIONS OF EARTH COLLECTIVE (NEC) SUCCESSFULLY TESTS AHB, FACILITY TO BE BUILT ON MARTIAN MOON PHOBOS

RETRACTION: SPACE LASERS NOT BUILT BY JEWS

FYI: BTW, TBA ETA OF NEC AHB TBD

After the war against the robots ended, the two victorious nations couldn't share their newfound superpower status. Tensions rose, and a whole new conflict began. The former ally of Mars suddenly became our new enemy.

With two AHBs in play, the threat of total devastation loomed. People of the NEC and Mars lived in fear, knowing their lives could be wiped out in an instant if some petty worlds leader had their ego bruised. Still do.

A PSA circulated across Mars featuring a cartoon hermit crab—which made no sense, considering no one on the Red Planet had ever seen one. When the spot first aired, there was a 5000% spike in searches for "shell claw bug thing."

The animation showed the cheerful little crab side-stepping along a beach—until a sudden bright light reflected off its shell. Its eyes bulged. The frame panned to reveal the source—an AHB detonation. An all-consuming, periwinkle explosion expanded at the tip of a thick, violet beam of condensed energy fired from space. It annihilated a sandcastle city.

The cartoon crustacean retreated into its shell as a fierce

shockwave howled around it. When the gust passed, the hermit crab poked its head out of its shell, looked both ways and then straight into the camera—giving a thumbs up with its claw.

Bubble letters bounced onto the screen:

Don't get charred. DROP AND GUARD!

As if scrambling under a desk would offer any protection against an AHB detonation. But the Martian government's white lie eased the public's fears—and kept the consumers buying and purchasing!

Yet not all threats came from hundreds of millions kilometers away.

Some were much closer to home.

CHAPTER FIFTY

NOT ANOTHER STATE FUNERAL

As 2116+ rolled into 2117, things were looking up for Mars—nothing jumpstarts an economy quite like the military-industrial complex. But for some, things stayed exactly the same.

Even after serving in Martian conflicts, clones were still treated as second-class citizens—and so were their children, despite being born naturally and nowhere near Warehouse Five. Everything was separate—schools, neighborhoods, businesses.

The *very serious* divide was based entirely on a *very silly* discrepancy. The divide wasn't biological. It wasn't physical. There was absolutely no way to tell the difference between a clone and an original.

Yet, the divide remained, and Cheddar had had enough.

She launched the clone rights movement—organizing nonviolent strikes, boycotts, and protests. Clones banded together, demanding equal rights under the law.

And some of the more enlightened humans stood with

them—Rizz joined her cause after he had resigned from the Ministry of Mars.

Of course, the movement wasn't without a little pushback—death threats cluttered Cheddar's Chattr account. But it didn't stop her. She kept pushing, spreading her ideology of love and respect, dreaming of a future where humans and clones could live together peacefully.

After my father fired the AHB himself, it felt like he'd knocked me down—stripping away the adult I'd become and leaving the child I used to be, right in front of everyone. If that's what he wanted, then that's exactly what I'd give him: Flip the troublemaker. Flip the rebel. Only this time, it wouldn't be anonymous. It'd be loud, pointed, and public.

I joined Cheddar's cause, hoping to ruffle his feathers.

As well as get clones equal rights and stuff. It was the right thing to do.

The movement culminated in a march on Town Hall. Almost every clone on Mars was in attendance, standing shoulder to shoulder with thousands of open-minded humans. Even some Native Martians surfaced—wrapped in protective clothing—to stand with their fellow oppressed. All packed so tightly not a single blade of grass on the lawn could be seen.

I stood on stage with Rizz, Cheddar, and a dozen other clones, who each stepped up to speak before the massive crowd.

Cheddar gave the final speech. One that would go down in history, even without the—

Zap.

A spade discharged, its energy pulse ripping through the air.

Cheddar ducked. Rizz and I threw ourselves over her, all three of us hiding behind the podium.

Screams of terror. Shouts of confusion. Panic. Shoving. Trampling. People flooding any exit they could find.

"Come on," I said, grabbing Cheddar. Rizz and I shielded her, guiding her off the stage in a crouch.

The frantic crowd nearly bowled us over. We hit the ground and hunkered down, bracing against the tidal waves of bodies surging past.

Slowly, the bumps were fewer and fewer. The fleeing crowd thinned out.

Rizz and I helped Cheddar to her feet.

Pockets came charging through the hysteria, practically tackling people out of his way. Ravi was right behind him, his face drained of color.

"Oh my god . . ." Ravi whispered, staring at us.

We hadn't even had a moment to assess. Blood covered our hands and stained Cheddar's shirt—she'd been shot in the shoulder.

She swayed and we caught her.

I wasn't losing Cheese—I wasn't losing Cheddar, not on the Town Hall lawn. Again.

"We need to get her to the hospital," I said. "Right now."

The four of us carried her across the town square. Before we even reached the hospital entrance, a team of doctors rushed out to meet us, a hovering gurney gliding between them.

We barely had time to lay her down before they whisked her inside. We followed, staying close, but we were shooed away as they hurried into the intensive care wing. All we could do was watch, as Cheddar disappeared through a sliding door.

Left in the waiting room with nothing to do but wait.

Forty-five minutes later, Pepper burst through the entrance, almost running right past us.

"Pepper." Rizz stopped her.

She spun, eyes wild, seeing us for the first time.

We stood from our chairs just as she fell into Rizz's arms.

"Is she alright?" Pepper asked, her voice muffled against his shoulder.

"We don't know," Rizz answered.

Pockets didn't say anything—just wrapped his arms around both of them, joining the hug, and I followed suit.

"Uh . . . Hi," Pepper said.

Ravi was standing awkwardly off to the side—not sure if he should join in, watch, or walk away altogether. With everything happening so fast, I hadn't even introduced him.

I stepped back from the hug. "Sorry—this is Ravi. Ravi, this is Pepper, Rizz, and Pockets." Introducing them by their nicknames suddenly felt weird at our age. "Uh, I guess I should say Pepper, Marco, and Hector. Ravi and I were in the same unit during the war."

"Nice to meet you," Pepper said, shaking his hand. "Thank you for keeping Flip safe out there."

"More like the other way around." Ravi chuckled, moving down the line—shaking hands with Pockets, then Rizz.

All three of them turned to me with surprise. And maybe a little pride?

"So you really did do the things your dad said?" Rizz asked.

I shrugged. "I guess that depends on what he said."

"Hector Martinez?"

A doctor stood outside the sliding doors.

"That's me," Pockets said, shuffling forward slowly, like the Crocs on his feet were heavier than usual, afraid of what he was going to hear.

"Your friend is alright," she said.

We all let out a sigh of relief.

"Do you want to see her?"

Pockets nodded, and we followed the doctor down the hall. Cheddar was already awake when we walked into her sterile hospital room—a white bed surrounded by white machines inside white walls.

"Hey, look who it is," she said. "The whole gang's here."

It had been a lifetime since we were all in the same room together.

Pockets took her hand at her bedside. "How're you feeling?"

"I'm fine. Just nicked me." She glanced at Pockets, then Rizz, then me. "Thanks for coming to my rescue."

It was nice to hear a thank you, but I wasn't expecting it. I rubbed the back of my head, pursed my lips, and gave her a slight nod.

"I don't think I could've handled another state funeral," Pepper said.

"State funeral?" Cheddar raised an eyebrow. "I don't think I'm that important."

"You have no idea," a nurse murmured while checking Cheddar's bedside monitors.

Cheddar turned to them, pausing for half a second before nodding—like she could tell they were a fellow clone without them having to say it.

"Hey, Marco, can I talk to you outside?" Pepper asked.

Rizz gestured for Pepper to lead the way. They were still together, but ever since Rizz resigned from the ministry and Pepper stayed, they had a strict rule of not talking politics. It worked, for the most part. At times when a good friend was almost assassinated, I'm sure it was more difficult.

"Do you have to stay here long?" I asked Cheddar.

"They're keeping me for a couple sols," she told us. "But I know a guy who's pretty good at helping people escape."

We smiled.

After I'd introduced Ravi to Cheddar, the door slid open again. Pepper and Rizz walked back in. And behind them—Freckle.

"I came as soon as I heard," she said.

I choked. "Freckle—"

"I'm not here for you," she cut me off. "I'm here for her." She nodded toward Cheddar.

We stayed until we got kicked out at the end of visiting hours—all seven of my closest friends, in the same room. Together for the first time.

And the last.

CHAPTER FIFTY-ONE

UNLUCKY NUMBERS

On my twenty-eighth birthsol—and Pepper's—May 5, 2117, we were gathered in her and Rizz's apartment. When they had gotten back together, Rizz moved back in, and I took his old place. Between the Olympics and the military, I'd earned enough to afford my own apartment—but those two things also meant that I'd barely spent any time there. Which was fine, because I didn't like living alone.

I'd much rather be crammed on the couch with my friends, watching the same broadcast as everyone else on Mars.

"Two-forty a.m. to two forty-nine a.m.," announced a man in a suit on a soundstage, reading from a small white ball in his hand.

Beside him, a woman in a silky red dress—deep neckline, high leg slit—flashed a dazzling smile and motioned toward a giant spinning sphere filled with hundreds more bouncing white balls, spitting them out one at a time. With red gloves up to her elbows, she reached into a basket underneath, retrieved another ball, and handed it to the man.

"Seven-fifty p.m. to seven fifty-nine p.m.," he read.

Energetic music swelled in the background—upbeat, major key, drum rolls galore—but no one was excited.

The same woman picked another ball from the basket. The man in the suit took it and announced, "Nine-ten p.m. to nine-nineteen p.m."

We were watching the Martian lottery—a lottery no one wanted to win. If your birth time was called, you were forced to join the fight in CHARLIE (Cybernetic Holographic Alternative Reality Lucid Interactive Environment).

The metaverse had finally arrived—after a century of failed startups, tech crashes, and science fiction beating the concept into the ground. Users were plugged in through their cerebral cortex and cerebellum, their bodies kept alive with external life support machines while their minds were uploaded to the simulated world. Inside, the possibilities were endless—socializing, events, virtual experiences. A lot of mini golf.

But the developers behind CHARLIE couldn't agree on how it should be run—mostly how to monetize it. They split into two ideological camps, forming rival virtual societies. Despite the limitless expanse of digital real estate, both sides wanted control of the whole thing. It didn't take long for tension to escalate into a full-scale armed conflict within the metaverse.

Neither Mars nor the NEC had built CHARLIE, but both nations decided to intervene—investing some skin to claim their share of the new frontier, backing opposing sides simply because they were opposing. Citizens were recruited, plugged in, and deployed into the simulated world to join the cyber war.

At first, the hyper-realistic virtual reality world thrilled the gaming community, whose members eagerly enlisted. But few ever returned. Not because of some overused, hokey sci-fi trope—if you die in the virtual world, you die in real life. That wasn't the case. This was real life, not an unoriginal debut novel.

Instead, soldiers inside CHARLIE became so immersed in its vivid, naturalistic environment, that they lost all ability to distinguish the digital world from the physical. When troops were unplugged, their bodies and minds couldn't readjust. Lungs forgot how to breathe. Hearts stopped beating. Brains decayed into mush. Those who *did* survive the disconnection without physical complications were never the same—plagued by flashbacks, insomnia, and an uncontrollable urge to drink heavily and smack their kids around.

Fear and confusion surrounding the war kept others from volunteering. Before long, Mars—and Director Buzz Buchanan—were forced to instate a draft.

Rizz was in his sofa chair, Pepper curled up on his lap. The rest of us—Pockets, Cheddar, and I—were squeezed together on the couch, silent, watching the lottery in tense, nervous anticipation.

"Only a few more left, folks!" the man in the suit teased, oblivious to the mood, trying to inject excitement but only provoking dread.

The bright white smile of the voluptuous woman beside him never wavered. She reached for another tiny white ball, taking it delicately with her elbow-length gloves.

"Five-twenty p.m. to five twenty-nine p.m.," the man announced. A bright graphic of the time slot flashed across the broadcast.

Five more time slots were picked that night.

First ball: Safe.

Second ball: Safe.

Third ball: Safe.

Fourth ball: Safe.

Fifth ball . . .

My jaw dropped.

If I wasn't already sitting, my knees would've buckled. My stomach lurched—I wasn't sure if I was about to puke, shit my pants, or pass out.

And if I was feeling that way . . .

I turned to Pepper. She was ghost-white, staring at the sparkling time slot graphic flying across the broadcast.

"Pepper." Rizz tapped her thigh. No response. "Pepper." He tapped her again. "Pepper. It's alright. You won't have to go. You're part of the ministry. They won't make you go."

Still nothing.

If I'd been born five minutes earlier instead—and hadn't disappointed my father—it'd be my brain going into the simulation, not hers.

But she was born first. And she was the one facing CHARLIE alone. I wasn't the one going to war. Pepper was.

And that was so much worse.

My heart broke. I didn't know what to do. "He's right, Pepper," I said, grasping at any reasoning I could find. "You won't have to go. They wouldn't send a ministry member in there."

"We'll get it all sorted out," Pockets added. "Everything will be fine."

"I'm sure we'll all be here next week, already having forgotten about it," Cheddar said.

Pepper stood, paler than I'd ever seen her.

"I have to go," she said. "The Martian people can't see a ministry member getting let off the hook. It's wrong. I have to serve, the same as everyone else."

She accepted her fate with controlled, quiet resignation—just like her mother. Just like Pepper.

That night, none of us left. It didn't feel right. Even after Pepper and Rizz went to bed, we stayed. Pockets and I let Cheddar take the extra bedroom. He took the couch. I crashed on the floor—which, honestly, was still more comfortable than any night I'd spent in a Spurt Yurt.

Not that it mattered—I still didn't sleep. I don't think any of us slept.

The next morning, we said goodbye to Pepper, trying to make it as normal as possible, like we were going to see her later that sol. And watched her leave the apartment to report for CHARLIE.

Pepper wouldn't let any of us come—didn't want our last memory of her to be the moment she lay down and got wired into the virtual world, her body left behind, motionless.

* * *

Over the next few months, Rizz and I committed ourselves to the countermovement, organizing protests and demonstrations—which we had plenty of experience doing.

We stood at the center of a sit-in protest on the Town Hall lawn—a donut of blankets surrounding us. It reminded me of the time I threw a French Cruller at my father. My rebellion had become a lot more public since then.

"Everyone—all people on the spectrum—are suffering!" I shouted. "We have no business in CHARLIE. Ceasefire!"

"We need to de-escalate the situation with hostile confrontation and antagonizing opposition," Rizz yelled. His rhetoric was . . . slightly more aggressive than mine. "Our pacifist agenda must be achieved at all costs, by whatever means necessary. I don't care who we have to kill, we will have peace!"

I let him take the reins while I checked our sound equipment. Then I spotted Cheddar, Ravi, and Pockets sitting down on the blanket I reserved for them closer to the front.

I popped a squat and joined them, watching Rizz do his thing for a while.

"Room for one more?" a voice asked.

I twisted around. Freckle stood there—at least, I assumed it was Freckle—all wrapped up in fabric from head to toe.

"Hey . . ." was all I managed to get out as I jumped to my feet. "I didn't think you were coming."

"I didn't think I was either," Freckle admitted. "But I recently had an amazing burger at The Gnukka Nook, and when I gave my compliments to the chef, all he talked about was you. I didn't know if I'd be allowed to eat there again if I didn't show up."

I looked at Ravi and nodded my thanks. I might've mentioned Freckle when we were walking along the bottom of the ocean. We had a lot of time to kill.

"I've only heard of *one* blanket being big enough for five people,"

Cheddar said as she stood. "And that didn't end so well for Better Mars. Lucky for us, I brought another one—and it looks like there's a great patch of grass . . ." She scanned the packed lawn without finding a spot. "Somewhere else."

Cheddar kicked Pockets, who was still lounging on the ground, oblivious, and he groaned as he got up to follow her and Ravi to another spot.

An extremely subtle, hardly detectable, silky smooth maneuver leaving Freckle and me alone.

I gestured to the blanket with both hands, semi-bowing in invitation.

It took me a long minute to figure out what to say, so we sat there, watching Jizzy struggle to set up his DJ deck on grass—it was technically my job to monitor the sound equipment, but I had more important things to tend to.

Freckle certainly wasn't going to ease the tension by speaking first. Probably relishing my anguish, leaning back on her hands while I sat curled up, arms wrapped around my legs—for comfort, or protection, or both.

"I have a lot I want to say," I finally told her.

"I could tell from your 'Hey' text before you left," she said.

"Yeah, I don't usually know how to say stuff. So I don't."

"We can sit here and not say anything. That's fine with me."

Normally, I would've taken her up on it—a younger version of me, certainly. But not anymore. She needed to know how I felt. And I needed to say it.

"There was never anything with Pepper. At least, not anything real." I plucked a few blades of grass, tossed them aside. "There was just so much history there. It *seemed* like we were destined to be together, but we weren't. We never were. It was the stuff of stories, not real life. But I was young, and I guess I thought my life was this grand story. A legendary romance. A relatable coming-of-age. A lost hero who finds his way. But my life isn't any of that. It's just life."

I paused, making sure she felt free to hop in at any time. She didn't hop in.

"You might not have been my first love. But you were my second. And I don't know, that feels like it means even more. The second time around, you have a better idea of what it's supposed to be."

Freckle scoffed. "So now that Pepper's gone, you're coming crawling back to me?"

"No. It's not like that. I've felt this way for a long time. I wanted to tell you all this before I left for Earth. And I've been texting you ever since I got back, even when you don't respond."

"You can't say there were never feelings there."

I wished I could read her face, but the clothing hid everything.

"You're right," I admitted, picking at more grass. "There were. I loved her. I still love her—as a best friend. As a sister. I think I just got those feelings confused when I was younger. Her too. But Pepper was always meant to be with Rizz—not me. She knows that. I know that. And I'm good with that."

Freckle eyed me as best she could with her empty eye sockets beneath thick fabric. "Oh, really? So suddenly you're over it? Now that Pepper's gone? Now that she's out of the picture?"

I let go of my knees. "She's not 'out of the picture.' She's not 'gone.' She's gonna come back."

She paused. "Sorry," she said quietly. "I didn't mean it like that."

"It's okay."

Her guard was dropping, slowly.

She tried to lighten the mood. "You have to stop texting me if I'm not responding. It's getting embarrassing."

"I guess that means you'll have to start responding. You don't want to embarrass me."

She bumped her shoulder against mine, and we smiled at each other—at least, I hoped she was smiling. And that smile lingered for a sixtieth-of-a-minute longer than was typical for friends—especially the kind who dated, broke up, didn't speak, tried again, imploded again, and slowly reassembled something like friendship over the course of eight years.

"Flip!" Rizz's voice shattered our moment. He pointed straight at me. Everyone's eyes followed. "The son of the director stands with us! Say it with me: Peace and love, or death! Peace and love, or death!"

The crowd rose, chanting. After a moment, so did we.

As I looked around—some eyes still locked on me—it dawned on me: I *was* the son of the director. I had direct access to the man in charge. And all I'd done was help organize a concert on a patch of grass.

My father had been making the decisions from the beginning. He had set everything in motion. And we let him—we handed him the wheel and sat back, willing passengers at the mercy of his reckless driving.

Madison Chen tried to steady the ship, and it got her killed. Cliff was dead. My mom was dead. Cheese was dead.

Pepper wouldn't join them.

Freckle's voice was distant. "Flip, where are—"

Before I realized what I was doing, I was suddenly at the center of the donut, and every person in attendance was looking at me, waiting for me to say something.

I gulped. But everything I had done prepared me for this moment. Everything had led me there. Whether I wanted to be there or not, I needed to be.

"We're yelling into a void," I started. "These protests are necessary. They're important. But we can chant and scream all we want—it won't change anything. It won't change policy. It won't change Buzz Buchanan's mind. It won't change my father."

I cleared my throat, raising my voice to a climax, ending with the theatrical gravitas I'd learned from the man himself. "Words are great. Action is better. We need to change his mind for him. March on Town Hall. Go into that boardroom and demand an end to the fight in CHARLIE. Demand progress. Demand different!"

I paused for a rousing round of applause and cheering.

"And what better time than now? Town Hall is right there. We're here. We're ready. The claws are coming out. Our gaskets are primed to blow. Lids are gonna be flipped!"

CHAPTER FIFTY-TWO

DRUNK ADULTS

I stood outside the Town Hall boardroom, an army of civilly disobedient Martians packed into the hallway behind me. Six of them tipped a vending machine, lifting it to ram the door, but I waved them off.

My eyes fell on the keypad. I typed in 05-05-2089. My birthsol.

The lock clicked. The door opened. My father hadn't changed the code.

I looked to Freckle, Ravi, Pockets, and Cheddar at the front of the crowd—each offering silent support. Rizz met my eyes. Then—a nod.

I was going in alone.

Inside, my father flinched in his seat, startled as I stormed in. Maybe he was shocked to see *anyone* come in—he was alone too. And that shocked me, making *me* flinch.

I hesitated, mid-ambush. "Where is everybody?"

"After the NEC developed a hyperbeam so quickly," my father explained, "I knew the ministry had been infiltrated by spies. I couldn't trust any of them." He swiveled in his chair. "Listen, now's not really a good time." He motioned to the six live feeds projected on the back wall—bodycam footage of something indiscernible, maybe an operation of some kind.

I didn't care. It wasn't important. I had hundreds of Martians behind me, and they were depending on me to get shit done. Nothing was going to interrupt this confrontation. It felt like my whole life had been building to this moment. It was happening whether it was a good time for him or not.

"It doesn't matter." I took a deep breath, gearing up to yell, the veins in my forehead already pulsing, teeth clenching—

But my father held up a hand, cutting me off. "I heard about your girlfriend."

"She's not—" I exhaled sharply. "She's like a sister to me."

"You're dating your sister?"

"We're not dating. And you know she's not my biological sister." I held my hand to my forehead and closed my eyes, trying to remain calm. "And things are kinda sorta looking like I might've sorta kinda patched things up with Freckle."

"Right, that Cavernese girl with the cyst."

"It's benign! We got it checked out—" I held out both hands, physically stopping him from derailing the conversation further. "So you know Pepper got drafted into your pointless war?"

"It's a shame," my father said apathetically, standing to refill his glass of red malt from the bar cart in the corner. "She's a valuable ministry member. But we can't make any exceptions. I have a duty to do what's right for the people, and so does she."

"What's right for the Martian people?" I scowled. "Are you kidding me? You really believe that's what you've been doing?"

He poured me a glass of vodka and handed it to me without a word.

"Maybe I haven't been perfect," he said, eyes narrowed, "but I'd like to see anyone else do a better job."

"Low bar to meet!" I spat. "Your whole reign's been mistake after mistake after mistake." Ugh, I sounded like *him*. "Mistakes that have gotten people killed. Just because you've done a few things right doesn't mean you're not doing terrible things too."

My father leaned back in his seat at the head of the table. "I know how you feel about what I've done," he said flatly. He waved his hands condescendingly, spilling a little of his drink. "I've seen your little demonstrations. Complaining and criticizing as loudly as you can, when you kids have absolutely no idea what you're talking about."

I was too charged to sit. "At least we're trying to do the right thing!"

"You don't think I'm trying?" my father barked. "I've been trying this whole time. And I've actually been doing it. Look at this country. Look at the planet you live on."

He stood up, strutting over to loom over me, trying to play the height card. But he didn't have it anymore—he was sixty-six, and he was shrinking.

I stared back at him, unfazed. "Look at what our planet has done. Look at what *you've* done."

"We would all be dead," he said, spreading his arms wide, gesturing vaguely to everything around us. "We wouldn't have this planet, this life, if I didn't do the things that I did—if I didn't do the things everyone *wanted* me to do. The worlds are harsh, and people know that. Sometimes you have to get your hands a little dirty to make sure you get the best of the best. You can't have one without the other. You gotta take both or nothing at all."

He took a smug sip from his glass. I set mine down on the table—to feel holier-than-thou while I told thou how unholy thou was.

"Don't act like you didn't have a choice," I said. "You had options. You were there at the beginning. You had a clean slate—the chance to build something totally new, from the ground up. Something better than everything that came before it."

He returned to his seat, placing his hands on the table. "If I recall correctly, so were you. You could've done something, but you didn't. That's the thing with people these sols—they don't want to get their hands dirty. They don't want to be bothered. They just want someone else to handle it, someone else to blame. But me? I'm the one who handles it. I built this place. You happily lived in it. I gave you nothing but opportunities and resources. You shat on them. I did something. You didn't."

I picked up my drink and downed it, wiping my mouth with my arm. "You wouldn't *let* me do something. Your ego couldn't take it. You've always hoarded power over me. You've hoarded power over everyone."

My father shrugged, holding up his hands. "I've been sitting right here, Flip." He swiveled in his chair, side to side. "Why haven't you taken it? You can't blame me for all your problems, pal. You're a grown-ass adult. That responsibility falls on you."

"Take some fucking accountability!" I yelled.

He tilted his head and raised an eyebrow—shouting my own words back at me without saying a thing.

And he was right.

For most of my life, I let him and everyone else control me, control Mars, while I stood back and watched, criticizing without ever stepping in to change anything myself.

But I had changed things.

Maybe I hadn't been in the spotlight, but my fingerprints were all over Martian history. I inspired Martian independence. I discovered aliens. I helped the clones escape. I warned my father about an incoming army—on two different occasions. I beat the robots at the Olympics. I blew up a *fucking* volcano.

"Just because my name isn't in the headlines doesn't mean I haven't done shit." I met his stare. "I'm not like you. I don't care about fame. I don't care about power. I'm proud of who I've become—even if I end up forgotten. Because we all do eventually. We're all just blips."

I stepped toward him. "I might not have been doing anything in your eyes . . ." I pulled out a chair and took a seat at the table. "But I'm doing something now."

He leaned forward, smirking. "And what's that, exactly? More yelling at your big bad dad?"

I leaned in too. "I'm running for director."

He chuckled, settling back in his seat and taking a sip. "You'll just come in second like always."

"At least I'll try." I sat up straighter, resting my hands on the armrests. "That's the thing about first and second. In second, you've always got something to reach for. You're always trying to do better. In first? You're just clinging to the top, desperately holding on, pushing everyone else down."

We sat in silence for a moment, both sipping our drinks, each of us trying to come up with one last quip. Not one that would solve anything or win the argument—just something catchy and cutting, soundbite-worthy.

Neither of us came up with anything.

"Well, are we having another drink?" I asked.

My father stood and grabbed our empty glasses to refill our drinks. He handed one to me, then sat back down and raised his in a casual toast before taking a sip.

He stared off into space. "You know, there was a time when I thought I knew everything too. I was a wise guy. Thought I had it all figured out. And everyone says that as you get older, you get wiser—so I figured by this age, I'd be the smartest guy on Mars. But the older I get, the more I realize I never knew as much as I thought I did. And I probably still don't."

I took a sip. "I think that realization comes from a lifetime of getting wiser."

My father cocked his head. "You might be right."

"Mars could've used that epiphany a long time ago. Yet here we are—on a planet consumed by spite, regret, and disillusion."

At the same time, we both said, "And it's all your fault."

Then we leaned back in our chairs and took a drink.

"Arriving on the surface of Phobos," said one of the operatives in the grainy bodycam feeds playing on the back wall, drawing my attention. The lighting was dim, the image hard to make out. "Successful landing. All agents accounted for. Approaching enemy AHB."

"What is this?" I asked my father.

He put his finger to his lips, leaning forward to watch.

On video, the strike team crept toward a short, metallic facility. They peered through the windows but only saw darkness.

"Lights are off. Appears to be unmanned," reported the commander in the main feed.

My father's heart looked like it was beating out of his chest. He nervously chewed the inside of his lip and picked at the skin around his fingers.

"Is this what I think it is?" I asked.

Without taking his eyes off the feed, he explained, "I don't know if the interstellar program will work. If they beat us to another planet, we have to maintain our dominance another way."

The operatives exchanged glances, communicating with sharp hand signals.

"Checking around back," said the agent in charge.

As the squad moved into position, I caught a glimpse of shadows in the corner of one of the feeds. A few enemy BOARs—Beam Operations Antimatter Regiment—springing up from a nearby crater. At least, I thought it was.

It was.

After ripping the agents' propulsion packs clean off—the very packs keeping them anchored to the moon's surface—the BOARs hurled each of them off the floating rock. With Phobos's relatively non-existent gravitational pull, all it took was a gentle fling for their bodies to drift away, untethered, into outer space.

"Mayday! Mayday! All agents compromised. Mayday! May—"

The feed cut.

One by one, the other five feeds followed. The agents were never seen again. More than likely, all six of them sailed into Martian orbit—lifeless bodies, tracing a silent path around the Red Planet.

Still circling to this very sol. And will be until the end of time.

My father's head dropped into his hands, elbows on the table.

"Were you trying to take out the NEC AHB?" I asked.

He nodded, slowly, without lifting his head from his palms.

The mission had failed. And it wouldn't stay a secret for long.

There used to be a thirty-minute delay between Earth and Mars communications. But a new method for real-time interaction had recently been developed—something about spatially distorted bubbles transmitting signals faster than lightspeed. Whatever the science, the result was the same:

The NEC would know at the exact moment we did.

"They're gonna kill us," I said.

My father nodded again, still buried in his hands.

CHAPTER FIFTY-THREE

THE APPLE AND THE TREE

My father rubbed his face with both palms, then slapped his hands against his thighs and pushed himself up to stand. He walked over to a side table in the boardroom and pressed his thumb to a fingerprint scanner. A drawer popped open, and he pulled out the AHB detonator and the circular key. He brought them both to the table and set them down beside each other as he dropped back into his seat.

"You can't," I told him.

"Flip, we can talk more later," he said. "You don't have to be here for this."

I checked the massive red countdown timer on the back wall—ticking away the seconds until the Martian AHB would be in position to fire on the NEC. Just below it, a smaller timer marked when the NEC's AHB could fire on the four Martian biospheres.

Of course, by some statistically impossible twist of fate, at that precise moment, the two timers were synced—down to the second.

The forces of the universe manufacturing a contrived, melodramatic sense of suspense, that, under any other circumstance, would've had me rolling my eyes instead of raising my blood pressure, drenching me in a cold sweat, and sparking a lightning storm of anxiety in my gut.

Five minutes.

"You're making a huge mistake," I said, trying to stay calm. "Another one."

"I'm saving the Martian people from oblivion."

"You're *guaranteeing* oblivion," I shot back. "We don't know where their AHB detonator is. They could have more than one. Maybe you hit the perfect target. Maybe you wipe out every detonator and every NEC official. But more likely than not, the sixtieth-of-a-minute you fire that weapon, they'll fire right back."

He picked up the circular key and pressed it into the front of the gray box. Its edges lit up. The glass shield retracted. The detonator was primed.

"You're naive to think we can just sit here and hope they do nothing," he said.

Four minutes.

"You'll go down in history as the man who sent humanity back to the Stone Age," I said.

"This is your problem, Flip," he said, voice rising. "You're too afraid to make the hard choice. Too afraid to take action. We don't know what'll happen if I press the button, and we don't know what'll happen if I don't. Sometimes you don't get the luxury of certainty. And you can't just sit and watch, waiting to pop in after the fact so you can say what was right or wrong."

He was going to press the button, and I wasn't going to convince him otherwise. I had to take the option away from him.

My eyes shifted from the detonator to my father to the timer.

Three minutes.

"I'm saying this is wrong right now," I told him.

I lunged for it.

My fingers grazed the side of the detonator—barely—before my father snatched it, lightning-quick, and held it out at arm's length. He moved around the table, keeping it behind him, his eyes locked on mine.

"I'm glad you're finally trying to make moves, kid," my father said. "But this isn't your moment. Don't try that again."

Two minutes.

"I *will* try it again." I stood from the table and slowly stepped around it, closing the distance between us. "It's like I said—when you're not at the top, there's always something to reach for. So I will keep trying. I will keep coming. I will keep reaching. While you're busy playing keep-away."

He backed up a step as I approached.

One minute.

"I've been at the top my whole life," my father said. "I've kept people away. I've done it. I like my chances."

"Just because you've never had to struggle doesn't mean you never will."

Time was running out. I made one final plea.

"Don't press that button."

Both timers hit zero. A soft ding echoed through the boardroom—the AHBs were in position. The countdowns reset to five minutes, the numbers turned green, and they ticked down once again.

My father lowered the detonator in front of him, eyes locked on me. "It has to be done, Flip."

He slammed his hand down.

But it struck plexiglass. In the split-second I had my hand on the detonator, I'd plucked the circular key from the gray box. And with his eyes fixed on me the entire time, my father never noticed the circular light fade away, never saw the glass shield quietly return to cover the button.

The device was deactivated.

Confused, he looked down at the detonator—then snapped his eyes to me. "Give me the key."

There was no way I'd willingly hand it over. He'd have to tear it from me. "I won't let you do this."

Four minutes.

"The longer we wait, the more likely we'll die," he said, trying to reason with me. "They're going to fire their laser and kill us all."

"They won't."

"I have to protect us."

"You only want to protect yourself."

My father darted around the black table, but I sprinted the other way, both of us circling in a high-stakes game of tag. He moved clockwise. I countered. He reversed. I matched him step for step.

Three minutes.

We paused, studying each other, trying to guess the next move. I smirked. "I remember playing this exact game with Pepper when we were ten. And you yelled at me to quit it—called me an embarrassment, a disappointment. Right in front of my best friend." I gestured vaguely at the room. "Now look at you. A little hypocritical, don't you think?"

Two minutes.

My father dove across the table and tackled me to the ground, landing on top of me. He clawed for the key, but I twisted and jerked my arm away, dodging his grasp again and again.

"Give it to me," he barked.

"No!" I shouted back, wrestling away as best I could.

"They're going to kill us all!"

"No one has to die!"

One minute.

He caught my wrist and pushed it to the floor, holding it down. With his other hand, he pried at my closed fist.

I tried to force him off with my free arm, but he didn't budge.

He peeled back two of my fingers. The edge of the key poked out of my grip. He started lifting a third.

Thirty sixtieths-of-a-minute.

I was fighting a losing battle. There was only one thing I could think to do.

Grunting through clenched teeth, I said, "History . . . is best served . . . by those . . . who swallow their pride."

With my free hand, I snatched the key from my loosening grip and shoved it into my mouth.

Ten sixtieths-of-a-minute.

"Flip." My father stiffened. "Don't."

I swallowed it.

Beep. The timers hit zero.

No one had fired their AHB.

For a moment, neither of us moved. Not a blink. Not a twitch. Not a word.

Then I exhaled.

"Look at that," I said, breathless. "We're still alive."

My father got off of me, but I stayed on the floor, letting out a huge exhale.

He poured himself another red malt from the bar cart. "We got lucky."

I pushed myself up, brushing myself off. "Luck had nothing to do with it. That was me."

I stepped toward him, each step steadier than the last. "It might not have been the way you wanted it, but I *have* made something of myself." I took one more step, and for once, I towered over *him*. "And I'm done trying to prove it to you."

I shook my head and made my way to the door.

"You have," my father said quietly.

I stopped—but didn't turn around.

"You have no idea how much I've enjoyed watching you grow up," he said. "I push you so hard because that's how I was raised. That's all I know. I saw your potential, and all I wanted to give you were the tools to build something better for yourself."

I heard the clink of his glass as he took a sip behind me.

"Your life is my life," he added. "*You* are my legacy. I wasn't going to fire that laser to protect myself. It was to protect *you*."

His voice came closer. "Do you know why you were in the second wave of the Earth invasion? I was so proud of you for enlisting—but I wasn't going to lose you. You're the only family I have. I knew the first wave would be slaughtered, so I made sure you were in the second. I was trying to keep you safe."

"What?" I said, spinning around to face him. He stood in front of me. No posturing, no bravado—just him.

"I've done a lot of things," he went on. "Made my share of mistakes. And yeah, maybe some of them were self-serving—I'll admit that. But a lot of it's been for you. I manufactured the clones to rebuild the colony because I couldn't bear the thought of you suffocating or freezing or dying of thirst. I sent you into the Cavernese tunnels to toughen you up because the worlds are unfriendly and unfair. I tried to give you the best life possible, the most resources in Better Mars. Everything I've done was for you."

I grimaced. "Now you're putting all of this on me."

My father sighed. "That's not what I'm trying to do. I'm trying to explain." He motioned to the table, inviting me to sit down again.

I stayed standing.

"I know you're upset about Pepper," he said, placing his hands gently on my shoulders. "But would you rather it was you getting hooked up to those machines?"

I didn't answer.

"I was never going to let that happen, Flip. You were never going to be drafted."

I furrowed my brow.

"Your birth time slot wasn't even in the lottery," he said quietly. "I had it removed."

Every emotion fought for the spotlight—confusion, hatred, gratitude, grief, guilt, relief, bitterness. On one hand, my father had ensured I'd never be drafted. On the other, he'd only saved me—instead of ending the war altogether. And by pulling my white ball, he'd increased the odds—even if only slightly—that Pepper would be drafted alone and never come back.

Which is exactly what happened. Maybe Pepper would've been drafted anyway. But maybe, if my father hadn't meddled, neither of us would've ended up in CHARLIE.

But I was alive. My brain wasn't being turned into mush. And that was because of him.

"We should've never gotten involved in this war in the first place," I said.

"Maybe," he replied. "But, then again, maybe things would've been a lot worse if we weren't. I control the things I can, and I always make sure those things keep you safe."

"You've only ever looked at me with disappointment."

"That's not disappointment," he told me. "That's fear. Fear I'll let you down. Fear I won't give you everything I can."

It was a lot—an overwhelming emotional bombshell, a clarifying reveal that was more confusing than heartwarming. In the moment, I didn't know how to feel. Tosol, I still don't. My relationship with my father will take a lifetime to unpack—as well as a renowned therapist and a cocktail of mental health medications.

If I had a prescription . . .

"This isn't going to end in a hug and an 'I love you,'" I assured him.

"You never expected it from me," he said. "So I won't expect it from you."

He held out his hand.

The extended olive branch lingered between us. I wasn't sure if I wanted to reject it or return it with one of my own. But he had just revealed he'd saved my life—on more than one occasion. And I had just saved his. And, arguably, all of Mars.

Then again, you could say the same about some of the things *he'd* done. The ends might not have justified the means—but I couldn't deny the ends his means had achieved.

I shook his hand.

It didn't feel like an apology. Or forgiveness. It didn't feel like redemption or acceptance. As we held each other's gaze, I didn't know what it felt like.

"Let me know when you pass that key," he said.

CHAPTER FIFTY-FOUR

BAR TRIVIA

Nobody would ever know what happened between my father and me, how close humanity came to complete annihilation. It would only cause panic—though, if someone happened to publish a salacious, tell-all, hit piece a year or so after the fact, I think it would be fine.

Even I didn't have time to properly replay my wrestling match with my father—no internal slow-motion recap with critical analysis and negative self-talk commentary—because I announced my directorial campaign to my crowd of supporters as soon as I left the boardroom. The election was only months away, in 2118+, and there was no time to waste.

But a week later, Pepper was officially relieved from active duty. Good news—except she was deemed too dangerous to unplug from CHARLIE. There was a high probability her brain would fail to regulate essential bodily functions if she was removed.

Military medical personnel transferred her to a facility entirely devoted to keeping veterans like her alive—bodies in beds, minds still trapped inside the virtual world. They'd live out full lifetimes, but never return to reality—eventually, forgetting it altogether.

She lay motionless in a row of a dozen beds, each patient tethered to a web of machines—in a coma, or something like it.

It was the first time I'd seen her since I watched her walk out her apartment door.

Rizz sat beside her, slouched in a chair. When he saw me, he held up a finger—*give me a sec*—and typed something into a monitor in front of him before standing to say hello.

"Hey man," he said, pulling me in for a hug. "She's a little forgetful. Not quite herself. Just a heads-up. But she'll still love to hear from you. I'll let you two talk. Take as much time as you need."

He left the room, and I took his chair.

The machine he'd been using was designed to let people on the outside—in the real world—communicate with patients inside CHARLIE. Whatever I typed on the monitor would be transmitted directly into Pepper's brain. I wasn't sure whether she heard a voice, saw words, or what—but it worked. She could respond with her own text.

Me:	Hey Pepper! It's Flip. How are you? I miss you.
Pepper:	Flip! Oh my god. I miss you too!
Me:	How's it going? Are you okay?
Pepper:	Hanging in. Everyone's coping the best way they know how.
	I probably drink too much. Picked up smoking too.
Me:	Is that stuff even bad for you in there?
Pepper:	In where?
Me:	CHARLIE.
Pepper:	Oh.
	I don't know.
Me:	It kind of feels like we're talking in Flipper Code.
Pepper:	Five soft thuds. Four loud thuds. Two soft thuds.
Me:	Ten soft stomps. One loud stomp. Three loud stomps. Two soft stomps.
Pepper:	Haha good one.

I missed her laugh. It wasn't the same without the audio.

I typed in all caps, throwing in as many exclamation points as I could, hoping the sheer force of my transcribed shouting might somehow jolt her awake.

Me: PEPPER!!!!!!!!! GET UP!!!!!!!!!!!!
COME BACK TO REALITY!!!!!!!!!!!!

Nothing.

Repeatedly pressing the up-arrow key didn't wake her either. Neither did a line of carets. They just confused her.

Worth a shot.

Pepper: I actually have to go.
They're calling me over for trivia.

Patients tended to improve—at least, regress less rapidly—if they regularly exercised their hippocampus and other parts of their temporal lobe by challenging their memory, recalling facts and dates. So, every veteran in CHARLIE was prescribed a steady regimen of bar trivia at least every other hour.

I'd talk to Pepper another time. I had a date with Freckle anyway, and cancelling because of anything Pepper-related wouldn't be the best way to kick off our rekindling.

But when I stood to leave, there she was—Freckle, watching quietly from the doorway.

"Oh—hey, I was just leaving to meet you," I said.

"It's okay," she replied. "I was already on the surface handling some trade negotiations when I heard." She pulled up a chair next to mine. "We can stay here however long you like."

The two of us sat in silence by Pepper's bedside. Freckle reached over and took my hand.

* * *

At first, Pepper's cognitive functions noticeably improved. She seemed like herself again, recalling things with ease. It was nice to create a few more good memories with her—even if she'd soon forget them.

Sometimes, we just played trivia together. While she sat in a virtual bar, she relayed the host's questions to me in real time. We didn't usually do very well, but our best category was always 2090s to present.

Pepper:	Next question: What animal's meat was the main food source of the Native Martian peoples in the Pre-Hectorian era?
Me:	Haha no way they named an era after Pockets!
Pepper:	I guess so! Gnukka right?
Me:	You got it.
Pepper:	Okay. We're rolling now. Next question: Before clones of Paul Kingsley attacked the biosphere, one of them hosted an orientation video covering all aspects of Mars, including the difference of gravity between Earth and Mars. How much would a 100-kilogram person on Mars weigh on Earth?
Me:	Damn. Do you know this? I know my Crocs are way heavier than the shoes on Earth so would that make a person heavier or lighter?
Pepper:	That would mean people weigh more on Earth, right?
Me:	That sounds right? Must be something like 150 kilograms.
Pepper:	Oh, we were so off. It's 260 kilograms.
Me:	260??? That's insane! I should've paid more attention.

Pepper: Haha I think we were a little preoccupied with the ride.
Here we go. Last question: How old was Pluto the donkey when she was attacked and killed by a warring Earth nation?

Me: Not old enough. Is that a viable answer?

Pepper: Haha I think they're looking for a number.

Me: I don't know. She was always here. Ever since we were kids. Maybe 31? 32?

Pepper: 44! Damn.

Me: Whoa. I didn't know donkeys could live that long.

Pepper: Me either.
I guess 6 out of 10 isn't so bad.

Almost thirty years—the span of our entire lifetimes, everything we had ever experienced, everything we'd lived through—boiled down to ten trivia questions.

And we only got six of them right.

* * *

I visited Pepper at least once a sol, and most sols, Freckle joined me. Though Pepper seemed to get better—thanks to the endless hours of bar trivia—it was still only a matter of time. She started to fade. And after a month, her regression accelerated.

Me: I've been meaning to tell you—I'm actually campaigning to be the Director of Mars. The election is only a few months away, but we're ramping things up fast.
I'm already ahead in the polls. I'm BEATING the one and only Buzz Buchanan.

Pepper: Oh my gosh. That's incredible. What's your slogan?

Me: Since I'm going up against my father, I went with "Vote practical, vote prodigal."
Like the prodigal son?

Pepper:	I don't think that means what you think it means.
Me:	I guess I should've looked it up before we made the signs.
Pepper:	Do you have a platform?
Me:	Haha platforms! Cheese would be proud.
Pepper:	What?
Me:	Cheese. One of our best friends from when we were kids?
Pepper:	You mean Cheddar?

I didn't want her to spiral—wondering whether she forgot Cheese, whether she was forgetting other friends, whether I was upset that she forgot, whether—

I didn't want to spiral either—wondering whether she was spiraling, whether I should be upset that she forgot Cheese, whether she would forget me, whether—

Nope. Not doing that.

I moved on. Quickly.

Me:	Yeah. Cheddar. Sorry. I'm just being dumb. My platform is kind of the everysol guy. Nobody really cares who our politicians are or where Mars stands in the worlds order. People just want a better life—more freedom, financial stability, safety. Less worry. I'm not trying to be powerful. I'm not trying to be famous. I'm just trying.
Pepper:	I love it.
Me:	Thanks. Cheddar and Pockets are helping me with the campaign.
Pepper:	That's amazing, Flip. I'm really proud of you. I wish I could give you a hug.
Me:	I wish I could give you a hug too.
Pepper:	My mom better keep an eye on you. You're coming for her job!

She didn't remember her mother dying. And she probably thought her dad was still alive too.

I typed and deleted a dozen different responses. I didn't know how to tell her.

After erasing my thirteenth message, I realized there was no point. It would only upset her. And then she'd forget all over again.

At least she wasn't mourning them anymore.

Pepper:	Flip? Hello?
Me:	Sorry. Went to grab another coffee. I'll tell your mom to watch out!

* * *

A few sols later, doctors gave her one last week before she'd forget everything—and everyone—she ever knew. Before that happened, Rizz made a decision: he was going to plug himself into CHARLIE and join Pepper in the virtual world.

He'd forget us too, eventually. But the two of them would be together, in a simulated reality that would become their only reality.

That morning, Cheddar, Pockets, and Freckle came with me to the facility to say goodbye. We took turns hugging Rizz, tears in our eyes.

"I'm not dying," he reminded us.

He wasn't. And neither was Pepper. But the people we knew were.

They'd have a life—I just wouldn't be part of it. Which, I guess, happens to most friends eventually. I just didn't think it would happen to us. And I didn't think it would be so final.

"I'm gonna miss you so much," I said.

"I'm gonna miss you too, Flip-Flop."

Maybe. But it wouldn't be for long. Once he forgot me completely, it'd be like I never existed.

"You don't have to go," I told him.

"I didn't stick around when she lost her mom," Rizz said. "And I'm not going to make the same mistake again."

I nodded. "Take care of each other in there."

"You know I will."

He lay down on the bed beside Pepper, gently taking her limp hand in his and weaving his fingers through hers. Doctors inserted wires into the back of his skull and slipped IVs into his veins. He gave us one last shiny white smile.

Then he fell asleep.

It was his sacrifice to make—not mine. Not for Pepper. The two of them were always meant to be together. And whether in reality or a simulation, they always would be.

Through blurry, watery vision, I typed my last messages to Pepper.

> Me: Hey Pepper! We'll all miss you so much.
> *I'll* miss you so much.
> Rizz told me to tell Two-Shoes that he was on his way.

She never replied. She was already gone.

Outside Warehouse Five, she had once promised she'd never forget me. And before I left for Better Mars, she promised again.

My best friend broke her promise.

Saying goodbye was harder than I imagined. I thought I was prepared. I thought I'd said goodbye gradually, over time. But there was still a part of me that hoped that one of my desperate tears would trickle down my face, drip onto her motionless body, and magically snap her out of her false reality. Then she'd blink, spring up, and throw her arms around me as all her memories came rushing back in a flash.

It never happened. Not for lack of trying. Not for lack of crying.

I pulled out our shared snow globe—the one she'd stolen for me twenty years earlier. It had been everywhere. All four biospheres, Warehouse Five, the Native Martian tunnels, outer space, Earth, the bottom of the ocean—and it had survived it all.

I placed it on her bedside table, handing it back for the last time. Then I typed one final message in Flipper Code:

Me: I don't know if you'll ever see this.
I don't know if you've seen any of my last few messages.
I guess this is more for me than it is for you.
You've always been there for me. I can't think of a time when you weren't in my life.
You're my friend, you're my family, and you're so much more. In my happiest moments, all my favorite memories, you were there.
I loved Two-Shoes. I fell in love with Pepper. And I will miss you for the rest of my life.

I let one last magical tear fall.

No luck.

I stood from her bedside, sniffling.

Pockets handed me a phyco, then gave one to Cheddar and Freckle. "Plankton Punch for Pepper," he said. "And for Rizz, I think we need to shotgun it."

That got a chuckle out of me. Pepper and Rizz wouldn't have had it any other way.

We punctured the cans and held them together in a circle.

"To Rizz and Pepper," I said.

"To Rizz and Pepper," they echoed.

And we chugged—a toast to our two best friends.

CHAPTER FIFTY-FIVE

THE SECOND SECOND WORLD

After saying goodbye to Rizz and Pepper, I didn't have time to process any of it—I had a rally that afternoon. Freckle and my two campaign managers walked with me to the Town Hall lawn, where a stage was set up—in the same spot it had been so many times before.

"You're gonna be great," Freckle said in the wing.

"I can't wait to see your dad lose," Pockets added.

"You've united so many different people," Cheddar said. "I don't think anyone else could've done that."

I smiled. "I think there's at least one other person."

Then I walked onstage and up to the podium. Before I said a word, I looked out at the crowd, letting the moment sink in. I'd been a part of the audience so many times—it felt strange to be the one on stage. Our campaign had worked. We were so far ahead in the polls, it was virtually impossible for us to lose.

I was going to be the Director of Mars. Number one.

And my father would be nobody.

I looked past the crowd, across the lawn, and saw him—standing on his own rally stage. And my stomach was calm. That's when I knew I'd made the right decision.

"Hi," I said to the sea of people. "I'm truly honored to be standing here tosol. We've come so far in such a short time. We might not be perfect, but I'm proud to be a Martian. I'm proud of our home."

Though, without Rizz, Pepper, or my mom, Mars didn't feel much like home anymore. And it didn't feel right leading a place I didn't truly belong to.

"This was not an easy decision. But I know it's the right one. Because this race was never about me—it was about us. About humans, clones, and Natives alike. It was about Martians. And I'm overwhelmed by how many of you trust me to represent this planet."

I think I could've done it. Maybe not the best director, but not the worst—decent. But I didn't want to. I didn't want to be my father. I wasn't chasing first anymore—not power, not fame, not legacy. That's not what my blip is about. That's not me. I never wanted to be Director—the only reason I ran was to make sure my father lost.

"But I think there's someone better suited for this responsibility. Someone I trust, admire—and someone you will too." I cleared my throat. "It is with a heavy heart that I am dropping out of the race."

Gasps. Murmurs. Flashing cameras.

There was one other person who could unify all Martians—maybe even more than I could. Beloved by clones, Native Martians, and humans—at least, the humans who weren't Buzz Buchanan supporters.

"That's why I'm proud to throw my full support behind Cheddar. I've seen firsthand her integrity, her resilience, and her commitment to justice—rescuing clones through the Native Martian tunnels, standing up for the rights of so many, refusing to back down when her life was on the line. She's the leader Mars deserves. So let's stand together—behind Cheddar—and let's finish what we started. Thank you."

Cheddar walked onto the stage to a roar of applause. We shook hands at the podium, and I stepped aside—gladly. I knew she would take care of Mars better than anyone.

Freckle and I said goodbye to Pockets in the wing, and then we went home.

I'm not sure we said a single word on the walk. Freckle hung out at my place for a while, too, and I don't remember much conversation happening then either. But I was glad she stayed.

Suddenly, I had the space to unpack everything—Rizz and Pepper, the campaign, my showdown with my father. It would've been better to give each thing its own time, but once my compartmentalized mind starts introspecting, all the compartments come sliding out.

I poured myself a glass and sank into the sofa chair—just like my father used to, night after night when I was growing up.

And just like that, I spiraled into an endless loop of rabbit holes.

Rabbit:	I won't become my father.
Hole:	Who do I want to become?
Rabbit:	Politicians are the worst. I'm not a politician. But sometimes stepping up is necessary.
Hole:	I've done that. Now what?
Rabbit:	No matter what I do, it's always because of my father—for him, against him, in spite of him, despite him. Any way you spin it, it's still about him. And on Mars, it always would be.
Hole:	Should I leave Mars?
Rabbit:	That's a big decision. Should I pour another drink?
Hole:	I should pour another drink.
Rabbit:	Ugh, I definitely don't need this drink.
Hole:	It's already poured. Might as well drink it. Cheers to Mars.

Rabbit: Mars might not feel like home anymore, but Freckle does.

Hole: Oh shit—I'm staring at her and not saying anything.

Rabbit: It's okay. She knows you're dealing with a lot. Just smile.

Hole: She's not even fazed by the creepy, silent smiling. She's the best.

Rabbit: She and I should make a new home—together. Somewhere else.

Hole: There's the interstellar mission. We could go on that. Start something completely new.

Rabbit: Something free of my father. I'd just be Flip—not the son of Buzz Buchanan. Building something better. For Freckle.

Hole: Can I end on a rabbit? Or does it have to be a hole?

After pouring myself another drink—and grabbing one for Freckle—I sank back into the sofa chair.

"Let's leave," I said.

"What?" she asked.

"I think we should leave."

"Okay," she said gently. "We can go out tonight if that's what you want. Or you can go for a walk by yourself. Whatever you need."

"No. I mean—leave for another planet. Leave Mars."

The interstellar mission had been fast-tracked after scientists successfully expanded a communication distortion bubble large enough to envelop an entire spacecraft, using the power of a controlled antimatter reaction. It meant a ship could theoretically zip across light-years in the blink of an eye.

Both Mars and the NEC were racing to implement the tech—each side scrambling to prove its technological dominance, hoping it would force the other to surrender and finally end the AHB stalemate.

"Flip," Freckle said cautiously, "I know you're going through a lot right now. But don't run away again."

"It's not like that," I told her. "This isn't about escaping. It's about taking responsibility—for my future, for everyone's. It's about building something better than what came before." I exhaled sharply. "There's nothing left for me here—except for you. Which is why I want you to come with me."

I hesitated, then added, "I know you've got your ambassador work, but Pockets has been helping you for years. He's already respected by humans and the Native Martian clans. He could take over. You've already built the relationship. You did the hard part. Since then, you've just been maintaining it. And I don't think you want to keep doing that for the rest of your life."

"You're serious?"

"Depends on your answer."

I started to say something else, but she held up her hand—*just give me a second.*

So I let her fall into her own silent maze of rabbits and holes. Definitely more boring from the outside. Until—

"Okay," she said.

"Seriously?" I nearly jumped from my seat. "You'd do that for me?"

"I'm not doing it for you," she clarified. "I guarantee I'll be the only Native Martian woman on that ship." She leaned in. "And if we don't work out—whatever *this* is—that's fine. I'll still go down as a legend who founded a new Native Martian society in another solar system."

"I was thinking I could do some of the founding and stuff," I said.

She waved me off. "You can do some of it, sure. Whatever you want. I'll probably be a little busy."

She was already lost in thought, planning.

"Fair enough," I said.

* * *

A few months later, we stood on the departure tarmac in Curiosity, which had been fully rebuilt after the attack. The dome had perseverance—even if its neighbor was the one named after that particular rover.

Space elevators fired up and down, carrying passengers into orbit to board the ship. Gusts from the lifts whipped my hair around, while the rumbling and revving of machinery charged the air with launch-sol adrenaline—a perfect backdrop for a climactic departure.

Cheddar—newly-elected, first clone Director of Mars—came to see us off. And I'm sure we were the only reason—it had nothing to do with the highly anticipated, astro-politically loaded launch of the interstellar mission. Pockets and Ravi came too.

Pockets bowed his head to touch Freckle's, saying goodbye and thanking her for entrusting him with the Native Martian ambassadorship.

Cheddar handed me the Better Mars flag I had once hung over the hole she dug in the lithium mine—she'd kept it all this time.

And Ravi had packed lunch for both of us from The Gnukka Nook for our trip.

As I hugged each of them, I spotted my father in the crowd—lined up with all the other spectators packed behind the perimeter railing. After losing the election, he was just an ordinary citizen. I was surprised he'd come at all. Maybe, for once, saying goodbye meant more to him than his pride.

Freckle touched my arm. "I'll let you have a moment." Then she backed away and disappeared into an elevator.

I strode up to my father. With the space elevators firing off unpredictably, the commotion came in bursts—forcing us to shout one moment, then leaving us caught yelling dramatically into silence the next, our hair falling flat as the air abruptly stilled.

"*You got everything you need?*" he asked.

I tapped my carry-on. "*I've learned how to pack light!*"

He nodded. "*I never said 'I'm sorry'!*"

The tarmac went quiet. So did he.

"Do you want to now?" I asked.

He waited until the next elevator roared to life, then shouted, "*I also never said 'thank you'!*"

"*Do you want to now?*"

He said nothing.

"Thank you for what?" I asked.

Again, he waited for the noise to protect him. "*Swallowing your pride!*"

He stared at me—windblown and silent, his thinning hair dancing around his face.

"Last boarding call for flight 05-05-2089," the intercom announced.

"Take care of yourself," I told him. "Cut yourself some slack—it's okay if you're not first. Doesn't mean you don't matter."

He pursed his lips, like he didn't believe me. "Make good decisions out there."

"I'll do my best."

"Me too."

We didn't say anything else. He just gave me a nod—subtle, but genuine.

I stepped into the space elevator, and the glass door slid shut. We didn't take our eyes off each other. His gaze followed me upward as I ascended into the sky, and mine held his, shrinking smaller and smaller—until he was gone.

* * *

All of it, my whole life—my friends, my family, everything—brought me here. On this space elevator. And my life story was just long enough to last me the whole ride.

Ding.

I boarded the ship, and we launched—away from Mars, toward another planet. As we traveled faster than light, I stared out at the stars. At that speed, they looked more like billions of streaks of white fire, flooding the viewport in a solid blaze. And for the first time, I felt what Pepper had all those years ago, when we were just kids gazing up at the night sky:

Not insignificance—but an overwhelming sense of possibility.

And also a desperate need for sunglasses.

My father had screwed up Mars, but I was sure I wouldn't do the same with our new home.

Right?

If I had a prescription . . .

EPILOGUE

"New news with Newt Newman is new at noon," reported Newt Newman from behind his anchor desk. "Tonight is a monumental night—not just for Mars, but for the entire human race. In mere moments, humans will land on a planet light-years outside our solar system for the very first time. Together, we'll witness this pivotal, historic occasion. Never in my four-decade career have I broadcast an event of such profound importance. And I am honored—from the bottom of my heart—to be sitting behind this desk tonight."

Live feeds from the interstellar spaceship showed its descent toward the exoplanet. A final engine thrust slowed the landing.

The ship touched down smoothly, dust pluming around it. The news banner read:

BREAKING NEWS: NEW PLANET, NEW US

"Wow . . . Unbelievable," Newt said, taking off his non-prescription glasses and blinking in awe. "I mean . . . I'm speechless. There are no words. But—wait a minute—yes! The doors are opening. Passengers are preparing to disembark. My god. The first human to ever step foot on an exoplanet—far beyond the solar system we call home—is none other than . . . Rebecca Armstrong! Descendant of the most decorated cyclist of all time."

A beat passed.

"And right behind her—it looks like Flip Buchanan has just become the sec—oh, hang on. Rebecca Armstrong is about to speak."

The news banner read:

BREAKING NEWS: ARMSTRONG FIRST HUMAN ON EXOPLANET, DOES IT HERSELF, ONE-WOMAN TEAM

ACKNOWLEDGEMENTS

Only one name gets slapped on the front of a book, but it really takes so many people to create the final product—at least for good books, which I hope this is, though I have yet to find out. Fingies crossed.

First and foremost, I have to thank my friends who've supported me—both throughout this process and across the rest of my stumbling writing career. When I worked for a famous writer—who then fired me—these friends gave me a beautiful pocket notebook. On the first page, they wrote an inspirational quote:

"Never give up, never surrender."
—Tim Allen, *Galaxy Quest*

That notebook has a permanent home on my desk. Dominic Buccieri, Anthony Phillips, Alex Shenkman, Allan Duso, Kevin Simcox, Anthony Dibiase, and Sean Vadas—thank you, Lads. The last four of you—in addition to my longtime friend Mike Emer—were subjected to some truly terrible early drafts. Thank you for your sacrifice. It has not gone unnoticed.

To all my friends on the East Coast, West Coast, and in my hometown in the Midwest—sorry Mountain Time, I got nothing for you—thank you. For your support, your encouragement, and all the laughs. My friends have always been my family.

And thank you to all my other beta readers who generously gave their time and feedback on one or more versions of this book. It wouldn't be what it is without you.

To Andrew Colaprete, another longtime friend and the talent behind the cover and Martian maps: I trusted you to create the face of this book, and you exceeded every expectation. Thank you. No matter how many copies I sell, I know it would've been far fewer without your work.

Thank you to Tim Heller and Samantha (Sam) Damiano at Audiobook Bonanza by Tim Heller Creative, and to narrator Ted Evans for bringing Flip's voice to life in the audiobook. I couldn't have asked for a better performance. And if he's narrating the acknowledgements right now . . . stop complimenting yourself. It's so unprofessional. The author didn't even write this paragraph—I'm Ted Evans, and I added it myself.

To the Books Forward marketing team: thank you for taking on this project. Though I'm writing this before launch, I already feel lucky to be working with you all. If someone's reading these acknowledgements, then I guess you did a pretty good job. And thank you to your sister company, Books Fluent, for making the interior of this book look so gosh darn pretty.

I already gave my dad half the dedication, and I don't want to make him cry more than he can handle, so I'll keep this short. Dad, I wouldn't be the writer I am today if it weren't for the stories you made up on the spot at sleepovers, for us kids giggling in our sleeping bags. So as much as you grumble about my career choices—it's kind of all your fault.

To my brother, Ryan Korell—a fellow writer (in music)—thank you for always being there, whether I needed to vent, brainstorm, or just talk shop. You've supported me since we were kid brothers creating a summer-long epic with our action figures in the basement.

Thank you to Dewey, my dog, who napped by my side every day while I wrote.

And finally, to McCauley Braun, my partner in life: your love, patience, and unwavering belief in me have kept me going for the past decade. Celebrating the little wins with you has meant everything. Without you, I probably would've given up and moved back home a long time ago. THANKS BOO. I LOVE YOU!

Other than that army of people, I did it all myself.

www.ingramcontent.com/pod-product-compliance
Lightning Source LLC
Chambersburg PA
CBHW020010120726
47903CB00004B/1218
* 9 7 9 8 9 9 9 6 3 9 0 0 4 *